I0616066

Vanilla
After
You

Vanilla After You

DEVIN EM

Book Summary

Vanilla Without You
By Devin Em

Brokenhearted and reeling after Ronan's betrayal, Thandi Elowen is forced to confront the fallout—both to her heart and to the company she's fought to build. As old wounds resurface and new threats emerge, the carefully balanced life she's created begins to fracture.

For Ronan Thorne, regret is no longer enough. Desperate to prove that he's worthy of Thandi's love and trust, he's willing to risk everything to make things right. But as danger closes in from all sides, Ronan may have to confront the possibility that love, once tested, doesn't always wait—and that the woman he loves may already be slipping out of reach.

A powerful conclusion filled with romance, suspense, and hard-won healing, Vanilla After You delivers the second half of Thandi and Ronan's unforgettable love story and their fight for each other.

Tropes:
- Enemies to lovers
- Female billionaire
- Found family
- HEA

Trigger Warnings

- Angst
- Childhood trauma
- Emotional abuse
- Parent sickness and death
- Explicit sex
- Violence

Acknowledgements

This book would not exist in its current form without the generosity, insight, and care of a few extraordinary people.

My deepest thanks to my beta and sensitivity readers—**Kaycee, Jennell, Whitney, and Amanda**—for lending your eyes, your expertise, and your honesty to this story. Your feedback sharpened the work, strengthened the characters, and helped me see what the book was truly trying to become.

A special and heartfelt thank you to **Kaycee**, whose thoughtful, incisive, and deeply constructive feedback has strengthened my craft by leaps and bounds. Working with you has been a gift, and I am profoundly grateful for your care, clarity, and rigor. If you're an author looking for exceptional beta reading support, I cannot recommend Kaycee highly enough: https://retrospect-publishing.com/betareading

Finally, an unexpected but essential note of gratitude to **Rosemarie**, the nurse at my local urgent care who quite literally helped make the end of this book possible. Two weeks, three steroid shots, and a great deal of kindness later, the manuscript is finished. Thank you for your skill, your patience, and your compassion when I needed all three.

Table of Contents

Projection

Hemorrhage
Thandi

"No one is questioning her leadership, but we can't deny the optics of this."

"Come on, Niko, let's not overreact here."

"The stock lost twenty percent of its value in the last twenty-four hours. You're telling me that's not a crisis?"

"We opened thirty percent above offer. Even after yesterday's correction, we're still trading close to the issue price. Let's not start screaming fire yet."

"Why not? The house is already burning!"

Niko and Trent can't stop sniping across the table. Spread between them are the morning headlines—the fallout from a press conference that was supposed to be about hope, yet ended in disaster:

IP-Oops! Immerscent Public Offering Hijacked by Scandal

Love and Lies: Immerscent's CEO in Bed With the Enemy?

I stopped checking my phone last night, but #ThorneGate was still trending when I went to bed.

The Washington Post's front page cuts the deepest:

Fails the Smell Test: Immerscent's Halo Evaporates as Its Ties to Astor Come to Light

The article begins: *The revelation that founder Thandi Elowen's partner is Astor Pharmaceuticals heir Ronan Thorne has peeled back the gloss on scent-tech's most celebrated disruptor, exposing an industry awash in pink washing and performative inclusion.*

Christopher's byline is front and center. Of course, the photo is unflattering—me dashing across the stage, desperate to escape.

The world thinks I'm a fraud. And now I'm a fraud who's hijacked attention away from Daysha.

My fingers clench in my lap. I'm bruised, raw from the accusations, from the damage to my reputation—from Ronan's betrayal. Yet beneath it all is a strange numbness. I'm frozen while a storm barrels toward me, threatening to consume everything I've built.

I stare across the boardroom to the window overlooking Chesden's streets as Niko's and Trent's barbed voices fill my ears. Outside, the world is just stirring to life, but the emergency meeting of the board started in the grayest hours of the morning, before the first school bus rumbled to the corner waiting for kids with heavy backpacks and cold fingers.

Fall has arrived with premature vengeance.

I tug my jacket tighter around me. How long have we been at this? One hour? Two? I need to focus, but all I can think about is Daysha.

And Ronan.

I haven't eaten or slept since Christopher's bombshell. Every time I try, the betrayal turns to bile in my stomach. And now my company is on the line. How do I fight for it when I've failed at the very reason for its existence?

I couldn't remember Tess' kidnapper, and now Daysha is gone too. I thought even if my shortcomings were undeniable, that I was at least helping others find closure—safety. But now, I wonder: Have I just been deluding myself?

"—show a steady hand to *avoid* affecting morale."

"Thandi? Thandi, are you listening?" Clara Yuen's voice wrenches me back from the darkness.

"I'm sorry," I rub my eyes. "Can you repeat the question?"

Clara frowns, lips parting, but whatever she sees in my face makes her pause. Her gaze softens with something akin to compassion. "I was asking how the team is doing. If we overreact, we could trigger attrition, and that's harder to recover from than a bad news cycle."

I blink as the first frisson of life surges through me at the mention of Immerscent's staff. Not a single one blanched when I updated them on the situation on the team call this morning. If they're still fighting, I can't give up—no matter how painful it is.

I lean forward against the table, meeting each pair of eyes around me. "They're worried. They're exhausted. But they're still committed—just like we should be."

"What about the mood of investors?" Niko is back, bullish as ever.

"I spoke with both Fowler and Yanovich this morning." My hands clench on the table. "I expressed confidence in the fundamentals and the team's resilience. They understand the noise will pass. They're not running."

"Tom's notes support that." Lami Nduka, Immerscent's CFO, interjects. She glances down at her tablet, scrolling. "We've seen some trimming among mid-tier funds—standard flight-to-safety behavior. A few retail holders have liquidated, but not in large volume. At the same time, we're seeing new entrants picking up shares at the dip."

She looks up, composed. "It's contradictory behavior, but not irrational. Some investors are taking shelter, others see an opportunity. The heavy hitters—Fowler, Yanovich—are still positioned long-term. Their teams believe Immerscent's advantage only widens if Astor falters."

Trent leans back in his chair. "So the floor's shaky, but the foundation's solid."

Niko goes silent, jaw tensing.

Dani rises to pour herself some coffee. "That contradiction," she says, "is borne out in public sentiment." Her eyes are warm as they meet mine. "The ecosystem is doing some very… *interesting* things right now."

"What do you mean?" Trent demands.

Dani leans against the cabinet, lifting the cup to her lips. "The talking heads are crucifying us on the roundtables—Abby Phillip, Fox and Friends. But the financial and tech press are holding steady; the fundamentals story is still intact. And the lifestyle outlets—Cosmo, The Cut, even Rolling Stone—have latched onto the human drama. The press conference clips are everywhere."

She takes a slow sip. "Half the world's dragging Thandi; the other half's calling her and Ronan the Romeo and Juliet of tech."

Romeo and Juliet.

Emotion clogs my throat at the thought of what Ronan and I have lost on top of everything else. Maybe they're right. Maybe we were star-crossed. Doomed from the start. I swallow, stifling the sob threatening to explode from my chest.

I want to hide, run away again, but I focus on Immerscent, on Daysha—on all the people counting on me. "So," I say, lifting my chin, "have we come to a decision?"

Trent nods, satisfied. "No major changes as long as Thandi steps back from the spotlight."

"Agreed." Clara Yuen raps her knuckles against the desk. "Niko?"

"Fine," he growls. "But we've got to keep this tight. We can't afford a wrong move."

"Excellent." Trent stands and rests a hand on my shoulder. "Then we're adjourned."

The boardroom empties in a shuffle of papers and muted voices. Trent squeezes my shoulder once before striding out, already on another call. Clara and Lami follow, murmuring to each other about the next steps.

I wait until the door shuts behind them before I finally take a breath. My pulse is still racing. I pull my phone from my jacket pocket and see two missed calls and one new text.

All from Ronan.

I'm not one for the silent treatment. Not really. After I ran from the press conference, I went home and cried myself to sleep. And with the emergency board meeting this morning, I haven't had time for much else.

But now that this hurdle's cleared, I have to face Ronan and decide what, if anything, comes next. The problem is, I'm still so broken, so raw, that I don't trust myself to make the right choice.

It's not the fact that Astor's blood runs in his veins that's unbearable; it's that he kept something so important from me while I was baring my soul about Tess, Ricky, and my amnesia.

While I was welcoming him into my family—and my heart.

I thought we were building something together, but what kind of foundation is built on lies and secrecy?

I'm gutted. Confused. Even though I know we've come to the end, something keeps holding me back. I can't reconcile the two— the Ronan who hid his past, and the one who saved me in the lab and at Fia's party.

I can't forget how he gave me the courage to pursue the Sugar Hill concept; how he looked at me and held me—

How he loved me.

I moan, pressing a hand to my eyes as tears well up again. Heart clenching, my fingers hover over the phone.

I swipe to my messages before I can talk myself out of it.

Baby please. I need to see you.

I love you. I'm not giving up on us. Can we talk?

For a moment, all I can do is stare. The words blur and sharpen again through the sting in my eyes.

"Hey."

I blink as Dani's reflection appears in the glass. She's leaning in the doorway, voice softer than I've ever heard it. "You did great in there."

I fumble to lock my phone, wiping at my eyes. "Thanks."

Dani crosses the room and sinks into the chair beside me. She leans in, nudging me with her shoulder. "You okay?"

"Yes." The word escapes me even as it twists into a broken laugh. Who am I kidding? This is Dani, who knows me, who sees everything.

"No." I bow my head under the weight of the truth. "It hurts so much, Dani."

Then I'm crying again, hiding my face in my jacket. I'm so embarrassed that I'm such a mess, so ashamed that everything that mattered to me has come to this.

When Dani's arms come around me, I freeze. Dani is the best, but she doesn't do physical affection. Ever. It's enough to stop the rain of my tears for a moment.

"What are you doing?" I manage, fumbling for a tissue. "You don't give hugs."

Raising a brow, she grabs the box of Kleenex from the center of the table, presses a wad into my hand, and tugs me back against her shoulder.

"That's why you're going to stop trying to be so damn brave and accept it," she says gruffly. "This is a once-in-a-lifetime opportunity."

A startled laugh escapes me.

I lean into her, feeling both her softness and her strength. "Thanks, Dani," I whisper.

Her arms tighten. "Anytime, Thandi. We're family now, you know that." Her voice gentles. "What do you need? How can I help? Evelyn and I would love to have you if you need a change of scenery. It's hard being alone during heartbreak."

"I don't know. That's the problem," I admit. "For the first time in my life, I don't know what to do. I don't have a plan to find Daysha or to fix any of this."

"That's okay," Dani murmurs. "That's why we're here. Trent, me, your parents—we're all here to support you. You only have to let us."

I nod, sniffling.

For a while, neither of us speaks. Rain has begun to fall, its soft drumming against the windows filling the silence between us. Somewhere down the hall, an elevator dings. The air smells of coffee and the faint sweetness of Dani's perfume, rising from her expensive wool suit. It's delicate, almost imperceptible, but this close, I catch traces of orange blossom, almond milk, and orris wood—gentle, warm, and as comforting as her arms around me.

I close my eyes, trying to absorb the quiet, to practice the acceptance she spoke of.

"Have you heard from him?" she asks softly.

My throat clogs with tears again. I can't trust my voice, so I unlock my phone and hand it to her.

Her sigh shudders through her frame. "You should talk to him."

"What?" I jerk back. She's right, of course, but I can't admit it—not when I'm still so afraid. It feels safer to exist in this painful limbo than to face the truth that the most beautiful love of my life might be over.

"I—I'm not ready," I mumble.

Dani's gray eyes pierce mine. "Can you ever be, for something like this?"

My shoulders drop. "I'll text him back."

"Good." Dani pats my hand. "Did it really never come up before? His family?"

I shake my head, a glimmer of guilt prickling at the edges of my exhaustion. "No. But he tried to tell me before Austin. I didn't let him. Trent was talking about Fowler and Yanovich. I didn't have the headspace. I just never thought it would be *this*."

Dani turns toward the window, watching lightning stitch across the gray sky. "Do you still love him?" she asks, facing me again.

"Of course, I could never…" I'm quiet, throat working.

Dani smiles. "Then hear him out, for both your sakes. And if it isn't meant to be, it'll hurt like hell. But you know what Evelyn taught me?"

"What?" I whisper, trembling—fragile, shaken, like the foundation I thought Ronan and I were building our love on.

"Love is never a mistake," Dani murmurs. "Even if it isn't returned. Even if it is, but doesn't turn out the way you want it to." She squeezes my hand. "And sometimes it's the only truth left when nothing else makes sense."

Dani's words hang in the air, soft and heavy as the rain. I can feel them settling in the space where hope and pain live next to each other. *Love isn't a mistake*. Not even mine and Ronan's. Whatever becomes of it.

I nod, brushing the last of my tears away. "Thanks, Dani—for everything."

Before she can answer, my phone vibrates against the table. The screen flashes with the only other name that can make my heart race: Detective McNamara.

Dani glances down, rising before I have to speak. "You should take that." She gives me one last hug before heading for the door. "My offer still stands. Come spend some time with Evelyn and me."

I nod, shooting her a grateful look before I reach for the phone.

"Hey, Dani," I call out before she can leave. "You're a pretty good hugger, you know that? You've been holding out on me."

Dani winks. "Don't get used to it."

And with that, she slips out of the room, the brisk rhythm of her heels fading down the hall.

Steeling myself, I raise the phone to my ear.

"Hello?"

"Ms. Elowen." Simone McNamara's crisp voice vibrates on the line. "I need you to come to the station. Immediately."

Shadows
Ronan

Fowler couldn't have picked a worse time to insist on a meeting.

I feel like shit.

I probably look like it, too.

The bell over the door jingles as I step inside the café. The owner, too chipper for this hour, greets me with a bright, "Good morning!"

I grunt in response, pulling my cap over my eyes. I slide into a corner booth, back to the wall. It's early, but the place is already crowded, bodies hunched over mugs and sizzling platters. The TV above the counter is blaring—one of those morning shows that thrives on someone else's disaster.

Two perky hosts beam into the camera.

"Let's turn to the scandal rocking the scent-tech industry. Not only does James Astor have a son, but he's dating Astor rival Thandi Elowen."

The brunette in a pink pantsuit nods. "That's right. Let's look at footage from the press conference."

I wince as the replay of Christopher's gotcha moment loops. Thandi's haunted face fills the screen as she flees the stage.

I did that to her.

The knowledge claws at me. I want to go to her, hold her, fix what I shattered, but her words in the elevator are a cancer in my chest:

Don't come any closer. Let me go.

Let me go.

I press my palms against my knees until they stop shaking. I can't believe she meant it. Not when I can still feel her heartbeat against mine.

Not when I can't live without her.

At the counter, a balding man with two stubborn tufts of hair jerks his fork toward the TV. "That's the problem with all this DEI bullshit," he says to his companion. "Yesterday, she was a genius. Now we find out she was just screwing the competition."

He snorts. "Figures."

I jolt to my feet, ready to yank him off his stool, make him take it back. Then I stop. My anger won't do anything except hurt Thandi's reputation. Besides, what would Fowler think? The last thing I need is to alienate her most important investor.

I slump back in my seat. It's the only reason I'm here. The only reason I came when I just want to be at Thandi's side, begging for her forgiveness.

"Coffee?" A middle-aged server with a razor-sharp gaze appears at my side.

"—a great point, Rebecca," the morning show drones on. "But shouldn't the real question be: Can Thandi Elowen be trusted?"

My throat tightens.

"Can I sit outside?" I ask abruptly.

The server shrugs. "It's forty degrees out there, but sure."

"Please," I say, grabbing the menus.

"No problem." She tucks her notepad into her apron. "I'll get the heat lamp going for you."

My mood doesn't improve even with a pot of coffee and an order of wheat toast. I can't seem to keep anything richer down this morning. It downright worsens when Fowler ambles up with a grin on his face.

He unwraps his scarf and settles in the chair across from mine. I wait as the server takes his order—steak and eggs, and coffee. I'm glad one of us has an appetite.

"Beautiful morning, isn't it?" Looking around, Fowler inhales deeply. I haven't seen him since Fia's party. He looks relaxed. Happy. The opposite of me.

My brows lower.

"You're a hard man to get a hold of, son. You also look like hell."

"Gee, thanks." I flick the straw wrapper off the table. "I assume you didn't call me here just to kick me while I'm down."

Fowler's eyes dance over the rim of his mug. "No, I wanted to give you this." He slides a creamy embossed envelope across the table.

I turn it over in my hands. "What's this?"

"Open it."

I break the seal. Inside, a matching card announces in looping gold script:

You are cordially invited to the marriage of Amber Lark and Johnson Fowler, Esq.

My mouth falls open. "Wait, what? You and Amber? How? When?"

"Next month in Tuscany." Fowler's grin widens. "She insisted on a villa with cypress trees. How could I say no?"

I set the invitation down beside my plate, struggling to contain the emotion clawing its way up my throat. *This* is the future I wanted with Thandi. Not Tuscany specifically, though I'd do that too if that was her dream. I'd marry her in her parents' backyard, at the courthouse, hell, even in Sugar Hill Park. The place doesn't matter. Only that we'd be together.

Looking at Fowler's easy posture, his serene expression, I'm confronted by a visceral recognition. I know what he's feeling. For one fleeting, perfect moment, I had that too. I think of the last two months with Thandi: her laugh, her brilliance, the unending well of kindness that seems to flow from her.

Her passion.

Knowing that I might have thrown it all away makes my stomach churn. Wind rushes through the patio, and a cough tears through me. I call the waitress over, desperate for water.

It doesn't do much to wash away the bitter taste in my mouth.

"Congratulations." I swallow, draining my glass until only ice clinks at the bottom. "But—no offense—why am I invited?"

Fowler chuckles. "Because if it weren't for you, there wouldn't be a wedding."

I stare, confused.

"Amber was my date to that infernal garden party," Fowler reminds me. "I didn't think I could want her after the way she behaved towards Thandi." He stares beyond the patio, his eyes soft with memory. "But you were so clear that Thandi was the only woman you needed, it humbled Amber, I think. Forced her to consider what really matters."

Fowler's gaze brightens as he turns back to me. "That gave us just enough space to find our way to each other. My girl isn't easy to love," he chuckles, "but once she apologized, I realized there was gold beneath the bluster."

The other man leans back, pleased. "Besides, if you hadn't sold me so hard on Immerscent that night, I'd never have invested. I've paid for the wedding many times over since Monday." He winks. "Two good turns make you a friend in my book."

A knot forms in my chest—the hard, bitter residue of irony... and jealousy. Festering beside it is the petty judgment of a Ronan I thought I'd eviscerated. I can't believe that *Amber*, of all people, has managed to cinch what I can't. I hate myself for thinking it. Hate myself more for realizing that even with everything I feel for Thandi, I still have so much more growing to do.

"Thanks." I manage a thin smile. "I'll be there."

Fowler slaps his hand on the table. "Excellent."

Before I can answer, a couple walks by, their voices carrying on the wind. The woman stops mid-sentence, eyes locking on me with startled recognition. She murmurs something to her partner, who raises a brow before gently steering her onward. I tug my collar up, stiffening in my seat.

Fowler watches them go. "It shocked me too, you know." His gaze meets mine. "Learning you were James' boy."

My jaw clenches. I didn't even know he and James knew each other.

"The more I look, though, the more I see the resemblance. The coloring is different, and no one ever called James affable." Fowler laughs. "But the stubbornness—that bulldozer instinct to plow through obstacles—is there."

"John...." My tone rises with a threat I can't bury. Good turns or not, he's treading on thin ice.

Unfazed, Fowler waves his hand. "Oh, you've packaged it differently, but it's the same stuff. Just kinder, smarter, less obsessed with being right. More intent on connection—version 2.0, if you will."

His blue eyes sharpen. "I see why you hate each other. He's your shadow, and you're the man he couldn't become."

I flinch as if struck. No one has ever compared me to my father. I take pride in that. I'm Rosalind's son. I've made sure of it. But once Fowler says it, I can't unhear it. I think of James and me brawling on Whitlow's pavers—his grudging respect, and my disgust.

Maybe that's why he never loved me.

Maybe that's why Mom pushed me so hard.

Because she saw that without intent, *without effort,* he is what I could become.

Fowler keeps talking, as though he hasn't just tilted my world off its axis.

"Don't fret about the noise around you and Thandi. Every public company gets its bruises. Immerscent's performing exactly as I expected—better, actually. Real fundamentals. The Street will settle once they realize the product's the story, not the scandal."

I sigh, wishing I could believe him. The talking heads above the counter don't seem to think so either.

"I'd be more concerned about Astor."

"Yeah," I say tiredly. "I'm sure investors weren't thrilled by the press conference."

"No, it's more than that." Fowler's expression darkens.

"More?"

"The truth is, I'm shorting Astor now, and I'm not alone. I used to be one of their defenders. Then I got burned. I won't make that mistake twice."

I stare at him, suddenly alert.

My instincts flare.

This is the missing piece—the thread connecting Micah's invoices, the *irregularities* Mrs. Jackson hinted at, the desperation that drove James to confront me at Whitlow—

And his decision to ruin Thandi.

I lean forward, bracing my elbows on the table. "Tell me more."

"For years now, Astor's been a paper lion," Fowler says. "James is a genius when it comes to sniffing out opportunity. That's what made him so damn successful."

He shakes his head. "But success breeds arrogance. Your father never did learn how to hear no. When the world started changing, he couldn't tell the signal from the static anymore, and he refused to adjust. He stopped listening to the people trying to help him—board members, analysts, even his own shareholders. Thought every correction was an attack, every skeptic a traitor."

I hold my breath, sensing there's more. But this isn't a smoking gun. James has always been king of his castle.

"James isn't alone in that, though, is he?" I press. "Plenty of CEOs are assholes."

"Yes…" Fowler rubs his thumb over his coffee mug. "I shouldn't be saying this, but I used to sit on Astor's finance committee. On paper, the investor reports look rosy. But that's the trick of it. The balance sheets don't show how deep the debt runs."

"Debt?" I jerk my head back.

"Massive." Fowler grimaces. "When James pivoted from petrochemicals into pharma, he financed the whole reinvention on borrowed money. That's when the problems started."

"What do you mean?"

"Petrochemicals was bleeding. Too much regulatory scrutiny, too much activist pressure."

Fowler drums his fingers on the table. "That's why he needed your mother's company. Thorne Therapeutics was supposed to be the linchpin, offering high-end drugs, formulations for cancer and other rare diseases."

"But?" I can barely get the word out now that he's spelled out the link to my mother.

"But he couldn't stand sharing the spotlight. He drove Rosalind out and gutted her research. The new division never got off the ground. He could've spun it off, taken the hit—but James was too proud to admit he needed her. So he doubled down. What started as debt ballooned into a full-blown crisis."

"He was digging his own grave," I murmur.

Fowler nods. "That's when he started the lifestyle-therapeutics push."

I pick at the blackened edge of my toast. "WhiffRush?"

"Sniffz, PlayMist, all of it. He saw what Immerscent was doing and caught the AI bug. But the foundation just wasn't there. James wouldn't see it."

I frown, thinking about Prime, the pods, the data collection—the hollow mimicry of Thandi's protocols.

So that's what was behind it.

"What did the board do?"

"We pushed for a full audit," Fowler says. "I wanted to see the real exposure, but it's hard to be a one-man activist."

"Others supported him?" I ask.

"Yes. We all knew it was unsustainable, but the returns were seductive. Too many wanted to ride out the bubble until it burst." Fowler sighs. "That's when I knew I had to step back."

"You left?"

"Yes. I didn't speak to James until I ran into him after your mother's funeral. I was shocked. I'd never seen him like that—jittery, jumpy, looking over his shoulder. I told myself it was grief."

I let out a bitter laugh. "Hardly."

Fowler's eyebrows rise, but I don't want to linger on Mom's pain or James's neglect.

"What happened next?" I ask.

"Things had gotten worse. He asked for help. I didn't want to, but I sympathized." Fowler swallows hard. "I lost my first wife to cancer, too."

"I'm sorry," I say softly.

He hesitates. "I'm the one who's sorry for staking a piece of my reputation on your father. I opened a short-term credit line to fund that new AI division he couldn't shut up about. I dragged Yani in, too. James swore it would revolutionize diagnostics, that Astor would finally come out on top. What it did was vaporize money."

"Shit." I shake my head. Is there no one James isn't willing to screw over?

Fowler gives a humorless laugh. "Now, with this kidnapping mess, the risk exposure's through the roof. I've seen this movie before, and I know how it ends."

I'm floored. Finally, it all makes sense.

It's so clear now, I can't believe I missed it. This was never about me or my private life. James was terrified of my association with Immerscent because Astor was cracking long before the kidnapping. Any hint of no confidence could've sent the whole edifice tumbling.

And what's more damning than your son falling for your rival?

The connection to the vineyard also clicks at last. If James was buried in debt and facing a liquidity crisis, no wonder he started dipping into Mom's coffers. She must have suspected, too:

In light of my declining capacity during my final year, I hereby direct that any profits, revenues, or benefits derived from its operation during the twelve months preceding my death be fully audited and, if found improperly allocated, returned in full to my son.

During the will reading, I couldn't understand why she'd been so insistent, but now it's obvious. With her too sick to manage the day-to-day, the vineyard was an easy target. James lived at Whitlow. No one would question his signing contracts or moving funds he had no right to touch.

Now I need to figure out how much he stole.

"Yani and I are predicting a collapse." Fowler's voice cuts through my thoughts. "We're just missing the final domino."

He studies me over the rim of his glass. "That's the other reason I wanted to talk to you."

I narrow my eyes. "What's that?"

"Your companies are the only things even remotely tied to the Astor name that are still yielding phenomenal returns." He refills his coffee. "Sure, your reputation's a little battered right now, but you'll survive it. You've still got the science—and the love of the most brilliant woman in the industry."

I flinch, the words twisting like a knife in my gut. I can't forget Thandi's shattered look or her tears. *Do I?* It sure as hell doesn't feel like it.

Fowler grins. "She's got you by the nuts—and the heart—son. When a man's that miserable, he either self-destructs or he fixes it. And something tells me you're not going to let a woman like Thandi slip away."

His smile fades, replaced by something sharper. "In the meantime, the field's wide open. Astor's on the ropes—"

The patio door slams shut as Yanovich strides up to the table.

"So, what's your move?"

Rainbow
Thandi

Even though I rush to the station right away, I have to wait for Detective McNamara when I arrive. A uniformed officer leads me down a narrow hallway into a small office that looks like it hasn't been updated since the early 2000s. The lights overhead are too bright, bathing everything in a gray-white wash.

The air smells like stale coffee and a cheap air freshener. I shift in my seat, trying to get comfortable in my damp clothes. I dashed to my car as soon as I hung up with McNamara, not bothering with an umbrella. Immerscent's parking deck wasn't a problem, but there's only street-side parking in front of the precinct. I hadn't realized how soaked I'd gotten until now. The vent above me, blasting cold air onto my neck, doesn't help either. Why is the air conditioning even on in forty-degree weather?

Shivering, I fold my arms to keep warm. On the wall, a corkboard displays faded notes and a curling flier for a community self-defense class. My reflection stares back at me from the dark computer monitor: tired, eyes rimmed in red.

I rub my hands together and glance at the door again.

Where is she?

The longer I wait, the more ice builds on my skin and in my veins. Is there a new lead? Surely if it were good news, McNamara would have told me.

What if—

No. I clench my fingers against the armrests. Daysha has to come home alive. I can't imagine the worst.

Desperate for a distraction, my mind ping pongs to Ronan, but there's no relief there. I consider responding to his text, but I'm too much of an emotional wreck in the face of McNamara's news. I decide to wait until after I leave the station.

That doesn't stop me from thinking about him, though. I'm hurt, and I hate that I miss him so much. I'd never describe myself as lonely before, yet the thought of navigating Daysha's kidnapping by myself feels … daunting. Terrifying, if I'm honest. Yesterday, I assumed we could rely on each other's strength.

Just twenty-four hours later, life is radically different.

I glance at my phone. It's already been fifteen minutes with no sign of the detective. I'm just about to leave when McNamara strides through the door, face harried. She's carrying a manila envelope in one hand and a tan file folder in the other.

"Ms. Elowen, I'm sorry for keeping you waiting," she says, settling herself in the chair on the opposite side of the desk. "I just spoke with the team managing the tip hotline."

McNamara smooths a hand over the folder before meeting my eyes. "First of all, thank you for the press conference and for financing the reward. The right people are finally paying attention to this case. That means all eyes are on me, but I'll take it."

"It's the least I can do for Daysha." I shake my head. "I wish I could do more."

"Well, you might be able to." McNamara leans back, a trace of fatigue in her voice. "That's why I called you here."

"What?" My heart jumps to my throat. "What is it? Did you find Daysha?"

McNamara raises a hand. "We haven't found her, but we've got a possible sighting. A young mother said she stopped at the Petrocor off Route 9 for milk and saw a girl in the backseat of a gray Subaru Outback—late model, probably 2019. The driver was a white male, average height, early thirties, face obscured by a hoodie. No clear plate."

"But that's good news, right?" I can barely catch my breath. "It means she's still alive."

"Yes. The witness accurately described her features and the outfit she was wearing at the time of her disappearance. She said the child appeared distressed but unharmed. That gives us a shot."

McNamara sighs. "The station's only about two miles from the park, but if he's fueling up for travel, we'll lose the advantage of containment."

"So what do we do?" My voice breaks.

"The CCTV footage is crap, and the suspect paid with cash, so that's a dead end." McNamara opens the manila envelope and pulls out an evidence bag. "But there was something else." She slides it across the desk. Inside, a dull brass clip glints under the canned lights.

"You were Daysha's mentor," she says. "Do you have any idea what this is? We found it outside the pump. Mrs. Howard didn't recognize it."

My heart clenches. The moment I see the clip, I'm not in the precinct anymore. I'm back at my parents' dining table, the scent of roasted vegetables in the air. Daysha and Ricky are hunched over a half-finished kite, the frame wobbling every time they tug the string. The earlier stress of the evening has faded to quiet companionship.

Ronan is laughing softly, his head bent close to theirs. "Same problem as last time, huh? We'll need a better way to secure it."

I remember how he'd straightened and kissed me before reaching for his keys. "I'll be right back."

Ten minutes later, he'd returned to our scientists with a hardware store bag in hand. He'd knelt between the kids, pulling out the brass clip.

"This will keep your line from twisting," he said, showing them how the swivel turned with a flick of his finger. "See? Even if the air moves, you'll stay steady."

Daysha had squealed, high-fiving Ricky. Ronan had grinned, glancing at me with warmth in his eyes.

Now, staring at the clip in McNamara's hand, I fight back a rush of tears. That was the night I realized I couldn't live without him—because he didn't just fix the kite. He steadied me, too.

"I…" I clear my throat as waves of sorrow and loss threaten to drown me. "It's a bridle swivel; at least I think that's what it's called." I trace the hook through the bag. "It's used for kite frames. That was Daysha and Ricky's science project. They were going to show it off that morning."

"Bridle swivel?" McNamara repeats, brows knitting.

"Yes. Ronan—Mr. Thorne—bought it for the kids. He'd be the best one to confirm." My voice falters. "I'll text him."

Just saying his name sears through me, even as I remember his unanswered messages burning a hole in my pocket. But this will give me something solid to hold onto, something graver than my own pain. The frame that will keep me from falling apart.

McNamara shoots me a sympathetic look. "Thank you."

I nod, fingers trembling as I lift my phone to take a photo of the clip. Then I send it to Ronan. My hands are shaking so badly, I have to get it all out in one rush:

> *With McNamara. Daysha was spotted at a gas station. She needs to ID this object found at the pump. It's the bridle swivel you gave her, isn't it?*

And then, before I can lose my nerve:

> *It hurts too much to talk now.*
> *I'll meet you tomorrow.*
> *But I can't make any promises.*

There is a pause. Three dots blink, stop, then start again.

My stomach twists with hope and dread. I can't think, can't breathe as I wait. I can't look away as they flash for what feels like eternity—three bullet wounds puncturing my universe. My alpha, theta, and omega.

Then:

Thank God she's still with us. I knew she'd be a fighter.

And yes, that is the bridle swivel from their kite project. Does McNamara need me to come in? You think Daysha left it as a clue?

Just seeing the words guts me. I can imagine Ronan's expression, the way his large hands cradle his phone, and the rough whisper of his voice, as if he were speaking right in my ear.

Closing my eyes, I take a deep breath.

I don't know. I hope so. You know how clever Daysha is.

It's surreal how easily the exchange flows despite the rift yawning between us. I stare at the screen, bracing for what comes next.

I know you're hurting, and it kills me that I'm the reason.

Thank you for meeting me tomorrow. Just give me one more chance. Please.

I love you, Thandi.

The words are at the tip of my tongue and emblazoned on my heart, but I can't type them. I set the phone down and cover my face with my hands.

I love you, too.

After texting with Ronan, I feel tender, vulnerable. I hate myself for it, but I just want to go hide in a safe place away from all this heartache. I didn't think I'd need it, but between McNamara's news and agreeing to meet Ronan tomorrow, I'm ready to take Dani up on her offer to spend the night.

I text her to let her know I'll grab a bag and come over this evening, and the pain in my chest eases just a little. I need to check on my parents and Ricky first, but it will be good to be with them.

I'm reaching for my purse, ready to head back to the office, but it turns out the detective isn't done with me yet.

"Ms. Elowen, I need to ask one more favor. It's a bit... unconventional."

"Please," I say, waving a hand. "Call me Thandi. And if it's for Daysha, the answer is yes."

McNamara studies me. "The boy's family has agreed to release his MRI scans to the task force. Our neurologist confirmed significant impairment, but the origin is unclear. He couldn't say whether what we're seeing is trauma-related, developmental, or the result of chemical exposure."

"And you think WhiffRush—"

"Might explain it. You're one of the few people qualified to interpret what we're seeing. If you're willing, I can have you listed as a technical consultant so the files can be shared legally."

McNamara slides the tan folder across the desk. "I need to know whether this drug could cause similar patterns in the kidnapper. If it can, the man who took Daysha might not be thinking clearly. That changes how we search for her."

The weight of her words presses on me. My heart goes out to Daysha and her cousin Stephan, who are both unwitting victims of something that should never have been on the market.

Once again, Ronan's face blooms in my mind along with a bittersweet ache.

Dani said to trust in love, but right now, Astor's destruction feels so vast that I don't know how we can heal the breach. Still, there's no other answer to McNamara's request.

"I'll do it," I say, even though I'm not sure how I'll find the strength.

"Thank you." The rigid line of McNamara's shoulders softens. "It's a standard confidentiality agreement and a one-page consultant form. Effective as soon as you sign." She hands me a pen. "You've already done so much that I hate to impose upon you further, but I don't know where else to turn."

"I'm glad you did. Whatever you need, I'm here."

We shake hands, and I fill out the paperwork. If I doubted the detective's sense of commitment or urgency, I needn't have. The MRI scans are in an envelope right beneath the forms.

McNamara catches my expression and shrugs. "I didn't know if you'd accept, but I had the scans cleared for release. Just in case…"

I slip the films out and stare, stunned for a moment by what's in front of me.

The scans are a rainbow of color—vivid swirls of orange and violet bleeding through gray matter. To anyone else, it might be beautiful. To me, it's injury made visible.

The symmetry tells me everything. Trauma doesn't strike both hemispheres evenly. This is chemical and systemic, the signature of something that floods the entire network at once. I've seen milder versions in adults who tried to self-medicate with WhiffRush, desperate to trigger lost memories before coming to Immerscent. But they were older, their prefrontal cortices fully formed. Even then, the damage was limited—spatial disorientation, maybe mood instability.

Stephan's scans are different. His reward centers glow too hot. The frontal networks are muted and thinned.

Some of it can heal. Synapses can re-route, and inflammation can fade. But seeing what WhiffRush did to this young man makes the blood run hot in my veins. Alongside it is desperation as I think of all the children being dosed on WhiffRush and PlayMist.

This was Ricky's brain, too, before I intervened.

I close the folder, fingers clenching in my lap. "The damage is extensive, but reversible."

McNamara's lips thin. We discuss what this might mean for Daysha's kidnapper and how it might manifest. On the positive side, the witness described an adult well into his thirties. What I don't know is whether age's protective mechanisms hold with extended use.

Needless to say, I'm exhausted by the time I leave the office. I'm ready for warm, dry clothes and a steaming mug of tea. Pulling the door shut behind me, I step out just in time to see someone even more worn out than I am, leaning against the coffee station.

It's Daysha's mom, Aliyah.

Her eyes are swollen, her gaze fixed somewhere beyond the wall. The coffee she meant to make sits abandoned mid-prep. The empty sugar and creamer packets are scattered beside the cup, spoon untouched. Her soft curls are pulled into a hasty plait over one shoulder, and she's wearing sweats and a T-shirt printed with Daysha's photo—the emergency special run from the youth center.

It's the first time I've seen her out of scrubs.

Something inside me breaks.

"Aliyah!" I rush over, and we embrace, both dissolving into tears.

"How are you holding up?" I squeeze her again. "I'm so sorry."

Aliyah pulls away from me, wiping her eyes on the back of her sleeve. "You heard about the hotline tip?"

I nod, still choked up. "It's amazing news. There's hope. She's still with us."

Aliyah trembles. "Thank you for everything, for the reward, for using your voice. I haven't slept a wink since yesterday. When they told me about the gas station—" her voice crumbles into a sob.

I hold her fast, murmuring words of comfort while I rub her back. "I know. But we have to believe in our girl. Daysha's a fighter." I press a pack of tissues into her hands. "We already have her bracelet and the bridle swivel. She's trying to tell us something. I can't believe it's a coincidence."

Aliyah's gaze is bright with tears. "You think so?"

"I know it. I feel it here." I press a hand to my heart. "She won't give up, and neither can we."

"I'm so worried about her." Aliyah's voice trembles. "She only likes sleeping over at Ricky's, nowhere else. And it's so cold now. It makes her so sad when she can't do her hair nice and fresh every morning. I just…"

She collapses against me, and her quiet tears break my heart even more than her sobs.

I know what she's trying to say. I've felt it before with Tess. When you've lost someone, the darkest, most terrifying thoughts pierce as deeply as the tiniest, most intimate fears.

I hug her close and guide her toward a row of folding chairs outside an empty office. We sit, grasping hands, both crying our eyes out. I don't know who's comforting whom, only that we're holding on for dear life.

Outside, the rain gathers force, blurring the world beyond the glass. Streetlights dissolve into watercolor streaks, the parking lot vanishing beneath a sheen of silver. A crash of thunder splits the air, so loud it reverberates through my chest. For a moment, it feels like the sky is mourning with us—like something vast and unseen has cracked open too.

Neither of us speaks.

How can we when our fears are so heavy?

When nothing can fill the space that Daysha left?

Eclipse
Ronan

Do you know what it's like to lose the sun?

I do.

I can't believe she's gone.

It's been two days since the disastrous press conference.

Two days since my world fell apart.

Forty-eight hours, 2880 minutes, 172,800 seconds that have become a lifetime.

No. An eternity.

A lifetime suggests I'm alive, but there is no living without Thandi. Going through the motions, yes. But every bright, vital thing in my world is gone.

I'm merely a shell.

I wish Thandi were the kind of woman who threw tantrums or gave the silent treatment. Because rage indicates investment and in the blankness of silence is room to imagine other possibilities—a future where all of this is behind us.

But instead, she's been in touch. We'll meet tonight, and in her own words, nothing is guaranteed.

Meanwhile, she'll own me for the rest of my life, no matter what happens.

Forty-eight hours.

There's another reason that timeline is so weighted with grief—Daysha.

The gas station sighting is a beacon, but it's hard not to think about what the two-day mark means. I've read the statistics. If she's not back home by the end of today, the chances of her returning safely to us plummet. Yet all we have now is a witness tip, a bridle swivel, and a couple of used inhalers. It hardly seems like enough to beat the clock.

And if we don't….

I cover my head with the pillow. It's too awful to contemplate.

"Come on, Roncito, we're not doing this again." Fia's voice pulls me out of my spiral.

Groaning, I flop against the sheets. I refuse to open my eyes as she wheels up to the bed. How did she even find me? I need to have a word with Hensley.

I didn't go back to my place last night. I can't leave Whitlow. Can't bring myself to abandon the memory of Thandi in my arms or our breakfast together. I wish I'd seen that we were already unraveling. I could have prevented this, but I was too afraid. Too afraid to lose her, and too afraid to leap.

And now if I can't fix this, I'll never hold her again.

"Ronan," Fia's voice is sharper now.

"What?" I crack one eye open. "Stop yelling at a broken man. Also, don't you have work? Why are you here?"

"I'm not leaving you like this." Fia's voice gentles as she rests her head against my arm. "And you're not broken. Don't ever say that. You might be hurting, but you're not broken."

It sure as hell doesn't feel that way. James' old insults echo in my mind, words I'd thought I'd long buried: Soft, weak, useless. He repeated them so often in my youth that it felt like they'd replaced my name.

Today, I almost believe him. My throat works as I feel the familiar sting behind my eyes. "I don't know if we can survive this, Fia. I'll do my best, but what if I'm too late?"

"You can't be too late. You love each other. That has to mean something." Fia cuffs me under the chin. "Besides, I can help."

"How?"

"I'll talk to Thandi. She's my friend too. I hate to see you both like this. Besides, I feel responsible. I told you not to confess when you wanted to."

I sigh. "None of this is your fault, Fia. I fucked up. I should have done more research and seen the connections to Astor sooner, but you know my method. I've never had to dive deeper before. And once I knew, I was so happy with Thandi, I kept waiting for the right moment. That was my biggest mistake."

I trail off, staring out the window at the sunlight dappling through the trees. What a fool I was.

"Ronan, you're human. It's natural not to want to disappoint the people we love. All you can do now is make it right." Fia's gaze pierces mine. "Have you spoken to her?"

"A few texts about Daysha's case. I asked to see her, though." I press a hand to my eyes.

"And?"

"And she'll meet me for dinner. That's it. No promises." My voice cracks.

God, I miss her.

"What if I can't win her back?"

"Stop it. You can't think like that. This is a rough patch—a big one—but you *can* get through it."

"He came to Whitlow, you know," I say.

"Who did?" Fia pats the mattress, and I help her onto the bed with me, settling her against the pillows. I pull the covers up around us.

"Isn't this wrinkling your suit?" I ask, eying her navy Prada blazer.

"I have a handheld steamer in my trunk. Who came to Whitlow?"

"James. He had that *Daily Graph* article about your party. He was angry at me for dating Thandi, ranting and raving that she was the competition—as if I owe anything to Astor." I frown. "I should have known he'd try to destroy us. He's killed everything else important to me."

I clench my fingers in the sheets as anger explodes in my chest. This is the unending cycle I've been locked in since the press conference: immobilizing sorrow followed by blinding rage at James, his pettiness, and his malice. Even in this, he could not be a father. What kind of man destroys his own son to save a company?

Wasn't Mom's suffering enough?

Hasn't he taken enough from me?

I've tried to strike my own path and be the man that my mother wanted, but last night, in the midst of my torment, I realized the truth: If I must live without Thandi, only one thing will console me.

Vengeance.

I will take James down surgically. I'll leave him with nothing, just like he tried to leave me with nothing. When the knife twists, I want him to know it's my hand wielding it.

Fowler and Yanovich are waiting for my move.

I've decided.

This has to end.

And I have to do it before I absolve my sins with Thandi.

"Wait." Fia stiffens beside me, her lips parting in shock. "James had a hand in this?"

"Yes," I say grimly. "I saw Greg Owens at the press conference, but he was wearing a press badge. I thought maybe he'd quit, and that was why James was so erratic on Monday. I should have known better."

I bite back a curse. "I saw him. He fed that question to the Post reporter."

"That dirty—" Fia mutters the expletive I didn't. "You have to take him down, Ronan. This isn't just about you and Thandi now, but Ricky, Daysha, and all the other people he's hurt."

She goes silent, but what she doesn't say echoes between us.

Her, too.

Nodding, I hold her tightly to me. This is long overdue, for so many reasons beyond Thandi and me.

And thanks to Mom, I finally have the tools to do it.

The house creaks, shifting on its foundations. Outside, wind howls through the trees, the branches rapping against the glass in a sharp, urgent rhythm.

Fia's right. I can't stay here wallowing.

Time to get shit done.

The cold hitting my lungs is the jolt I need to kickstart my system. Fia provided the emotional charge; now all I need is the dopamine rush to carry me through to the end.

My feet strike the spongy asphalt that loops around Whitlow and descends into the quiet neighborhood below. As soon as Fia left, I called Aamir to tell him we were pulling the trigger. I know he would have liked more time, but to his credit, he didn't say a word. He just got Dr. Rhee, the patent lawyer, on speed dial.

The truth is, she drafted the complaint days ago.

Aamir wasn't just being a perfectionist. I'd held on filing until I could tell Thandi….

I suck in a deep breath. The cold burns my throat as a wave of pain assaults me. I ride it, reminding myself that I can't afford to lose momentum.

I need to keep moving. No more crying over spilled milk.

I think of Thandi, so small and delicate in front of the sea of reporters. Yet she projected strength far beyond her stature—voice clear and chin notched high even through her pain.

I can't stop fighting, not only because it's right, but because it's what Thandi would do, too.

The path curves toward Whitlow's back gate, where a camellia bush has exploded into bloom. Its pink petals gleam against a backdrop of dying color—maples burning red, oaks fading to bronze. Life opening, even as the rest of nature prepares to retreat.

Becca, one of the summer hands who'd worked the vineyard register, waves to me from across the lane. I lift a hand in return. She grins, braces flashing, then ducks into her car. Music spills from the open window as she drives past.

For a moment, life feels sweet again.

The footsteps aren't out of the ordinary at first; just another runner on the lane. I swerve to the side, making room for them to pass.

Except they don't.

They realign, moving behind me instead.

Frowning, I keep running even as the hair pricks on the back of my neck. The footsteps behind me sound lighter, the stride shorter—someone smaller, but keeping pace. A man, probably.

The question now is whether this is a coincidence or a threat. I'd be hard to pin in hand-to-hand combat, but strength isn't everything if my pursuer is fast or agile. Besides, I have no idea if he's armed.

Abruptly, I break left, taking the narrow path that leads to the pond. For a moment, I think I've lost him, but after a few minutes, the footsteps pick up again, more distant, given my headstart but steadily closing in.

He's fast.

Fuck.

There's no question now that I'm being followed. I pick up the pace, glancing around for something I can use as a weapon.

Did James get wind of the filing?

Could he be desperate enough to take out his own son?

Sadly, after everything he's done, I wouldn't put it past the bastard. I think of the many beatings I endured as a child, and the punch he didn't hesitate to throw on Monday. Even putting aside the worst-case scenario, he's never been above physical intimidation. He's just hired it out, now that he's too weak to do it himself.

My breathing deepens. My mind is suddenly sharp, infinitely clear, as I enter that surreal headspace I always inhabited before tournaments. Adrenaline pumps through my veins, and my muscles contract, activating—tensing for confrontation.

This is a shit situation. I'm isolated and exposed with nothing to defend myself. I could stop, grab a rock, or break off a branch, but I'm pretty confident in my endurance. Giving myself a longer lead and wearing this motherfucker down seems like the better option.

For now, at least.

I keep running. Leaves rustle and twigs crack under the man's feet. He's not even trying to hide his intent anymore.

I listen hard, weighing my next move.

Now that I'm running faster, my stalker hasn't faltered. His breaths have become audible, though not ragged. If I push to max speed, I could probably lose him.

His breathing also suggests something critical: even if he's armed, he doesn't have a gun or a long-range weapon. If he intended to use one, he would have by now to avoid falling further behind.

Am I certain? No.

Am I willing to take the chance? Yes.

I increase my pace, my footfalls pounding the path in a furious rhythm. It's imperceptible at first, but the faster I run, the more I hear it.

His steps slow, then quicken again. He's struggling. *Good.*

I toy with outrunning him, but I'm no fool. I know that won't eliminate the danger. Bullies don't fight fair. When they can't defeat strength, they go after someone more vulnerable. And there are only two people in my life who could be used as leverage: Thandi or Fia.

I'm not about to let that happen.

I decide in a split second, slowing enough for James's thug to catch up. He's gasping and wheezing; pathetic, just like the man who hired him.

He finds his second wind and regains his stride. The gap narrows. I resist the urge to bolt, letting him approach. His footsteps are so loud now that I can almost smell his sweat. He surges forward, and finally, he speaks.

"Stop—"

I don't let him finish.

I pivot, drop my shoulder, and tackle him.

Catch

Ronan

We hit the dirt hard, and everything that happens next is reflex, pure instinct. I roll James' thug beneath me. He fights, flails, bucking up against my greater strength. I lean into him, my weight pinning his chest until his struggle falters.

His foot kicks out once, then stills. A panicked whine seeps from his lips.

"Who are you and what the fuck do you want?" I growl.

"Please," he gasps. "I'm not—" His chest heaves under me.

"Not what, you bastard?" I brace my arm, increasing the pressure. He gurgles, eyes rolling in fear.

Seriously? This is the best James could do?

"Well?" I demand, and the man whimpers.

Now that I have him subdued, I get a better look. He's not what I expect: hazel eyes, thick dark brown hair, pale, mousy features. His white button-up is rumpled. A sticky-note pad and a pen bulge from his shirt pocket. He's a little taller than average and lean—exactly what I'd guessed from his stride. Normally, I'd call it a runner's build, but that clearly isn't his forte.

His lips tremble. For the first time, I spot a backpack and a pair of cracked tortoiseshell glasses a few feet away—clear casualties of our tussle.

Who the fuck is this dude, and what is he doing here? There's no way James sent someone like this to shake me down.

"Speak," I grit. "Or you won't like what happens next."

"Please," he croaks, hands lifting helplessly. He swallows hard. When his gaze finds mine, his eyes are glassy with unshed tears. "Please, you have to believe me. I'm not here to hurt you. I need your help."

"Sorry about earlier," I say, pressing a mug of coffee into Dr. Patrick Linny's hands.

The scientist makes a grateful sound and brings the cup to his lips. He still looks shaken from our encounter.

Turns out he *was* hired by James, but not as a thug. He's a neuro-data scientist in Astor's Cognitive Therapeutics division. Instead of chasing me, he is literally on the run—a man terrified for his reputation and his safety.

Dr. Linny is a whistleblower. Once he started speaking, I knew I had to get Aamir and Frederick here immediately. Given what he's uncovered, his fear isn't paranoia; it's self-preservation.

James will stop at nothing to keep this buried.

I pour myself coffee and sit across from Linny at the kitchen table. We're at Whitlow, but not in the main house. Though Patrick has never been here before, he's convinced someone might recognize him, so we're holed up in the pool house, a place that hasn't seen a guest in years.

The doorbell chimes, and Patrick jerks upright, nearly sloshing his coffee. He's already half out of his chair, eyes wide with panic.

"Hey," I say softly, showing him the security camera feed on my phone. "It's okay. It's just Aamir and Fred."

"Oh." He sinks back down, hands shaking. "Okay."

"You can breathe easy," I tell him. "You're safe here. I won't let Astor touch you."

The other man's throat works as he nods. I'm not sure I've allayed his fears, though. He stares into his mug, shoulders hunched, the surface of his coffee trembling almost as much as his hands.

Once again, I'm stunned by the number of lives James has poisoned. He robs everything of goodness and innocence. But no more. It ends now—and with Patrick's testimony, the final blow will be sharper than I ever imagined.

That is, if I can keep the poor man from having a heart attack first.

The doorbell chimes again, and I head for the entrance. I let Aamir and Fred in, ushering them toward the kitchen.

"This better be good," Aamir mutters. "We need to submit the filing soon if you still want to announce today."

"Trust me," I say. "This will be worth your while."

He grunts but follows me down the hall. Fred, less skeptical, clasps me on the shoulder. He looks steadier than when I last saw him—grief still present, but no longer devouring him.

"Good to see you, son. I hope I can help."

"Me too," I murmur.

Both men stop cold when they see the frightened scientist. Despite my reassurance, Patrick has retreated to the French doors that lead to the garden. His backpack is slung over his shoulder. A knife trembles between his fingers.

"Hey." I approach slowly, palms raised. "Remember what I said? You can trust me. Aamir and Fred are here to help."

"Jesus Christ," Aamir mutters under his breath.

I shoot him a warning look. "Patrick, put the knife down. No one's going to hurt you here."

The room is taut with tension; the knife glints under the pendant light. Then all at once, the fight drains out of Patrick. He flings the blade aside, and it clatters to the floor. He grips the counter, chest heaving.

"I'm sorry. So sorry." He drags a hand over his face. "I'm not normally like this, but someone broke into my office, and my tires were slashed this morning. What if they come after my family? I just—" He draws a gasping breath. "I don't know what to do."

"Should we call the police?" Fred's tone is deliberately even. "If what you're describing is accurate, that's targeted intimidation, and it's a felony in most jurisdictions."

"No!" Patrick shrinks back. "No cops. Not yet. Velma was convinced they were on Astor's payroll."

"How about a compromise?" I offer Patrick my hand and guide him back to the table, easing the backpack off his shoulder. "I'll call Equinox, my private security firm. They're highly trained and can provide round-the-clock protection until you're ready to involve the authorities. Since your home may be compromised, you can stay here."

Patrick stares. "You-you'd do that for me?"

"Dr. Linny, it's the least I can do, given everything you've endured."

"I'm sorry," Aamir says, pulling out a chair. "Can someone please explain what's going on?"

"Yes." Patrick straightens. "I'm Dr. Patrick Linny. My background is in neurodata science, and I analyze brain-imaging data to find patterns. I'm currently the head of Cognitive Therapeutics at Astor Pharmaceuticals."

"Patrick is a whistleblower," I tell Aamir and Frederick.

"Fuck." Aamir's eyes widen. He's already digging through his briefcase for his MacBook. "Hold on. We'll need to document this."

"What happened?" Fred asks, leaning against the counter. He turns an apple over in his hands.

"My research partner saw it first," Patrick says quietly. "Dr. Velma Koenig—she was the neuropharmacology lead who ran the early WhiffRush animal studies. When the mice started showing cortical thinning and erratic maze behavior, she called it neurotoxic stress."

I nod, but Fred and Aamir both frown.

"What exactly is that?" Aamir asks, pausing his note-taking.

Patrick rubs the back of his neck. "The drug overstimulates the brain. At first, everything speeds up—memory, focus, even reaction time—but the system can't handle that pressure. The circuits that are supposed to calm things down don't. It's like a motor that won't shut off until it burns out."

Frederick's brows jump to his hairline. "So you're saying it damages the brain?"

"Yes," Patrick says. "Tiny injuries that build up over time. Velma tried to stop the product launch when she saw the pediatric trial MRIs."

I glance at him. "Let me guess: Astor did not like that."

He shakes his head. "A month later, her access to the database was revoked. Two weeks after that, they accused her of falsifying assay data."

Patrick's eyes are haunted as he stares into the mug in his hands. "It was completely false, of course, but that wasn't the point. Pushing her out was. Compliance opened an investigation. She fought it, proved every result, but the damage was done. They settled out of court—NDA and non-disparagement baked in. Officially, she 'resigned to pursue other opportunities.' Unofficially… her career's over."

He swallows hard. "I didn't speak up then. I told myself it wasn't my fight. But when I saw Dr. Elowen's press conference—and that little girl's face on the news—I couldn't stay quiet anymore."

"I'm glad you didn't. But why come here? Why me?"

"Once I started asking around, there were whispers that Velma wasn't the first to raise the alarm. But no one was powerful enough to take on Mr. Astor."

Patrick's expression darkens. "When I saw you on TV, I realized the only person who might be able to stop him is his son."

I blink. Hearing his conviction strengthens my own. If I needed a sign that I must go through with my plan, this is it.

"There's more," I say after a moment.

"More?" Patrick frowns.

I nod. "Before you arrived, Aamir and I were preparing to file a suit against Astor Pharmaceuticals. We know their products are harmful, but I discovered that my father stole Dr. Rosalind Thorne's formulations to produce them."

I take a steadying breath. "She was my mother."

Patrick gasps. "Son of a—"

Fred's lips part. "So you figured it out. Just like she said you would."

"Yeah," I croak. I tell him about my conversation with Fowler, about how Mom's company wasn't the only thing James stole from her. About how Astor's already unraveling, and it's up to us to pull the final thread.

I stare at my hands. Mom gave me this gift. I hope by the end of today, I've lived up to everything she wanted.

Aamir stops typing, a grin spreading across his features. "This is huge. With Dr. Linny's testimony and what we already have, we can file the civil suit immediately. There's even enough to support a criminal inquiry if the feds take an interest."

"Perfect," Frederick says, biting into his apple. "Son, you've clearly done your homework. Why did you need me here?"

"There's one thing I need to clarify before we file," I say, forcing myself to focus. "I reviewed the old merger language. There's a clause suggesting all data and inventions developed under Thorne Therapeutics passed to Astor."

We've spent two weeks working on the complaint, but anxiety still grips my chest. Everything else is damning, but so much hinges on this detail. "That wouldn't invalidate Mom's IP, right?"

"It couldn't." Fred shakes his head. "When your mother founded Thorne Therapeutics, she didn't assign the patents to the company; she licensed them. She was cautious about your father's motives and kept ownership to herself. Her formulations never legally belonged to the company, only to her."

"That's Mom for you." I manage a small smile. "Always a step ahead."

Fred's gaze softens, his expression wistful. "Your mother was no fool."

"Neither is her son," Aamir says, closing his laptop. "We'll draft the final filing today. Then we move."

I frown, rocked by a sudden thought. What if James misunderstood? He's still a bastard, but what if I've been assigning him more malice than he deserves?

"Wait—did James actually understand all of this?" I ask.

"Oh, he knew." Fred's tone hardens. "He simply convinced the board that since Rosalind was his wife, Astor had 'effective ownership' anyway." His mouth twists. "I refuse to believe any of those people thought it was legal, but who was going to question him? With that much profit on the line…" He shrugs.

"And Mom was too sick to fight it." My fists clench. "They were all complicit."

"Exactly."

The knowledge settles over me like a shroud. For a moment, all I feel is rage—raw and searing—followed by a wave of grief so sharp it leaves me bereft. How many times did he betray her? How much did Mom suffer, watching him strip her work bare?

"This…" Patrick's voice breaks through my torment. He's been following the exchange, eyes wide. "This is so much." He swallows hard. "But you're saying there's hope? That we can actually take Astor down?"

I clench my jaw. "And we're going to win—if I have anything to say about it."

Patrick's shoulders relax. The desperation that's been dogging him since we collided begins to fade, replaced by something fragile but unmistakable.

Faith.

"Thank God," he breathes. "It was a risk—" He shakes his head, clutching his backpack to his chest. "I've got all my notes, all the datasets right here. Whatever you need, just say the word. This is for Velma, too."

"We've got this," I murmur, thinking of Thandi, Daysha, Fia, and Ricky.

Through it all, Mom has always been the catalyst—for hope, for love, for change, even in the darkest moments. I hold onto that as I think of what the day will bring. And most of all, my dinner with Thandi.

"I'm sorry about you and Dr. Elowen." Patrick smiles for the first time, as if reading my mind. "To be honest, I've had a bit of a crush since I met her at the Society for Neuroscience Annual Meeting last year. Just professionally, of course—" he adds quickly when he sees my expression. "She's brilliant, and she gave me some valuable feedback on my latest model."

Damn right she is. She's sweet, and sexy, and kind—

And Patrick isn't a threat, I remind myself, forcing my body to relax.

Besides, how can he be, when I'm not even sure Thandi still wants me?

Patrick ducks his head, cheeks coloring.

I clear my throat and reach for my coffee, pretending it suddenly requires all my attention.

The corners of Aamir's mouth twitch, though his eyes, when they meet mine, are warm with empathy.

"Well," he says dryly, "now that we've all bonded, shall we discuss next steps?"

Breadcrumb
Thandi

"How many more posters do we need?" Janice holds the picture of Daysha up to the light. The youth center director isn't in her usual crisp business suit but in jeans and a sweatshirt.

I'm dressed down too. I haven't been in the office much since Daysha's kidnapping. I've been working from home, starting at the crack of dawn, so I can leave early enough to make it to the youth center by four for our daily search party.

It doesn't matter how many days have passed, or how many news articles say the window to find Daysha is closing.

We're not giving up.

"I think we need about fifty more," I tell Janice, handing a stack to a somber-looking Mya and Romero. Normally, they'd be all over the basketball court, but like so many others, they've come to help.

Across the gym, a young woman kneels to photograph a smiling group of volunteers, her camera strap brushing the floor. I recognize her a second later as Alyssa Grant, one of our former youth center kids, now reporting for the *Kenleigh Gazette*.

She catches my eye and jogs over, her press badge bouncing against her sweatshirt. "Ms. T! It's so good to see you. I'm just putting together a quick community story about the search—how everyone's pitching in."

I manage a small smile. "That's wonderful, Alyssa. Thank you. The more attention we can draw to Daysha's case, the better."

Alyssa beams. "Can I get a quote?"

"Maybe not today." I shake my head. "I'm trying to keep my nose clean—keep the focus on Daysha."

Alyssa laughs, unoffended. "Fair enough. I guess your reward speaks for itself." Winking, she slips me her card. "Just in case you change your mind." Then she moves off, camera clicking as she captures another group near the poster table.

I sigh, turning the card over in my hands. I haven't forgotten McNamara's words about what's needed to keep a case relevant. A quote from me would probably be huge for Alyssa's career, too.

But I had good intentions with my last press conference—and look how that ended. I can't afford another distraction or to risk the board's ire with another PR disaster.

Besides, there's more than enough to do here.

I grab my badge and get moving.

Across the room, Ricky is hunched over a sheet of poster paper with my parents. This has been hardest on him most of all. He hasn't spoken much since Monday, and he's barely eaten. Today, he's wearing Daysha's favorite navy hoodie that says *Science Superstar* on the front. I don't blame him. I'd want to keep her close, too.

"Hey, how's it going?" I say, jogging over to them.

"Hanging in." Mom sighs, enfolding me in a hug. Without letting go, she looks around the gym where we've set up our makeshift command center. "It's good to see so many people here."

I swallow past the lump in my throat. "Yeah."

Dad's organizing the bright pink wristbands we'll use to identify everyone in our group. He looks up with a tired smile. "Hey, Peanut. Almost done with our poster."

While all the other fliers are printed, Ricky insisted on making his own. He's meticulously drawing a border of yellow stars as I come up behind him.

I have to fight back a rush of tears when I see what he's created.

The poster is a beautiful collage of images: Daysha in a lab coat and oversized goggles, holding up a beaker of blue liquid. That was the day we learned about copper ions and how a little ammonia could turn them into something new. Daysha sticking her tongue out in concentration as she winds the spool of a kite. Daysha grinning in front of a giant bowl of ice cream. Daysha throwing her hands up after a cartwheel.

At the top of it all, in big purple letters, Ricky has written: **PLEASE FIND MY BEST FRIEND.**

He's included all the critical information—Daysha's height, weight, eye and hair color, and when she was last seen. He's so intent on his work that he doesn't even hear me come up behind him.

I want to hug him, but I don't want to smudge the stars, so I lean in and kiss his cheek instead. "How are you doing, sweetie?" I ruffle his hair.

"Good," he mumbles, not looking up. "I'm almost done. This is my last one." I glance across the table and see that he's already completed three posters, each with its own unique, loving design.

Heart clenching, I smooth the curling edge of the orange one on top. "These are so beautiful, Ricky. They'll grab everyone's attention, and that's exactly what we need to find Daysha."

"You think so?" He raises his head, staring up at me with wide, wounded eyes.

"I know so," I choke out, but I'm not sure if I'm trying to convince him or myself.

"Thandi, over here."

I turn around, and Fia waves to me as she rolls up to the equipment table. Ms. Ortega is stationed there, clipboard in hand, checking people in with her usual efficiency.

The table in front of her is a patchwork of supplies: bottled water glistening with condensation, neatly wrapped foil sandwiches stacked in boxes, rows of flashlights with fresh batteries, and folded route maps weighted down by a bowl of candy. A stack of reflective vests sits at the corner—only a dozen or so—set aside for team leads or anyone wearing dark colors.

Ms. Ortega lifts one of the vests and holds it against Fia with an appraising look.

"You're definitely a small, not a medium."

"Only if we're talking size, not personality," Fia quips, and the nearby volunteers chuckle.

At the far end of the gym, the emergency exit doors are propped open, the alarm temporarily disabled so Fia's SUV can back halfway into the space. The cool evening air seeps in through the doorway, carrying the smell of cut grass and the earlier rain.

The van's hatch is open, its interior glowing under the gym lights. Inside are rows of thermoses, pastry boxes, and a folded sign that reads **COMMUNITY INFO BOOTH — TIPS & COFFEE.** Carmen and Fatouma are crouched at the rear bumper, packing up the last few boxes before they head out to the rendezvous point near Anchor Park.

Fia won't be out on the trails tonight, but she's running the coordination hub at the park entrance—collecting community tips, logging check-ins, and keeping the volunteers fueled. Ms. Ortega calls it an "information station," but everyone knows it's more than that. It's where you go for updates, directions, or just a cup of something warm when the search drags past sunset.

"Don't worry, I'll make sure everyone stays caffeinated," Fia says, tapping the rim of her travel mug with a wink. "And I brought the big percolator this time—none of that instant nonsense."

"Good," Ms. Ortega nods. "You'll be our anchor there. Once the teams check in, they'll come straight to you for updates."

I move toward Fia as she adjusts her lanyard over the electric-orange vest.

"Hey, girl."

She looks up, and before either of us can say another word, we pull each other into a tight hug. For a moment, the buzz of the gym fades, the murmur of volunteers blurring into a soft hum around us.

I'm so glad she's here. I'd worried that when everything with Ronan fell apart, I'd lost not only the love of my life but my newest friend too. When Fia texted to say she'd be at the gym tonight, that she wanted to help, I almost wept. I can't stand to lose anyone else.

We're both crying a little as we pull back from each other.

"You holding up?" Fia asks.

"Not really," I admit, and we both chuckle.

"Real talk." Fia swipes under her eyes. "This has been the worst." Her gaze softens. "We'll talk later, yeah?"

I duck my head. "Yeah."

"Oh, Thandi, you're here," Ms. Ortega calls, glancing up from her clipboard. "Good. Got the only XS vest left for you."

"Wow," I say, folding my arms. "I'm not *that short*."

Fia and Ms. Ortega share a look.

"What?" I demand.

Fia grins, then makes a motion like she's sealing her lips.

Ms. Ortega mutters something that sounds suspiciously like she could fatten up Fia, but even her *pozole rojo* couldn't help my situation.

Before I can fire back, Carmen appears, hefting another box of sandwiches onto the table. "Who called the cops?"

Fia blinks. "What do you mean?"

Carmen jerks her chin toward the gym doors.

I turn, my pulse jumping. Standing just inside the doorway are Detective McNamara and the younger officer I recognize from the night at the park. They're hesitating, McNamara scanning the room, Hayes shifting her weight beside her, unsure where to start.

My heart thuds as a dozen possibilities crash through my mind. *Please let this be good news.*

"That's Detective McNamara," I murmur. "She's in charge of Daysha's case."

Fia's eyes widen. "You think…?"

"I don't know," I whisper, just as McNamara spots me. Her eyebrows lift, and she waves.

"I think they want to talk to you, Thandi." Carmen rests her arm on Fia's chair. "No rush, Sis, but we're all loaded up. Just waiting for your final check."

Fia spins her chair around, nodding. "Let me take a look." She pauses. "You'll be okay, Thandi?"

"Yeah." I swallow, even as I glance over my shoulder, trying to read McNamara's expression. She looks grim, but then she always does.

What if it isn't good news? What if it's no news at all? I ball my fists, nails biting into my palms. At this point, I don't know which is worse.

"I'll see what they want," I say, leaving Fia and Carmen to finish their prep. My heart pounds as I approach Hayes and McNamara.

"Detective. I wasn't expecting to see you here."

McNamara gives me a tight smile. The collar of her dark field jacket is turned up, emphasizing her simple pearl studs. "Sorry for the interruption. Just didn't know who was in charge here."

"In charge of…?" If she needs permission for something related to the case, Daysha's mom isn't here. She wanted to be, but I convinced her to sit this one out and get some rest.

"I don't have much manpower to spare," McNamara says, "but Hayes will lend whatever support she can from the command tent. She'll help coordinate communication with your teams and relay any credible tips that come in."

I blink, surprised. "That's… really kind of you."

McNamara adjusts her jacket. "Kindness has nothing to do with it. You're organized and committed. We should've looped you in sooner."

She glances toward the open door where Fia's SUV waits, ready to go. "That's your friend out there—the one setting up the info tent?"

I nod.

"Good. Hayes will check in with her, make sure lines stay open."

Hayes flashes a thumbs-up and moves toward Fia's station, tucking a small notepad under her arm.

I wait, my hands twisting together. "Detective—" I blurt.

McNamara sighs. "We're still giving this everything we've got, but we haven't found her yet."

My shoulders droop. I'm not surprised… yet, I'd hoped. I try to keep my composure, even as devastation creeps in. I'm starting to understand just how long the wait to bring Daysha home might be. I can't keep shattering at every disappointment.

I suck in a breath. "Okay."

"There is something small, related to your contract, though." McNamara shifts her weight. "That's why I wanted to talk to you."

"My contract? Do you need me to look at more of Stephan's scans?"

"No. We pulled more evidence from the gas station," McNamara says. "There was a coffee cup in the trash—near one of those self-serve stations. The kidnapper must've poured himself a cup before paying for gas."

I feel a tiny surge of hope. It's not much, but it's something.

"I told you before that the exterior footage was a wash, but we just got the in-store feed. We can't see his face; the register cam only caught him from behind. But the timestamp matches the clerk's memory."

"You're sure it was him?" I try to hide my skepticism. I'm no detective, but hundreds of customers must use that kiosk every day.

"We ran DNA off the cup's lid," McNamara continues. "And it matches what we found on the WhiffRush inhaler Hayes recovered near the park."

"Matches?" I whisper, glancing over my shoulder at Hayes, who's now huddled with Fia. God, what if she hadn't thought to bag that extra inhaler?

McNamara nods grimly. "It's the same person, Ms. Elowen. Which means whoever took Daysha is also using WhiffRush. I just need your expert opinion on how unstable he might be."

I feel so lightheaded I can barely stand. I jerk my thumb toward one of the benches. "Can we sit?"

"Sure." McNamara follows, taking her seat beside me.

"But does this mean you know who he is?" I press, ignoring her question and the sinking feeling in my stomach, for the moment.

McNamara presses her lips together. "We're running it through CODIS, our DNA database, but so far—nothing."

I'm quiet. I don't know what to say. I lean forward, cradling my head in my hands. It's a breadcrumb, a glimmer on the path to justice, but it feels so insignificant in the face of what Daysha is enduring.

I wanted more.

"I know it's not much." McNamara's lip twitches. Her expression softens, caught somewhere between defensiveness and embarrassment.

"No, it's important." I force out, seeing her face. There's as much at stake for her as the rest of us. No need to kick her while she's doing the best she can. "Thank you for telling me."

She nods, jaw tight. "And the behavioral pattern?"

I shake my head. "Impossible for me to say, without more information about his previous use. WhiffRush has no dosage guidelines. Two inhalers in two days is frequent, but not unreasonable." I meet McNamara's gaze. "Sorry, Detective."

McNamara is quiet for the space of two heartbeats. Her gaze drifts across the gym and lands on Alyssa, photographing the quilt Mrs. Marshall has been piecing together in Daysha's honor. A half-dozen volunteers lean in to help her stretch the fabric flat, the flash catching on bright patches of yellow and purple.

The detective's expression softens for just a moment, then she looks back at me. "Then we'll keep working. Thanks, Ms. Elowen."

"Thandi, please." My voice comes out soft. "And thank you, Detective. Truly. From all of us here."

McNamara zips up her coat. "I'll be in touch."

Her gaze drifts toward the bleachers, where Hayes is still talking with Fia.

"Officer Hayes," she calls, and Hayes glances over. "You've got point here. Keep me updated if anything solid comes in."

"Yes, ma'am," Hayes replies.

McNamara turns back to me. "Good luck out there," she calls and heads for the exit, pulling the door shut behind her.

I watch her go, shaken, disappointed, and unsure what to do or think next. I'm grateful when Romero comes up to me, clutching a stack of pens.

"Ms. T, Jenny says we're out of release forms."

"Shit." The word slips out as I jerk back to the present, scanning the room for Janice. "Janice had some, but I don't see her."

I stand, rubbing my hands down the front of my sweatpants. "Right. I'll go make more."

"Thanks, Ms. T."

Romero's easy trust steadies me, at least for the next few minutes.

I sprint across the gym and down the hall. Janice's office door stands half open, the light still on inside. She's nowhere to be found, but I can't help smiling when I spot a fresh stack of release forms on her desk. I brush my hand over the top sheet. It's still warm from the copier.

"Of course," I murmur, shaking my head. Leave it to Janice to be ten steps ahead.

I grab the stack, pivot on my heel—

And slam straight into Ronan.

Falling
Thandi

Of course, he catches me.

I wanted to fall.

Then I wouldn't have to remember what it feels like to be in his arms.

"Careful." Ronan steadies me, pulling me against his chest as the consent forms slip from my hands, fluttering to the floor in a shower of white.

The moment our bodies touch is electric. I feel it all the way to my toes. He's just as warm and strong as I remember—just as solid. Worse, for all his strength, his tenderness is the same too. That's the part I have no defenses against. That, and the way that even now, when my heart hurts so much, he still feels like home.

I'm trembling. I stiffen and try to pull away, but he doesn't let go.

"Don't run from me, baby. Please." His voice is rough, his eyes searching mine. There is so much pain there that I'm frozen for a moment.

I don't know how to process it. I don't want to know he's suffering, because I still don't understand how a man who claimed to love me deceived me so easily.

Was it easy? My traitorous heart whispers, reminding me of his desperation at the park, his anguish during breakfast. *Didn't he warn you?* It presses. *And look at you now. Aren't you doing exactly what he feared?*

"Please," I whisper.

"Please, what?" Ronan cups my face, his thumb stroking my cheek. Sparks ignite from his touch and blaze down my neck, inflaming me in a torment of desire and confusion. "Tell me. Anything you want, anything I can do to make this right, the answer is yes."

"Don't." I jerk away from him. "I can't do this. Not right now. I need to focus on Daysha."

Ronan nods sharply, releasing me. "Okay."

"What are you even doing here?" I say, wrapping my arms around myself.

Ronan steps back, shoving his hands into his pockets. "I'm on the mailing list. They added me after my pickup game donation. When I read about tonight, I wanted to help but..." He trails off, jaw clenching.

"But what?"

"I knew you'd be here, and I didn't want to make you uncomfortable, so I told Janice I'd drop by with a check instead. Besides—" Ronan's gaze darts away from mine. "Something's come up, and I need to head to an event."

That's when I notice what he's wearing. A fine wool charcoal suit molds to his powerful frame. Platinum cufflinks glint at his wrists. His blush tie is a soft, unexpected touch. *Pink,* just like the old nickname he had for me before we became something far more intimate to each other.

My throat aches. Something inside me hardens as I glance down at my sweats and scuffed sneakers. I've been barely holding it together—too gutted over Daysha, too hollow from missing him—to manage anything beyond survival. And here he is, pristine and composed, moving on with business. Meanwhile, I'm still walking a tightrope with an Immerscent board that already doubts my leadership.

I'm such an idiot. The pain I saw in his eyes earlier? Who says it has anything to do with me? He didn't even want to see me today. He said so himself.

The papers are everywhere. I drop to the floor, blinking hard, gathering them up.

"Thandi."

I move faster, crawling across the carpet, crushing forms under my knees. Two have slid beneath Janice's giant speckled dieffenbachia. I reach for them, hands shaking.

"Thandi, please."

There's one left, half-hidden under the coffee table. Or maybe beside it. I can't tell anymore. My vision blurs. I pat blindly at the rug.

Not there.

Not there either.

"Where is it?" I whisper. The words hitch as a sob tears loose from my chest.

The tears won't stop. Ashamed, I twist away, hiding my face in the crook of my arm.

Pain. That's all there is. Pain everywhere. I don't know how to stop it. All my strength is gone. I can't get up. Not even the thought of Tess can rouse me. For the first time, I want to stop fighting and just sink into the darkness that's been chasing me for the last two decades. My fingers clench the carpet.

What has fighting gotten me anyway?

Tess is still gone. Daysha is now in danger.

An animal sound fills the air, guttural and wounded. It takes a moment before I realize it's coming from my lips.

Oh, God.

I scramble backward, desperate to escape, but suddenly I'm caught, pulled into Ronan's arms again.

"Stop it, Thandi, please. You're hurting yourself."

His voice is ragged. His arms tighten around me—unyielding as stone, comforting as a caress. He draws me close and slides to the floor, his back braced against Janice's desk. He rocks me as if we're both orphaned—rootless.

"Don't cry, baby. I'm sorry," he murmurs into my hair. "I'm so sorry you're hurting. I never wanted it to be like this."

My tongue is a stone. I close my eyes, too tired to do anything else.

"You'll still come tonight?" Ronan whispers in my ear.

I stifle a laugh, almost delirious with sorrow. Maybe that's what Tess has been trying to tell me all this time—that it will never get better until I shatter into a million pieces. That I have to break to start over again.

Just give up, the voice in my head coos—the one that's afraid, the one that's heartbroken, the one exhausted from carrying a debt I can never repay.

So I do as it says.

I say yes.

Crisis
Thandi

I didn't have much energy for the search in the end.

So I'm here in the community tent with Fia and Evelyn, handing out coffee and backstopping Hayes as she interviews community members and files paperwork.

The evening has been a flurry of activity. The tent is filled with the aroma of coffee, hot cocoa, and fresh pastries. Fia's stationed at a folding table, swiping through a tablet as she logs which search teams have checked in. Hayes moves between her and a cluster of volunteers, jotting notes in efficient shorthand, police radio crackling at her shoulder.

Evelyn is beside me, rosy-cheeked in a scarlet sweater and a mustard polka dot scarf wrapped around her halo of dark curly hair. She keeps morale up, doling out coffee and banana muffins from a tray and encouraging newcomers to fuel up. Quiet spoken and curvy, Evelyn is as soft as Dani is strong. On the surface, at least. You won't meet another woman with a stronger spine of steel—or a bigger heart.

After tonight's run-in with Ronan, I'm not ready to return home and will spend another night at her and Dani's place. I'd go to my parents', but they have enough to deal with without putting up with my heartbreak. At least with Evelyn and Dani, I won't be alone or have to put on a brave face. It hurts a little, seeing their love when mine is in shreds, but I'd never begrudge them their joy. Not when so little in this life is guaranteed.

"Hey, love." Dani shakes the mud off her boots and ambles over to our fuel station. In one seamless motion, Evelyn presses a coffee cup into her hands while Dani leans in to kiss her forehead.

"How's it going?"

"Good." Evelyn nudges me with a conspiratorial wink. "Thandi and I make a good team. We've gone through four canisters of coffee and about fifty muffins already."

"Jesus," Dani mutters. "No wonder everyone's so revved up."

I let out my first laugh since we left the youth center. "Nothing like sugar and caffeine to keep the trains moving."

"Yo, Dani!" Fia calls across the tent. "Stop distracting my workers and come make yourself useful. Hayes is drowning over here."

She jerks her thumb toward the line of folks waiting to be screened. Hayes and Fia have worked out a color-coded sticky-note system—green for solid leads, yellow for maybes, red for rumors that don't check out.

Dani rolls her eyes, but I catch the gleam in them as she abandons us for Fia. Now I'm really laughing. It's like watching two mastodons butt heads. Those two live to rib each other.

"This level of bossiness has to be an OSHA violation," I hear Dani say, and Fia cackles. A second later, their heads are bent together as Fia walks her through the color-coding system.

"Quick break?" Evelyn murmurs, her gaze soft as it drifts toward Dani.

"Yeah." I grab a cup of hot cocoa, dumping in extra marshmallows—I've definitely earned them—before following her to the makeshift "lounge" area on the other side of the tent. In reality, it's nothing more than three folding metal chairs, but I'll take it.

Evelyn eyes me over her mug. "Did something happen at the youth center?"

"What?" I jerk my head up. "Why do you ask?"

"You weren't on the roster for the tent tonight, and when you came in, you looked... shaken."

"I…" I bow my head.

"Hey, don't do that," Evelyn says gently. "I'm glad you're here. I would've been bored out of my mind by myself."

I nod, my fingers tracing the rim of my cup. "I went to Janice's office to get some extra consent forms … and Ronan was there."

"What? What did he say?"

I startle as Fia rolls up to us. Her chair hums as she maneuvers across the uneven ground, the power assist kicking in when the grass dips. She lifts a thermos. "Hayes and Dani have got the line covered. Can I join you?"

I give her a tired smile. "The more the merrier."

"Don't sound so excited," she teases. She leans her head against mine. "Talk to me. How can I help?"

When I don't answer, she sighs, going quiet. "I know it's … complicated. Ronan's my best friend, but I care about you too, Thandi. And I've known that man for a decade. He's the happiest he's ever been with you. You belong together."

"Stop." My eyes sting. I drop my gaze to my trembling hands. "I don't know if that's in the cards for us anymore, Fia."

"Why?" Evelyn prods gently. "Is there really no repairing what happened?"

"I don't know." My voice cracks. "It's not just that he's an Astor— though it is. It's that he said he loved me, but still kept it from me. I don't understand why."

"I'm biased. Of course I am," Fia says, her voice uncharacteristically unsteady. "But I know Ronan loves you. Just give him a chance to prove it." A short laugh escapes her. "That's kind of his superpower. He's not perfect, but he never makes the same mistake twice."

She stares toward the fluttering tent flap, her eyes distant. "He's one of the few people who actually does what he says—and he'll sacrifice everything for the people he cares about."

She squeezes my hand. "He did it for me once. I know he'll do it for you, too."

I wipe my eyes on my sleeve. I *want* to believe her. God, it would be easier when I miss him, when I need him so much. But I don't know if I'm ready yet. I don't even know if I can be.

"I—" I start just as Dani rushes over, jaw tight, face ashen.

"Thandi, we have a problem."

Oh, God. What now? I can't take any more surprises.

"What is it?" I ask.

"Check your phone. I just sent you an alert. There's a breaking news story." Dani's expression is grim. "And you're in it."

All I can think is I told the board I'd keep my head down.

That, and how did this happen?

"Complicit or Compassionate? Questions Emerge Over Immerscent Founder's Role in Daysha Howard Kidnapping"

Private conversation with Detective Simone McNamara sparks speculation about CEO's involvement.

I stare at the headline in disbelief. But it's the picture that guts me.

It's a tight shot, zoomed in from across the gym. McNamara leans forward, elbows on her knees, her expression sharp. I'm beside her, shoulders rounded, face tight with worry. In the frame, it looks like I'm confessing something, not fighting for a child's life.

I already know how this will play out. After Monday's press coverage, I'm guilty until proven innocent.

I frown up at Dani. "Alyssa? I can't believe she'd—"

"Not her. Her editor." Dani shakes her head. "Her own piece was lovely—no mention of you. I reached out, and the poor girl was practically in tears. She's on our local interest media list, remember? And I was her reference for the Gazette."

She scrolls and holds out her phone, showing me Alyssa's frantic text.

"She shared her camera roll, and the photo of you and McNamara was in there. I know Larry. He's not a bad guy, but he's under a lot of pressure with the drop in circulation. My guess is he saw the photo and thought he struck gold."

Gold means my life. My reputation. But no one cares about that.

"What can we do?" Evelyn asks. "This is insane."

"I'm already reaching out, trying to get this contained, but AP has picked it up. We may need to bring in legal." Dani curses under her breath. "I can't believe Larry would be this reckless."

Fia folds her arms, her expression darkening. "I know the chair of Quill Media Group. I doubt their investors will appreciate the optics of the Gazette exploiting a child's kidnapping for clicks. If Dani gives me the contact chain, I can apply pressure on the financial side—a quiet word about reputational risk usually gets attention faster than a cease-and-desist."

I shake my head. "We don't have time for that. We need to reach out to Trent. If we don't manage the board—"

The words are barely out of my mouth before my phone buzzes. Somehow, I know what it means before I even look.

Trent's text is brief. Perfunctory:

Come to HQ. The board is calling an emergency session.

Shattered
Thandi

"I hate to admit it," Clara murmurs, "but this does not look good."

"Our one stipulation was that you keep a low profile. Now we're dealing with another scandal in less than forty-eight hours," Niko barks. "What happened?"

"It sounds like you're accusing me of wrongdoing," I bite back, irritated that Niko and the board are doing the Gazette's work for them. "This is sensationalism at best, possibly defamation, yet I'm on trial here?"

Marisol rubs her temples. "Please, everyone, this is not helpful. Thandi, can we go through what happened one more time?"

I nod, throat tight as I stride to the window. My reflection stares back at me. The crisp navy pantsuit is one of my favorites, but this evening it does nothing for my complexion. Even in the fading light, I look wrung out, desperate.

It's not just exhaustion. That same creeping dread from Whitlow is back, its cold tendrils caressing my spine.

I take a deep breath before pivoting back to the table. I don't sit; my fingers trail over the polished wood.

"The youth center has organized search parties since Daysha disappeared two nights ago. I was there to volunteer, just like everyone else. I had no idea McNamara would show up. She brought one of her junior officers to help the effort."

Trent nods. "That all seems quite straightforward."

"And the photo?" Clara presses.

"There was a local reporter at the event," Dani says, stepping in before I can. "Alyssa Grant, from the *Kenleigh Gazette*. She took the photo, but it was one among dozens she submitted for a feel-good community feature. Her editor's the one who twisted it into something salacious. The one who's suggesting that the photo is some kind of admission of guilt."

I sink into my chair, the fight abruptly draining from me. "We sat together because MCPD confirmed that the second inhaler from the park belonged to Daysha's kidnapper. McNamara wanted to know whether WhiffRush could affect his behavior." I shrug. "I told her I didn't have enough data to make an assessment."

The room falls into uneasy silence.

Trent leans forward. "Lami, where does this leave us? What's the immediate impact on the stock?"

Lami makes a soft sound, scrolling on her tablet before tapping the clicker. Charts bloom across the wall screens.

"Minimal movement for now. Fowler's holding steady, which helps stabilize perception. But Yanovich is the one to watch."

Trent's brow furrows. "He's trimming?"

"Three percent this morning." Lami's tone is clinical. "Not enough to spook the market, but enough for people to notice. He's the unicorn that put us on the map—the one analysts pointed to when Immerscent's valuation exploded. If he starts to bail, others will follow. He doesn't just move capital—he moves confidence."

"Are we compromised?" Niko is dogged. "We have to address the elephant in the room."

"Come on, Niko," Trent says wearily. "Let's all take a step back and bring the temperature down a notch. You've made your point."

"No." Niko's chair scrapes against the floor. "I'm done with your excuses, Trent. I listened to you last time, and look where that got us. We have a fiduciary responsibility to this company, no matter how *sweet* or *kind* Thandi is." He folds his arms. "You think I'm the bad guy, but I'm only saying what everyone else is thinking. If I'm so wrong, let's put it to a vote."

Fiduciary responsibility.

It's funny how the most sterile words can mask the crudest intent.

When Immerscent was private, our returns were solid. Safe. Now we're public, everyone's addicted to the rush. The IPO is a gold mine, and volatility is the monster under the bed threatening portfolios, bonuses, and vacation homes.

Monday's earnings should've been cause for champagne, not panic. But loyalty has a shorter half-life than fear—and even in the fairytale, they killed the goose that laid the golden egg.

Trent's eyes meet mine across the table. He opens his mouth, then presses his lips together.

I nod once, sharply, even as my heart sinks to my stomach. This isn't Trent's fault. Once again, I've failed. Forcing him to side with me will only undermine his legitimacy as board chair. No matter what happens, I'll need him here—championing the dream I fought so hard to build.

I look around the room at the faces of the people I once saw as co-conspirators, even friends. Of course, it was always business, but the rigidity—the lack of grace—is so startling that I feel whiplash.

"I built this company on the ashes of my sister's memory," I say slowly, meeting each board member's gaze in turn. "Every decision I've ever made has been in Immerscent's best interest. Time and again, I've delivered, often despite the odds. I proved that with the IPO. And more importantly, I've proved it with my own sweat, my own pain, every single day for the past three years."

I lift my chin. "If you can't see that, it's a reflection of *your* leadership, not mine."

Chairs shift uncomfortably. Niko's jaw is set.

Trent hesitates, waiting for someone to speak up, to stop this runaway train.

Papers rustle. A cart rattles somewhere down the hall. Inside, the HVAC roars to life, then quiets.

No one protests.

Trent sighs. "Very well, then. The board will vote on whether to request that Ms. Elowen take a temporary leave of absence—pending an internal assessment of company leadership and public communications."

The words are a gavel strike. *Temporary leave of absence.* But we all know what it really means. It's the beginning of the end. Immerscent is slipping through my fingers.

Niko leans back, satisfied.

Trent swallows, visibly shaken. He turns toward the board secretary, steadying his voice by force of will.

"For the record, please note that this action is not disciplinary in nature. It is procedural, pending the outcome of the internal review."

Procedural. I almost laugh. *Procedural* is what you call it when you're afraid to say *betrayal.*

The secretary nods, fingers poised above the minutes. "Noted for the record."

"All those in favor of requesting Ms. Elowen take a temporary leave of absence pending internal review, please indicate."

Niko's hand goes up first, no hesitation.

"Lami?" Trent prompts.

Lami stares at the table. My CFO. We built the first investor decks slide by slide, shared takeout from the same styrofoam box during those endless all-nighters. She hesitates, jaw clenched—

Then raises her hand.

The breath leaves my lungs in a gasp I can't disguise.

Marisol speaks up, voice wavering. "I vote no. We will all regret this."

Trent's throat works. Behind him, the financials glow on the projector. "I also vote no." His hand tightens on the clicker. "Clara?"

Clara glances at me, eyes full of apology. She mouths *I'm sorry*—then lifts her hand.

Trent keeps tallying, but I don't need to count. I already know how it ends.

I've been cracking since the youth center, and this is the final shard that will bring the whole edifice down. The darkness closes in, smug and victorious. This isn't the oblivion Ronan offered. This is cold and permanent. I know I'll never return from here.

A few more hands rise. Quiet. Reluctant.

All vote yes.

Besides Trent, only Niko and Marisol meet my eyes—Niko in defiance, Marisol with genuine regret, and dear Trent with all the hurt and sympathy of a friend.

My life's work is going up in flames. How can I ever make things right for Tess when I'm no longer running Immerscent? If I thought living without Ronan hurt, nothing compares to this. The room tilts. My vision tunnels. I think I'm going to be sick.

Dani's fingers find mine under the table. "Chin up," she whispers fiercely. "Don't let them break you. We'll find a way to fix this."

I do laugh then—brittle, half-crazed. She has far more faith in me than I do.

I look around the room at the polished walnut table, the ergonomic black chairs curving like ants around its circumference. Dusk spills over Chesden through the floor-to-ceiling windows, turning the glass towers outside to molten gold. On the far wall hangs a framed photo of the staff cutting the ribbon on the new headquarters. I'm laughing, Dani's and Sammie's arms slung around my shoulders. Next to it hangs the portrait Dani insisted we display—a photo of me posed against a wash of Immerscent's lavender branding, smiling with a confidence I no longer possess.

Over the last three years, I've probably spent as much time in here as I have in my own living room.

Two out of ten.

After all the work, after all the relationship-building, after all the sacrifices—after every crisis I steered us through—that's all I could muster.

Two out of ten.

When my gaze returns to the table, every face is shadowed with the gravity of what is about to happen. Even Niko sobers for a minute.

I keep my head up for Dani's sake, because I have no willpower of my own left. Hard to think this is how it all ends.

I close my eyes, steeling myself.

I'm so sorry, Tess.

Trent clears his throat. "The motion carries, eight votes in favor, two opposed." He pauses, swallowing audibly. "Effective immediately, Ms. Elowen will take a leave of absence pending the board's internal review."

I collapse against Dani.

That's when my world shatters around me.

Dry Down

Game Day
Ronan

I have a speech, but I can't remember it.

I'm pacing. My hands are shaking. I stare at the page, but the words keep blurring together.

This is it, the moment of truth.

Do we have enough evidence to take down Astor? Absolutely.

Will it be enough to win back Thandi and clear her name?

I don't know.

All I can hold onto is hope—and the promise of our dinner tonight.

I've let her down as a lover and a friend. I think of Fowler and Amber—how improbable their connection seemed. If they can find their way to each other, maybe there's still a chance for Thandi and me. She said it herself—no guarantees. But I'll do whatever it takes to be worthy of her love and trust again.

I glance around the room, at the crowd rushing in, at the swiftly-filling seats. The stage seems vast and imposing. The podium is empty, a single mic waiting to be seized.

I'd agonized over where to hold this press conference, but in the end, only one place made sense:

Mom's new wing.

The *Rosalind Thorne Innovation Center for Sensory Science* stretches before me, finally complete. The scientific equipment gleams in the background. In the converted main area, endless rows are divided into sections designated by audience—media, scientists, investors—the people who can turn the tide of public opinion and restore Thandi's future. On the far wall, a portrait of Mom, calm and dignified, watches over everything.

I remember the night I first showed Thandi this room. Then, the grand entrance, swelling now with jostling guests, was nothing but a frame, a threshold of possibility. It was the same between Thandi and me. We stood behind the cellophane, shielded under the veil of new love, still figuring out what we meant to each other.

I uncurl my fist, flexing my fingers. Her hand was so soft in mine, her eyes so bright with compassion and conviction.

I pull out my phone and swipe through photos, landing on the one from Sugar Hill Park. It's been my meditation these last two days—a reminder of the love and joy I hope we can have again. A wistful laugh escapes me as I trace Thandi's features. She was so beautiful, so brave that day, trusting me with her truth.

I didn't do enough to honor it.

It hurts so much to be without her, and her suffering in the youth center tore my heart out. I hate that she's paying the price for my failures. I was so focused on loving her, so focused on not losing her, that I didn't do enough to protect her. Now she's facing a storm—a hurricane fueled by my fear—all alone.

That ends tonight.

I straighten my papers and commit the words to memory. This has to be seamless. After everything I've destroyed, Thandi deserves perfection. That starts with the suit, which we filed at 2:17 this afternoon, well before the deadline.

Across the room, the lawyers huddle together, deep in prep. Aamir, Frederick, and Dr. Rhee, the patent counsel, are all here. There's a newcomer, too. Lydia Kassan from Marsten & Chase sits shoulder-to-shoulder with Aamir, fingers flying over the MacBook in her lap.

The hotshot lawyer represents the only other person here who is more nervous than I am—Dr. Patrick Linny.

The scientist is perched in the front row, lips moving silently as he practices his lines. The paper trembles in his hands.

I don't take his sacrifice lightly.

Licensing violations, copyright claims—those are the wrecking balls I'll swing at Astor's empire. Yet, compared to the physical risk Patrick faces, they're bloodless. I'll demolish the company's foundations, but Patrick's testimony will show the world that James wasn't just greedy; he deliberately chose to harm children. We had to make sure the scientist was protected.

None of us had the background to handle a criminal case, so Aamir brought in Lydia to take Patrick's formal statement—anonymized for the court as a protected witness. The emails, lab notes, and scans he handed over were mirrored to Equinox's encrypted servers, with the originals sealed in a vault at Marsten & Chase. The security team is also here tonight, invisible until needed. I've learned the hard way that you don't walk into a storm without a backup plan.

"Mr. Thorne, we're ready for sound check." A technician waves at me.

"Of course." I gather my notes and follow him onstage.

He's adjusting my earpiece when my phone buzzes with a message from Fia. I feel guilty for not telling her about the presser, but I know how much she wanted to be at the Park for Daysha and Thandi. I couldn't take her away from that.

Besides, she's already supported me so much. I'm ready to show her that I can stand on my own two feet.

Well, there's no fucking time like the present because my heart stutters as soon as I read her text:

Where are you? Thandi's in trouble.

A link to a Kenleigh Gazette article quickly follows the words. As soon as I open it, rage explodes in my chest. It's an ugly smear piece, insinuating Thandi is complicit in the kidnapping. The most disgusting part is the photo, captured just hours ago. In it, Thandi is huddled with Detective McNamara, her face twisted with worry.

How could anyone see that and pervert it for clicks—for rage bait? I'm sick of these bastards tearing Thandi down when she's sacrificing everything to bring Daysha home. Now, even the youth center isn't sacred.

There's no time to swallow my fury as another text comes in, this time from Dani:

> *At Immerscent for an emergency board session. It's not looking good for Thandi's leadership. If you have an ace up your sleeve, now's the time to use it.*

What? I stagger to my feet. I won't let that happen. She can't lose everything because of me.

I glance at my watch. We're fifteen minutes early, but the room is already packed. Our two special guests aren't here yet, but there's no time to waste.

"We need to get started," I say sharply to the technician.

He nods, signaling to RT Laboratories' head of communications. Voices swell, cameras begin to flash.

I tap the mic and step up to the podium.

Thandi, hold on, sweet baby.

I've got this.

This time, I won't let you fall.

Funeral March
Thandi

Through my haze of pain, I catch fragments of conversation: Trent calling the board into an additional emergency session to discuss communication with staff and interim leadership. Lami's shell-shocked expression when Clara says it's typical for the CFO to take the reins during a transition. Niko blurting something about being relieved to enter a period of stability.

It all sounds surreal, distant. I'm floating through the darkness, watching it unfold from somewhere far away.

I'm underwater again, but this time no one's coming to the rescue.

"Thandi?"

I blink to find Trent kneeling in front of me, his hand on my shoulder. My lips move. Somehow, words emerge.

"Yes?"

"Thandi, honey … I'm sorry. We need to start the meeting."

At first, I don't understand. I scan the room, searching for context, for something solid to hold onto.

Dani looks like she's fighting to remain in her seat. Marisol is flushed with anger. Clara won't meet my eyes. She's fixated on the earnings chart glowing on the screen. And Niko, chest puffed out, suddenly looks smaller. Now that the decision is made, the confidence that filled the room minutes ago has drained away.

"Thandi?" Trent repeats, his brow furrowed, his hand tightening around mine.

That's when I get it.

He's asking me to leave.

Of course. I'm no longer part of the board, and Dani needs to stay to manage the internal and external announcements.

I'm the only one redundant here.

I jerk to my feet and grab my handbag. *One foot in front of the other.* I'm proud of myself for making it to the door without crumbling.

I need to go home. I want my parents. They'll understand, even though I'm coming home one more time to tell them that I lost something precious.

The doors shut behind me with a sharp click.

For a moment, I just stand there.

The corridor is empty. It's late enough that most of the staff have gone home. Only a few stragglers will still be in the labs, but that's on the fifth floor, not here.

I walk slowly, committing everything to memory: the gleam of the glass partitions, the framed patents lining the wall.

I pass the staff lounge, where the team crowded around me after I collapsed from the ice-cream experiment. Next to it is the sick bay where Aisha tended to me and where, cradled in Ronan's arms, I realized there was more between us than rivalry.

Now I have nothing. Not Tess. Not Ronan. Not Immerscent.

It feels strange to be so empty-handed. Immerscent has been my compass for so long that I don't know what tomorrow even means.

The youth center. I'll go to the youth center. They still think I'm useful there.

I pass Sammie's office and catch my reflection in the window. I look like a ghost. A laugh escapes me. No wonder. This isn't a walk of shame—it's a funeral march.

A pang of disappointment hits when I realize Sammie isn't here. We're usually the last ones standing, but tonight the universe seems to be telling me that she, just like the board, has moved on.

Unlike the other darkened spaces, the light is on in her office, papers pushed aside on the desk in uncharacteristic haste. Her coffee mug is still on its warmer, suggesting I just missed her. I can't decide if that's a mercy or a curse. I want to say goodbye, but I probably couldn't hold it together anyway.

I slip inside, a wistful smile touching my lips as I turn off the warmer. I take in the familiar space, tucking away the details like mementos: the photos of her five-year-old son plastered on the upholstered pinboard, the extra scarf on the coat rack because she's always cold. A crystal prism etched with her name—Dr. Samira Bennett, DIA Global Inspire Award for Excellence in Patient Engagement—refracts blue light across the surface of her desk. Next to it is the custom Funko Pop she made a bigger fuss over when I gave it to her for her work anniversary last year.

God, I'll miss this place.

And my people.

Sniffling, I grab a neon pink sticky note and start scribbling a message for Sammie. I tap it onto the screen of her laptop before closing the case.

I'm tempted to linger, to do the same for all the research leads— Jared, Julia, and Ashanti—but I force myself to leave. I'm not wanted here anymore.

I've got to keep moving.

My heels echo against the tile, the sound thin and lonely. I'm crying now, but I'm not ashamed. If I'm owed anything, it's my grief.

I'm halfway down the hall when the boardroom doors slam open behind me.

"Thandi!"

I freeze.

"Thandi!" Dani's voice is breathless. "Thandi, come back. You need to see this!"

Revival
Thandi

I don't know what to expect when I enter. It certainly isn't the board transfixed to the screens around the room.

Clara is frozen.

Marisol is standing, her hand clasped over her mouth.

That's when I realize something is happening.

And Ronan is at the center of it.

My heart contracts just at the sight of him.

On screen, the room is packed with journalists, scientists, and executives. Bodies overflow to the back wall, camera crews pressed shoulder to shoulder in the new wing of RT Laboratories. A giant plaque gleams behind the podium: *The Rosalind Thorne Innovation Center for Sensory Science.*

Flashes burst in quick succession. Voices rise. The crowd shifts and jostles, but the eye of the storm is Ronan—composed, his eyes narrowed in focus.

As always, he towers over everyone, handsome and painfully masculine. It's not just his stature; he'll always be larger than life to me. Tonight he's wearing the same gray suit and pink tie he wore at the youth center. The detail shouldn't matter, but my heart stumbles when I remember how he held me.

On his left stand Aamir, Yanovich, and Fowler—familiar faces. On his right, two newcomers: a plump, formidable red-haired woman with eyes like tempered steel, and beside her, a thin dark-haired man who looks like he might faint under the bright lights.

What's going on?

I move to the table, heart galloping in my chest. It takes a moment to register that Ronan is speaking.

"—which is why we're pleased to make this announcement here, in the newest wing of RT Laboratories," he's saying. He pauses, amber gaze flashing. I've never seen him this serious, this intent.

"And now," he adds quietly, "to less pleasant matters."

Ronan gazes over the crowd. "First, and I need to be clear, James Astor is my father."

The room goes still. In the quiet, the only sound is the rustling of the papers on the podium.

"But I am not him. And I never will be."

Ronan presses the clicker, and the screen behind him splits in two.

"Tonight I present tangible evidence that Astor Pharmaceuticals has illegally built its entire line of scent-based products—Sniffz, WhiffRush, PlayMist, PlayMist EDU, and PlayMist Platinum—on stolen intellectual property."

The room erupts. The roar through the TV speakers is so loud I can't imagine what it's like in person.

"Holy shit," Dani mutters.

Clara stands. Trent lets out a low whistle.

I can't speak. I grip the table. My emotions are in shambles.

On the left is a grid of microscope slides, each tagged with the label of a different Astor product. Under magnification, a compound glows with an indigo dye that seems to shimmer. Most won't understand what they're looking at.

I do.

It's an allosteric modulator, and it's clearly unique. Yet, even to the untrained eye, the pattern is clear: every one of Astor's products contains it.

The right side of the screen is filled with a set of legal documents, its key clauses highlighted in yellow:

Rosalind Thorne, primary patent and license holder.

Intellectual property not transferred in the sale of her company.

And never the property of Astor Pharmaceuticals.

It's stunning. Damning. Impossible to believe a CEO could be this reckless.

A short, bitter laugh escapes me. Crazy, isn't it? Meanwhile, here I am, sidelined and stripped of my life's work, even after all of my care.

Only Ronan's voice keeps me from sliding deeper into sorrow and rage.

"The formulas behind these products are not Astor's. They represent the life's work of my mother, Dr. Rosalind Thorne. Work she refined until her last breath. I will not let my father sully her reputation by repackaging it into poisons marketed to children."

Ronan leans forward, the cameras catching the fire in his eyes. "What kind of man steals the research of his dying wife and turns it into an empire built on addiction and harm? That ends tonight."

I can't believe this is happening. Every word fills me with a storm of emotions—shock, pride, and tremulous hope.

I close my eyes, pressing a hand to my chest.

Every day since Astor became Immerscent's competitor, I've done everything I can to warn parents about the risks associated with their products. But none of it was enough to stop them. Astor's reach only grew, hurting Ricky, Stephan, Daysha, and so many others along the way.

Tonight, in one fell swoop, Ronan hasn't just cauterized the rot. He's dismantling his father's empire, word by word, image by image.

And he's not done yet.

"RT Laboratories holds the intellectual property rights to every one of Rosalind Thorne's formulas, as stipulated in her last will and testament. That includes the bespoke and proprietary allosteric modulator you see behind me—RT3."

Ronan's expression darkens. "That is why, as of this morning, we have filed a federal suit for patent infringement, trade secret misappropriation, and unjust enrichment against Astor Pharmaceuticals and James Astor. We are seeking a permanent injunction to halt production, seize all infringing inventory, and claim full restitution of profits."

Pandemonium reigns. At this point, I expect the conference to end. Astor's theft exposed, and its products stripped from the shelves? Surely this is the final blow.

But that's when the slim dark-haired man leaves Ronan's side to take the podium. He sucks in a shaky breath.

"Hi, I'm Patrick—"

The mic squeaks, and he flinches. "Sorry."

He clutches the podium, knuckles white. "I'm Dr. Patrick Linny, head of Astor Pharmaceuticals' Cognitive Therapeutics Division." He swallows hard, "And I'm a whistleblower."

Dr. Linny straightens the mic. "For years, I oversaw neurodata analysis for Astor's adaptive scent therapies," he says, his voice gaining strength. "My colleague, Dr. Velma Koenig, was the first to identify damage to developing brains in early product testing. When she tried to stop the pediatric expansion, she was silenced, and her reputation was destroyed."

He glances down at his trembling hands, then lifts his gaze again. "I didn't speak up then. I told myself it wasn't my fight. But when I saw Dr. Elowen's press conference and that little girl's face on the news, I realized it was. I can't undo the harm we caused. But I can tell the truth."

"*Jesus fucking Christ,*" Niko murmurs.

There are no words to describe what we've witnessed—justice and retribution delivered in a single stroke. Domino after domino, falling in an avalanche that will leave Astor buried beneath the rubble of its own greed.

And the instrument of destruction is James Astor's own son.

Ronan Thorne.

The love of my life.

The knot in my chest begins to loosen. Fia's words in the tent suddenly ring in my ears:

He'll sacrifice everything for the people he cares about.

He did it for me once. I know he'll do it for you, too.

That's when it finally sinks in. He's not just doing this because it's right.

My vision blurs.

He's doing it for me.

As if by some sixth sense, Ronan's body language shifts. He stares straight into the camera, eyes fierce and full of longing.

I shiver. I'm such a freaking mess. It's ridiculous. He doesn't know I'm here. Doesn't know I'm watching. So why do I feel like he's looking right into my soul?

"Lastly," Ronan says, his voice thick with emotion, "I need to address the insinuations made about Immerscent and its founder, Thandi Elowen—the woman I love."

The woman I love.

Love.

I fold over the table, sobbing now, deep, hiccuping cries that flow from me, unstoppable as a rushing tide. After everything I've been through today, after feeling so empty, so *alone*, his support ravages me.

Trent and Dani abandon all protocol and rush to me, steadying me. Their arms wrap tight around my shoulders.

"In just forty-eight hours, she has been called a hypocrite. She's even been cruelly accused of complicity in a crime she was once a victim of."

Ronan makes a sound of disgust. "And now, in the most ludicrous twist, her leadership is in question, despite steering her company through the most successful public offering the tech sector has seen in a decade."

Across the table, Niko coughs in embarrassment. I barely hear him. I'm too focused on the man I love, and the way he's lifting me, healing me piece by broken piece.

"Thandi, baby, I'm sorry. I never meant to hurt you." Ronan's voice roughens. "I love you. I need you. I thought my life had a purpose—and then I met you. You showed me what true kindness, sacrifice, and determination look like. Because of you, I'm a better man. A stronger man."

He draws a breath. "Ten years ago, I gave up the Astor name and my inheritance because I was ashamed of what it stood for. I'd do it again—twice over, twenty times over—if it meant having you by my side. Thorne Consulting, RT Laboratories—all of it is worthless if you're not in my life. That's what tonight is about. I want us to build a life together, not just as lovers, but as friends and partners."

"About that," Fowler steps up to the podium. "Look, I know I'm jumping the gun here, especially since we're dealing with matters of the heart."

He grins. "But I've had more fun since Monday than in the last fifteen years, thanks to Thandi and Ronan. And I'm a hell of a lot richer, too."

Laughter ripples through the room. I'm shell-shocked, but even I can't help a watery chuckle.

"Thandi, my girl, if you're listening, I'm calling first dibs on any future venture between you and Ronan. In fact, Yani and I—"

"Agreed."

Yanovich, stoic as ever, prowls toward the podium to stand beside Fowler. He pauses, then breaks into a grin, earning a gasp from the crowd.

"Count me in," he says with a wink. "Actually, I'll double whatever John invests."

I have to sit down. It's too much. Trent helps me into the nearest chair as I drag my sleeve across my eyes. I don't know whether to laugh, scream, or cry. All I know is that I feel like I'm *rising, rising* far above everything. Like that day on the Dragon of Doom at Sugar Hill Park, the world shrinking into insignificance around me...

Except for Ronan at my side.

On screen, he's shaking his head at the two investors. Then he steps back to the podium, gaze locking on the cameras. He leans in slightly.

"Thandi, come back to me. *Please.*"

Rally
Thandi

The feed freezes. The press conference ends.

"Wow," Dani breathes, grinning as she squeezes me. "Just—wow."

Trent raps the table with his fist. "Goddammit, I've got to hand it to Thorne. That was a hell of a move."

I'm barely listening. I'm filled up; love vibrating through every nerve, every cell. I don't recognize this feeling. I'm so used to pain, to sacrifice, to holding everything together. I've never known this kind of warmth, this safety—this joy of someone risking it all for *me*.

Dani rubs my shoulder. "I knew it would be alright." Her voice is fierce. "What will you do now?"

That's the million-dollar question, isn't it?

I frown, twisting my hands together in my lap. "I—"

"We interrupt to bring you continuing coverage of tonight's shocking announcement by RT Laboratories CEO Ronan Thorne…"

I jolt as a dramatic news jingle blares from the screen. Two talking heads appear beside a replay of Ronan's press conference. Along the bottom, a glowing ticker scrolls after-hours data on Immerscent's stock value.

A bright red banner flashes: **ASTOR EMPIRE IN CRISIS.**

I blink, dazed. The commentator's voice barrels on.

"If you're just joining us, Ronan Thorne—yes, the estranged son of James Astor—has publicly accused Astor Pharmaceuticals of patent theft and filed a federal suit against the company. Let's bring in our legal analyst, Dr. Susan Kearney…"

A woman in a navy blazer appears. "This is unprecedented," she says. "A direct, public accusation between father and son, paired with tangible evidence—including testimony from a whistleblower claiming deliberate negligence. If Thorne's documentation holds, this could not only bankrupt Astor Pharmaceuticals but open the door to criminal charges."

The male commentator laughs. "You ladies are stronger than I am. I'm still focused on Thorne's declaration of love to Thandi Elowen. Destroying your father for the woman you love? Forget the stock value. This is headed straight for Hollywood."

"Okay, Tom, before we start placing bets on who'll play Thorne and Elowen, can we talk about what's also at stake for Immerscent here?" His partner, a woman in a bright red sheath dress, says.

Kearney nods. "You're right, Carol. First—"

The anchors frown on screen. They nod, fingers to their earpieces.

"Susan, I'm sorry to interrupt, but we have another development in this story," Carol says. "A leaked internal memo appears to show that Immerscent's board, shortly before Thorne's conference, asked Thandi Elowen to take a leave of absence, citing stability concerns."

Tom shakes his head. "Incredible."

The screen splits to show a scanned letter, columns of signatures filling the page.

"Folks, this is a *News 5* exclusive. Immerscent staff have drafted a letter of no confidence in board leadership. I repeat, Immerscent staff are requesting that the board step down after what has to be a stunning misfire in judgment. Let's go live to Chesden, where employees have gathered outside the company's headquarters."

"I'm Dr. Samira Bennett, head of patient engagement at Immerscent," Sammie begins. "I'm speaking not as management, but as one of hundreds of employees who believe in what our company stands for.

The board's decision to remove Dr. Elowen was made without consulting those of us who built this organization from the ground up. We're scientists, engineers, and field staff—and we stand with her. Our work reflects her vision, and we will not let fear dictate our future."

My heart lodges in my throat. This team has been my life—my heart. Just an hour ago, I thought I'd been discarded. Now I see how wrong I was.

Eyes stinging, I leap to my feet and sprint down the hall, Dani and Trent close behind. The cafeteria window overlooks the back lot, and sure enough, they're all there—hundreds of familiar faces gathered in the cold, Sammie at the center.

Behind me, the rest of the board pours in. Marisol grabs the remote and flicks on the TV above the coffee station. Onscreen, the anchors exchange wide-eyed glances.

"Wow," Carol murmurs.

Tom clears his throat. "For context, staff letters of this nature are non-binding, but organized pushback will have Wall Street paying attention. The optics aren't good."

Carol shakes her head. "Susan, what's your take? We just saw Fowler and Yanovich one-up each other to invest in anything Thorne and Elowen touch. How could a board fail so spectacularly at reading the market?"

Susan nods, listening through the satellite delay. "Look, we have to remember, this is a young company. Immerscent is only three years old. I'm sure it seemed sensible not to complicate things with a governance shake-up right after the IPO, but what happened tonight is actually quite common."

She presses her lips together. "We saw it with Etsy, even Pinterest. Boards that make sense for a private company often aren't fit for purpose once it's public—too conservative, too risk-averse, not bullish enough about the company's own potential."

Tom leans back in his chair, half-smiling. "Sounds like Immerscent needs Fowler or Yanovich on its board—stat."

A heavy silence settles over the cafeteria.

Niko, to his credit, is the first to break it. "Thandi, I'm sorry. It appears we jumped the gun." He turns to Trent, eyes uncertain. "Trent... how can we fix this?"

Trent reaches for the remote and turns off the television. Crossing his arms, he leans against the counter.

"Well, the first thing we need to do is take control of the message. Dani, do you think we can do that?"

"Of course." Dani snaps to attention, fingers already flying across her phone. "Luckily, the external statement never went out, so we only have to deal with the staff leak..." Her eyes dart to mine with a quick wink before she turns back to the board.

"Trent, if we get you on air in the next half hour, we can chalk this up to a misunderstanding. We'll need a mea culpa, obviously, around the process, but I think we can manage it. Focus on next steps. Thandi, you can—"

"Sorry," I say, already pushing back my chair. "You'll have to do it without me."

I break into a run. There's only one place I want to be right now.

And that's with the man who loved me enough to save me.

Care
Ronan

The camera crews are packing up, and the guests are leaving, faces alight with excitement. The mood is still electric.

Fred and Aamir are grinning, clapping each other on the shoulders. Fowler and Yanovich are talking a mile a minute on their phones. Lydia and Dr. Rhee exchange information, and for the first time, Dr. Linny looks relaxed.

He crosses the room, his tie already loosened, hazel eyes bright. "Mr. Thorne—" he extends his hand. "Thank you for helping me do the right thing."

I clasp his hand. "I should be the one thanking you. If you hadn't come forward, we wouldn't have a criminal case."

Fred joins us, his voice warm. "You should both be proud. Thanks to you, Astor won't hurt anyone else." He rests a hand on my shoulder. "Rosalind would be proud of you, son."

I nod sharply, staring at Mom's portrait. My throat works.

God, I hope so.

Lydia calls to Patrick, and he gives her a thumbs-up before turning back to me.

"Well… this is it. I've got to run." He rubs the back of his neck. "Thanks again for everything—and for putting my mom up in that hotel. After the break-in…" He trails off.

"Patrick, it doesn't matter that the press conference is over," I say. "We're in this with you until the end. Security, legal support—whatever you need, you'll have it."

His relief is palpable. "Thank you, Mr. Thorne."

I shake my head. "Just Ronan."

"Thanks, Ronan." Patrick grins.

"Ready?" Lydia asks, and he nods, giving one last wave. I watch as they leave, heads already bent together, two of Equinox's security detail trailing close behind them.

"Well, son, you did it." Fred shoves his hands deep in his pockets. "I—" His voice cracks, and he has to turn away for a moment.

"Oh, Fred…" I pull him roughly into a hug. His shoulders hitch against mine. I blink hard, feeling the wetness of his tears against my neck.

He sniffles and pulls back, embarrassed. "Sorry." He presses a hand to his eyes. "It's just—she went through so much. I felt so powerless." He straightens his jacket. "Now I know she's at peace."

We sit together then, side by side, quiet. Each wrestling with Mom's love and the legacy she left behind. One that, finally, feels untainted.

It's the only thing I have to hold onto now.

I look around the room at the empty doorway, the scattered chairs. I know how deeply I hurt Thandi, how much I cost her. I never expected tonight to erase that. Still, I'd hoped—prayed—it might open a door. That it might be enough to let love in again.

I was wrong.

She isn't here.

And I have no one to blame but myself.

"Have you heard from her?" Fred asks.

I ball my fists together in my lap. "No."

He covers my hand. "Give her time. And don't give up. Healing isn't linear. It has to happen in its own way and its own season, but your love will see you through."

"You think so?" I bury my face in my hands. "I'm so scared, Fred. What if I've lost her? I can't—"

"Ronan," Fred says sharply. He jerks to his feet.

"What?" I frown up at him. "What is it?"

He smiles. "I'll leave you to it," he says. Then he turns and walks away.

I blink after him, confused. That is, until I stand.

Then I see her.

Standing in the doorway.

The first thing I notice is her bright pink hair. She's wearing a navy suit that makes her look exactly as I remember—soft and strong, impossible and real all at once.

But it's her face—her sweet, beautiful face—that stops my world.

My heart squeezes so hard I gasp for air.

Her eyes find mine. She's crying. Smiling.

Thandi.

My baby.

I bolt toward her, pushing past the tech crews with their gear, vaulting over a stack of chairs. She's moving too—running—but I get there first. I have to, after the pain I've made her bear.

I sweep her into my arms, pulling her close, fighting the urge to crush her to my chest. She needs only tenderness now, the gentlest of care. Her body molds against mine as she wraps her arms around my neck.

"You came," I breathe, kissing her face, catching her tears with my thumb.

"Yes." Her voice breaks. "They took everything from me … said it was my fault… I thought—" Her face crumples, and she shudders as sobs tear through her.

I cradle her close, hating what this has done to her.

"It's alright. I'm here. I love you, and I won't let them hurt you anymore. Whatever they've taken from you, I'll get it back," I vow, kissing her fiercely.

I carry her to a chair and sink into it, pulling her onto my lap. She curls into me, trembling. I rub her back in slow circles and wait for the storm to pass.

After a long moment, she takes a deep, shuddering breath.

"Okay?" I ask softly, stroking the back of her neck.

She nods.

"Good." I kiss her cheek. "Now, who do I need to fight for you?"

"Silly." A laugh bursts from her lips as she nestles closer, wrapping her arms around my waist and resting her head against my heart.

"You're sure?" I murmur, teasing.

"It's all fixed now," she whispers. "Thanks to you."

"Is it?" I cup her face, searching her features. "I know I let you down. I'm sorry, Thandi."

Thandi shakes her head. "None of that matters anymore. Not after tonight. Thank you for believing in me. For standing up for me."

The way she says it twists something inside me. There's sadness there, and wonder—like no one has ever risked it all for her before.

It's appalling. I don't understand how it's possible when she's so beautiful, so extraordinary.

She doesn't have to thank me because I never had a choice.

Not when she's the blood in my veins, the heart in my chest, the breath in my lungs.

"I love you, Thandi," I whisper. My arms tighten around her. "More than life itself."

She smiles, eyes luminous. "I love you too."

God. My heart is beating so fast, I can hardly think. Forget Fowler and Amber. There's no way their love can feel like this—like joy sweeter than honey, like the first rays of the sun after a lifetime of night.

Like home.

Thandi gives a shaky little sigh and takes my hand in hers. "What now?"

"Now," I say, standing and gathering her into my arms, "we go home."

Lover's Special
Ronan

I canceled the dinner reservation, took Thandi to her condo, and made love to her instead.

Now, after a shower, we're curled up on her couch, an open box of Tino's pizza on the coffee table. It's half pepperoni, half mushroom with white sauce, just like that time at RT Laboratories. There's also a bonus pie in the kitchen—a special gift from Tino. As soon as he heard my voice on the line, he insisted.

I reach for the last slice of mushroom, closing the box and carefully tearing off the oil-stained note Tino slapped on the lid:

I piccioncini,

You almost gave an old man a heart attack. I'm glad you found your way back to each other.

Enjoy your favorites on the house.

In your honor, from now on, we'll be offering half white mushroom, half pepperoni every Wednesday as the Lover's Special.

Don't make me rename it the Fool's Special if you make the same mistake again.

—Tino

I can't help chuckling. The old man is a piece of work, but his heart is in the right place. I could hear the joy in his voice even on the phone. All he wants is for Thandi to be happy.

We have that in common.

It's all I want too.

"Full?" I ask, tugging Thandi against my side and kissing the top of her head. "Should I grab the other pizza?"

"No," she groans, snuggling into me. "I don't think I can eat another bite."

I tighten my arms around her. I love how she clings to me, seeking my warmth—my support. I hope she now knows that I'll always be there for her. And if not, I'll prove it to her again and again.

Of course, having Thandi close only makes me want to touch her. Earlier, I helped her rub scented shea butter into her skin. Now she smells like a chocolate-dipped strawberry, and her legs have that glow I love. Unable to resist, I slide my hands up her thighs, caressing brown skin and feminine curves.

She sighs with pleasure, and I'm already soaring. My heart speeds up. My dick is hard in my sweats, and it's easy to tug Thandi up and shift her until she's straddling my erection.

I love the way we fit together. Unlike her, I'm not wearing underwear, so I can feel the living heat of her through her panties. How am I supposed to resist heaven? Groaning, I rock up against her.

"Are you trying to tell me something?" Thandi cracks an eye open and peers at me.

"Mm," I caress her pulse with my thumb. I slide down to pluck the buttons on the oversized shirt she's wearing, popping one after another. "*I'm* still hungry. I'd love another bite."

"So now I'm on the menu?" Thandi laughs.

"Tino did call it the Lover's Special." I roll us over, pinning her beneath me. "You object?"

She loops her arms around my neck. "Never."

I moan. There's a part of me that can't believe she's back in my arms, but this is real. *She* is real, and every moment with her is a little taste of ecstasy. I slip my hand under her shirt, and heat rushes through me.

I need her again.

"Ronan?" Thandi stares at me with wide brown eyes.

"I want you," I murmur, smoothing my hand over her hip. She whimpers when I nuzzle her breast through her shirt. The peak immediately hardens. "Feels like you want me too."

"I do," she gasps, squirming beneath me. She tries to say something, but her breath catches on a cry as I capture her nipple through the soft cotton.

I tug her panties down, notching my hand between her thighs. She's like satin—wet and still soft from our earlier lovemaking. I'm a fucking Neanderthal, but I can't help the possessiveness that washes over me. I remember how snug she is, how her little pussy stretched around my dick, taking everything I had to offer. Now, feeling how she's changed for me ignites all my baser instincts. She's *mine*, and I'm never letting her go.

"You're so perfect here," I whisper, parting her and slowly fingering her petals. I love that she's drenched—that I'm the one who called forth all of this sweetness.

"Ronan, I..." Thandi jerks against me, her thighs clamping around my hand. Her voice rises as I caress her entrance. Her helpless, gentle contraction makes my head spin.

Fuck. I want everything with her.

I drag the neckline of her shirt down one shoulder, exposing her breast. She's soft, full—perfect—her nipple a taut velvet peak. I fondle it, and her response is just as passionate and sensitive as I expected.

I've been with dozens of women, but none of them is as beautiful as Thandi. None of them made me feel like we were made for each other. None of them made me feel like there's fire in my touch.

When I roll her nipple between my fingertips, Thandi gasps and rewards me with a rush of wetness. I follow it, moaning as she blooms for me.

I crush her mouth to mine, breathing in her cries as I keep caressing her. Our tongues tangle, and her desire flows over us like honey. I make a ravenous sound, thrusting into her mouth the same way that I'm desperate to claim every inch of her pussy.

Thandi nips my lips and writhes against me. Her soft scent fills my senses—soap, strawberries, and the tang of arousal. Intoxicated, I double my attentions, plucking and teasing her nipples even as I find the bud of her clit.

"Ronan, *please*," Thandi groans, pushing at my shoulders.

"What?" I nudge her thighs wider.

How did I survive these last few days without her? She's the hunger I will never satisfy, the thirst I will never quench. I've only begun touching her, and I'm already hurtling towards the edge.

"I want you …" Thandi flops against the throw pillows with a groan. "But, I'm a little sore."

"What?" I jerk up. "Did I hurt you earlier? Why didn't you say?"

"Stop." Thandi smiles, resting a hand on my shoulder. "Don't be so dramatic. I'm not injured. I just didn't realize we'd be ready for action so soon. Besides, how could you hurt me? I'm the one who couldn't wait, remember?"

How could I forget? I'm still reeling from the way she shoved me against the door as soon as we got home. You won't hear me complaining, though. I love it when she plays rough.

I grin down at her. "You're right. I'm the victim here."

"Okay, let's not get carried away." Thandi rolls her eyes.

"Mm," I brush my lips against hers. "Tell that to the scratches on my back." I tighten my hand around her pussy. "I'm a wounded animal."

"Oh god—" Thandi makes the most adorable noise—a combination of a squeak and a gurgle. "I'm so sorry."

"Don't be." I lick the seam of her mouth, dipping to trace the fullness of her bottom lip before suckling the soft flesh. "I love it. Scratch me up, baby. Mark me. Make me yours."

"Oh, Ronan…" Thandi breathes.

I'm hard as a rock just from that plea. This is what it's come to. I'm nothing but her plaything. She controls me with the slightest sound, the barest touch.

"Say my name again," I growl, grasping the lapels of her shirt.

"Ronan," she moans.

The heat inside me builds to a crescendo. I bend to her again, kneading her breasts. For a moment, I just admire her. I love how she feels in my hands, love that she has no defenses against this. It's a weakness I intend to exploit.

Thandi gasps as I rub slow circles around her areolas.

"Don't look away," I chide as her eyes flutter shut.

She whimpers, but she obeys, staring helplessly at me as I call forth her pleasure.

I pinch her nipples, drawing the movement out— savoring her beauty, I release her so slowly that her breasts quiver.

Thandi shouts, her hand tangling in my shirt. A delicate shudder seizes her. When I repeat the caress, her movements completely disintegrate. She's so frantic, she can't decide whether to tug me closer or push me away.

I'm happy to give her another option. I take her into my mouth, suckling each swollen peak. I swirl my tongue around her nipples, and she cries and twists in my arms, even as her pussy spills more sweet nectar over my fingers.

She is exquisite. The sounds of her desire are tiny, incoherent things, but they're music to my ears—proof that this passion can't be a mistake.

That we belong together.

She opens for me, and our breaths mingle, her tongue tangling with mine in a frenzied dance of desire.

"Baby, you're so amazing. Does it feel good?"

"Yes," she whines, shuddering again. "*Please.*"

"Please, what, sweetheart?"

"I want—" She makes a frustrated sound and arches, offering me her breasts.

Fuck, she's so sexy.

"You want my mouth on you again? Is that it?" I whisper, tracing the whorls of her ear with my tongue.

She nods. "Please, Ronan."

"Of course, my love."

I cup her breasts until she overflows my hands and her nipples jut forward. God, she has the prettiest tits. Her nipples are perfect, and engorged like this, I can't get enough. My tongue steals out to lave one bud and the next, and Thandi shouts, her entire body collapsing into mine.

"Ronan, I thought...." She shakes her head, unable to catch her breath.

"I'm not going to make love to you—" I smile against her skin. "But a hellcat terrorized me earlier. I'm still owed compensation."

"Compensation?" Her eyes are wide, unfocused.

"Mm hmm." I slide my fingers back and forth over her pussy. Grasping her thighs, I push them wide apart. Her labia are flushed, unfurled, glistening with her desire. I caress her there, and she gives a hoarse cry, arching like a strung bow.

I groan. Did I mention she's perfect?

"Fuck, Thandi, you're so beautiful," I praise her between kisses to her hip and her thigh. I lick a burning trail over her abdomen. "Baby ... you tempt me so badly. I need to taste you."

That's when I reverse our positions, guiding her so she's straddling my face. Her thighs are warm against my cheeks; I'm nestled in her softness.

Ah, this is what heaven must feel like.

I take a deep breath, inhaling her scent. I said I wasn't going to make love to her, but that doesn't mean I can't worship her.

"Ronan..." Thandi's thighs tense, and the look in her eyes is far too tempting as she stares down at me.

"Come here." My fingers dig into her hips, tugging her downwards.

I make a ragged sound as I'm enveloped in her sweetness. Her wetness bathes my face. The faint freshness of soap mingles with the hotter perfume of her desire. I press my nose deeper, licking along her slit, easing my tongue into her channel.

"So damn delicious," I purr, dragging her closer.

I think she screams then, but her thighs are pressed so tightly against my ears that everything is muffled. She's a fucking feast. Who needs oxygen? If I'm going to suffocate, there's no better way to go. For Thandi, I'd die a thousand deaths.

I suckle the satiny folds of her labia, and her hips undulate in a wild rhythm. When I swirl my tongue around her clit, her back arches like she's been lashed by a whip. She jerks up, but I pull her back down again.

"Where are you going?" I chuckle. "I'm not done yet."

"Ronan, please," Thandi whines. She grips the back of the couch with white-knuckled strength. She throws her head back as I attack her clit in earnest. Her voice is almost anguished as she pleads with me to let her come.

But I want more. I latch onto that sensitive nub, making a sound of protest.

"Ronan … *Ronan*…," Thandi moans. Her voice rises, then twists into a shout as I thrust my tongue into her pussy again. "*Please! Oh, God!*" She throws her arm over her eyes.

"Mm." I only tighten my grip around her and nurse happily at her clit.

"Enough," Thandi whines, tugging my hair. "I can't … I need…."

I pause against soft, scented flesh. "Are you sure? You said—"

"Ronan," Thandi says sharply.

"What?" I lick the inside of her thigh.

Thandi leans back, shifting away from me. She takes my hand in hers.

"Could you please stop arguing and fuck me?"

I grin and whisk her away to the bedroom.

"With pleasure."

Breaththrough
Thandi

This time when I wake up, I'm not alone. In fact, Ronan has transformed into an octopus overnight. I'm half pinned beneath him, his powerful legs tangled with mine. One hand is curled around my waist, the other cupped possessively between my thighs. I try to shift, and he protests, mumbling in his sleep. His hand tightens intimately, and I flush as last night's memories rush back to me.

The board's decision, the press conference, the staff protest— and then the fierce, consuming way Ronan and I found each other again. Not even the wildest ride at Sugar Hill Park could match the whiplash of it all. I still feel the echo of that storm inside me. But today feels like a tremulous new start—a light in the darkness after an endless night.

And it's all thanks to the man beside me.

I turn my head toward the window with a sigh.

The rain has passed. Outside, the trees blaze in autumnal glory. Unlike Whitlow or Ronan's mansion across the river, my condo in Willowburn overlooks downtown and the ordinary rhythms of life. Across the street, Patty from the pastry shop props up a chalkboard sign with today's specials. A metro bus with a giant injury-lawyer ad—**77-HURT-HELP**—rumbles by.

I'm full of too many feelings to name, but I'm mostly grateful not to be alone anymore. Even when she was gone, it's always been Tess and me. I relied on her memory for so long that I didn't realize it could be different. Last night, Ronan, Dani, Sammie, and Fia showed me that I don't have to carry the weight alone—that others are ready to support me. I just have to let them.

Maybe that's what Dad means when he asks me to trust the process, to believe in the pull of the moon—in the hidden processes of the universe. Like quantum tunneling, where particles slip past barriers they have no business getting through.

It feels right; it's almost perfect.

Except for one thing:

My heart is still breaking for Daysha.

She deserves her happy ending, too.

We have to find her. I don't know how, but if yesterday taught me anything, it's that the impossible can happen. Ronan taught me that hope can survive in the face of immeasurable odds.

I have to hold onto that.

Thinking of Daysha reminds me of my parents. I haven't spoken to them since the youth center. I'm sure they saw the press conference. They must be beside themselves not hearing from me.

I have to fix that.

After some concerted wriggling, I wrest free from Ronan and pad over to my phone.

I have three missed calls—one from Mom, one from Fia—

My breath catches.

And one from Detective McNamara.

"You're sure you're okay with this?" Ronan asks as we enter the police station. His hand envelops mine.

I nod. "McNamara said they turned up something at the information booth last night. If there's anything I can do, I want to help."

"Alright." Ronan kisses my forehead. "Just know that you don't have to push yourself too hard. I'm here."

"Thank you," I murmur. I lean into him, closing my eyes for a second, absorbing his strength. It feels so different being here with him, so much better than when I looked at Stephan's scans and sat with Aliyah.

"Ms. Elowen, I'm glad you could make it." Officer Hayes waves us over. She's holding a metal *Orioles* coffee mug in one hand. "We'll meet in Interview Room Two."

"Great." I squeeze Ronan's hand, and we fall in step behind Hayes as she leads us down the hall.

Morning has settled over the station, but it's a tired awakening—voices are still hushed, daylight is barely creeping through the windows. An older officer balances a box of donuts on his forearm, offering it to a cluster of detectives hunched around a bulletin board. A public defender with a loosened tie and a crumpled suit jacket trudges toward the exit. Someone yawns behind a stack of paperwork. The whole station seems to carry the weight of a night that didn't let anyone rest.

"In here." Hayes flips the switch and nods toward two empty chairs. "I'll let McNamara know you're waiting. She's still with the witness."

"Thanks," I say, twisting my hands together. Ronan gives me a soft look and pulls me closer.

"No problem." Hayes pauses at the door. "Oh, and Ms. Elowen?" Her expression shifts into a rare smile. "Glad to see you two are back together."

I blink, startled. Ronan chuckles.

"Thanks, officer," I say.

Hayes winks, then heads down the hall, her stride quick and purposeful.

My thoughts spin. *Please*, I beg Dad's quantum tunnels. *Let this be the breakthrough we need.*

I can't sit still. I shift in my chair and drum my fingers on the table.

"She said McNamara was with the witness. What do you think they found?"

"I've been wondering that too." Ronan leans back, thinking. "Last time they discovered the bridle swivel. Maybe Daysha left us another clue."

I inhale, my throat closing around the fear I don't want to name. I'm grateful Ronan still talks about her as if she's here—as if she hasn't stopped fighting.

"It'll be okay." Ronan kisses me softly. "It can't be over."

"I hope so. I just—" My shoulders cave under the weight of it all. I can't hide the tremor in my voice. "I'm so scared for her. What if—"

"Don't," Ronan's voice is warm but firm. "We have to hold on. We have to believe she's okay."

"Mr. Thorne is right."

McNamara enters the room, her eyes weighted with dark circles. "I haven't given up on this case, and neither should you."

I sit ramrod straight. "Detective."

"Thanks for coming in." McNamara lowers herself into the chair across from us. "We got something last night thanks to your friends' information booth."

The breath leaves my lungs in a rush. So our little task force *did* matter. I could kiss Fia.

"What is it?"

"At about nine last night, a young woman ran into the tent, claiming a man tried to grab her in the same area where Daysha was taken."

Ronan stiffens. "You're saying the kidnapper was at the park last night?"

"The young woman's description matches the original tip from the gas station." McNamara folds her arms. "When we first got that report, we worried the kidnapper might be on his way out of town. But now we know he came back."

A chill prickles down my spine. "But why?"

"It's not typical behavior," the detective continues. "Most offenders flee. Staying close to the abduction site usually means the location holds something for them—past trauma, unresolved fixation, or a connection to another crime."

"What are you saying?" I grip the edge of the desk.

"Whoever this man is, I now believe he is connected to your sister's kidnapping. There is no other reason he'd be so fixated on the park."

McNamara leans forward. "Now we just need proof."

"Hold on," Ronan's brows lower. "I thought the suspect was a man in his thirties. How could he be the same kidnapper from two decades ago?"

"I'm not saying he is," McNamara replies. "I'm saying he may be tied to Theresa Elowen's disappearance. We're looking for the link between the two cases—the common thread."

My pulse thunders. "What do I do?"

"Hayes took the witness's initial statement, but we brought her back in this morning for a full account and to work with the sketch artist. I'd like you to hear her story and look at the drawing. See if anything stirs a memory."

I slump back, stunned. After all this time, after the years of searching, the prototypes, the failures, the hours spent trying to force my memory to yield something—the truth crashes in like an avalanche.

Daysha's kidnapper is connected to Tess.

It doesn't seem possible. And yet that's what McNamara is saying. The implication is doubly damning. It means every dead end, every failed experiment, every moment my technology couldn't pull that day into focus—all of it might have cost us the chance to stop the kidnapper sooner.

Now, both Tess and Daysha are slipping through the gap I could never close.

The room tilts. My breath won't come. I push away from the desk, struggling to stand.

"Sorry, I…" My voice breaks. "I think I'm going to be sick—"

"Thandi." Ronan rushes to my side, pulling me into his arms. "It's okay, baby. Deep breaths. I've got you."

I cling to him, gasping for air.

"I'm so sorry." McNamara's expression softens. "I know this is a lot. I won't push you if it's too much. I've got officers combing the park right now. We'll throw everything we have at this. Maybe it'll spark something."

I breathe in Ronan's scent. It anchors me, and in an instant, I'm back in the cafeteria where he once caught me—where he protected me from my shame. He's my mountain, I remind myself. The one steady point when everything else gives way. No matter what happens, I'm not alone anymore.

"No." I ease out of Ronan's hold so I can stand on my own two feet. "This is too important," I say. "I'll do it."

Full Circle
Thandi

"Okay, she's in here." McNamara pauses outside her office. "She's still a bit rattled, so we'll tread lightly. I'm not asking you to confirm an ID. I just want to know if anything she describes feels familiar to you—tone, behavior, pattern, anything."

I nod even though my hands are clammy with sweat. "I'll do my best."

McNamara smiles. "That's all I ask, Thandi. Thank you again."

Her reassurance steadies me a little as she leads us inside. With five people in the room, the office feels more claustrophobic than I remember.

A Black woman about my age sits closest to the desk, clutching a coffee cup. She has a heart-shaped face and full, expressive brows. Her knee bounces in an erratic rhythm. Beside her, the sketch artist—a willowy blonde with streaks of violet in her hair—leans over a drawing pad. Charcoal smudges her hands as she traces the contours of a second sketch.

On the desk in front of the two women lies the first drawing: a profile of a man in a hoodie, shadowed and impressionistic, as if caught mid-movement.

"No," the witness says, leaning in to study the emerging portrait. She chews on one fingernail, then forces her hand back to her lap. "His eyes were closer together, I think."

The sketch artist nods and begins adjusting the detail.

"Amanda," McNamara says gently, "this is Ms. Elowen. She's assisting us with the case."

The young woman lifts her head. Her eyes widen, darting from me to Ronan. "Oh—oh. When the detective said Elowen, I didn't think she meant *that* Elowen."

"Sorry—" She half rises from her chair and thrusts out her hand. "Where are my manners? I'm Amanda. Amanda Colefield."

"Hi, Amanda. I'm Thandi. Good to meet you." I touch Ronan's arm. "This is Ronan."

Ronan offers a smile. "Thank you for helping, Amanda. I know last night must've been terrifying."

Amanda's throat works, but she nods.

McNamara watches the exchange with a satisfied look. "And this is Katarina, our sketch artist. Why don't you all make yourselves comfortable?"

Hayes brings in a few white plastic chairs and arranges them in a semicircle. We settle in, McNamara in her usual spot behind the desk, and Ronan and I squeezed together on the flimsy seats. I can't help reaching for his hand. His fingers close around mine at once, warm and tender.

I force my shoulders to relax. "So … where do we start?"

"I thought Amanda could take us through what happened one more time," McNamara says. "If that's alright with you, Amanda?"

"Yeah." Amanda inhales shakily. "Yeah … okay."

"Good." McNamara steeples her hands under her chin. "And remember, you've done nothing wrong. You're not on trial. We're just trying to put the pieces together."

I tense as we wait for the other woman to begin. A weight hangs in the air between us. I feel like I'm on the edge of a cliff, staring into the abyss—waiting for the monster below to claw its way to the surface.

Amanda stares at her hands. "I'm the receptionist at Mayview Apartments. Yesterday, there was a regional management event, so most staff got to leave early. I'd seen the fliers about the community search—and you guys on television." She offers a small smile to Ronan and me. "I wanted to help."

I think of all the fliers we printed and Ricky's hopeful posters. It feels good knowing they reached the right people. I squeeze her hand. "Thank you for coming out."

Amanda gives a jerky nod. "As soon as I got to the park, I signed in at the booth and got my gear. They put me in group five, but halfway through, I realized I'd left my phone in the tent."

Ronan tilts his head. "So your group left without you?"

"They offered to wait, but I had the map of the route. I told them to go ahead." Her voice trembles. "It was only a few minutes. I didn't think...." She breaks off, fists clenching in her lap.

"Hey," I say gently. "You can't blame yourself. You didn't do anything wrong."

"Thandi's right." McNamara's jaw tightens. "That's why we have to catch the bastard."

Katarina sets her sketch pad aside and begins making a fresh pot of coffee at McNamara's makeshift station—the top of an old metal filing cabinet. She offers some to us, but I'm too wound up to have any caffeine. When she refills Amanda's cup, the young woman gratefully accepts.

Amanda is quiet for a moment as she nurses the dark brew. Then she lifts her gaze.

"Everything was fine. Someone at the tent had already put aside my phone, so I grabbed it and headed out to find my group again. My family's lived in that neighborhood forever. My BookTok group even meets there every Sunday." She gives a thin, broken laugh. "I didn't need the map. I thought I could save time by cutting through the bathrooms—"

She stops. Her hands tremble so much that she has to set her cup down. Tears well fast, spilling over as she presses her hand to her mouth. "Oh, God."

"It's okay." McNamara leans forward and passes her a tissue. "Take your time."

"Sorry." Amanda wipes at her nose. "I just … I still can't believe this happened. I'm so shaken."

My own vision blurs, and I sniff as a wave of sympathy crashes over me. She's so afraid, still in so much pain. I know better than anyone that once you stare terror in the face, you are forever changed. Nothing will ever be the same for her again.

"Now that I think about it," Amanda whispers, "it's terrible that those stalls are set up so the taps are outside."

She blows her nose again. "One minute I was walking past them, and the next—" Her voice fractures. "—an arm was around my neck, and someone was dragging me toward the bushes."

Fresh tears spill. She breaks down again, shoulders shaking.

"Should we stop?" I turn desperately to McNamara. "I can't bear to see her like this."

McNamara nods. "Maybe we should reschedule. Amanda, I'll have Officer Hayes—"

"No." Amanda straightens, crushing the tissue in her fist. "No, I can do this. Please … I want to get it over with."

"Would it help if fewer of us were here?" Ronan asks. "With this attack…." He hesitates. "I'm the only man here. I understand if it's helpful for me to step out."

My heart lurches. That kindness is exactly why I love him, but fear slams into me. I'm too raw, too hollowed out from everything that this week has taken from me. The thought of him leaving—even for a few minutes—steals the air from my chest. Embarrassment and panic collide, and before I can think, my hand shoots out to grab his.

"Please don't leave," I whisper.

Ronan is already rising, but he freezes the instant I touch him. His eyes widen, and he folds me into his arms, holding me tight.

"McNamara, we should stop," he grits through his teeth. "They're both hurting too much to do this."

The older woman glances at me, then at Amanda. She sighs. "Okay."

"Stop, please." Amanda grips the edge of the desk with both hands. "No one needs to leave. I can finish."

McNamara turns to me. "Thandi?"

I meet Amanda's gaze, and something quiet passes between us—the shared recognition of trauma and the cost of being brave enough to face it. I reach out and squeeze her shoulder.

"Let her speak. She's come this far. We owe it to her."

Amanda gives me a tremulous smile, and I manage one in return.

"Keep going," I say softly. "He grabbed you. How did you get away?"

"I have three older brothers." A ragged laugh escapes her. "I fought like hell. I used everything they ever taught me. Got him good in the nuts, too."

Even Ronan laughs at that. "Good for you."

"He was so fucking creepy. And his eyes…." She shudders. "They were so vacant."

"Should I be capturing any of this?" Katarina asks suddenly, and I jump. I'd forgotten she was in the room.

"No, not yet," McNamara says, shaking her head. "Amanda, tell us again what he said to you."

"He kept saying, '*Come home … we're waiting. Dinner is ready.*' Over and over." Amanda wraps her arms around herself. "And he stank of those cherry inhalers—Sniff Rush or whatever they're called. My cousin uses them sometimes, but this was different. On him, it was overwhelming. I thought I was going to be sick."

McNamara turns to me. "Does any of that make sense to you, Thandi?"

I shiver as the kidnapper's words echo in my skull: *We're waiting.*

Waiting for whom? For Daysha? For someone else?

God. A sob clogs my throat. I can't let myself imagine what it means if he has an accomplice—and all of it magnified by Astor's poison. Will Daysha really be okay?

"Baby?" Ronan murmurs, rubbing my fingers between his.

"No." I try to swallow my fear. "I'm sorry. None of it makes sense."

I bite my lip, tamping down the frustration, the gnawing desperation of another roadblock. *If I could just remember even one detail....*

My gaze drifts to Katarina. "Maybe if I could look at the sketch?"

Katarina glances at McNamara. "Detective?"

"Go ahead."

Katarina takes her seat, sliding the sketchpad over the desk. Remember, this is just a best guess."

I nod, studying the drawing. Unlike the other image, this one is a close-up portrait. A young white man with a thin nose and sharp cheekbones stares back at me. Amanda is right, there is something empty about his eyes. Like someone snuffed out whatever spark used to live there. It unsettles me more than I want to admit.

I trace the edge of the paper, grounding myself. My gaze drops to his shoulders, swallowed by the hoodie. He's lean but broad-shouldered. With everything rendered in shades of gray, his frame feels like the only solid thing about him.

I grip the pad and let out a breath. Nothing. Not a twinge. Not a flicker of recognition.

I'm already shaking my head, sliding the pad across the desk, when my thumb skims the page, catching on a patch of charcoal. It smudges the drawing just enough to blur the line of the man's jaw.

"Shit, sorry." I jerk my hand back. *Great, now I'm erasing Amanda's memory too.*

"It's no problem. That's an easy fix." Katarina smiles and restores the line with an elegant flick of her wrist.

"Thank goodness," I breathe.

My gaze drifts back to the kidnapper's face, and I notice the faint stippling on his cheeks. It's barely a spark, but something flares, deep in the reaches of my memory. It's fleeting—a moth fluttering through the darkness. I frown, trying to hold onto it.

"What's that?" I ask quietly. "There. On his cheeks."

"What?" Katarina looks up.

"Those marks."

"Something was wrong with his skin," Amanda says, crowding closer. "I saw it when I kneed him."

My pulse stutters. Cold rushes down my spine.

Ronan glances at me. "Something wrong, like what?"

"I'm not sure. Acne scars, maybe?" Amanda pauses, brows knitting together. "Actually… there was something else. He had a rash on his hands, and he had something smeared over them. Like calamine lotion."

"Calamine lotion?" I echo in disbelief. "Who is covered in bug bites in the middle of autumn? I—"

I stop. Everything in me goes very still.

Because that's when the strangest thing happens.

I don't know anything about calamine lotion, and nothing Amanda says triggers anything related to Tess. Yet, as I stare at the sketch, an earthquake ripples through me.

White male, mid-thirties. Hair that's neither blonde nor brown. Acne scars on his cheeks. Hooded eyes that are slightly too close together….

The spark niggling at the edge of my consciousness bursts into a conflagration.

"Amanda," I say sharply, "did you happen to see his eye color?"

"Yes." Amanda bites her lip. "Green, I think."

I gasp.

I've seen this face before. But it has nothing to do with the park or Daysha.

I shoot to my feet.

I know him. I knew him long before the kidnapping or even before I met Ronan.

It's the patient who came to Immerscent for a consultation.

The one who ignored all protocols and arrived hopped up on WhiffRush.

The one Sammie and I turned away.

Last Known Address
Ronan

Thandi is as still as a stone next to me. The thin packet of emer-gency-release copies from the patient file is crumpling under her grip.

She looks so small, swallowed by the Maybach's quilted leather seats. She hasn't uttered a word since we left Immerscent, and she con-firmed that the kidnapper is the rejected consultation patient. I know the woman I love well enough now to guess the pain she's carrying.

This time, I won't let her break again.

It's taken me my whole life to sharpen my awareness—to put my privilege aside and center those most in need. Sometimes, I wish I could give Thandi some of my old selfishness. She shoulders too much and always takes more blame than she deserves.

I hate what this week is doing to her. I hate that even when she gives everything, the world keeps demanding another pound of flesh.

"Come on, baby. Talk to me." I glance at her while shifting gears.

The car surges over the country road. We have a lot of ground to cover as we head to the address listed in the patient file, deep in Spotsylvania County. We've been traveling for more than an hour already. Chesden's glass buildings have faded into rolling fields, old silos, and cows grazing by the ditch.

I remember McNamara's warning about the kidnapper's fixa-tion on Anchor Park. Out here, miles from anything familiar, doubt creeps in. Could he really be this far away?

I glance at the GPS mounted on the console. The clipped British voice announces that the next turn is still fifteen minutes away.

"Sweetheart?" I try again.

This time, Thandi looks over with wounded eyes. "Sorry. I'm not trying to shut you out. I just…."

She breaks off. "I keep thinking … we turned him away. What if—"

"Baby." I reach across the console and lace my fingers through hers. "Don't do that to yourself. You are *not* responsible for what this man did. Turning him away isn't what made him dangerous. Letting him in wouldn't have fixed him." I lift her hand and kiss her knuckles. "Please. Trust me on this."

Thandi nods, swallowing. Her fingers tremble in mine. "I—"

A sudden vibration rattles the cupholder.

It's my phone. Before I can reach for it, the Maybach's center display lights up, McNamara's name flashing across the console. I curse under my breath and tap the steering-wheel control.

"Detective, what is it?"

"Ronan, I'm ahead of you on Route 2. I want you to keep your eyes peeled for the old Milkwood Farm distillery sign. You'll see it on the right about three-quarters of a mile before the Oak Ridge Road turn. That's your cue: Oak Ridge to your left, gravel drive just past the tree-line."

"Understood. We're roughly ten minutes behind you," I say as my cell service wavers between five bars and three. The reception is shit out here.

"Good. Listen, I want to go over the plan. I'm not expecting him to be at the house. His pattern keeps him circling the woods around the park. But as his last known address, what we're looking for is evidence. Thandi, your role is pivotal. If you recognize *anything* on the property, we need to document it then and there."

"Okay," Thandi manages in a small voice.

I glance at her. God, she looks fragile. I wish more than anything I could turn the car around, take her home, hold her, make love to her—show her that she can put the weight on my shoulders instead. But right now, all I can do is pray that this will finally give us what we need to put this monster away for good.

"When you arrive," McNamara continues, "you'll wait in the clear zone. It's the empty lot about two hundred feet from the house. One of my team will meet you in a patrol cruiser."

"Got it," I say, unwrapping a protein bar and offering it to Thandi, who still looks far too frail for my comfort. We haven't had anything since breakfast. She takes it and nibbles at the corner.

"Ronan, you stay at Thandi's side. No one enters the house. My team is clearing the main structure and the surrounding barn. Dogs and tech are already sweeping the property. I want you two in that space, protected—out of the house but close enough that we can call on you if needed."

"Sounds good. We'll see you in a few."

McNamara's voice softens. "I know how much you two have already done. Thandi, thanks to you, this could be our big break. Stay sharp. I'll see you in ten."

The line goes silent.

I reach over and stroke the back of Thandi's neck. "McNamara's right. Every bit of progress we've made so far has been thanks to you. I'm so proud of you, baby."

Thandi's shoulders hunch, curling inward, but she nods.

I sigh. I won't push her. Even this is progress.

As we crest a gentle rise, we pass the distillery McNamara indicated. The sweet, heady scent of charred oak and mash drifts across the road—a deep, warm smell that feels at odds with the dread pressing against my chest.

A wooden sign appears on the right, **MILKWOOD FARM DISTILLERY** scorched into the planks in heavy letters.

Even though it's not yet noon, a cluster of locals is already gathered outside the squat brick-and-timber building. Two older men in camo jackets sit on stools fashioned from old whiskey barrels, sipping drams from tasting glasses. Another pair chats against a split-rail fence, gift store bags in hand. In the typical way of country folk, they all stare as we drive past.

Next to me, Thandi tenses as the group of blank faces scrolls by. "What's wrong?"

"Nothing." She shivers. "I just hate places like this—rural, insular, and not another Black or Brown face in sight. I don't feel safe."

My jaw clenches. She's right. There's no guarantee she's welcome here. It's just one more way the world makes her vulnerable in ways I'll never experience.

It's just one more reason I have to keep protecting her.

I lean over and kiss her softly. "I'm sorry, baby. I won't let anyone come near you, you know that, right?"

She nods, and I kiss her again, hoping that if she can't believe in the world, she'll at least believe in me.

I gun the Maybach's engine, speeding us along the dirt road. Soon, we're in front of the property, and it's just as McNamara described. The house is a modest ranch, once beautiful but now sagging under years of neglect. A looming red barn rises behind it, weirdly in better condition than the main building.

Two patrol cruisers are parked near the front steps, lights still pulsing. McNamara's sedan is closest to the door, trunk popped open, evidence kits and gloves spread across the bumper. A K-9 SUV idles farther down the driveway, the dog whining and pacing in a tight figure-eight as its handler murmurs commands. Two other officers walk the perimeter, one sweeping the tree line with binoculars.

A cruiser is already waiting in our safe area—the steep dirt driveway of the abandoned house next door. Clearly, this neighborhood has seen better days.

I turn into the lot and ease the Maybach into a patch of flattened grass where Hayes waits, directing us forward with a quick wave. As soon as we pull up, she steps toward us with a grin. I'm surprised by how relieved I am to see her.

"Officer Hayes."

"You made it," she says, looking inside the SUV. "Thandi, you holding up?"

"Trying," Thandi says with a tired smile. "Let us know where you need us. I brought the copies you asked for under the emergency protocol." She hesitates. "As much as I hate this man, he's still one of our patients. If you need his full record, I'll need something more official."

"Got it." Hayes shrugs and checks her watch. "McNamara will sort that out. For now, nothing to do yet. The detective and the team are about to go in. The initial sweep should only take about twenty minutes. Just sit tight."

I take a deep breath.

Twenty minutes, and I get to take Thandi home and make sure she's okay.

I can manage that.

"Thanks, Officer Hayes," I say with a smile.

"Don't mention it." She jerks her thumb at the cruiser. "Hey, you met my partner yet? Brooks! Get out of the car and show your sorry ass."

"Jesus Christ, Hayes, this is a sweep, not a fucking meet-and-greet," a gravelly voice grumbles from inside the cruiser.

The door opens, and a heavyset officer with sharp blue eyes steps out. He looks like a man who trusts nothing. But even through the grousing, he casts Hayes a look of unmistakable respect.

He raps on the roof of the Maybach with a beefy hand. "Morning, folks. Glad you're here." A smile breaks across his face. "Any tips for dealing with her? Ever since she and I became partners, she's convinced she's in charge."

I bark out a laugh, and beside me, Thandi grins for the first time since we left the station. I'm grateful to these two for that more than anything.

"Congratulations," Thandi says, her smile widening. "Last time you mentioned your training officer. Partners means a promotion, right?"

Hayes rubs the back of her neck, but the pride in her eyes gives her away. "Yeah," she says quietly. "It does."

"Well deserved," I say. "I don't know what we would've done without your help—" I shoot Brooks a mock-apologetic look. "Sorry, Officer. No tips from me on how to rein her in."

Brooks' radio crackles.

The shift in him is instant. His smile vanishes, his face snapping back into a watchful mask. His hand drifts toward his holster.

"Look alive," he mutters. "They're going in."

Hayes straightens beside him. The tension that had lifted for a precious moment settles back over us like a shroud.

As they head back to the cruiser, Hayes pauses beside us, lowering her voice. "Hey. We've got eyes on you. Nothing's happening on my watch."

Then she gives a thumbs up—a soft, wordless promise—and heads back to her post.

I sigh, my eyes drifting to the clock on the dash.

And now we wait.

"Come here, baby," I say, tugging Thandi onto my lap. I tilt her chin so I can see her eyes.

"Now tell me, truly. How are you doing?"

Mehen
Ronan

Thandi's asleep.

It happened sometime between her whispering that she was fine and me telling her I'm here for whatever she needs. I guess she took me at my word. The patient packet lies forgotten beside her hip, its edge bent where it presses against her leg. She's curled into me like she's finally allowed herself to take as much as she gives.

God, she must be exhausted to sleep here, inside a police perimeter, with lights strobing against the trees. Not to mention the specter of the kidnapper hanging over this place—and the knowledge that whatever is in that house could make or break things for Daysha, and for Tess.

I tighten my arms around her, careful not to wake her. Twenty minutes has never felt like such an eternity. I want this finished. I want Thandi home. I want her warm and safe and far from all of this.

I'm not a religious man, but I lift my gaze, praying to Mom, the heavens—whatever deity is out there—to let this be our turning point. My baby can't go on like this. She's trying to push through, but every day without Daysha is slowly killing her. I can't bear to see it.

A tap on the window startles me, just as I'm adjusting Thandi so she doesn't wake up with an arm tingling with pins and needles.

I catch Hayes' reflection in the sideview mirror. She's standing outside, and her eyes soften when she sees Thandi sleeping. She lowers her voice as I crack open the window.

"They'll be out soon," she murmurs. "They just needed a few more minutes. Officer Patel wanted to sweep the back room one last time."

So I'm not going crazy that this is taking longer than expected.

I nod, my hand still cupping the back of Thandi's head.

"Thanks," I whisper.

Hayes gives an understanding smile, then pivots on her heel.

A shadow passes in front of the porch window. I glimpse a black uniform and the sputter of a flashlight flicking off.

Movement.

McNamara steps outside, peeling off blue nitrile gloves. Clear evidence bags are tucked under her arm, rectangular items inside. Her hair is slightly mussed. A streak of dust is on one sleeve. She comes down the walkway toward us, her stride clipped and sure.

"Thandi." I brush her cheek. "Wake up, baby. They're coming out."

"Hm?" She stirs, blinking. "What?"

"They're done with the sweep. McNamara's coming to brief us."

In an instant, she's upright, jolting so fast she almost hits my chin. She reaches for the patient packet, already shifting toward the center console.

"No, stay." I guide her back with a kiss to her forehead. "Lean on me. No more heroics."

Her eyes widen. "I'm not—"

I lift a brow.

She ducks her head, then relaxes. "Okay. You're right."

Something warm expands in my chest. This is all I've ever wanted—this quiet trust. To not just be her lover, but her protector.

I know Thandi said the past was behind us, but the mind and the heart have different rhythms. I hurt her. I nearly lost her. I wouldn't blame her if her guard were still up. But she lets me hold her. She lets me help her. She reaches for me without hesitation.

That's my Thandi. A heart bigger than the sun.

Forget Shezmu, I'll be her Mehen.

Her shield.

Her living fortress.

The one who holds back the darkness so she never stops shining.

McNamara's at the fender, waving to us as she approaches the driver's side window.

"Ready?" I say to Thandi.

She smiles. "As I'll ever be."

"Good." I kiss her, blocking the world out for a moment, savoring her sweetness—the soft press of her mouth against mine.

Then I roll down the window. "Detective, what do you have for us?"

"I'll give you the bad news first." McNamara lets out a weary breath.

Since Thandi is still curled on my lap, the detective takes the passenger seat. She perches on the edge, one leg outside the SUV, like she doesn't want to linger enough to be pulled under by whatever she is about to say.

"When you shared the patient information with us, we looked up the deed associated with this address. The suspect's name is Damian Patrick, but the home is registered to an Arnold Patrick—his father. We didn't find anything here tied to Daysha or Tess. But—" She raises a finger when Thandi tenses. "This isn't a dead end."

"How?" Thandi demands, voice trembling.

"For the first time, we have conclusive evidence that our suspect is reenacting trauma from his childhood—trauma which may be connected to him being a witness to his father's crimes."

My stomach churns.

Thandi's fingers twist in the front of my shirt.

"Fuck," I breathe, tightening my hold on her. "What kind of evidence? What exactly are we dealing with here?"

McNamara hesitates. "Are you sure you want to hear this? It isn't pretty."

"Yes," Thandi answers quickly. "Tell us, please."

"There were children." McNamara grimaces. "Dozens. Hayes ran the photos through the database. At least a third match missing child cases going back to the eighties—too far back to make these artifacts from our current suspect. Most of the kids were from rural counties or neglected urban pockets—places with low visibility and little funding. The father knew they'd slip through the cracks."

Thandi looks gutted, the color draining from her face. I feel sick. Somehow, I didn't think any of this could get worse, and yet it has.

"But that wasn't Tess." Thandi stares at her hands.

"What do you mean, baby?" I ask, rubbing her back.

She lifts her chin, eyes brimming with tears. "She wasn't neglected. Our neighborhood wasn't depressed. She was loved—" Her voice breaks. "*We* loved her so much."

"You're right." McNamara's voice is soft. "Tess doesn't fit the earlier profile. And that's exactly why you matter to this investigation."

The detective shifts, leaning back slightly. "There's something else," she says. "In the kitchen, we found a photograph of a woman pinned inside one of the cabinets. The picture was in surprisingly good condition compared to the rest of the house. And there were fresh handling marks along the edges. Someone's been taking it down, touching it, and putting it back."

"A memento," I mutter. "Do we know who she is?"

"Not yet." McNamara sighs. "Our working theory is that she was the father's domestic partner. There's no marriage license, no shared lease, no joint mortgage—nothing that ties her to the father on paper. That makes a positive ID tricky."

She folds her arms. "Women in informal partnerships can disappear in rural records. No deed, no shared bills, no name on file—she could be functionally invisible. We've got a facial recognition request running, but without a confirmed name, it may take time."

McNamara's gaze sharpens. "The important thing is that some- one loved her enough to keep that picture safe for decades. That tells us she mattered—to Arnold Patrick, and likely to his son."

"I'm sorry," Thandi shakes her head, her voice uncharacteris- tically impatient. "But how is this connected to Daysha? Shouldn't that be our focus here?"

McNamara looks toward the horizon as a bird cries out some- where beyond the barn. A shimmer of starlings wheels above the treeline, rippling like a dark ribbon.

"I didn't understand why he went for Amanda," she says slowly. "Jumping from a child to an adult in less than a week is an extreme break in typology." Her fingers tap the dashboard. "Then I saw the photo."

McNamara turns towards us. "The woman in the image bears a strong resemblance to Amanda—Black, soft features, petite frame, roughly the same age. We think this is part of his regression."

"Regression?" Thandi murmurs.

McNamara nods, folding her hands in her lap. "When offenders relive formative trauma, they often start reenacting the emotional landscape of that period. Not the exact events, but the *feelings* tied to them. In this case? We think the woman in that photo played a pivotal role in his childhood. Maybe a caregiver. Maybe someone he even called 'Mom.' Someone he lost."

Her brows lower. "That kind of attachment, unresolved, can turn into fixation. And fixation isn't rational. It shifts targets. If he's spiraling, slipping into a state where he's trying to 'find' her again…" McNamara's gaze sharpens. "Then he'll latch onto anyone who resembles her. Amanda fit the pattern."

A sudden breeze sweeps through the clearing, catching on a torn, dingy white sheet hanging from the abandoned clothesline at the edge of the property. It snaps loudly, drowning out the starlings overhead.

The wind gusts through again with more force, cracking the sheet like a whip. Both evidence bags lying face down in McNamara's lap lift at once. One skitters toward the open door, the other slides to the floor near her boot.

"Shit." McNamara lunges.

She catches the first bag just before it can blow into the dirt. And for a second—just one—its contents tilt into view.

I see the photograph.

Of a man and a woman.

The woman is soft-faced and pretty, smiling into the camera with a gentle tilt of her head. She's young; in her mid-twenties, maybe. Her hand rests on the man's chest. The man has his arm around her, but he isn't smiling. His eyes are narrow, wary—watching the photographer like he expects danger from behind the lens.

I shiver, suddenly unable to chase a chill.

I see what McNamara means. The woman *does* look like Amanda. But something about the photograph fills my lungs with dread.

If you soften the edges … imagine another hair color … something even more feminine. *Brighter.*

She looks a lot like someone else.

I suck in a shaky breath.

Thandi.

Instinctively, I tighten my arm around her.

The resemblance isn't exact—not enough to sound an alarm on its own—but the echo is there, and it unsettles me. I tell myself I'm overreacting, that stress is making ghosts out of shadows. But something in my chest stays tight, like a wire pulled too taut.

McNamara snatches the bags up, slipping them back into her pocket. But the damage is done. I hate to even think it, yet once it's there, the seed takes root. Fear looms like a specter, unwelcome and impossible to ignore.

If the kidnapper is searching for a stand-in for that woman … and Amanda slipped through his fingers … then he isn't done. He'll keep looking.

If that's the pattern, then someone who shares even a passing resemblance—someone petite, gentle—could drift into his crosshairs without ever knowing it.

It's probably paranoia.

God, I hope it is.

Still, I'll call Equinox when we're back, just as a precaution. As an extra layer of vigilance in case this man is more desperate than even McNamara realizes.

"—a separate briefing," the detective says.

"Ronan?"

I jerk upright. Thandi is staring at me, her pretty mouth pursed with concern.

Shit. Was I starting to spiral?

I shake my head. "Sorry, what?"

"Detective McNamara says there's more, but it … might be too much." Thandi clenches her fists. "Potentially connected to Tess. She's wondering if we want to break for today and schedule another briefing tomorrow."

"Baby, it's not about what I want." I lift her hands and kiss them, even though my heart is still stuttering from the echo of fear. "This has always been hardest on you. How do you feel? If you want to stop, we'll turn back. It's nothing to go to the precinct tomorrow. I'll support whatever you prefer."

Thandi shifts against me, her eyes fixed on McNamara with that aching determination I've come to recognize.

"Then we stay," she says firmly. "Let's finish it."

I smooth my hand along her back, grounding myself. Then I take a breath, tightening my arm gently. Anchoring her.

"All right," I say to McNamara, "What else did you find?"

Echoes
Thandi

"Okay, nobody panic—but we brought snacks," Hayes announces, rounding the front of the SUV with a family-size bag of Hot Cheetos raised like a trophy.

Brooks trails behind her with two water bottles and a bag of pretzels, wearing the expression of a man who has accepted his fate. The contrast makes me laugh under my breath. I'm learning that the younger officer has far more spark than I realized, and I'll take any bright spot I can get right now.

"We should stretch our legs," Ronan murmurs, easing me upright.

He's been so loving and tender with me since we got back together that my heart almost aches with joy. As worried as I am—as terrified about Daysha—it helps to know that he's in my corner.

I nod, and we step out into the cool air just as Hayes tosses the Cheetos onto the hood.

McNamara approaches from the side, tucking her gloves into her pocket. "I don't know how you eat this junk," she mutters—then, grabs a handful of Cheetos and pops them into her mouth.

Hayes chuckles. "If you say so, Detective."

Brooks hands McNamara a bottle of water. "Detective, what's next?"

She takes it, wiping orange dust off her hands. "Next, we wrap up. Most of the perimeter teams can stand down. Tell Patel and

Morales to start packing up the evidence kits. We'll keep the sedan and your cruiser here for now."

"On it." Brooks nods and heads toward the house.

Hayes trails after him, pausing long enough to call over her shoulder. "I'll help them get things together. Holler if you need anything."

McNamara turns to us. "Should we continue?"

"Please." I slip my hand into Ronan's, and he meets my eyes with a smile before lacing our fingers together.

In the distance, I see the other officers packing up. The K9 unit drives off, followed by the second patrol car, leaving the detective's navy sedan in the driveway.

McNamara grabs another handful of Cheetos. "We think the father's partner came into the picture about a year before Tess' disappearance. That's when his pattern shifted," she says, leaning against the Maybach's fender. "After that, he couldn't vanish for days at a time. He had to hunt closer to home—places where he could blend in. Suburban parks. Community spaces."

"That's how he ended up in our neighborhood." I shudder.

When Tess disappeared, it felt like a horrible twist of fate, a fatal throw of the dice. There was no explaining it, so in our hearts, we believed it was a crime of opportunity. Learning that Arnold Patrick planned his atrocities with such calculation leaves me gasping. I'm horrified and enraged that he dared to bring his evil into our lives.

I'm heartbroken that his soulless existence cost me the other half of mine.

I close my eyes as a tide of grief threatens to drown me.

"Baby?" Ronan squeezes my hand.

"Sorry," I whisper, "This is just ... a lot."

McNamara nods. "Take your time."

"It's okay." I shake my head.

I can't afford to unravel, not now. Not when Daysha's life might hinge on what we learn next. My heart may be collapsing in on itself, but the rest of me has to stay upright. We have to move forward. She's counting on us.

"I'm fine," I say, forcing a breath through my lungs. "Let's keep going."

McNamara watches me for a moment. Then, her expression darkens.

"There's something else."

"I'm almost afraid to ask," Ronan mutters.

As he speaks, a gust sends a scatter of dry leaves skittering across the gravel, the sound thin and papery. It feels like the world is holding its breath with us, waiting for the next crack in the ground beneath our feet.

McNamara follows my gaze to the drifting leaves. "When we looked at the dates, we found three other children whose disappearances overlap with Theresa's. Same general timeframe. All from different counties."

The detective sighs. "We believe Arnold Patrick had some of these children in his custody. Not necessarily all at the same time, but close enough that it would have affected his access and mobility." Her voice drops. "So he would have needed another strategy. A different way to approach kids in safer neighborhoods."

"A different way?" I echo.

"Yes." McNamara's expression turns grim. "We're still combing through the evidence, but it's possible he even used the children he already controlled to lure new targets."

I stiffen. For a moment, I cannot speak. The thought of Tess—bright, gentle Tess—caught anywhere in this man's twisted orbit rips apart something inside of me. She deserved so much better than Arnold Patrick and his darkness.

"Let me get this straight," I manage, my voice shaking. "You're telling me this man may have gotten to Tess because he used *his other victims as bait?*"

McNamara nods. "It's a working theory only, but we can't rule it out."

She reaches into her breast pocket, retrieving one of the evidence bags the wind scattered earlier. I couldn't see what was in them before, but now, she hands the bag to me carefully, as if the photos inside could bruise from the lightest touch.

"I want to show you something," she says. "We found these in a box in the basement alongside children's toys and clothing."

My stomach churns as I gaze at three Polaroid photos, all of them old and overexposed, their white borders smudged with fingerprints. Three girls, ranging from seven to eleven years old, stare back at me.

The youngest is Black with neat cornrows. She's wearing a white shorts set. The second girl, likely the eldest, has long dark hair and the gangly build of a child on the cusp of puberty. The last is a redhead with wide, fearful eyes.

"These were all taken within a year of Theresa Elowen's disappearance," McNamara says. "I need to know if anything about them feels familiar. Were any children matching their description near the park the day she went missing?"

My hands tremble as I grip the edge of the thin plastic. Familiar? How could this ever be anything other than sickeningly *foreign*?

Recoiling, I wonder what happened to the girls' families. Did they move on, or are they, like me, still praying for closure—still clinging to their memories with every waking breath?

"Thandi?" McNamara prompts again.

"Sorry. Yes. I'm looking." I drag my eyes back to the photos. Forcing myself not to look away, I scan for any detail that might lead Daysha home to safety.

The Black girl sits stiffly on a threadbare armchair, her hands folded in her lap. The tall girl stands in a hallway I don't recognize, her expression blank. But the redhead—

Gasping, I curl into Ronan, unable to shake off a frisson of terror. What he sees must unnerve him, too, because he holds me fast, murmuring soothing words in my ear.

Each of the photos, and what they represent, is awful, but the picture of the redhead is the most disturbing. Because she is standing outside on a porch, her face splotchy from crying.

The same porch that is just two hundred feet away from us.

The warped slats and the crooked post were straight then. The white paint on the siding was still bright—not today's yellowing peeling mess. And the shutters were cobalt, not a tired blue-gray. Yet, there's no mistaking the property. It's the same house, down to the rusted horseshoe nailed to the post near the flower boxes.

Coldness seeps through my limbs. These photographs aren't just sick mementos from another time and place. They are proof that Arnold Patrick brought children *here*. Some of them, all of them—maybe even Tess.

A sob threatens to break free from my throat. Blindly, I shove the bag back at McNamara, even as I press my hands to my mouth.

This is why I've always clung to science, to reason. Because no deity, no higher power worth worshipping could convince me that this brutality had a divine purpose. All of these children, spanning so many decades, were robbed of their futures.

I blink, fighting tears. There was no brighter ray of sunshine than Tess. I'll never understand why she had to suffer so much.

"You alright, baby?" Ronan asks, rubbing my shoulder.

"I don't … they're not—" I shake my head. "I don't remember any of them at the park."

"No problem." McNamara sighs, putting the photos away. "It was a long shot anyway. We'll keep looking. But we're getting closer. I can feel it."

I nod as the rain of tears threatens to fall again. I'm glad one of us feels confident because I'm hollow. Exhausted.

Losing Daysha, seeing these photos…. For the first time, I'm not sure that hope is enough to carry us through. Not when I'm staring at an evil so wilful, so deep that its claws have reached across generations to harm the people I love.

Four days.

It's been four days since Daysha's been in the clutches of a madman whose own father provided the template for his cruelty. Can anything truly stop this? Will we ever see her again? Or will she be another sad Polaroid, lost to a brutal legacy?

"Detective, is there anything else?" Ronan sounds as weary as I feel.

"No, that's it for now." McNamara rocks back on her heels. "I'll reach out if forensics turns up anything else. Thanks for coming out here. And I'm sorry—truly."

The detective dips her head and begins making her way to the rest of her team.

"Come on, love," Ronan murmurs, guiding me to the SUV's passenger side. "Let's get out of here."

I turn, staring at the porch one last time. At the front step where a little girl with red hair once stood, terrified, praying for help that never came. I think of the two other girls, trapped, so far from home, likely used as bait.

It's too horrible to contemplate.

The tears do come then, and I cry. I cry for all the children taken, and all the innocence that has been lost, including my own.

"Oh, baby, I'm so sorry." Ronan holds me close.

I lean on him, savoring the gentleness of his hands. I don't know what I would do without him here—without his love and his support. Suddenly, the only place I want to be is in his arms, with nothing between us, his body melding with mine, giving me the pleasure that makes me feel whole again.

My entire life, I've been trying to remember.

He's the only man who lets me forget.

"Take me home, please," I whisper.

"Of course, my love." He cups my face and our lips meet, softly, fiercely.

I cling to him as the wind whistles through the cul-de-sac, feeling even colder and more desolate than before.

Ronan opens the passenger door for me. He's kissing my forehead, guiding me onto the runner, when something jolts me.

Not a memory. Not quite.

Something else.

More like a concept.

A terrifying realization.

I still don't remember those girls, but the idea of other children at the park explodes in my mind like a stick of dynamite. I go rigid, as I'm flung back to twenty years ago.

The sun is hot, and I'm sweating as I play with my LEGO blocks. Tess has just finished her dismount from the swing and is racing off to buy us vanilla cones. Time refracts. The sequence concentrates through the prism of time and the hindsight of maturity:

Just before I go back to my blocks, a little boy with dark blond hair starts talking to Tess.

I've never seen him before. I don't think he goes to our school.

And then:

"Hey," I say, hurrying over to Maisha and Bobby. "Did you see Tess?"

Maisha licks the side of her hand and nods. "Yeah. She was just at the truck. She got two vanilla cones. Said one was for you."

"She was talking to some boy," I say.

Oh, God. I grip the edge of the door.

How could I have missed this? After all this time? After all these years?

"Thandi? Baby, what's wrong?" Ronan steadies me against the door.

I start to tremble. For twenty years, I've fought to conjure something, *anything* beyond the moment Tess left to buy ice cream. I've catalogued every second, every interaction leading up to that terrible juncture. I spent decades building technology to trigger even a glimmer beyond the dark, murky period in the woods afterwards, where everything fragmented.

And now the key to it may have been something I hadn't forgotten at all—something I'd known all along but simply discounted.

Because of all the horrors of that day, it always seemed the least significant.

I was wrong.

There was another child.

There has always been another child.

Not a girl.

Not any of the three in the photos McNamara presented.

But a boy.

An unfamiliar boy with dark blond hair.

Something terrible, yet so clear—so terrifyingly certain—dawns on me. I lunge forward, scrambling onto the seat.

"Thandi, what's going on?" Ronan asks. "Come on, baby, talk to me."

I barely hear him as I find what I'm looking for. The patient folder is tucked between the dashboard and the windshield, exactly where I'd left it. My hands shake as I flip the file open and stare at the passport-sized image on the intake form.

Green eyes.

And dark blonde hair.

Suddenly, I don't have to guess who the little boy at the ice cream truck was or what he might look like. I grip the folder so hard that it bends beneath my grip.

"Call McNamara back," I gasp.

Daysha's kidnapper wasn't just groomed by his father.

Twenty years ago, he was the bait Arnold Patrick used to grab Tess.

Target
Thandi

"Let's go through it one last time," McNamara says.

We're in front of Hayes' and Brooks' cruiser, Damian Patrick's patient file open on the hood between us.

It's him.

It's always been him.

I nod, but I'm shellshocked from the force of my discovery. It's hard to think, hard to see anything through the iron grip of guilt. Immerscent, β7, the Sugar Hill formula—they're laughably redundant in the face of what I've missed.

I built a company to find justice for Tess.

It turns out I had everything I needed all along.

"The last time I saw Tess," I say, "she was standing at the ice cream truck, talking to a blonde boy. The same kids visited the park every week. He stood out because he was new."

I rub my hands up and down my arms. "He didn't go to our school; he didn't live on our street, and he wasn't playing on the grass earlier with the rest of us. It … felt like he popped up out of nowhere just to talk to Tess."

I close my eyes. "Now I know he did."

"Christ, to think he was the one who helped—" Ronan starts, but even he can't finish. Cursing, he stands behind me and wraps his arms around me instead.

"It's despicable, but highly plausible. Many criminals force their children to assist with their crimes." McNamara's energy has shifted to a tense kind of excitement. I can't resent her for it. If she didn't love her job, there'd be no chance of finding Daysha.

"We have no proof that Damian Patrick was the child you saw." McNamara's hand brushes her holster. "But, it explains how his father grabbed these children without anyone raising an alarm."

Her eyes narrow. "If Damian was used by his father as bait, his trauma and his fixation with the park make even more sense."

"Detective, you said there were multiple cases, right?" Ronan tugs me closer. "The three girls in the photos were taken around the same time as Tess. Even if the kidnapper's father used him as bait, why is he fixated on Anchor Park? Why this specific case?"

I close my eyes. He's asked what I've been afraid to.

I wondered the same thing, but didn't dare to name it. Because what if it wasn't Damian? What if I'm wrong—*again*?

"I don't know yet," McNamara says. "But I believe there was something specific about the period Tess was taken. Something that changed the family dynamic."

The detective leans against the cruiser. "Now that we've confirmed Arnold Patrick had a partner at the time, I think she may be tied to it. Whatever happened with that woman could be the trigger behind Damian's spiral. That's why my team is working to identify her. She might be the missing key."

Relief surges through me. Maybe I haven't completely screwed this up yet. "So what happens next?" I ask.

"My team is pulling the case files for the other three girls," McNamara says. "We're looking for any mention of a young boy present just before they vanished. Even a vague note matters now that we know what we're looking for."

She pauses, gauging our reactions. "We'll also reach out to their families again. Maybe one of them remembers a blond boy near their daughter that day. Thandi, you didn't see his face, right?"

I shake my head. "Not fully. They were at the ice cream truck. I saw them from behind—maybe a flash of his profile when he said something to Tess." The uncertainty, the uselessness that's clung to me for twenty years, wells up again.

"Hey." McNamara's voice gentles. "You've given us more than you realize. With the photo from the patient file, we can run an AI-based child-age regression to generate what Damian looked like then. We'll take that image to the families and see if it jogs anything."

I sag against Ronan, wrung out, terrified to hope. And yet, despite myself, the naive part of me—the part that believes kindness and the right people, no matter how few, can still change the world—stirs.

I see the steel in McNamara's eyes, the drive that refuses to let this trail go cold. Near the porch, I see Hayes ribbing Brooks while she types on her laptop, and I want to believe again.

For Tess, Daysha, and the little girl I used to be.

"You'll let us know as soon as you find something?" I ask.

McNamara nods. "You have my word."

"Good." I turn in Ronan's arms, pressing myself against him. "Then we're going home."

"Oh, sweetheart," he breathes.

When I look up, his eyes are aflame with such tenderness that it almost erases the horror of today. I rise onto my toes and kiss him, telling him with my lips, my hands—my heart—how much I love and need him.

McNamara chuckles. "All right, lovebirds. I need to go over a few safety details with you, and then I promise I'll leave you to it."

"Better make it quick." Ronan winks, and a soft laugh escapes me. It's one of the things I love most about him—how he can bring light into the unlikeliest places.

Still holding onto each other, we gather around McNamara as she radios Brooks for her tablet.

He jogs over with the sleek case. "Here you go, detective. We're just doing one last check. Hayes is on the line with Financial Crimes now. She's checking whether any of the father's outgoing payments can help us identify the woman he was living with."

"Roger that." McNamara taps her earpiece and speaks into it. "Hayes, good thinking on FC. You working with Mellon?" She pauses, listening. "Okay, I'll come over and look at the pulls with you."

She turns to us. "This is a precaution only, but I want to show you the kidnapper's active radius."

McNamara sets the tablet on the hood, tapping an app until a blank grid fills the screen. Using a stylus, she sketches out a rough square of streets, adding boxes to mark points of interest.

"These are the places we've confirmed he's operated in," she says, circling the cluster. "The park, the gas station, and the two side streets between them." She pinches the screen, zooming in. "All of it is within about a two-mile radius. He doesn't stray far. His movements are predictable—almost obsessive. It fits the profile we're building."

The detective sighs. "That should make him easy to find, but the woods surrounding Anchor Park are enormous and irregular. Without a directional lead, we're burning hours we can't afford to lose."

I tamp down the anxiety rising in my chest. "They still haven't found anything?"

McNamara shakes her head. "Teams are out there every day, but they can't grid-search every square foot of that vegetation. It's a needle in a haystack. And based on what we found in the house, it doesn't help that Damian Patrick is skilled in hunting and camouflage—just like his father."

I bite my lip. "Are you sure the woods are the only option? He's been here, and this isn't anywhere near Anchor Park."

"You're right." McNamara draws a single box far outside the circle, in the upper right corner of her map. She taps the lone square. "This is where we are now. The only outlier."

Ronan frowns. "Because of his childhood?"

"Exactly," McNamara says. "But we think this home is tied to his past trauma, not his current pattern. The evidence inside seems to confirm it. He visits the house, but he hasn't been here since he took Daysha."

She drags her stylus back to the tight cluster of streets. "Everything he's done since Monday is in this zone."

I peer at the area she's indicated, and a bitter taste fills my mouth. I know those streets like the back of my hand—Alemu Hair Design, where Ms. Hanna braided my hair every summer, Yoon's Cleaners, the tiny shop that's been there longer than anyone can remember, and of course, Shimmy's 24-hour diner. All places full of warmth and community—now turned into a kidnapper's hunting ground.

"One more thing," McNamara says over the crackle of her radio. "Based on Damian's profile, I want you to steer clear of this radius until we have eyes on him. The failed grab on Amanda would have made him more unstable. She fought him hard. That kind of rejection hits the same nerve as whatever happened with his father's partner."

"Avoid the area?" My voice rises. "How am I supposed to see my parents? Ricky?"

The man lured Tess. Now I'm supposed to let him keep me from the only family I have left, minus Ronan? I pause, trembling in anger.

"I'm sorry, Thandi. I know this isn't what you want to hear." McNamara grimaces as she meets my gaze. "But your parents' home is here—" she sketches a box near the rim of the circle "—which puts them right on the edge of the red zone. Until we know where Damian is, I recommend you stay away. He's targeting young women your age. I don't want you anywhere he might see an opening."

I turn to Ronan, hoping for backup, but his features are shadowed with concern.

"I hate to say it, baby, but the detective is right. We can bring your family to your place or Whitlow until we find Daysha."

I swallow hard. If Ronan is this worried, I'll listen, but none of it feels right.

"What about my family?" I ask. "Will they be safe? We can't leave them in harm's way either."

"I understand your concern, but I do not believe they are in immediate danger." McNamara's brow furrows. "Neither your parents nor Ricky fit the age or gender profile for Damian Patrick's victims. His behavior may seem erratic, but it's not random."

She slips her tablet back into its case. "Unfortunately, he is replicating his father's pattern of targeting girls. And now, of course, there's the escalation with Amanda."

"No disrespect, detective, but I can't just take your word for it." I hesitate, trembling.

"What is it, baby?" Ronan asks.

"I'm not discounting your profile, but we're forgetting something important."

McNamara folds her arms. "What's that?"

"WhiffRush." I press my lips together. "The scans from Stephan, Daysha's cousin, showed serious damage. And while Stephan is younger, he wasn't dosing at the extreme levels of this kidnapper."

I step closer to Ronan, hooking my finger in his belt loop. "Under these conditions, we should expect a wider degree of variance in any behavioral models we're using for Damian Patrick."

"In other words," Ronan says grimly, tightening his hold on me, "expect the unexpected."

He looks up. "She's right, detective. The data Dr. Linny shared from the Astor trials showed catastrophic harm in kids, but prolonged exposure produces similar effects in adults."

McNamara nods. "Alright. I still want you to avoid the area, but I'll increase patrols across the entire radius. Given your family's connection to the earlier case and the offender's fixation on this zone, we'll put an extra unit near your parents' street."

She glances across the clearing. "In fact—" McNamara jerks her thumb toward Brooks, who's back in our safe zone. "It looks like Brooks and Hayes just got their next assignment."

"Oh, thank God," I breathe, sagging against Ronan. "Thank you, Detective."

"Not a problem. You were right to raise it."

"Anything else, Detective? Or can we head out?" Ronan asks.

McNamara flashes a grin. "No. This time, you really are free to go."

She tucks the tablet under her arm and waves as she crosses to the house, already huddling with Hayes.

"Shall we?" Ronan murmurs, cupping my face in both hands.

"Please," I whisper, pressing my cheek into his palm.

He nods, and hand in hand, we make our way back to the SUV.

I feel so off balance, torn between hope and an awful sense of dread. We've made progress today; I know we have. And yet, the echo of panic clings to me. We need to move faster. I can't shake the feeling that we're still too far from finding Daysha.

Overhead, the swallows wheel once more, their calls thinner now, distant, as if they, too, feel my despair. The wind shifts, and I clutch my sweater tighter about me, shivering.

I glance at the sagging house and the barn behind it. The decaying exterior of both buildings seems to represent something so much more sinister now that I understand what transpired here.

I'm chilled to the bone, and this time it has nothing to do with the wind.

I grip Ronan's hand, eager to return home to warmth and our little bubble of normalcy.

The trees shake, ablaze with dying color. The woods seem to breathe as we keep walking towards the incline that leads to the Maybach. Now that the adrenaline has faded, the distance between the cruiser and Ronan's SUV seems wider than I remember.

A crunching sound drifts on the breeze. At first, it seems like nothing more than the whisper of dried branches and the dance of leaves hitting the ground.

But it returns—faint, yet regular.

I glance over my shoulder. Just at the edge of my vision, a shadow ripples through the underbrush.

A twig snaps, the crack echoing through the clearing.

An animal? I wonder.

I pause, heart in my throat. I know nothing about wildlife, but I don't do deer, coyotes, or God forbid, bears.

It could be something worse, an internal voice reminds me.

I think of the faces at Milkwood Distillery, cold with suspicion as we drove past.

We need to leave.

We've spent too long here.

"Ronan…." I squeeze his hand.

"Hmm?" He smiles down at me.

"Did you hear that?"

"Hear what, baby?"

"There." I point at the dense thicket of trees. I can barely get the words out. "I think there's something out there."

Ronan frowns, tensing. His hand goes to my shoulder. "Where?"

"There, I—"

"Hey! What the—"

Ronan turns just as Brooks stiffens, hand flying to his holster.

A figure explodes from the bushes—hoodie flung back, face pale, body crouched close to the earth.

At first, I don't know what I'm seeing. I can't process anything except the panic seizing my lungs.

Then I see the shock of blonde hair, the scarred cheeks, the wild green eyes.

I gasp.

Terror freezes my limbs.

It's Damian Patrick.

The kidnapper.

He rushes forward, a snarl ripping from his throat. He moves like a madman … or a hunter trained to stalk shadows.

Metal flashes. Brooks doesn't even get his weapon out before the knife arcs downward. Steel rakes across the back of his hand in one vicious slash.

Brooks roars, stumbling back, blood dripping through his fingers.

"Knife! Knife!" he bellows.

Damian pivots and charges.

Ronan starts.

I scream.

Because the kidnapper is sprinting toward us.

And that's when I realize:

He's coming straight for me.

Coward
Ronan

The moment I see Damian, only one thing matters.

Keeping Thandi safe.

If this loser thinks I'm going to let him grab her, he's out of his goddamn mind. Not when I've just won her back. Not when I've vowed never to let anything—*or anyone*—hurt her again.

I don't think. I don't breathe.

I shove her behind me and launch myself at him.

We collide, my shoulder smashing into his ribcage with a sick crack.

Once I was too strong to be bullied, James used to sneer that I was "big for nothing," but years of training tell the real story. At six foot six and two-twenty, heavyweight was never a euphemism. I barely feel the impact as Damian Patrick goes airborne, sprawling in the dirt.

He hits the ground with a grunt. For a second, he just lies there, gasping—a shocked wheeze bursting from his lungs.

Good. He didn't expect this.

He didn't expect *me*.

His eyes roll back, whites flashing before they return to me, wide and unfocused.

I glare, and for the first time, I see that Amanda was right: There's something wrong with his skin. His forearms are blistered and smeared with streaks of pink lotion. In his fallen state, against the backdrop of the dirt and leaves, it looks like failed camouflage.

For a heartbeat, he seems less like a predator and more like prey—a deer frozen in headlights. He scrabbles at the dead leaves, unsteady and disoriented.

But when my gaze drops to his hand, something cold crawls up my spine.

Because even stunned and gasping, even with pain written across his face, his right hand is still locked around the knife. He's prioritized the blade over his own safety. A thin trickle of blood streams down his wrist where the edge bites into his palm.

That's when I know nothing about Damian Patrick is normal.

Thandi screams my name.

Resisting the urge to turn, I grit my teeth, bracing for Patrick's next move. The fear in her voice tears at me. I can't believe this asshole is putting her through this.

Her voice is *my* reason for being.

And for him, it's gasoline.

The second she cries out, something jolts through him—a grotesque spark snapping him back to life. He lurches upright with uncanny speed, eyes locked not on me, but past me.

On the woman who is everything I live for.

Shit.

"Come on, you sick fuck," I growl, stepping into his line of sight. "Face me like a man."

"Mama!" he screams, launching himself at me.

We hit the dirt in a twisting knot of limbs, his knife hand jerking wildly. The reek of sweat and artificial cherry slams into me, sweet, nauseating, and feral.

"Baby! Get in the car—windows up, doors locked. Drive off if I'm not there in five!" I bark, grappling with Patrick, trying to pry the knife from his fingers.

He fights with a berserker's strength, and even with our size difference, I'm struggling to hold him down.

"But—" Thandi's voice breaks.

"Now!"

Thandi's sob rips through the clearing, and something in me fractures as I hear her soft footsteps pounding toward the Maybach.

Patrick goes mindless as he bucks and snarls beneath me. He fights like a cornered animal. But I've waited my whole damn life to use my strength for something that matters.

I get him under me and drive my fist into his jaw, once, twice, trying to break his grip. But he's a man possessed. He isn't fighting me.

He's fighting everything between him and Thandi.

"Mama!" He cries out again—a sound so wild and primal it barely qualifies as human—and wrenches his arm free.

The blade flashes. Then drives deep.

Pain detonates in my side, white-hot and brutal enough to rip the air from my lungs. I grunt and jerk for half a second, but I don't go down. Not with Thandi still exposed. Blood gushes down my torso, soaking my sweater.

"Ronan!" Thandi's anguished voice ricochets across the clearing. "Oh my god! Someone help, please!"

Please let her reach the SUV. I don't care how bad this is as long as she's safe.

I rain blows onto Patrick, pummeling him with everything I've got. His cheekbone caves under my fist. A sickening crunch, and blood erupts from his nose. He gurgles, coughing like he's drowning.

His arm jerks up.

He stabs again—wild, uncoordinated. The blade glances off my ribs, piercing shallowly.

I grunt, faltering.

My grip loosens.

And he slips free.

"Thandi!" I choke out. "Run!"

Patrick bolts, wriggling out from under me. It's horrifying how fast he shakes off his injuries the second he spots Thandi scrambling up the incline toward the car. She's almost there, but Damian is far too close for comfort.

I pivot, giving chase.

Brooks is yelling something, but he's too far away. He fumbles for his gun with his left hand, blood streaming from the other.

I guess it's all up to me then.

"Ronan! Fall back!"

Movement explodes from the front of the house. McNamara sprints across the yard, Hayes outpacing her in seconds. Both women have their pistols raised.

I glance from Patrick, closing in on Thandi, to the two officers still more than a hundred feet away.

Fall back?

That's not fucking happening.

I roar and surge forward. With a running leap, I slam into Damian from behind. The knife goes flying into the underbrush. He scrabbles for it, but I wrench him backward, driving a brutal punch into his kidneys.

We roll, dirt and dead leaves sliding down the back of my shirt. Damian grunts and elbows me in the side. Fire tears through my wound, a fresh gush of blood spilling fast, but I push past it.

My pain, the injury, all of it is irrelevant. I'm pure adrenaline now. There is nothing I won't do to stop this man from hurting my baby.

We grapple with each other. My fists rain down again, and Patrick groans. For the first time, he hesitates. Fear and uncertainty cloud his gaze.

I have no idea what he's thinking, if he's even lucid under the haze of WhiffRush, or if his own psychosis is driving his response. But even with my stab wounds, he looks the worse for wear.

I am sure of one thing, though: As long as he's trying to hurt Thandi, I will fight him until my last breath.

Our eyes meet. In a split second, he seems to make a decision.

He twists hard and drives his elbow straight into my wound.

Agony sears through my side. My body hunches on instinct, every muscle seizing around the injury. I try to keep hold of him, but fuck—my grip slips.

It's all the opening Patrick needs. He wrenches free and rolls out from under me. Before I can recalibrate, he's already on his feet. Bloodied and panting, he breaks into a sprint.

This time, however, it's in the opposite direction, away from Thandi.

I clamp a hand over my wound, gritting my teeth as I force myself upright. I can't falter. Not with Thandi still exposed. I push toward her even as Patrick tears off toward the edge of the property.

He veers to the left, aiming for the sagging clothesline and the cover of the woods.

Goddammit. My priority is Thandi—*always* Thandi—but watching this monster slip away again sends rage burning through me. I scan for Hayes or McNamara while still moving toward her.

Can anything be done to stop him?

To keep him from getting back to Daysha?

"Dispatch, we have an officer down and a civilian injured. Knife in play! Suspect still active!" McNamara shouts, sprinting toward us. "All units converge on the Patrick property! Stage EMS at a safe distance until the scene is secure!"

I know then that we've lost Damian. Not because anyone screwed up. But because the detective's got two injured men and one terrified civilian. No way she'll leave us to chase a knife-wielding kidnapper into the woods.

"Jesus Christ!" McNamara approaches me just as I reach Thandi. "You okay? Let me see the wound."

"I'm fine." It's a lie, but I lift my sweater anyway, peeling back my shirt.

Thandi gasps. Her whole body shakes as tears spill down her cheeks. "Oh my god... oh my god... Ronan, why did you engage him? I can't—" She chokes, sobbing.

I pull her close. "Shh … shh … it's okay. Just a couple of flesh wounds. Looks a lot worse than it is."

"A lot worse than it is? You're soaked in blood." She balls her fist into my sweater. "Don't you ever do that again, you hear me? I can't lose you, too!"

That hits me right in the heart. This is too much. We have to bring Daysha home. We have to end this nightmare before it steals anything else from her.

"Okay, okay," I murmur. "I'm not going anywhere, baby."

I kiss her forehead, trying to soothe the panic radiating from her. "It'll take a lot more than a scrawny dude with a knife to do me in," I whisper, brushing away her tears with my thumbs.

She only shakes harder, a broken sound escaping her as more tears spill down her cheeks.

My gut twists. I hate seeing her like this. "Don't cry, Thandi. I—"

"Damian Patrick! MPD! Stop right where you are!"

Hayes barrels past us. Whatever I was about to say dies as she brings her pistol up, sightline locked on Patrick's retreating form.

"Oh no, you don't," she mutters, long legs devouring the ground. "I'm not letting you off that easy."

McNamara's head snaps up. "What? Fall back, Hayes! Priority is securing the site and protecting Brooks and the civilians."

The detective starts to follow, then stops short when she realizes she can't leave us. Frustration rips through her voice. "Hayes! Are you listening?" She yanks up her earpiece. "Hayes, I repeat. Do not pursue!"

She might as well be speaking to the wind.

Hayes is already gone. Her breath clouds in the cold air as she rounds the SUV, gun raised—eyes flashing fire. She streaks past Brooks, who's still clutching his bleeding hand.

"Fuck!" Brooks barks, staggering. "Hayes! Stand down! That's an order!"

"Sorry—partners now, remember?" Hayes steadies her weapon with both hands. "I've got a visual. I'm taking the shot."

Damian bolts, racing across the yard until he reaches the sagging clothesline and the mouth of the woods. He crashes through the torn gray sheet, fabric tangling in his shoulder. He wrenches free and ducks behind it, desperate to vanish into the brush.

Hayes veers left, fighting the fluttering cloth as she tracks the shadow slipping behind it.

He's almost gone. Almost swallowed by the trees.

Hayes plants her feet.

She fires.

Red bursts across the cloth—startling, vivid—a violent sunset. Damian jerks, then stumbles, tearing through the tattered fabric. He vanishes into the thicket, branches cracking like bones beneath his feet as he disappears into the deep green darkness.

The wind gusts.

The swallows cry overhead.

The cloth flaps in the wind, the single bullet hole outlined like a bullseye against a widening halo of crimson.

Mixtape
Ronan

The door clicks open, and a man in gray scrubs steps inside, a tablet tucked under one arm and a folded page clipped to the front. He's in his late forties with dark hair going silver at the temples. He nods at me as he approaches the bed.

"I'm Dr. Nathan Kline. I've been overseeing your tests."

"Good to meet you, doc." I shift in the stupid hospital gown, smoothing the sheets around me.

Let's just say the standard patient outfit was not made with me in mind. I'm not sure what the ties at the back are supposed to do, because I feel like a sausage about to burst out of its casing. I'm pretty sure my ass would be hanging out if not for the second gown the nurse gave me to wear as a robe. At least it's cotton.

"You're a lucky man, Mr. Thorne." Dr. Kline pulls up a stool. "Your scans are clear—no internal bleeding and no fractures. We closed the more serious laceration on your side with twenty-four sutures. The smaller cut that glanced off your ribs is superficial."

I'm relieved—mostly for Thandi, who's still tearing herself up over the attack. She left me fifteen minutes ago for the hospital café.

"That's great," I say, easing the bed into a more upright position. I ignore the dull throb in my side. "How long will I need to leave the stitches in?"

"Two weeks. Your PCP can remove them for you." Dr. Kline taps the tablet. "You'll be sore for a few days. No heavy lifting, no sudden twisting. And given the pain medication, you shouldn't drive tonight."

He flips the folded page over. "Looks like you came in with your wife. Good."

Wife.

The word settles strangely—*beautifully*—in my chest. Some rushed admin staff must have looked at Thandi and me and jumped to the wrong conclusion. I like it, though: The idea of Thandi being my forever.

"We can't discharge you unless someone else is driving you home," Dr. Kline explains. "She'll need to keep an eye on you overnight. I'll have the nurse go over—"

"Babe, look what I got you."

The door swings open, and Thandi slips inside, balancing a cafeteria tray. A paper bag dangles from one wrist. She's gathered far more food than one person could reasonably eat: two cups of soup, a banana, a roll, a carton of milk, and what looks like a Jell-O cup. She stops short when she sees Dr. Kline.

"Oh—I'm so sorry. I didn't realize you had company."

Dr Kiline's smile is warm. "No apologies necessary, Mrs. Thorne. Your timing is perfect. I was just sharing care instructions with your husband."

"Hu-husband?" Thandi freezes, eyes wide. The tray wobbles in her hands.

"Yes," Dr. Kline murmurs. "He's being discharged. I've put in a short course of Tramadol in case he needs it. Your pharmacy is the one on Elk Street, correct?"

"Yes … yes, of course," Thandi stammers.

I settle against the pillows with a slow grin. No part of me wants to correct the physician. I pat the bed beside me.

"Come here, baby. Let me see what you got."

"Here you go." Thandi sets the tray on the rolling table next to the bed, arranging it so it stretches across my lap. "I also got you a change of clothes in the gift shop." She tucks the paper bag in the corner. "Please try to eat. You need to keep your strength up."

She slips away just before I can tug her close. I shoot her a dirty look and push the spoon around the bits of chicken in a soup that looks alarmingly colorless. Keep my strength up? If this is the key, I might be better off hungry. I bring the spoon to my mouth and grimace.

The chef needs to be fired, stat.

Thandi casts me a warning look over her shoulder as she turns back to Dr. Kline. "Doctor, you mentioned care instructions?"

"Yes." He shows her the tablet screen. "The nurse will print you out a copy of these before you leave. Keep his dressing dry for forty-eight hours. And I recommend taking the pain medication with meals."

Thandi jerks her head up. "Does that mean he needs another dose now?"

"No, not yet," Dr. Kline says, glancing at the chart. "But he'll need another one in about three hours."

"What about her?" I ask around the dinner roll. That's edible at least.

Dr. Kline's eyes widen. "Was Mrs. Thorne also hurt?" He flips back to the cover sheet. There are no notes—"

"No." I shake my head. "But, she hasn't been eating or sleeping well. I can't imagine that's going to get better with me injured. Is there anything that can help?"

"Ah." Dr. Kline smiles, rocking back on his heels. He gives Thandi a sympathetic look. "I see this all the time."

Thandi flushes, looking like she wishes the floor would swallow her. "I'm fine, but it's true. My appetite hasn't been great," she admits quietly.

Dr. Kline nods. "Low appetite under stress is completely normal. If eating feels like a chore, try small amounts throughout the day. And consider nutritional shakes. They can help you feel full without the effort."

"Alright, I'll try," Thandi murmurs.

"Good. Your body needs fuel—especially if you're going to be the one keeping an eye on him."

"And sleep?" I press. I extend my hand, and this time Thandi comes to me. She's careful, circling over to my non-injured side.

"I can't prescribe anything—not without evaluating her myself— but a small dose of melatonin in the evening can help reset things." Dr. Kline tucks the tablet under his arm. "But if the challenges persist, don't ignore them. Follow up with your primary care physician."

Thandi nods, her gaze shifting from Dr. Kline to me. Her back is ramrod straight, her expression faintly flustered and apologetic.

Internally, I kick myself. I've made her uncomfortable, and I'm sorry for it. I don't mean to put her on the spot. I just worry about how little she thinks of her own needs. My faux pas aside, I'm grateful for the information Dr. Kline has shared.

I bring Thandi's hand to my lips. I whisper an apology against her skin, and her spine softens.

"Thank you, doctor," I say.

"You're all set, then." Dr. Kline strides to the door. "The nurse will come in shortly. You both take care of yourselves."

As soon as he leaves, I turn to Thandi. "I'm sorry, baby. I didn't mean to make things awkward for you."

"It's okay." Thandi picks at an invisible piece of lint. "But our focus should be on your recovery, not me." Her voice cracks. "He stabbed you, Ronan. Twenty-four stitches isn't nothing."

"I know." I sigh, trailing off. "I'm sorry."

Thandi nods, blinking rapidly. She's fighting tears but still trying to be strong.

My heart twists.

"Come here, love." I fold her hand into mine. "I'll be okay. You heard the doctor. Please, no more guilt."

I kiss her forehead. "I know you don't want to hear it, but the truth is, if Damian Patrick burst in here right now trying to get to you, I'd face him down again in a heartbeat."

"Ronan, you can't—" Thandi begins to protest.

"I can. And I will." I meet her gaze. "Because that's what love is. Protecting the people we care about, no matter what. That's never going to change as long as I live."

I kiss the corner of her mouth. "Besides, I'm putting my life on the line right now by eating this soup. It's ghastly."

A watery laugh escapes Thandi. "Only you could be silly at a time like this."

"That's because you're serious enough for the both of us." I nudge the tray towards her. "You should have some, too. I can't eat it all, and you need to get something in you."

"Alright." Thandi perches on the edge of the bed. She takes the extra cup of soup and sips it, but her worried glance never leaves my face, eyes tracking every bite I take.

I pause, mid-slurp. "Baby, you're making me nervous as hell."

"Sorry," she sighs.

"Hmph." I kiss her again until the tension leaves her body, and the look in her eyes isn't so haunted.

Afterwards, we eat together. We don't speak. We don't need words to acknowledge what we just survived—or the bond between us.

Thandi leans gingerly against me, resting her head on my shoulder.

"What?" I murmur, brushing her cheek.

"That soup really does taste like shit." She grimaces, putting the empty cup aside.

I chuckle. "Told you so."

Thandi bites her lip. "Thank you for being there for me today. Seeing you get hurt…" She can't finish the rest.

"I know, honey." I pull her closer. "But I'm here. We made it."

Thandi glares as I shift her. "Please be careful of your side. You shouldn't be moving around like this." She tries to pull away, but I hold her fast to me.

"Uh-uh." I nuzzle her neck. "I heal faster when you're closer."

Thandi makes an exasperated sound. "You're a terrible patient, you know that?"

I grin. "But you love me anyway."

"I do." Thandi's gaze is soft, full of warmth. "How are you feeling?"

"I've been better," I admit. "The worst of it is tenderness. The pain meds are working, but things will be a lot less pleasant when they wear off." I push the tray table away. "But it's just discomfort. Nothing I can't handle. I'd rather have some stitches, Thandi, than not have you with me."

She slips under the covers with me and curls against my good side. "I hate this," she whispers.

I rub slow circles over her back. "Me too."

She's silent for a moment.

"Do you think we'll find Daysha?" she asks in a small voice.

After finding out how deeply this case is rooted in the past, I'm not sure what to think anymore. I'm daunted by the gravity of what we're facing, but I have to believe that we're getting closer. Anything else is too painful.

"I don't know," I say simply. "We know a lot more about the kidnapper now. Plus, he's hurt. Maybe that slows him down, creates an opening we didn't have before."

"But, hurt means desperate." Thandi clenches her fists. "There's no telling what he'll do in that state. I just wish—"

"Wish, what, baby?"

"McNamara said without a clue, they could be searching the woods forever. If I could remember *more*, I could help them find Daysha faster." She meets my eyes. "We're running out of time, Ronan."

I press my lips together. I hate to admit it, but she's right.

We've been clinging to each new scrap McNamara feeds us. But the truth is, we've discovered a hell of a lot about Damian Patrick's past, and not nearly enough about his *present*. Thumbing through old photos and chasing ghosts won't help us find Daysha. We need something tangible, a trail that will lead us to his lair.

"I hope she's okay." Thandi's eyes reflect my fear—and the one specter we're both too terrified to name.

What if we're already too late?

I think of Daysha's smile … her intelligence….

We have to do something. Fast.

"All right, good news, folks." A nurse bustles into the room. "Looks like you're being discharged, Mr. Thorne." She sets a plastic bag at the foot of the bed. "Your jeans are in here, but we cut your sweater. Do you need something to wear home?"

Thandi slips off the bed. "I got him a hoodie at the gift shop. It zips up the front since I know he can't raise his arms right now."

I feel a rush of tenderness at her foresight. Of course, my baby thought of everything.

"Good." The nurse nods. She wheels a small cart closer and begins sorting through the stack of papers. "Alright," she says brightly. "These are your discharge instructions. Wound care's on the first page.

She hands the packet to Thandi before turning back to me. "Your prescriptions have been sent to your pharmacy. Pain levels okay right now?"

"I'm fine," I say automatically.

The nurse steps to my side, checking the edge of the bandage. "Dressing looks clean. Still sore?"

"A little."

"That's normal. Just remember to move slowly." She taps the rail of the bed. "When you're ready, I'll wheel you downstairs."

The nurse ducks out, and I feel like a preschooler on the first day of class as Thandi helps me out of the gowns and guides my arms into the hoodie one at a time. I can't help but grin when she zips me up with a kiss.

"There," she says softly.

I hold her eyes. There's something so intimate about being cared for like this, and I'm grateful to her, so pleased to have her in my life.

"Thank you," I say, and I hope she can hear everything I mean by it. Not just the food, the clothes, or her assistance, but for her love. For transforming my life in ways she'd never guess.

I reach for my jeans and wince as my wound protests.

"Need some help with that?" Thandi asks.

"Please." I stop trying to be a hero and let her. Bending to get these on will only end in a world of hurt.

Smiling, Thandi helps me tug the denim on. It takes a little shimmying first—me lying back, then sitting on the edge of the bed. But in the end, I'm zipped, buttoned, and none the worse for wear. Thandi lends me a shoulder as I rise, my hand braced on the bed rail.

The minute I'm upright, a familiar face pops into the doorway.

"Good to see you on your feet." Hayes grins. "You gave us quite the scare. That was real bravery out there."

"Thanks, but I should be saying the same to you," I shoot back.

"Good to know she's concerned about someone," Brooks grumbles, edging in next to Hayes. He's in a fresh shirt; his right sleeve rolled to the elbow, arm bandaged and supported by a navy sling.

"Come on, a hardass like you?" Hayes pops open the uneaten Jell-O cup and spoons the green pudding into her mouth. "You're as tough as old leather. I knew you'd be alright."

"Well, we're grateful for you both," Thandi says with a laugh. "Officer Brooks, how's your hand?"

"Sore as hell," he admits. "No permanent damage, though. Doctor says I'll keep the sling on for a few days and maybe do a little PT once the stitches come out."

Hayes snorts. "Physical therapy? They're going to make you squeeze those foam balls like you're eighty."

Brooks rolls his eyes. "Anyway, we're heading out, but wanted to check in. You've been through a lot today."

I glance at Thandi. "We're still processing, but we're grateful to be safe—and I, for one, will be glad to be out of here."

"Understandable." Hayes nods. "I'm taking this guy home. He's out for at least a week." She jerks her thumb at Brooks. "Modified duty until that arm stops looking like a mummy wrap. The good news is it's forcing him to take his first vacation in years."

Hayes ignores Brooks's grumble and presses on. "Once he's settled, I'll head over to your parents' place, Thandi, to set up patrol like McNamara said. Another officer will join me since Brooks is out of commission."

Thandi looks stricken at the reminder of her parents' vulnerability. "Thank you," she says softly. "Please contact me if—for any reason at all—you're concerned for their safety."

"Agreed." I squeeze her hand. "They're not law enforcement, but my firm, Equinox, can be available at a moment's notice."

"I'll pass that along to the detective," Hayes says. "Though I doubt we'll have trouble tonight."

"Why?" Thandi asks.

"With his injuries, Patrick's likely gone to ground—at least for now. He'll attract too much attention unless he gets medical help. We didn't recover a casing at the scene. That could mean the bullet's still in his shoulder."

"Let's hope he's too incapacitated to hurt Daysha again," I mutter.

A heavy silence settles between us, thick with unspoken fear.

Hayes sighs. "Alright. We'd better get going. I'll be in touch with any updates."

"We're heading out too," I say. "Thank you for stopping by."

"Not a problem." Hayes tips her chin, and she and Brooks disappear down the hall.

"Shall we?" I turn to Thandi.

"Yes, but let's wait for the nurse to bring the wheelchair." She holds out her palm. "In the meantime, hand over the keys."

"I could drive," I grumble, adjusting my hoodie. "The Maybach barely needs me. With driver assist—"

"Ronan," Thandi says warningly.

"Fine, fine." I fish the keys from my pocket, but I pause before handing them over.

There's a small pink smear on my waistband.

At first, it barely registers, just a faint streak against the denim. But then I remember. It must be from when Damian and I grappled. Pink like calamine lotion—just as Amanda described.

Calamine lotion.

The words open a door in my mind.

Suddenly, I'm back in Anchor Park, surrounded by jostling kids in line for the ice cream truck. A mosquito dive-bombs my forearm. I scratch the bite, irritated, and a tiny old woman scolds me before reaching into her purse for a bottle of calamine lotion.

I go still.

The samples.

So much has happened that I'd forgotten about the samples I collected at Anchor Park. I remember Thandi's anguish after Fia's party and my desperation to help. My heart contracts as I realize it was also the day I first met Ricky and Daysha.

Later, working overnight at the lab, I'd channeled Shezmu, distilling each scent until I had a complete collection—my own brand of mixtape for the woman I love.

And I forgot to give it to her.

I'm a fucking idiot. But maybe now it can serve an even more urgent purpose.

"What is it?" Thandi asks, seeing my expression.

"You said you wanted to remember," I murmur. "To give McNamara something that might finally end this."

"Yes," she whispers, eyes dark with uncertainty.

"I think," I say softly, "I might have something that can help."

Mosaic
Thandi

"Ronan, are you sure this can't wait? You really should be resting."

He's been trying to play it off since the hospital, but he winces when he thinks I'm not looking. I know he's hurting.

I frown as I pull into Ronan's spot at RT Laboratories. I still can't shake the image of Damian driving the knife into his side. I can't believe how close I came to losing him.

Tess' disappearance has always been my nightmare. I never thought anything could be as terrifying as that. But seeing Ronan throw himself in Damian's path to protect me, watching helplessly as the blood gushed from his side, I know how wrong I was.

With Tess, there can never be a happy ending. But with Ronan, I've tasted what love, ecstasy, and partnership feel like. In that moment, the prospect of facing a lifetime without him—the yawning emptiness of that existence—sucked the very air from my lungs.

I almost didn't survive a week apart from him.

I can't risk a minute more.

But now, instead of focusing on his recovery, he's got us chasing some wild idea. Whatever this surprise is, it can't be more important than his health.

"We're here." I shut off the engine and turn to him. "Now, are you going to tell me what this is about?"

"Not yet, but trust me, baby. I wouldn't insist if it weren't important."

Ronan reaches for the door, and the moment he rotates toward the passenger side, he gasps. Brackets of pain line his mouth.

"Stop." I'm already unbuckling my seatbelt. "You're going to tear your stitches."

"I'm fine." He says too quickly, which means he absolutely is not. He grips the armrest, gathering his strength to push himself out.

And he calls me stubborn. What is he trying to prove? As if saving my life wasn't enough.

"Ronan, don't do that," I chide him. I lean across the console before he can push the door open. My palm finds his thigh, warm through the denim. Tension is locked in his muscles. "Just wait for me, please."

Ronan huffs. "It's just the angle. I've got it."

I slip out of the SUV and circle over to his side. When I open the passenger door, he tries to smile, but it's strained. The pain meds must be wearing off.

"So let's make a deal," I say, resting my hand on his arm. "I'll do better about taking care of myself if you do too."

I reach up to brush back the strands of hair that have fallen into his face. "You were already my hero before Damian Patrick, and you'll always be. There's no shame in admitting you're in pain." I cup his cheek, forcing him to meet my eyes. "Let me help you."

Something in him softens, then, just enough to melt into weary truth. He nods.

"Okay." Then that characteristic Ronan grin flashes. His hand slips down to cup my ass. "Your hero, huh?"

"Mm-hmm." I brush my mouth against his, and he leans in, deepening the kiss.

I feel both his strength and his exhaustion in the softness of his mouth, the gentle caress of his tongue against mine—and underneath it all the banked fire of his passion roaring to life. He moans, tightening his hold on me.

I pull away with a nip to his bottom lip. "Are you seriously groping me with your injured hand?"

His eyes dance. "My hand is perfectly fine. The doctor said no sudden movements to my side." He slides his hand lower. "He didn't say anything about this."

Heat rushes through my body. I close my eyes, trying to catch my breath. This man is far too tempting for his own good.

"Come on," I say, stepping back. "Let's get this over with so we can get you to bed." I tilt my head back, throwing him a meaningful look.

He's out of the car as soon as I offer him my shoulder. Amber eyes sparkle, and he's grinning from ear to ear. "Bed or *bed?*" he asks, almost clipping my heels as I fob into the building.

"I guess we'll have to make this quick if you want to find out." I wink.

"Tease," he offers me his hand—this time on his good side. "Come, I'll show you."

It's been weeks since the night he first brought me here and showed me his mom's wing under construction. Of course, I saw it during the press conference, but that was one room, with cameras zoomed in on the podium.

I gasp as we enter the new section. The scale of what he's done is incredible. There's the conference room I saw on TV—more like an auditorium, really—for lectures and TED-style talks. There's even a small area with equipment for live demonstrations.

But that's nothing compared to the rest of the wing.

A long corridor lined with paneled glass leads to a suite of laboratories. Two researchers are still inside the room on our right. Their faces are lit by the blue glow of molecular models rotating on suspended screens.

Farther down the hall in a second room, a temperature-controlled vault lines a back wall. Even through the glass, I can make out color-coded labels and cooling racks stacked with microtubes.

A smaller engineering space is next. Tools are laid out in rows, and a compact 3D printer idles in the corner. Prototypes sit mid-assembly, tagged with handwritten notes. This is where theory meets application.

At last, Ronan leads me to the lab at the end of the corridor where distillation towers, chromatographs, and calibrated precision scales flank a steel table. Vials lie in narrow drawers, all meticulously labeled.

My heart constricts.

Even before we step inside, I know this is where Ronan works.

Because on the shelf above the workstation is a photo of Rosalind—and the silly printout we took with Captain Funnel Cake at Sugar Hill Park.

"Ronan," I whisper, squeezing his hand in mine.

"What?" He gives me a lopsided smile. "I keep my inspiration close."

"We need to get a better picture than that one," I say, leaning against him.

"I love this one though," he murmurs, leading me to the workbench. "Because I'm pretty sure that was the day I fell in love with you."

I stare at him, heart full—melting, yearning.

"I love you so much," I say, placing his hand over my heart. "Thank you for loving me; for always being there for me."

"Always," he vows, and then I'm swept up in his kiss again. He is my lifeline, my haven, the eye of my storm.

The embers of this afternoon's adrenaline flare into passion. I want him. No, I need him so much.

I'm trembling by the time we pull apart, but we have a mission to complete.

I take a breath. "Okay, show me this surprise of yours."

"We should probably sit," Ronan says, pulling out a stool for me, then grabbing one for himself. He eases out a drawer with a row of vials. The entire set is labeled *Park Summer*.

I pick up one of the tubes and hold it to the light.

"Babe, what's this?" I gesture at the set. "What's all of this?"

"Fia's party was the first time I fully understood how much losing Tess affected you," Ronan says, brushing his hand over the row of vials. "I wanted to help."

"Help me, how?"

"You fainted because of the vanilla ice cream." Ronan rubs the back of his neck. "So I thought: What if another scent could trigger your memory?"

His gaze is hesitant, vulnerable, as it meets mine. "I went to Anchor Park hoping to replicate the scents from the day Tess disappeared." Sadness shadows his features. "That's how I ran into Ricky and Daysha with their kites."

I'm quiet as I stare at the drawer in front of me. It's crazy how much has changed. Crazy how much innocence we didn't know we had left to lose. Back then, with the IPO looming and our relationship budding, everything seemed so overwhelming. But looking back now, life was perfect. Daysha and Ricky were safe and happy. Later that week, dinner at my parents' house was a slice of heaven I'll always cherish.

Ronan may have fallen in love with me at Sugar Hill Park, but that's when I *knew* he was family.

And now, he's given me even more proof of his love.

For years, I've tried to recreate my memories alone. I've never had anyone see me so clearly, never had anyone love me enough to take that burden onto themselves.

I bite my lip. But it's even more than that:

I've never known anyone extraordinary enough to even try.

There are twenty-four vials here. Each represents hours of distillation, iteration, and refinement. The time and care Ronan has put into this undoes me all over again.

"You ... this is...." My throat is clogged with tears. "Thank you," I manage.

"Baby, every day you're in my life makes me happier and stronger. I want to be the kind of man who does that for you, too."

"You do," I sniff, clinging to him. "You do make me happy. And as for strength—" I laugh, wiping my eyes. "I think it might be the opposite. I don't know how to function without you anymore." I shake my head. "And this is more than I ever dreamed."

"Good." Ronan's throat works. "Lean on me, then. I love you, Thandi Elowen."

I cup his cheek. "I love you too."

For a moment, we just stare at each other. In the warmth of his gaze, I see the recognition of who we were, who we are—and how, bit by bit, our love has transformed us.

My heart hammers. I've failed so many times before that I tell myself not to hope, even as a spark ignites anyway: *What if this is it?* What if everything comes back? Will I know what to do? Who will I be when there isn't a gaping hole in my heart?

I'm afraid to find out.

But being trapped in the dark forever terrifies me more.

"Baby?" Ronan asks softly.

"I'm ready." I smile. "Should we start?" I hold up a tube to the light. This one is labeled *Fido*.

"Yes," Ronan looks sheepish. "But maybe not with that one."

"No? Why—" The moment I uncap it, an awful smell hits me. "Oh God!" I gag and slam the cap back on.

I don't know if to laugh or cry. Of course, Ronan captured even this to perfection. His genius aside, if *that* were the key to my memories, I'd be deeply worried.

"I warned you," Ronan says, grinning. He reaches over and rearranges the tubes. "Try this instead."

At first, I don't understand what he's done, but then I see it: a kind of geographic progression through Anchor Park, starting at the swings and moving outward to the street where the ice cream truck was waiting.

My hands tremble so badly I have to shut my eyes and breathe.

"It's okay," Ronan murmurs. "You can do this. And even if you can't, I'll be right here to catch you."

I crack an eye open. "Not with those stitches, you aren't."

We both laugh. But he's right. Just knowing he's here makes all the difference.

I curl my fingers around the first tube.

Earth. That's the first thing that hits me. The richness of soil and the tang of fresh-cut grass wash over my senses. Beneath it is the heat of a summer afternoon—the smell of land baked under the sun, and vegetation thirsty for rain.

I'm not in the lab anymore.

I'm on the grass, my knees stained green, my LEGOs scattered around me. The sun is bright. The wind ruffles the garland in my hair.

I take the next vial.

A grill—no, the rotisserie of a hotdog stand. I almost laugh. Mr. Moore's cart, manned now by his son, Danny. A generation may have changed, but the smell, mouthwatering, and savory hasn't. Underneath it is the hint of a prepared bun—Chicago style. No ketchup but all the fixings: mustard, onions, peppers, tomatoes, and briny-sweet relish.

My stomach actually growls. After that miserable hospital soup, a frankfurter sounds divine. I make a mental note to order in later, but for now, I move on.

Cotton candy, sweet clematis, rusted metal, and steaming asphalt.

I'm halfway through the set when my hope begins to crumble.

They're incredible. Each scent transports me back to that summer twenty years ago. Yet, they're all familiar terrain—safe and nostalgic. I bring another vial to my nose and tense, waiting.

Nothing happens.

Nothing at all.

The river of memory doesn't come rushing in. Tess isn't within reach. No missing piece slides into place.

All I have is a quiet, hollow stillness. And the knowledge that, despite the beauty of what Ronan created, none of it is enough.

I'm failing again.

"I should stop," I murmur, putting the vial that smells like sawdust away. I swallow back tears. "This isn't working. We should go home, let you rest."

Ronan's hand covers mine. "Come on, baby, I know this is hard, but I believe in you."

Should he? I'm not sure I believe in myself.

How long will I be locked in this cycle? For years, I vowed that I would never quit. Yet my effort has only brought more harm—Ronan hurt, and Daysha still missing. The line between persistence and delusion feels paper-thin.

My hand hovers over the next vial. I'm ready to pull back when I see Ronan's expression. His gaze holds so much love, so much hope, that I can't bear to disappoint him. Not after everything he's done for me.

So I don't stop.

Despite my doubt. Despite my fear.

I keep going because my respect for his craft and my need to honor what he's given me outweigh everything else. Because whenever my world has slipped off its axis, he's been the one constant I can believe in.

I hold onto that now.

The glass is cool against my fingers. One by one, I bring each vial to my nose: caramel popcorn, a park bench's peeling paint, sweaty sneakers, the rubber thump of a basketball against the court, a cherry lollipop, and a waffle cone with its chocolate ice cream already melted.

I keep going until there is only one left.

My hands tremble. I'm both gutted and relieved to reach the end. I stare at the drawer, and the truth is heavy in my chest.

My memory is still as blank as when I began.

Ronan created the perfect sample size, but we never had a chance at success.

So much for his faith in me.

I grip the final glass cylinder. This tube is named *Mosquito*.

I bring it to my nose, and the chalky scent of calamine lotion fills my lungs. I inhale, hold it, then release it slowly.

I'm disappointed.

This is the most banal of the set. It has none of the joy of the hot dog stand and none of the irreverence of *Fido*. I also can't remember the last time I used calamine lotion. Certainly not that summer. Dad preferred his herbal balms, and Mom, ever the scientist, thought other ointments were more effective.

My eyes sting. It's strangely deflating to end on something so flat and unfamiliar—like despite everything he's said, even Ronan gave up on me in the end.

That hurts more than anything else.

I'm lowering the vial back into its slot when another trace drifts upward. The duller top notes have burned away, revealing a hint of sharpness. I can barely detect it, but its ghost lingers, soft and elusive. Frowning, I breathe in again.

That's when I see Ronan's brilliance.

Underneath the medicinal blandness is the scent of skin: sunblock, lotion, and that note that's just beyond my grasp. Sharp, coppery metallic—

My head swivels towards him.

It's the smell of an abrasion not yet healed:

A single pinpoint of blood.

Every muscle in my body seizes.

I'm hurtling backwards through time and space.

Back to the uncanny cool of the woods and the crunch of twigs beneath my feet. Branches catch on my dress and scrape at my arms as I race through the vegetation. The salt of my tears fills my throat.

In the distance is a monster, and my beacon is Tess' bright yellow dress.

I run. Faster than I've ever run before. So fast my legs shake, and my lungs burn.

I'm closing in.

I think I can save her.

Closer … closer … until our hands almost touch.

He yanks her back; her beads scatter.

I sway as my vision narrows.

But this time the world doesn't go black.

A tiny spark.

Then memory explodes, hitting me like a truck.

Memory
Thandi

"Tess!" I scream.

I don't care what it takes. I'm going to save her.

"What the fuck is she doing here? Boy, I told you not to let anyone see us. We only need one this time, not two."

Boy?

Why is the bad man calling me that?

I try to run forward, but something yanks me back so hard I lose my balance and hit the ground. My palms burn. My knee smacks into a big tree root, sharp enough to make my eyes sting, but I don't cry. I can't. Tess needs me.

That's when I realize someone is behind me.

"I'm sorry, Papa."

I look down and see dirty sneakers. When I try to push myself up, hands shove me back down again. I twist and finally see him properly.

It's the boy who was talking to Tess.

He has green eyes and blond hair that lies flat against his head, like he hasn't washed it in a while. He's older than me. Bigger. Like a fifth grader. I'm strong, but I've never had to fight a big kid before.

He called the bad man *Papa*.

But I don't understand that. Daddies aren't supposed to hurt children.

"Don't push me!" I yell, shoving him hard. He stumbles, but he doesn't let go.

"Jesus fucking Christ," the bad man says. "Now you're letting her push you around? Where the fuck were you?"

"I had to go to the bathroom." The boy's voice shakes. He sounds scared. Like me. "I didn't know she was there."

"I told you to go before we left! Can't you do anything right?"

"I did go," the boy says, and then his voice breaks. "But my arm hurts. I thought the water would help."

He lifts one hand to his chest. The skin is scabby and red, spotted all over like bug bites that never healed. I'd feel bad for him, but his other hand is still pressing me into the dirt. That one looks the same, only it's smeared with weird pink stuff.

Did the bad man do that to him?

The thought makes my stomach hurt.

"I wasn't—"

"I don't want to fucking hear it. Look at you. Weak and useless, just like your mother. No wonder you've got her skin problems."

The boy drops his head. His lips wobble, and a fat tear slides off his chin and lands on my dress.

"Yes, Papa."

My heart is beating too fast. I'm scared. I don't like this. I don't like how mean this man is, or how his yelling at his son makes my chest feel tight. It makes me think he'll be mean to Tess, too. I have to get her out of here.

"Stop! Let my sister go. We won't tell anyone," I plead, shoving at Damian. "Pinky promise."

"Thandi," Tess whimpers, squirming in the man's grasp. She's crying again, and that makes me cry too.

"Please! Let her go!" I say, fighting Damian harder now. I'm doing good—he has to use both hands to hold me down. If I just keep trying, maybe I can get loose.

"Shut it. All of you." The bad man squeezes Tess's arm so hard she cries out.

He's hurting her, and I hate him. I hate everything about him. I wish my Daddy were here to stop him.

But he's not.

It's just me, and I don't know what to do. I don't know how to get to Tess.

"Damian. I will not say this a second time. Take care of this."

The bad man tosses something, and it rolls to the ground between us. I look down to see one of those big needles that they use at the doctor's office. It's already filled with liquid.

My blood turns cold. My stomach flips so hard I think I might throw up. I don't like needles. And if they use it on me, I won't be able to save Tess.

Damian's eyes go wide. He shakes his head, crying harder now.

"I don't wanna," he says. "She's just a stupid kid. Why can't we just leave her? Why can't I go back home to Mama?"

"Lana's not your fucking mother," the bad man snaps, "and she's not coming back. So stop calling her Mama. Now take care of it."

Daddy always tells us that if you meet a bully, you have to fight back. That bullies are scared people, and that's why they hurt others.

I don't know if the bad man is scared. But Damian is.

That means I have to fight with everything I've got.

I don't care that I'm wearing a dress. I twist and kick and punch. I scratch at his arms until some of his gross pink stuff gets under my nails. It's mixed with blood, and it makes me want to puke.

We roll in the dirt. He's trying to hold me down, but the grass scratches at his skin, and I can see it hurts. So I wriggle harder and kick him again and again.

The bad man is cursing. Tess is crying so loud, I hope someone hears her. I don't want her to stop. I hope a nice person—a good adult—comes to help us. Not someone like Damian's father.

"Ow, ow, ow!" Damian jerks back when I rake my nails down the arm he was using to hold me. I grab on tighter, my fingers digging in.

"Stop!" Tears spill out of his eyes. He curls both arms into his chest, and when he does, he lets me go.

As soon as I'm free, I scramble to my feet. My hurt knee wobbles, but I don't stop. I run straight for Tess.

"Damian Patrick," the bad man roars, "haven't I taught you anything? If you don't finish this right now, you know what will happen. Do you want to spend two hours in the shed again?"

"No, Papa," Damian sobs behind me.

There's a pause. Then I hear leaves crunch under his sneakers. I don't look back. I keep going, even though I'm limping, even though the cut on my knee burns like fire. Blood runs down my leg. I don't think even Grandma Moses' cocoa butter can stop this one from leaving a mark.

"Thandi! Run! He's coming!" Tess screams.

That's why she's my best friend—my favorite sister in the whole wide world. She always warns me when someone's about to tag me in freeze tag, even if we're on different teams.

I wish we were only playing now.

I'm about to tell Tess I'm coming, to not give up, but I don't get the words out.

Damian slams into me like a footballer. It's not fair that he gets a running start when he's so much bigger. The hit knocks the breath out of me. My knee buckles, my feet slip, and pain explodes as I crash onto my side.

My head slams against a root.

"No! Thandi! Thandi!"

I hear Tess, but her voice sounds far away. There's a bell ringing inside my head. I groan and clutch the dirt, dizzy like when Tess and I spin in circles on the carpet to see who falls first.

I guess it's me this time.

Big black dots swim in front of my eyes. I think I'm going to faint.

Mama says that when you feel faint, you're supposed to put your head between your legs. I try to move, but I can't get up. My body won't listen. Everything hurts, especially my head.

It's strange. It's not bedtime, but I'm suddenly sleepy. I blink, and my eyes go blurry.

That's not right. I need to stay awake for Tess.

I force my eyes open. I have to look around to remember where we are. I don't think I'm strong enough now, but once I'm better, I'll come back for her. I will.

I strain my neck, but all I see is green on green on green. Trees everywhere.

"—last time you did something worthwhile." The bad man's voice drifts over me.

"I—" Damian starts, but it's hard to listen. My eyelids droop again.

No.

I jerk myself awake.

I can't move my head anymore, so I use my eyes. I search for something—anything—that will help me find my way back. Back to Tess. Back to this place.

There.

My head feels so fuzzy that even though I'm scared, I almost giggle when I see it. A strange rock, sticking up like a stack of gray LEGO pieces. Not neat and straight like I'd build it—more like when you let a baby play with them.

Good.

I won't forget that.

"We're leaving … late … I expect you back … an hour." The words bend and stretch, like I'm under water.

I squint. My head swims.

"—Papa." Damian comes into focus, then drifts away again. He's just a blurry shape now. He moves, but I can't tell what he's doing.

I try to shake my head, to clear my eyes, but it won't work.

"—come to the lake. And don't you dare muck about in the water like last time. Made a fucking mess."

The lake.

That means there's one nearby.

I hold onto that, too.

Tess yells. The bad man shouts something back.

Then—nothing.

It goes quiet.

Fear squeezes my heart.

They're leaving.

He's taking her away.

"No…" I whisper.

"Tess!" Tears stream down my face. "Tess, come back! Bring her back, please. *Please!*"

I jerk to the side, trying to get up, but my body won't listen. It's not fair. She's my only sister. My twin. Mama says we're like two halves of an apple. Or a mirror. That means we need each other.

Why does he want to take her from me?

"Please!" I call again. My head throbs from crying.

But the bad man doesn't bring Tess back.

A shadow falls over me instead.

I look up.

Damian is standing above me, the needle raised high. His whole body is shaking. He's crying too—eyes swollen, snot dripping from his nose.

I stare at him, and I feel so sad. For me. For Tess. And for Damian, who didn't get a nice family like ours.

Maybe if he did, none of us would have to be hurt.

He lifts his hand. The needle flashes in the light.

This is it.

I scrunch my eyes shut, bracing for the prick. If I don't make it, I hope at least someone saves Tess. I'll wait for her in heaven—well, I think I've been good enough to go there.

It'll be hard to watch over her if I'm somewhere else.

Time stretches. My head pounds. I breathe and think of Mama, Papa, and Tess. I think it will be over soon.

But the jab never comes.

My vision goes fuzzy at the edges. I hear one last thing before I pass out.

"I'm sorry," Damian whispers.

Then his footsteps pound away from me as the world disappears.

Sillage

Repair
Thandi

"Alright, I have tea for everyone. This is a special blend," Dad announces, balancing a tray in his hands. "Tulsi, chamomile, lavender, ginger, and honey. To shore up the root chakra and calm our nervous systems. Ronan, I'll make you some soup in a second."

He places the tray on the coffee table and starts handing out mugs. "This is heavy emotional work."

No kidding.

We're back at my condo, huddled in the living room with the fireplace crackling in front of us.

McNamara's en route. We called her straight from the lab.

Ronan is stretched out on the long part of the sectional, and Mom is settled on the other end. I'm between them, leaning into Ronan's good side. I tried to tell him I'm fine, but he insisted.

He worries too much—and he's a cuddler. So there's that.

"Seriously. I need everyone to stop flirting with danger for one fucking second," Fia says, wiping her eyes. She's positioned near the glass hearth, one of my crocheted throws draped over her lap.

"Roncito, you've been stabbed, and now Thandi's been forced to relive this awful trauma. God. We haven't even caught up since you two got back together. That alone was a bombshell," Fia huffs.

"Sorry." Ronan shoots her a smile. "We thought we were doing a quick favor for the cops. We had no idea it would turn into this."

He looks down at me, and I feel his warmth, the weight of his arm, the way his presence keeps me tethered. I'm overwhelmed by everything he's done for me. I never knew love could be like this—that it could break you open and then knit you back together again.

Love you, he mouths, and the dark places in my heart ease a little.

I slip my left hand into Ronan's, squeezing lightly. With my right, I reach for Mom's.

She smiles at me, but there are lines of distress around her eyes and mouth.

Ricky is staying with Aunt Mariah tonight. He's already so torn up over Daysha that it felt like the right call, especially after everything I had to share.

This has been hard on all of us.

I'm still reeling from the return of my memories. I always imagined I'd feel relieved when they came back. But no one tells you that remembering is its own kind of death.

I look in Mom's eyes and see the sorrow I feel reflected there. It's not regret, but recognition. Our old selves are passing away. Everything we thought we understood before today is fading.

"You okay, Peanut?" Dad asks, handing me a mug and draping a heathered shrug over my shoulders. It's been my favorite forever. Whenever I visit in the winter, I make a beeline for it. Somehow, he remembered to bring it.

"I'm good, Dad," I say, managing a smile. "Just … worn out. Thank you."

He nods and squeezes my shoulder before moving on, mug still in hand. Mom's next. Hers comes with a kiss.

I watch him putter around the room, tending to everyone with quiet care, and my chest aches. The memory of Arnold Patrick's insults, his brutality, surges forth, battering at my defenses. I wonder at life's strange math—how one child was gifted a treasure like my father, and another a violent narcissist.

I shiver, despite the weight of the cozy shrug. I hate what Damian's done to Daysha. I'm terrified that she'll end up like Tess— terrified in the end that Arnold Patrick succeeded in carving up the humanity of the boy who ran away instead of hurting me.

Everything feels twisted. I don't know how to reconcile my anger at a kidnapper and the man who stabbed Ronan, with the knowledge that, in his own way, he too might be a victim.

I just know it hurts.

"I still can't believe it," Mom murmurs, and I can't tell if she's speaking to us or to herself. "We've lived with this for so long...." She stares into the fire. "Maybe now we can finally heal."

"Hey, don't sell us short." Dad sets the empty tray aside and goes to her, wrapping her in his arms. "Our scars might be deep, but we didn't stay frozen in place. We kept moving forward."

He nods once. "What Peanut's given us is closure. Not knowing what happened—that's always been the hardest part."

Mom tightens her arms around him. "That's true," she whispers.

"The universe isn't always kind," Dad says gently, "but it doesn't make mistakes. This is a deep karmic loop. How else do we explain Daysha's kidnapper being connected to our Tess?"

He kisses Mom's temple. "We have to trust that bigger forces are at work. Daysha will come back to us. I feel it."

I flinch, just a little, at his certainty, but I don't have the heart to contradict him. I can't imagine how suffering of this magnitude could ever be purposeful.

But he's the artist, and I'm the scientist.

I think of his sculptures inspired by Tess—some sprawling and hulking, made of twisted plaster and metal. Others are light and airy, gossamer-thin. Of all of us, he's always been the most hopeful.

Maybe it's because he has a way to transmute his grief. To work through it not just with his mind, but with his hands—with both sweat and tears.

Fia's stomach rumbles loudly.

"Sorry." She winces. "Long day. I skipped lunch, and of course, as soon as I left work, all I wanted was to get here."

I grin. "No apologies necessary. It's my fault for not being a good hostess. Let me grab you a snack."

"Snacks?" Dad shakes his locs like a lion's mane. He's on his feet in an instant. "What we need is real nourishment. Let me throw Ronan's soup together. We can all have some. I can rustle up some rock buns for dessert."

"Mr. Elowen, please don't go out of your way," Fia says quickly.

"Winston, that's really not necess—" Ronan starts.

Dad fixes them both with a look.

They go quiet.

Mom's laugh tinkles beside me.

I bite back a smile. Even I know better than to test Dad when he's in caregiver mode.

"I'll help, Dad," I say, standing.

"Pass me a little more celery? Some carrots, too."

Dad sticks his hand out without looking up from the pot bubbling on the stove. He stirs, then bends to taste the soup.

I'm on rubbing-in duty for the rock bun dough.

"I don't have anymore," I say guiltily, pressing the pastry blender into a stubborn chunk of butter. "Will celery salt work? I think I'm also out of fresh carrots, but I'm pretty sure there's at least one can in the pantry."

Now that we're cooking, I'm struck by how bare my refrigerator and pantry are. I haven't had much time for meals lately.

I bite my lip.

Maybe Ronan wasn't just being fussy at the hospital.

"Not to worry," Dad says, brandishing the spoon. "You've got plenty in here that we can work with."

He turns the heat down to a simmer, then opens the fridge, crouching to peer inside. A moment later, he's rummaging through the pantry. I hear jars clink. A can thumps against a shelf.

When he comes back, his arms are full. He sets everything on the counter with a flourish: an onion, a head of garlic, a container of chicken stock I'd forgotten about, half a lemon, a can of carrots, a bag of spinach that's a tiny bit wilted, and a lonely potato.

"See?" he says, already reaching for the knife. "Plenty to work with."

He rolls the onion toward me. "Mind chopping that up? I'll take care of the garlic and the potato."

"Sure thing." I drop the rock buns onto the baking sheet. Wiping my hands on my apron, I slide them into the oven. "Three seventy-five for fifteen minutes?"

"You got it."

I grab the smaller chopping board and start in on the onion.

Dad smiles faintly as he works. "You know," he says, "you used to make me read *Stone Soup* over and over when you were little."

I pause, knife hovering above the board. "I did?"

"Mm-hmm. You liked the idea that everyone brought what they had, even when it wasn't much. That everything worked better when we came together as a team."

He nudges me with his shoulder. "You haven't changed, Peanut."

Maybe it's the onions, but my eyes sting. I hear what he's really saying: life may throw us curveballs, but I haven't lost myself.

Somehow, he always knows exactly what I need to hear.

I swipe at my eyes with my sleeve. "Thanks, Dad."

"That's why I'm here." He winks. "Now, what do you think? Should we toss in that scotch bonnet I spotted in the crisper, or will Ronan be cursing our ancestors?"

I snort a laugh. "His spice tolerance is actually decent. And heat won't be a problem for Fia. I say we use half."

"ETA?" Ronan calls from the couch. "Whatever you're making over there smells incredible."

"What's it to you?" I call back. "I thought you didn't want any."

Fia's laughter rings out, bright and clear. "She got you there, Roncito."

Ronan mutters something I don't catch, but I don't need to. I can practically see the pout. Big baby. I'll make it up to him later.

My hands go still on the cutting board. For a moment, I let myself take it all in—Dad humming by the oven, Ronan and Fia bickering over the remote, Mom lingering by my bookshelf.

I close my eyes and draw in a slow breath. The shadows aren't gone, but suddenly the world feels a little brighter.

I'm so glad they're here.

The oven dings.

Smiling, I pull the rock buns out and set them on the cooling rack. I help Dad ladle out bowls of our soup.

We've barely started eating when the doorbell rings.

"I'll get it," I say, slipping away from my spot beside Ronan. Dad's already back in the kitchen, brewing a fresh pot of tea for dessert.

I hurry to the door and pull it open.

McNamara stands on the threshold, her expression sharp, trench coat cinched tight at her waist.

The small spark of magic I'd been holding onto vanishes.

"Detective," I say softly. "Come in."

"Rock bun?" Dad offers, holding out the plate of pastries to the detective.

"Detective McNamara, you remember my parents and Fia Beltrán Zamora?"

"Of course." McNamara nods. "Good to see you all again. And thank you—I will take one."

She settles back in her chair, nibbling at the bun. She chews for a moment before her gaze returns to me. "So," she says evenly, "you remembered something."

I nod, swallowing. "I ... yes."

How do I even begin to explain what triggered it?

I look up at Ronan, and he strokes my hand encouragingly.

I keep going.

"For years, I've had a visceral reaction to the smell of vanilla ice cream," I say. "It was the last thing Tess bought before she disappeared. Even when the scent took me back to that day, my memory always stopped at the same place—just before the kidnapper took her away."

I smooth my hand over the blanket Ronan and I are sharing. "That changed today. Thanks to Ronan."

McNamara's brows lift. "How so?"

"I have an unusually precise olfactory memory," Ronan says, folding my hand in his.

"Meaning?"

"Some people remember images," Ronan says. His thumb traces a slow circle over my pulse. "I can recreate almost any scent. When Thandi told me about her amnesia, I created a set based on Anchor Park. I was hoping one of them might jog her memory."

I take a shaky breath. "It did."

I tell McNamara everything—from the moment I sniffed the vial, to the memory of my struggle with Damian, to his father dragging Tess away.

The detective is quiet. She leans forward, bracing her forearms on her thighs.

"Detective?" I press.

"We've unearthed more information about Arnold Patrick," she says at last. "What you remembered confirms what we found."

"What do you mean?" Fia asks, wheeling closer. She reaches for the last of the rock buns.

"His wife, Selena Patrick, died when Damian was about nine years old—two years before the incident," McNamara explains. "That means the woman in the photo—the one Arnold called Lana—was likely Damian's first real mother figure after Selena passed. It makes sense that he was attached to her."

McNamara sighs. "I suspected something had shifted in the household. Based on Thandi's memory, it appears Lana left abruptly—which would have affected both Arnold and Damian."

Pain grips my heart. So Damian was a grieving child, dealing with yet another loss. Everywhere I turn, the tragedy only seems to multiply.

"So what now?" I ask.

"Tell me more about the location," McNamara says. "You mentioned a rock."

"Yeah. It was oddly shaped. Craggy." I turn to my parents. "Mom, Dad—did the cops find me near a strange gray rock?"

"A gray rock?" Mom shakes her head slowly. "No. A group of campers found you wandering about half a mile from where Maisha and Bobby said you disappeared." Her voice trembles. "When we couldn't find either you or Tess, my world stopped."

She tightens her grip on her mug. "Then you showed up—like a miracle. But Tess never came back."

Dad settles beside her, pulling her close. "You were bleeding and concussed," he murmurs. "You couldn't remember much, but you kept saying, *the bad man took Tess.* That's how we knew the worst had happened."

His expression grows distant. "We were terrified that he'd hurt you in other ways. That he'd—" He shakes his head. "But the doctor said you were okay. No one knew how you escaped, and we didn't care. We were just grateful the universe gave you back to us."

I can't stop thinking about Tess in Arnold Patrick's clutches. In some ways, it was better when I couldn't put a face to her kidnapper. It's devastating now that I understand who he really is.

"A distinct formation helps narrow our search," McNamara says, thumbing something into her phone. "We'll loop in the Park Service. They know these woods better than anyone."

My head snaps up. "I forgot one thing."

"What's that?"

"A lake."

"You saw a lake?"

"No. But Arnold Patrick mentioned it. He told Damian to return there when he was done with me." I take a breath. "I think that's where he took Tess. And if Damian is copying his father…." My voice wobbles. "Maybe Daysha is there."

"Shit," Ronan murmurs. "So how do we find it?"

"It's another detail we can share with the Park Service," McNamara says. "Every piece matters." She rises. "I'll reach out to the experts and start rerouting units. I'll have them keep an eye out for both the rock and the lake."

"What can we do to help?" Fia asks.

McNamara's expression softens into a weary smile. "For now, we stick to the plan. Thandi, avoid your old neighborhood. Fia, you too." She turns to my parents. "Mr. and Mrs. Elowen, I've got one of my best officers stationed on your street. You're in good hands."

Mom bites her lip, but Dad nods. "Thank you, Detective."

I squeeze Mom's hand. "Remember, you don't have to go back. You can always take the guest room. If one of us grabs the couch, there's even room for Ricky."

Ronan smiles. "And you're always welcome at Whitlow."

"No." Mom exhales. "We'll go back. This has already been so hard on Ricky. I don't want to disrupt him any more than necessary. As long as the detective thinks we'll be safe…."

"I do," McNamara says firmly. "And if it makes you feel better, I'm heading that way myself. I'm happy to escort you."

That makes me feel lighter. "Thank you, Detective."

"No problem, I—"

McNamara's radio crackles.

One hand goes to her earpiece. Her posture changes instantly.

"Where?" she barks.

A pause.

"How long ago?"

The detective begins moving towards the door. "Keep the building secured. I'm on my way."

I jump to my feet. "Detective, what about my parents? The escort—"

"Sorry, folks." McNamara's hand is already on the doorknob. "Change of plans."

"What happened?" Dad is right beside me, equally lost.

"We've got a male matching Damian Patrick's description at an AccessHealth urgent care clinic, about thirty minutes south of here," McNamara says. "He came in with a bullet wound."

She meets my eyes.

"He's not going anywhere."

Submerged
Ronan

I find Thandi in the bathroom in a tub full of water, suds up to her neck. Her adorable face is peeking just above the foam.

"Hey, you," she smiles when she sees me in the doorway.

"Hey, yourself." I ease myself onto the lip of the tub. "I'm mad these stitches mean I can't join you."

She reaches for my hand. "Two weeks isn't such a long time."

"It feels like a lifetime." I capture her fingers in mine. A protective instinct washes over me as I think of McNamara rushing out the door. *Maybe this is finally the end.*

Thandi sighs. "Is it awful that I'm glad everyone has left? At first, I was elated. Now I'm just … *tired.* I'm glad they stopped by, though."

"Nothing about you could ever be awful, Thandi. We've been through hell and back today. Naturally, you need a break—even from the people you love." I wink. "Except me, of course."

She laughs. "Of course."

I sober. "That said, I won't be offended if you need some space. Whitlow has an entire team who would be happy to fuss over me. I'll be all right."

"No." The words are barely out of my mouth before Thandi shakes her head. "You're staying. I won't hear anything else."

Warmth seeps through me like slow honey. I bend and capture her lips.

"Then I'll stay," I whisper.

"Perfect."

Thandi finishes up, and I help her out of the tub, insisting on wiping her down. Let's just say I'm very thorough, and by the time I'm done, she's limp and panting in my arms.

"Ronan," she whimpers.

I pull away, admiring her soft curves and smooth skin. "This doesn't have to stop here, you know."

She bites her lip. "We shouldn't," she says, but she looks awfully tempted.

Good.

"Why not?" I pull her gently to me. Her hair is still wet, and as I brush her temples, her springy curls smooth into silky tendrils. She looks so vulnerable, so fresh like this, that I can't decide if I want to bundle her up and tuck her away, or lift her onto the counter and make her cry out with pleasure.

Is both an option? Both would be great.

I saw the bottle of melatonin Dr. Kline recommended in the kitchen, but if I get her into bed, a couple of orgasms should put her right to sleep. Then I can watch over her until McNamara calls back with news about Daysha.

My hands are already sliding to her hip when she stops me.

"Maybe we should wait until you're a little more healed," she groans, clutching at my shirt.

"Honey, the parts I need for this are not broken."

She chuckles, leaning into me. Her hand pauses at my waist, then dips lower. I hiss as her palm curves over my dick.

"Trust me, I know."

"Then we're on the same page," I say, grinning.

"We have to be careful, though," Thandi murmurs, eyes tinged with worry. "I don't want you getting more hurt."

"Of course." I place a hand over my heart. "I'll be very careful with your little pussy."

"Ronan," Thandi sputters. She punches me in the arm—my good side, naturally. "You know that's not what I mean."

"Okay, okay, I'll be serious. We'll be careful." I hold out my pinky. "Scouts honor?"

Smiling, she loops her finger in mine. "Scouts honor."

Later, we're curled up in bed together. Thandi's skin glows in the warmth of the fireplace. It's nice that the bedroom has one too, especially on chilly days like this.

"You were amazing," I murmur, my hand settling at her hip.

"So were you," she whispers. "I needed this. Thank you."

Her words make me happier than should be rationally possible. It's such a simple thing—the certainty of our love, the ease of wanting each other—but to me, it's everything. I tighten my arms around her and kiss her again. She moans softly, her body moving against mine like a dream.

And yet, even as we cling to that closeness, dread seeps in at the edges. I'm afraid it will always be like this if we can't bring Daysha home safe.

I glance at my digital watch.

"She hasn't called yet," I say quietly.

"No." Thandi sighs. "Do you really think they got him?"

I stare at the window, at the lights twinkling beyond the glass. It's still early evening, but the night has already settled in, thick as velvet. I hate that about fall and winter—the way the darkness always seems to nip at your heels.

"I don't know," I admit. "But how many bullet-ridden men who look like Damian Patrick are walking around the DMV?"

Thandi is quiet.

I get it.

Despite the intimacy we just shared, my thoughts keep circling to McNamara, Damian, and Daysha. Thandi is the only thing keeping the monsters at bay—and even then, it takes effort to push my doubts aside.

No news is good news, I tell myself.

I shift on the mattress—and curse as Thandi eases away from me. Before I can protest, she's rolling over and on her feet.

"Where are you going? This is supposed to be snuggle time only."

"Hush." She leans back in to steal a kiss. "I'm just going to wash up."

"But what if I want to get you dirty again?" I counter, lifting a brow. My plans for the rest of the evening involved Thandi ... and more Thandi—specifically right here in this bed.

She shoots me a look before padding into the bathroom. A few minutes later, the water turns on. I swipe through my phone, waiting not-so-patiently for her to reappear.

When she does, she's wrapped in a fluffy towel, a curl of steam trailing behind her. The scent of body wash hangs in the air. I'm thrilled to see her—but she's abandoned me mid-cuddle, and now this infernal towel is blocking my favorite view in the world.

Am I pouting?

Maybe just a little.

I watch as she rifles through the closet. When she starts pulling on sweats and a hoodie, I sit up so fast I forget about my side.

Fuck. I wince.

"Baby," I say, trying to keep my voice even, "why are you getting dressed?"

She grabs her sneakers. "I should probably run to Harrington's before it gets too late," she says, settling on the edge of the bed. "Between the soup and the snacks, Dad and I used up everything I had left."

I kick the covers aside. "I'll come with you."

"No." She shakes her head. "You're going to stay here and rest. I'm just grabbing a few essentials to tide us over until morning. I don't think we have a single egg left, and you need to keep your strength up. Besides—" She lifts her phone, and the glow casts a cool blue light over her features. "I checked Cartly. All the delivery slots are booked. I'll only be gone a few minutes."

I bite back a protest. Maybe it's the lingering stress from Damian's attack, but my protective instincts are in overdrive. Unease stirs in my chest. After everything we've been through, I just want her close.

"Baby, we can order in tomorrow. Or go to the diner," I say. "Come back to bed."

"But what about—shit." Thandi's phone buzzes.

"What is it?"

"That was Janice from the youth center." She sighs. "I forgot ISO needs to be prepped for the exhibit tomorrow afternoon. It's science day." She bites her lip. "The first one without Daysha…"

"Oh, baby," I murmur, crossing the room to her.

She nods, blinking rapidly. "It felt wrong to cancel it outright. And the kids need something normal." A broken laugh slips out. "Who am I kidding? We could all use a distraction."

"It sounds wonderful," I say, wrapping my arms around her, my thumb brushing her cheek.

"I figured it's not every day you get to meet a genetically modified mouse," she says, hope lighting her eyes. "We've set up an obstacle course with timed, scent-based tests. Adults can even place bets— proceeds go to the center, of course."

Of course.

As usual, she's thought of everything. No—more than that. Somehow, in the midst of memory, trauma, and heartbreak, she's still found a way to put the kids first.

"I'll take tomorrow off," I say. "Not that I'd be much use in the office with these stitches anyway. We'll go together. It'll be good to be there." I hesitate, then add, "Besides ... maybe we'll have good news to share. It would make science day even more special."

"Maybe," Thandi says softly. She eases away from me. "I guess I should head over to the office and hit Harrington's on the way home."

"Wait, you have to go now?" My body tenses before I can stop it. "That means you won't be back for another hour."

"More like two." She crosses to the dresser, smoothing a dollop of moisturizer into her hair. "I need to check ISO's food, prep his travel enclosure, and review the instructions for the youth center team. Then I'll do a quick trial run with him using some of the compounds."

"Two hours?" I fold my arms. "Nope. I'm putting my foot down. There's no way you're doing all of this tonight." I soften my tone. "Baby, you've got to slow down. You faced a kidnapper *and* recovered buried memories today. ISO can wait until morning. Someone else can save the world."

Thandi lets out an indignant huff. "I'm not trying to save the world. I just—"

"You're deflecting," I say gently. "Throwing yourself into helping others instead of sitting with everything you've been through."

I pull her back into my arms. "Look at me," I say, tipping her chin up. "I get it. I really do. But someone has to remind you to take care of yourself."

"I haven't forgotten the rules," she says in a small voice. "Harrington's fifteen minutes away, and nowhere near my parents' neighborhood. Immerscent is even farther out."

I sigh. "You're stubborn as hell, you know that?"

"I know." Thandi buries her face against my chest. "And you're right." Her voice is muffled against my shirt. "It's just what I'm used to. I'll try to slow down. Take better care."

"Good." I kiss the top of her head.

She draws in a steadying breath. "This has been so hard, but I wouldn't trade it for anything. It's good to finally know what happened. To begin to put Tess to rest." She looks up at me, her eyes full of grief—and something gentler. "I'm so grateful to you."

My heart twists. Everything about this woman feels like my life's purpose. I think of how far I've come—from the Shezmu days to now. I never imagined that something I once treated like a clever diversion, a shallow way to make money, would end up helping heal the woman I love.

"You don't need to thank me," I say, brushing my nose along her cheek. "I just want you happy, baby."

She loops her arms around my neck. "Always—if I'm with you."

My heart pounds. I savor her warmth, her softness, the clean sweetness of her scent.

"Don't go out," I whisper, tightening my hold.

"Ronan…"

"I know." I swallow. "I'm being irrational. Overprotective." My hands clench against her back. "But when Damian came at you…"

I shake my head. "You didn't see his eyes."

"Tell you what." Thandi rubs my shoulder, trying to smooth the tension knotted there. "How about a compromise?"

I grunt.

"Sammie comes in early. I'll ask her to prep ISO so I don't have to go to the office tonight. And I'll skip Harrington's. I'll walk to the convenience store around the corner—stay close to home." She smiles. "Better?"

I ease off the panic button, though a niggling anxiety lingers. Of course, I'd rather she stay with me—but loving her can't mean putting her in a cage. And she didn't need to make even the concessions she just offered. She's right. She's sticking to McNamara's guidance, and if the cops are correct, Damian's at a clinic thirty minutes on the other side of town.

I frown, hoping for one better—that by now he's already been processed and sitting in a holding cell.

With a sigh, I relent.

"Fine," I grumble.

I walk her to the door—and then pull her back into my arms for another fierce kiss, a reminder of who's waiting for her at home. A little extra incentive to make it quick.

"We'll continue this when I get back," she gasps. Her gaze locks onto mine, full of a promise I know all too well.

"I'll hold you to that," I murmur against her lips.

"Scout's honor." She winks before slipping away. Her graceful form moves briskly down the hall, a reusable canvas bag swinging at her side.

I don't go back inside. I keep watching until the very last second.

She turns, lifts a hand in farewell, then disappears around the corner.

Crossroads
Thandi

I stand at the crosswalk waiting for the light to turn. The red hand flashes to the green man—white really.

A wistful smile touches my lips.

"Did you know some cities use women-shaped walk signals?" Daysha's *voice rings in my head. "Like Vienna, parts of Germany, Spain—and even Australia."*

I gasp, the cold night air rushing into my lungs. I press my hand to my mouth, stifling the sob that's trying to break free.

God, I'll miss her at science day.

She loved it so much—not the prizes or the costumes or the wacky cupcakes Ms. Ortega always bakes—but the problem-solving. The figuring things out.

I'd give anything to see her burst into the room tomorrow, goggles crooked, asking if ISO is ready yet. I just know she'd get a kick out of him.

The banded stripes of the crosswalk blur in front of me, and I scrub at my eyes.

Deep breaths, I tell myself. The cops might be booking Damian as we speak. I try to imagine them finding the gray rock and racing to the lake.

It's only a matter of time.

"She'll be okay," I whisper like a mantra. Yet when I pull my phone from my pocket, the only texts I have are from Ronan. They're emojis only—a heart, a smile, a kissy face. And then, beneath that—an eggplant.

I snort, fumbling for a tissue. This man is utterly ridiculous. And yet, he has me smiling again.

His searing kiss and anxious face as I turned toward the elevator loom in my mind.

I wish he wouldn't worry so much.

I text Ronan back a double heart. And then for the hell of it, a peach before tucking my phone away.

The bell over the door rings as I push into FreshMart.

I love these stores. They're not as sprawling as a supermarket, but they have a bit of everything. I can't count how many times this one has saved me in a pinch—flour, tampons, detergent, pantyhose. I once even found bra tape in the back when a dress threatened to fail me on a night out. And I've known the owner, Ashish, for years.

I smile, thinking of Ronan's text.

It was a good idea to skip Harrington's.

I wave at Ashish as I grab a basket.

I wander the aisles, mentally checking off my list—bread, milk, eggs, bagged mixed greens, a box of cereal, and a tub of the improbable yet shockingly good neon-yellow macaroni salad from the refrigerator case. Ashish's cousin up in Landover makes it, and locals come from far and wide just to get their hands on it. I'm shocked there's any left. I grab an extra for the heck of it.

Bananas go into the basket next. The fresh strawberries look like a crime, so I opt for frozen instead. Smoothies are good for healing bodies, right?

Of course, while I'm in the freezer aisle, my eyes slide to the ice cream. I shouldn't, but…

I shrug and reach inside.

What? It's not just for me. I picture Ronan beside me on the couch, sharing the carton, a dumb movie playing in the background.

I rummage toward the back for Rocky Road, but frown when I come up empty-handed.

Damn it.

"Hey, Ashish," I call, hauling my basket to the front. "You out of Rocky Road?"

He takes the basket from me and sets it on the counter. "Pregnant lady took the last one ten minutes ago. You just missed it."

"Ugh," I huff. "I'm not about to begrudge a pregnant mom her fix, but damn if I wasn't craving that."

Ashish laughs. The scanner beeps as he starts checking me out. "I keep telling you to call me. I can set it aside."

I prop my hands on my hips. "Okay, but the last time I texted you, you didn't notice for half a day. By the time I swung by, Rocky Road *and* Chocolate Chip were gone."

"I said *call*, not text. You young people and these phones—I don't do all of that mess." He gives as good as he gets, though it's immediately undermined by the extra chocolate bar he slips into my bag.

"Fine." I grin, waving my phone at him. "Tap to pay, or do you need me to write a check since you're so old school?"

A short laugh bursts from his lips. "You've got jokes, eh?" He shakes his head. "It's always the quiet ones."

"And still you put up with me." I wink, reaching across the counter to grab my bags—

And freeze.

Just behind Ashish, off to the left, a wire rack is stacked haphazardly with rows of WhiffRush inhalers, their lurid packaging screaming neon purple. A bright plastic sign hangs above them:

CLEARANCE — 80% OFF!

Ashish follows my gaze and shakes his head. "Yeah," he mutters, his expression sour. "They make me sick, too. Astor scammed all of us. I was just trying to keep the lights on, not harm anybody."

I nod, my throat tight. "I'm really sorry, Ashish."

He leans on the counter, tired eyes softening.

"What most people don't know is that it isn't just the products. Astor tried to push a whole franchise model—tie stores like mine into their supply chain. A lot of us won't recover from it."

My chest aches as I'm confronted by yet another cruel ripple of Astor's destruction. "That's awful."

"I'll be okay," Ashish says. "But my boy Ousmane's got it the worst. You know him—the shop just around the corner on Fifteenth."

I nod, and he continues.

"Business completely tanked, and he's still got two kids at Blair High School." He squints up at the ceiling. "Actually, Hawa's supposed to go off to college next year. Anyway, he went all in—invested in their luxury line, Prime. Took out a ten-year lease on a space in Chevy Chase and everything."

He sighs. "Now it's all worthless."

I reach over and squeeze his hand. "I'm so sorry. Every time I think I've seen the worst of Astor, I learn something else."

"You and me both." Ashish shifts away as another customer steps up, asking where to find WD-40.

I wave and leave him to it.

"Hey, Thandi," Ashish calls just as I open the door. "I texted Ousmane." He points to his phone with a proud grin. "He's got a couple of tubs of Rocky Road left. He'll hold them if you want."

I hesitate. Ashish is the best, and his showing off his newfound texting skills warms my heart. But the mood has shifted. My stomach churns with the knowledge of how Astor has harmed even these small businesses. I'm not sure I could keep anything down now—even ice cream.

"No pressure," Ashish says, setting his phone down with a shrug. "But he could really use the business."

Damn it.

My hand stills on the handle. I feel like Cinderella at midnight. My coach has definitely turned into a pumpkin. I just want to be back home in Ronan's arms, shutting the world away.

But I see the hopeful look in Ashish's eyes—and I can't forget the extra bar of chocolate nestled in my bag.

"Okay," I nod. "Tell him I'll be over in five minutes."

I slip into Ousmane's, determined to make it quick. This Fresh-Mart is identical to Ashish's, except for a little nook with a desk in the back. Ousmane's a notary public.

He's behind the counter, looking as regal as ever in his crisp white boubou, the fabric flowing softly as he stacks a few magazines. He looks up as I enter.

"Thandi, you made it." A smile splits his features. "Ashish told me you had a late-night craving. I'm glad we could help."

I can't help smiling, even though I still feel a bit out of sorts. "Thanks, Ousmane. I owe you one."

"Don't mention it." He frowns, glancing around. "Where did she go? Hawa!" He calls something out in Wolof, and a muffled reply comes from the back of the store.

"She's coming," he tells me. "We held it for you in the back."

I blink back another wave of emotion. This brand of Rocky Road is my favorite, its creaminess supposedly coming from Amish cows—though the label says *Made in Virginia*. But a tub still costs only $3.98.

The fact that Ousmane went to such lengths to protect this sale tells me how tight things are for him. I make a mental note to leave a little something extra on my way out.

"Don't worry about it," I say, already heading toward the rear of the store. "I'll grab it."

"Hey, Ms. Thandi."

I find Hawa stocking the freezer. My Rocky Roads are perched on the step stool beside her, already bagged. Unlike her father, she's dressed in all black denim, her braids piled into an elegant knot atop her head. She's so much taller than I remember—and she's sporting a new septum ring.

I glance toward the front of the store.

I wonder how *that* went over.

"Hey, Hawa." I lift the bag like a trophy. "Thanks for this."

"No problem." She grins. "I don't blame you. This one's my favorite, too. I'd stock up if I were you."

"School going okay?" I ask. Hawa came to the youth center for career day. If I remember right, she was on the computer engineering track—pen testing.

"Yeah." She shrugs. "I'm gunning for valedictorian. Got some early letters from Virginia Tech and Purdue…" She glances toward the front of the store. "But we'll see."

My heart sinks. Now Astor is jeopardizing even Hawa's future.

I frown. Maybe I should talk to Janice at the youth center, take a look at the science scholarships. Fia and I still haven't gotten that thing we were planning off the ground, either. I know she wanted to leverage some of the funds from Rosalind's inheritance.

I reach over and squeeze Hawa's hand. "Keep your head up. Things will work out."

She bites her lip and nods. "I'll ring you up front."

"Be right there."

I hang back, lingering long enough to grab some bills from the ATM.

Back up front, I can't help but notice that Ousmane also has a WhiffRush display. This one isn't behind the register, but off to the side in one of those fancy branded cardboard shelves. What *does* shock me is the pricing—**90% off**.

His expression shutters the moment he follows my gaze. He drops his head. "I know," he mutters. "You don't have to say it."

"Ousmane," I protest quickly. "I'd never judge. Astor's in the wrong here—not you."

Hawa rolls her eyes. "I keep telling him to get over it. He needs to mark them *up*, not down."

She slides my bag across the counter. "There's a whole subreddit of people trying to buy up the last stock. Yesterday, a guy came from Williamsburg—*Williamsburg*—to grab a ton. We're the only location with Cherry Smash. We should be capitalizing on this." She tilts her head at me. "It's always the first to go."

I glance from father to daughter, the tension sparking like a live wire between them.

"No," Ousmane barks. He gestures sharply at the display. "I'm sick of all of it. I just want it gone. My wife, Mariama, warned me. I should have listened."

I wince, trying to figure out a diplomatic exit when Ronan saves me. My phone vibrates.

Hey, do we have more gauze? The stitches are pulling a bit.
No rush.

Jesus. I need to get back.

"So sorry," I say to Hawa and Ousmane, who are still bickering. "The gauze is in aisle…?"

"Nine!" they say in unison, already back to sniping at each other.

I rub a hand between my eyes. I can't get home soon enough. Resting my bags on the counter, I head down the aisle in search of Ronan's first aid.

Of course, it's not where they said it would be, and with things still heating up at the front, I'm loath to ask for help.

I bend, trailing my fingers along the shelf. "Maybe I just missed it," I mutter.

I'm about to throw in the towel when the bell tinkles.

The store goes quiet.

A muffled male voice says something, but I'm too far away to make it out.

"The *fuck?*" Hawa blurts. Her voice drifts down the aisle, loud and clear. "This shit is creepy as hell."

"Look," Ousmane says. "We don't want any trouble here."

My blood runs cold. I hope to God this isn't a robbery. Ronan is going to be pissed.

I grip my phone. Heart pounding, I duck low, careful not to make a sound, and peer around the edge of the shelf.

And freeze.

Ousmane is glaring at a man in a gray hoodie, hunched over the WhiffRush display. I'm too far away to see his face, but unbelievably, he's wrapped his arms around the cardboard Cherry Smash shelf as though he intends to cart the entire thing away.

I stall, unable to process for a moment. I knew Astor's products were addictive, but this is something else entirely.

"Hey!" Ousmane's voice sharpens. "These are discounted, not free. You can't just grab them."

Hawa's at the register, clutching her phone, and from my vantage point, I see Ousmane's hand slip beneath the counter.

I edge closer, my thumb hovering over my phone's emergency call icon—just in case.

"Sorry," the man mutters, his voice slurred and rough. He grabs a basket and starts packing the neon inhalers into it. One handful. Then another.

Fist over fist.

Until the entire display is empty.

A chill races through me. *What on earth…?*

I'm two aisles closer now, but the man is still only half in profile. My hands shake as I lift my phone and snap a quick photo. It's a terrible angle, but I can't lean in without drawing attention to myself. If this escalates, even a bad photo is better than nothing.

The man shuffles forward and dumps the basket onto the counter in front of Hawa, his hands trembling.

She jumps as the plastic clatters against the counter. Ousmane steps closer, his stance protective. He mutters something almost inaudible in Wolof, and Hawa nods—but she doesn't shift.

She can't seem to move.

"Cash or card?" Ousmane snaps.

"What? Oh. Sorry." The man fumbles in his pockets. "Cash. I'll use cash."

When Hawa doesn't move, Ousmane gently nudges her aside. He checks the man out, inhalers beeping in rapid succession. He's moving so quickly—scanning so fast—that it sounds like one continuous, high-pitched scream.

Ousmane shoves the entire haul unceremoniously into a reusable shopping bag that reads **KEEP THE EARTH GREEN** above the FreshMart logo. He rips the tag off, not bothering to charge the man for it.

"Thirty-five dollars and sixty-nine cents."

The man pulls out a wad of bills. Now that I'm closer, I notice how stiffly he moves, favoring one side over the other—so much so that it seems to take an eternity for him to count off the cash.

Is he hurt?

I lean in, close enough to catch Hawa's reflection in the security monitor mounted above the counter.

She still hasn't moved. Her eyes are wide, fixed on the man's shoulder.

I frown, peering at the screen. My gaze follows hers, tracking the spot she can't seem to let go of.

That's when I see it.

On his shoulder. The one angled away from me.

A dark splotch.

An irregular stain.

Dark red.

No.

Blood dark.

I follow the line of it down to the counter, where his fist rests against the glass. From this distance, flattened by the grainy footage, it's barely perceptible, but it's there:

Two thin tributaries, trickling down his wrist, smearing the glass.

He's still bleeding.

My heart stutters. Fear slams into me so hard I gasp as the breath leaves my lungs.

A hoodie … a shoulder wound … a WhiffRush addiction….

No!

I whirl, ducking back out of sight, pressing myself against the shelf. My body shakes so violently I nearly drop my phone.

It can't be. It has to be a mistake.

McNamara said they had him. That he was at the clinic.

He can't be here.

He can't be.

Time warps. Seconds stretch into years.

It takes me three tries to unlock my phone. Two more to put Ronan and McNamara into a group text. I attach the photo.

> He's here.
>
> FreshMart on the corner of Fifteenth and Susq Ave. Come now.

I hold my breath. The store has gone eerily quiet. I didn't hear the bell tinkle, so Damian must still be inside.

What's going on?

I'm too afraid to move. Too terrified to risk calling out to Hawa or Ousmane.

Coins jingle, the sound muffled by fabric. Footsteps drag closer. A soft, rhythmic thump follows—the bag of WhiffRush knocking against Damian's leg.

Oh, God. He's coming this way.

I scrabble backward, crawling on hands and knees to the far end of the shelf.

"Hey!" Ousmane calls. "If you're finished, you need to move on. We have no more of that stuff, and there's no loitering here. Fifteen-minute shopping limit," he lies.

He pauses.

"Or I call the cops."

The footsteps stop.

The freezer hums. The world ceases to spin.

Then—a garbled retort.

Ousmane grunts.

The bell tinkles.

A car engine sputters, then fades away.

I don't even bother grabbing my things from the counter. Just outside the bathroom, there's a door that leads to the back entrance. I run for it without a word to Hawa or Ousmane.

I just need to get out of here. I need to go home to Ronan, where it's safe.

I'll figure out what went wrong, what happened to Daysha, once I'm back in his arms. That's the only thing that matters now.

I shove the door open and sprint into the empty parking lot. The streetlamps cast long pools of light over the asphalt, making it feel vast and forbidding.

I shiver, tugging the sleeves of my hoodie over my fingers as I jog, veering around the building, away from the direction Damian drove. I'm not far from my condo. At the intersection, I can cut through the shopping center and get back to Main Street.

I spot the stop sign ahead.

I round the corner towards it.

That's when a hand clamps over my mouth.

The smell of cherry fills my nostrils.

It's the last thing I register before the blow comes—and the world drops away as I'm dragged to the ground.

Agony

Ronan

She's been gone a long time.

Too long.

I pace in front of the window, checking my phone again. Outside, the world is infuriatingly banal: shoppers weighed down with bags crossing the street, teens clustered near the milk tea shop, a delivery guy on an automatic bike flying down the sidewalk so fast that an elderly couple shouts after him.

Nothing about my world feels normal.

How could it, when Thandi isn't here?

Her last text is the one that made me smile—the heart and peach emoji—but she read my message about the gauze. So what could have happened?

She should be back.

Something's wrong.

I feel it in every nerve in my body, visceral and electric, vibrating along the connection that Thandi and I share. I should have gone with her, made sure she was safe.

Now I hope my carelessness hasn't cost me my reason for living.

I begin shrugging into my coat, this time refusing to ignore my instincts. I'm halfway out the door when my phone lights up.

My hopes soar then plummet. It's McNamara, not Thandi.

False lead at the clinic.

Park Service confirmed Thandi's gray rock. I have approximate coordinates.

Units paused earlier due to visibility and K-9 fatigue. They're redeploying now.

Waiting on confirmation of the lake.

My sense of dread only deepens. If Damian is not at the clinic, we're back where we started—Daysha still missing and an erratic kidnapper at large.

I tell myself Thandi's neighborhood is miles outside the active radius; that Damian has no reason to be anywhere near her. McNamara profiled a man tethered to the site of his trauma—not a stalker with a single-minded fixation on the woman I love.

It doesn't help.

Because Thandi's own words keep echoing in my ears:

We should expect a wider degree of variance in any behavioral models we're using for Damian Patrick.

I close my eyes, and Damian's green stare, frenetic and intent, burns behind my eyelids.

Thandi is right.

Because I felt it myself.

No one understands what Damian is capable of like I do. Not McNamara, Hayes—or even Brooks. None of them was close enough to see the wildness in his eyes. They didn't wrestle him to the dirt and feel the obsession locked into every bone and sinew.

They didn't see the way he looked at Thandi.

And now he is still out there, his instability amplified by my father's greed and negligence.

I clench my fists.

Damian Patrick isn't the only monster who needs to be caged.

The door clicks shut behind me. Thandi said the FreshMart was just around the corner. That shouldn't be hard to find. I move quickly, my strides swallowing the distance to the elevator.

My phone buzzes again. I laugh as I see the notification. Thandi—finally!

Then, I freeze as the image loads on the screen.

No.

No.

This can't be happening.

Two words explode my universe: **He's here.**

Panic and rage knot in my chest. I don't wait for the elevator. I race downstairs to the Maybach and peel out of the garage, shouting the FreshMart's address into the GPS.

She's okay; she's okay; she's okay; I keep chanting silently.

Dear God, please let her be okay.

"Fuck!" I slam both hands against the steering wheel. If Damian harms a hair on her head, I'll hunt him down and make him regret the day he was born.

I weave through traffic, ducking between cars and taking short-cuts wherever I can find them. The console lights up. McNamara's calling. I ignore her and put Equinox on speed dial instead.

"Boss." Ethan, my head of security, answers on the first ring.

"Thandi's in danger," I say hoarsely. "I need your help."

"Okay," Ethan says. "Tell me what happened. Where is she now?"

I swing onto the next street, running the red light. "We were at her condo together. She left about thirty minutes ago to go to the FreshMart—said she'd be back in a few minutes." I forward him the photo and the text exchange. "Then she sent me this."

I haven't even briefed him since the stabbing. I tell him about the attack, my injury, Thandi recovering her memory, and the false lead at the clinic.

"I'm on my way to the store now," I finish. "She texted both of us, but McNamara's on the other side of town."

"Understood," Ethan says immediately. "I'm deploying a six-person Equinox team to your location." He pauses. "Mr. Thorne, I need you to understand that we may be facing an active hostage situation.

The best thing you can do for Ms. Elowen when you arrive is to *not* enter the building."

My phone flashes with another text.

"I've sent you a map of the property. Pull in behind the building on the west side. Remain in your vehicle and wait for my backup."

"Got it."

The FreshMart's cheery entrance comes into view, but I swerve as soon as I receive the map and swing around to the back side.

God damn it. I'm trembling, fighting the instinct to go in. But I won't. I'd never put Thandi in more danger.

"Okay," I say, taking a deep breath. "I'm pulling into the parking lot now."

"Roger that. ETA is four minutes."

I've barely hung up when a police cruiser swings into the lot, lights flashing but sirens off. It avoids the front entrance and pulls around back, stopping about a hundred feet from me, right beside the dumpster.

Thank God. McNamara must have called for help. They made better time than even Equinox.

Time to end this nightmare.

I'm still gripping the steering wheel as two officers step out and slip through the store's rear door, guns holstered. Sweat beads along my brow. My side throbs from the hard driving and sharp turns. When I press a hand to the dressing, my fingers come back wet.

I'll deal with that later.

"Come on," I mutter, drumming my hands against the curved leather. "Come on."

They're taking too long. It all feels too calm. No weapons drawn. No sign of backup. Is this it? Two cops strolling in like they're responding to a noise complaint?

I'd expected a goddamn cavalry by now.

The door opens, and I go rigid.

The officers emerge, still unhurried, murmuring into their earpieces. This time, they're followed by a tall Black man and a teenage girl. The girl gestures anxiously back at the door. The man's face is creased with worry.

Where's Thandi?

Where's Damian?

I lean forward, craning to see something—anything—through the open doorway behind them.

There's nothing there.

Thandi isn't there.

Panic crushes the air from my lungs.

I'm out of the Maybach before I remember opening the door.

"Where is she?" I roar, sprinting toward the building.

"Hey! What the fuck is this?" the cop closest to the cruiser yells. "Stop right there!"

I don't.

I shove through the door and bolt down the first aisle, skidding past rows of groceries, my eyes scanning for a flash of bright pink hair.

"Thandi!" I tear down the next aisle, pivot hard, and sprint again. "Thandi, baby, where are you? I'm here!"

Footsteps thunder behind me. Voices tumble over each other.

"Sir—stop!" Metal clicks. "This is your last warning. Get on the ground."

I whirl around.

Both officers stand with their weapons trained on me. Behind them, the man and the teenage girl hover near the entrance, frozen, their faces taut with fear.

I lift my empty hands.

"Where is she?" My voice breaks. "Where's Thandi?"

"MPD," the younger officer snaps, bringing his other hand up to his weapon. "State your name and your business here."

A cry tears from my throat—raw, desperate. "Tell me what you've done with her. *Please.*"

The officers exchange a look.

"Wait. Stop," the girl blurts, stepping forward despite the older man's hand on her arm. "I know him. I've seen him on TV." She points at me, eyes wide. "He's Ronan Thorne. Ms. Thandi's boyfriend."

There's no cavalry.

No brave rescue.

Just my heart ripping out of my chest.

We're too late.

He's already taken her.

The two officers weren't part of McNamara's response at all. They were just local patrol, drawn by a frantic call, as blind to the larger picture as I was when I first arrived.

Ousmane, the store owner, and his daughter Hawa had called them after Damian grabbed an entire display of WhiffRush from the shelves and Thandi vanished, leaving her groceries behind.

"I don't know," I hear Hawa tell one of the officers. Her voice trembles. "He was creepy. And there was blood dripping down his arm." A pause. Then, firmer: "Yes. That's him."

Beside her, Ousmane answers questions of his own. "We've never had trouble here," he says slowly. "My store—this neighborhood—it's quiet. Full of good people like Thandi." His voice breaks. "Inshallah, she is safe."

That's the only thing keeping me upright: Hope—or madness. I'm not sure which anymore.

I turn Thandi's phone over in my hands. It's still lying where it fell, exactly where it slipped from her fingers when Damian struck her and dragged her away.

I thought I knew pain. I was wrong.

Watching the security footage—seeing Thandi's body go slack—teaches me what agony really is. The wound in my side is nothing. It can't compare to the fire roaring through my skull, the violent churn in my gut, or the vise that keeps tightening around my heart.

I can't believe after everything we survived, after everything we fought for, he still took her from me.

"Ronan." McNamara kneels in front of me. Her voice is steady, but her eyes are full of shadows. "I'm so sorry."

"Sorry?" I snarl, dragging a hand through my hair. "What the fuck happened? You said she was safe."

The perimeter goes quiet. Heads turn. Even the radios seem to hush.

Of course, now—*now* that Thandi is gone—the place swarms with law enforcement of every kind: state police, federal, and finally, my own Equinox unit, black-clad and lethal, standing just beyond the row of cruisers.

McNamara flinches. "We followed protocol. I—"

"Mr. Thorne, we've got a hit on the license plate from the security footage." Ethan materializes at my side, a wall of muscle. He glances from me to McNamara. "Do you want us proceeding with the extraction plan, or are we taking our cues from the authorities?"

He folds his arms. "Time is of the essence. I need to know who's on first."

McNamara stands, her expression hardening.

"Ronan, I know you're scared," she says evenly. "And I know you want to help Thandi. But this is still an active police investigation."

She gestures at the scene around us. "This case was never about manpower. It was about direction—having the right information at the right time to narrow the search." Her gaze holds mine. "We have that now, thanks to Thandi."

She sighs, for the first time sounding truly weary. "You're right. Our profiles didn't sufficiently account for WhiffRush's effects. Damian *shouldn't* have been here, but he was."

McNamara notches her chin, eyes unflinching as she meets Ethan's. "Right now, we're heading into the woods, at night, with limited visibility. The last thing I need is a fractured chain of command or armed personnel my units won't recognize on instinct." Her voice is calm, but immovable. "This situation is volatile enough. Your team will need to stand down."

"Not happening," I say immediately.

"Ronan—"

"I'm not abandoning Thandi." I take a steadying breath. I unclench my fists, forcing myself to calm down. McNamara isn't the enemy, I remind myself. Damian is. She's been fighting this with us from the start.

"Look, Detective, I know you care about this case. I know how hard you've worked to show up for us." I meet her gaze. "But Thandi is my whole world. I can't sit on the sidelines while she's in a madman's clutches. If that puts me out of protocol, I'll deal with the consequences later."

McNamara stares at me for a long moment.

Then she swears under her breath.

"Here are my rules: You come with me and my unit. You follow my orders—no running ahead, no freelance heroics. You're under my command."

I start to speak, but she cuts me off with a look.

"Your Equinox team stays on the edge of the woods as backup only." Her eyes go to Ethan, then me. "We give ourselves forty-five minutes from entry to locate Thandi and Daysha and begin extraction. At minute forty-six, Equinox rolls in."

McNamara steps closer and extends her hand.

"Deal?"

I remember Thandi in my arms, kissing me goodbye at the door. I see her puttering about the kitchen with her Dad, creating the home and family I never thought I'd have—even in the midst of all this sorrow.

And once again, the security footage screams in my mind—her small form collapsing beneath Damian's blow.

If this is what it takes to get her back—to protect the beautiful, precious world we began building together—then I'll do it.

She's worth anything.

I meet McNamara's eyes and see the determination reflected there.

I step forward and take her hand.

"Deal."

Lake
Thandi

An engine sputtering off jolts me awake.

It's dark.

Pitch black.

The faint smell of gasoline fills my nose.

I don't know where I am. I blink, trying to make out shapes in the darkness, but my head throbs and my vision swims. Saliva floods my mouth. I moan, fighting the bile rising in my throat.

I'm curled onto my side, arms bent, legs cramped. The felt mat I'm lying on is scratchy and musty. Somewhere behind me, two plastic objects roll loose, clacking together before coming to rest near my temple.

A sickly-sweet scent fills my nostrils.

Cherry.

Nausea surges. I groan and try to lift my hands to my head.

But I can't.

My wrists are bound.

I jerk, panicking. My breath comes in too fast. Memory rushes back, alongside stomach-churning fear.

Damian.

There's no amnesia this time. I recall in excruciating detail the FreshMart, Damian grabbing the WhiffRush display, Hawa's and Ousmane's alarm—

And pain exploding behind my skull just when safety—just when Ronan—seemed within reach.

Ronan.

My heart clenches. He didn't want me to leave. He must be worried sick.

My phone!

I try to scoot in the dark, using my bound hands to feel around, but the moment I attempt to sit up, my head slams into metal, and pain, needle-sharp, splits my skull.

That's when it clicks.

I'm in a trunk.

The trunk of Damian's car.

A dull thump sounds from somewhere outside. Then the lid wrenches open.

Damian's face hovers above me, ghost-pale against a canopy of green. The FreshMart bag of inhalers is slung over one shoulder.

I flinch, curling inward.

"What do you want?" I gasp.

He doesn't answer. He only yanks me up by my arm and hauls me out of the trunk. I stumble, my knees sinking into the soft earth, and the world tilts around me again.

"Get up," he rasps. "It's almost dinner time."

Dinner time?

I'm afraid to ask what he means.

I totter on my feet. The moon is a luminous halo—the only light we have as we move through the darkness. The ground here is soggy, and with my hands bound, I fight to keep my balance. The air is dank, not quite fetid but thick and unpleasant with the smell of decay: dead leaves, stagnant water, and things that have not seen the sunlight in too long.

Damian leads me up an incline, and a marshy lake comes into view. The cold light reflecting off the water deepens the shadows of the vegetation around it, turning them into lurid shapes.

I stop short, trembling, frozen in place.

My memory failed me for so long that even when Ronan helped me recover it, I never fully trusted myself. Somewhere deep in my heart, I wondered if the gray rock and the lake were real—or merely the wishful phantoms of a desperate child.

Seeing the glinting water breaks something within me. A hot rush of tears spills down my face.

I found it, Tess.

Even if I'm too late.

"Hurry up," Damian grunts and pushes me forward.

I stumble ahead.

Shapes begin to separate from the darkness. The trees thin near the water, their roots clawing out of the ground like exposed knuckles. A building, half-collapsed, leans toward the lake.

It's nothing more than a shed, its warped boards dark with age and moisture. The roof sags in the middle, moss creeping along the shingles. One corner has sunk into the earth, as if the ground is trying to swallow it whole.

The sight of it unearths something in me. Another fragment, once buried, forces its way to the surface, as ghastly as the roots clawing at the water's edge:

Damian's small body, rigid beside me, and his father's voice cutting across the clearing:

"If you don't finish this right now, you know what will happen. Do you want to spend two hours in the shed again?"

I shudder, trying to imagine a child confined in there, nothing to keep him company but the dank and the sound of the living darkness. It's too awful to contemplate.

God, please don't let Daysha be in there.

I stumble again, a soft sound tearing from my throat.

Damian's fingers bite into my arm as he jerks me upright. "Watch it."

For all his roughness, he's limping, and clutching the loot of inhalers doesn't help. He keeps one arm tucked against his side, his movements uneven. The sour-sweet funk of cherry surrounds us, his breath fogging in the cold air.

We keep moving, and our path veers away from the water. Damian's steps quicken, steering us in an arc, until the shed recedes into a dark smear at the edge of my vision. At first, I think he's avoiding the worst of the mud, until we slosh straight through a murky seep pool.

I gasp as cold water floods my shoes.

That's when I understand.

It isn't the water he hates.

It's what's beside it.

The ground tilts upward, becoming firmer beneath my feet, mud giving way to packed dirt and pine needles. The air smells different here—sharper, cleaner, threaded with sap.

Damian yanks me forward, and I nearly go down as my shoes strike soft, loose earth. It's piled higher than the ground we just crossed, the surface uneven beneath a thin scatter of needles. The smell of fresh soil is thick here, and though the dirt is dry, it shifts strangely under my weight. I gasp as my foot sinks in, down to my ankle, the ground collapsing into an empty pocket. I clutch my arms to my chest, lifting my legs high, scrambling to stay upright.

Damian keeps moving ahead of me, barely visible. The clouds thin, and for a second, a shaft of moonlight illuminates the earth around my feet, bathing it in silver.

A scream claws its way from my throat.

The mounded shape ... the disturbed soil ... the way the ground hasn't settled....

This isn't an obstacle.

It's a grave—unmarked and freshly dug.

Oh god. Is that—?

Please. Please no.

Tears flood my eyes, and my knees threaten to crumple beneath me. I'm shaking when the clouds part again. Through the veil of my panic, I see the depth of the mound before me.

It's large. Too large.

Human-sized, yes—but too long for a child.

I don't know much about digging graves, but I know it's back-breaking work. Too hard to make it more challenging than it has to be. Only a madman would dig more than needed.

Damian's not far from that, my mind whispers, but I shove that aside.

In science, the simplest explanation is usually right.

An adult lies here. Who, how, and why don't matter. Only Daysha does.

And she isn't here.

I inhale and force my feet to keep moving.

I'm shivering from the cold night air and my wet socks sticking to my feet when we reach a narrow path between the trees. Dark and partly overgrown, I would have missed it if not for Damian. I can barely see my breath, but he moves without torchlight or lantern as if by some preternatural instinct, finding his way unerringly among the dirt and leaves.

Bit by bit, a larger structure emerges from the trees. This time, it's not another shed, but a cabin, small and squat, built of logs roughened with age. One side is piled high with firewood. In front of that is a plastic drum, its lid weighted down with a stone. A length of hose snakes from its base into a jerrycan of water.

Damian steers me toward the cabin, his grip tightening on my arm as we near the door.

Everything he needs is here—wood, shelter, distance from the world. No wonder he's been so hard to find.

My stomach lurches. My heart pounds so fast, my chest hurts. This will be my prison if I can't find a way to fight back. A way to free myself—and Daysha.

Daysha.

My mind flits back to the grave. Is she really here? Will I see her sweet face when that door opens? Or will she already be gone? Lost to me forever.

Like Tess.

I gulp in deep breaths. Yet, even now, even as Damian's fingers grip my skin hard enough to bruise, there is a part of me that believes I can endure anything if Daysha is here.

She is my hope. My redemption. If she's here—if I can reach her—then all of this suffering will mean something.

Just like Dad always says.

A heavy padlock hangs on the door's rusted deadbolt. Damian pulls a key from his pocket and slides it into the lock.

My heart hammers against my ribs as he twists it.

Damian pushes us inside, the floorboards creaking as we enter. The door slams shut behind us, and the lock clicks with a finality that steals the air from my lungs.

He sets the bag of inhalers on the floor, and I blink, eyes adjusting to the dim interior of the room before me. A meager fire burns in the hearth, and Damian shoves me forward before turning to stoke it, coaxing the flames higher. Even as they catch, the air remains cold.

A rough dining table anchors the center of the room. It's flanked on one side by a small kitchen with a cast-iron sink overlooking a window. On the other side is a lumpy loveseat. There is no television, only a shelf of yellowing books sagging against the wall. The farthest wall is stacked with crates, boxes, and what looks like a massive chest.

There's no sign of Daysha.

My gaze darts wildly from corner to corner, my heart lodged in my throat. Near the couch lies a rumpled sleeping bag with a single pillow. But that could be Damian's.

I don't see a small body. Don't see bright, curious eyes or a sweet, round face.

I sob, sinking to my knees, as pain familiar and paralyzing sears through me. It's the same agony, the same helplessness I felt twenty years ago when I chased Tess' yellow dress into the woods.

The same pain I felt when she never came back.

A deep animal sound tears from me. I rock back and forth, mourning everything that has been taken from me—the utter sense-lessness, the cruelty of it all.

"Be quiet," Damian snaps. "What's wrong with you? We have to get ready for dinner."

He tries to pull me to my feet, but my body is a stone. Even he can't shift me as I grieve the loss of Daysha's bright, beautiful life.

"I said stop. Don't make me—"

A door clicks softly behind me.

"Ms. Thandi?"

I freeze. For a second, even my heart seems to forget how to beat. Maybe I'm hallucinating. Maybe the fragile knitting that's held me together for so long has finally unraveled.

Blood roars in my ears.

Because that voice—

I squeeze my eyes shut, my breath shuddering in my chest.

Dear God, please let this be real.

Let *her* be real.

Slowly—fearfully—I turn. Inch by inch, I pivot, the wooden planks biting into my knees, every movement a quiet, aching prayer.

I stop.

I open my eyes and lift my head.

And there she is.

Standing just beyond the doorway of a room I hadn't noticed before.

Her hair is tangled. Her clothes are dusty, her favorite pink hoodie smudged with dirt. She looks exhausted, ashen beneath her warm complexion—and thinner than I remember.

But she's here.

Alive.

Whole.

"Daysha!"

I surge to my feet, running toward her, heedless of my bound hands or the darkness around us. It doesn't matter—because she's running too.

We collide halfway.

"Ms. Thandi!" she sobs, throwing her arms around me. Her tears soak into my shirt.

I understand. I feel it too.

I drop to my knees, pulling her with me, pressing my face into her hair. I wedge my hands between us just enough to cup her cheeks, kissing her forehead, then both of her cheeks. Somehow, impossibly, I'm smiling through my tears.

"I'm here, honey," I whisper.

"And I'm getting you out of here. No matter what."

Family
Thandi

Neither Daysha nor I wants to let go, so it takes some maneuvering to make it to the couch. We're half crying, half laughing as we shuffle to the old sofa, clinging to each other like we're afraid the other might vanish if we loosen our grip.

I don't forget about Damian, not for a second. Even as we move, I angle my body, keeping myself between him and Daysha. If he lashes out, he'll get me first.

The fear proves well-founded. The moment we sit, Damian barrels toward us, closing the distance with shocking speed despite his injuries.

"Behind me," I hiss at Daysha.

She nods and ducks, her small hands fisting in the hem of my hoodie.

"Hey!" Damian shouts, green eyes blazing.

I flinch, shrinking back. My heart lodges in my throat.

"Look," I say, my voice shaking. My hands, bound and useless, tremble in front of me. "You don't have to hurt us. I'll tell the police you were kind—good to us. We can forget this ever happened."

Behind me, Daysha nods furiously.

Damian's eyes narrow.

Then he lunges.

I whimper, squeezing my eyes shut. I curl over Daysha, doing everything I can to shield her with my body.

Here it comes—

Damian jerks my hands forward, and the rope bites into my wrists.

God, he's going to drag me off the couch. I'm too terrified to think of what comes after. The past and the present collide, and the image of a needle filled with poison pierces my memory.

He was too afraid to use it then, but that boy is long gone.

I wait, gathering my strength for what's to come. I have to stay strong for Daysha. She'll need me at my best—whatever that means, for however long it takes.

No matter what happens to me, I'll make sure she leaves here safe.

My heart trembles as I think of Ronan and what this will do to him, but I push that away.

The rope jerks again—

Then slackens.

My eyes fly open.

Damian is kneeling in front of me, the rope dangling from his uninjured hand. His expression has gone strange: soft, unfocused—empty of the fury that filled it moments ago.

"Yes," he says, his voice lilting upwards, bright and childlike. "Damian's a good boy, Mama."

He clutches my hand in his.

"Now," he says gently, "can we have dinner?"

"Everyone must get ready for dinner," I say, clasping my hands together.

I brush an imaginary speck off my apron. It's pink gingham with a ruffled bodice. Despite the dankness of the cabin, this piece is freshly laundered and pressed—meticulously cared for. Damian didn't pull it from one of the boxes lining the walls. He took it from the coat closet, where it was already hanging, waiting.

"Mama needs my help?" Damian asks. He sits by the fire, bright-eyed and expectant. It's a chilling contrast to the blood still dripping down his fingers and the bruising purpling his face.

I swallow. I've never been an actress, but tonight, our lives will depend on it.

"Yes," I say brightly. "Why don't you wash your hands and help me get the cans from the cupboard?" I tilt my head toward Daysha. "Your sister can help me set the table."

It's a risk. But Damian's regression is nearly complete. The only chance I have is leaning into it. The only chance Daysha has is if he starts seeing her as family, too. Because even hurt, I'm no match for him physically. Fighting him isn't an option—not with Daysha here, and not without a weapon.

I would give anything for Ronan's strength right now.

Ronan. He's all I've thought about besides how to escape. He's out there looking for us. I know it. He'd never give up on us.

I press my hand to my heart.

And my parents. God, I can't imagine what this is doing to them. They've already endured so much; I won't let Damian take even more from them.

So, now I watch and wait.

I buy us time so I can think my way out of this.

As soon as I speak, Damian springs to his feet. Now that the edge of my panic has dulled, I register the full extent of his injuries as he shuffles to the sink.

His nose and cheeks are a map of swelling and bruised color, the bridge bent at an angle that tells me it's broken. His left cheekbone looks oddly hollow, not to mention a near-black shiner blooming beneath his eye. He looks like he ran face-first into a bruiser.

Which, I suppose, he did.

Daysha tugs on my apron. "What happened to him?" She whispers. "He wasn't like that before. Now he's even scarier."

"He attacked Mr. Ronan earlier," I say, squeezing her fingers. "And the police hurt him too."

Her eyes go wide. "You met him before?"

"Yes," I murmur. I soften the truth, casting the encounter as us helping the police search for evidence at Damian's old home.

Damian turns toward us, water and blood dripping from his hands, leaving pink smears across the linoleum.

"What now, Mama?"

"Now we take out the cans," I remind him gently. "I need the beans, carrots, salmon, and spinach."

"Okay, Mama!" Damian says, already moving, humming softly under his breath.

Daysha edges closer to me, reaching for the stack of mismatched plates at the corner of the table. She bites her lip as her gaze darts over to Damian. "I'm so glad you're here, Ms. Thandi."

"Me too, sweetie." I move to hug her again, but she pulls back, shaking her head.

"I'm messy. I'll get you dirty," she whispers, her lip wobbling. She brushes her hand over her dusty hoodie and tries to tug back her hair.

My heart breaks into a million pieces. Daysha has always been organized—her lab station neat, her stickers and beaded bracelets color-coded—and just as Aliyah said, her hair without a strand out of place.

I gather her into my arms anyway, kissing her forehead. "Honey, you're the most beautiful thing I've ever seen." I smooth my hand gently over her hair. "But if you want, I can help you freshen up."

Her eyes brim again. "Yes, please," she whispers.

I clap my hands, drawing Damian's attention. "Son, when you're finished opening the cans, I want you to change into something nice and clean. This is a special dinner. It's our Thanksgiving, celebrating being together again." I stretch my mouth into a smile. "As a family."

He pauses in opening a can of stewed spinach. "Yes, Mama."

"In the meantime," I add. "Your sister and I will freshen up."

As soon as Damian returns to his task, Daysha points me to the bathroom. The room is narrow and cold, lit by a single bulb. I help her rinse her hands and face at the sink, dampening a clean kitchen towel to wipe away the worst of the grime. She stands patiently, letting me fuss over her.

There's a broken comb in the vanity. No brush, but it's enough. I part Daysha's hair, spritzing it with water, easing her coils loose until they shine again. Then I plait them into two pigtails, twisting each into a small Princess Leia–style bun—her favorite.

I tug off my hoodie. "May I do the honors?" I ask, holding it up.

She bites her lip. "But won't you be cold?"

"Not as long as I'm with you." I smile as I slip it over her head. "There." I kiss her cheek. "Even more beautiful."

Her eyes shine when she glimpses herself in the mirror. "Thank you, Ms. Thandi."

"Don't mention it." I fold her hoodie carefully. "What should we do with yours? Should I keep it safe so we can grab it when we go?"

"No." Her expression darkens. "You can throw it away. It's not my favorite anymore."

Oh, Daysha.

I'm so sorry for everything she's been through, but I understand. I ball up the pink jacket and drop it into the wastebasket.

"Good?" I ask.

She nods. Then, without warning, she slips past me. Before I can react, she darts behind the toilet, crouching low.

"Daysha, honey, what are you doing?" I whisper, glancing toward the door.

She looks up at me with a shy, conspiratorial smile and holds something out in her hands. "It's my mirror."

I blink. "Your... mirror?"

Daysha nods, waving me closer to the wall, showing me a flattened piece of metal. The edges are smoothed down, and a bit of wire is wrapped around a folded corner. She tilts it just so, angling it toward the bathroom window. A thin shaft of moonlight slips in, catching on the metal.

A pale flash blooms against the trees, small but distinct.

Oh. My. God.

"Daysha … this is…" My breath catches.

Daysha's eyes shine. "If you move it like this," she whispers, twisting her wrist, "the light jumps. I've been doing it whenever he leaves. It's my signal—to call for help."

I grab her and pull her into my arms, squeezing her tight. "You're a genius," I breathe into her hair. "Do you hear me? An absolute genius."

She smiles, small and proud, and tucks the mirror back against her chest like a secret. I'm still holding her when something clicks into place.

"Wait," I mutter.

I look around the bathroom at the rounded walls. The logs aren't flush. Instead, seams of darkness peek through the gaps between them, where the cabin has settled over time. I crouch, then straighten, eyeing a spot above the bathroom window—high enough to perhaps be seen by a search party from afar.

Unfortunately, it's too tall for Daysha or me to reach alone.

But I have an idea.

"Daysha," I murmur, my pulse quickening. "If I lift you, do you think you could slide your mirror into one of those cracks? Right above the window?"

Her eyes dart to the wall, and understanding blooms across her face. "Yes," she whispers. "I picked this room because he doesn't like it. It's wetter here. He never comes to this side of the house."

I think of Damian's pointed diversion away from the shed. Of course, he doesn't.

"Come on," I say.

Turning my back to the wall, I bend my knees. Daysha climbs onto my thigh, light as a bird, and I steady her with my shoulder. She stretches on her toes and carefully feeds the flattened metal into a narrow gap between the logs. The wire catches just enough to hold; the metal slips through, hanging on the other side. Then she lets go.

I lower her, and the second her feet hit the floor, we rush to the bathroom window. We press close, peering out.

For a heartbeat, there's nothing. Then a pale flash glints between the trees. Then another. And another. The metal swings, catching the moonlight as the breeze nudges it back and forth.

I squeeze Daysha to me as our beacon keeps flashing.

And hope—as fragile and trembling as a thin strip of metal—takes root.

When we return to the kitchen, Damian has changed.

He's wearing a clean plaid shirt, the sleeves rolled to his elbows, exposing the pink streaks along his forearms. His damp hair is parted down the middle, a single cowlick jutting up at the back of his head. A clean bandage is wrapped around his hand—not because it's injured, but to catch the thin trickle of blood still seeping from his wound.

Every can is open, just as I asked, lined up neatly along the counter.

My blood freezes when I see the hunting knife notched in his belt. I can't forget the moment he drove another knife, just as wicked, deep into Ronan's side.

The sight is a brutal warning and a reality check. For all of his confusion, all of his seeming regression, Damian still hasn't forgotten his instinct for violence.

His face brightens the minute he sees us, and for a second, I glimpse the bruised boy inside the man. I will never forgive him for what he's done to Daysha, my family, and me, but I wish that it hadn't come to this.

I wish that life had dealt us all different hands.

I move to the counter, keeping my grip firm on Daysha's hand.

"Thank you," I say, careful to keep my tone warm. "You did such a good job." I glance at the cans. "Now it's my and your sister's turn. Why don't you go sit by the fire while we cook?"

"You're welcome!" Damian straightens, clearly pleased. He hesitates, eyes darting between the stove and my face. "Dinner will be ready soon, Mama?"

My fingers tighten around Daysha's hand. "Before you know it, sweetheart."

Satisfied, Damian nods and drifts back to the hearth, settling near the fire like a boy waiting to be called.

Only when his back is to us do I let out the breath I've been holding. I guide Daysha to the counter, positioning her safely at my side. Together, we begin turning cans into something that looks like a meal.

This isn't mere compliance. It's care. Daysha looks exhausted— hollow in a way that says she hasn't been eating enough. Whatever comes next, she'll need her strength.

I open cupboards, working quickly. I find a few forgotten spices, salt, and a half-used jar of pepper. I add what I can, coaxing warmth and flavor from what little we have. I think of the fresh groceries I left behind on Ousmane's counter—bright vegetables, real bread, things that would be miraculous now.

I push the thought away with a sigh.

This will have to do.

And I will make it enough.

Countdown
Ronan

The woods are dark. Almost impenetrable. I hate to admit it, but I understand why McNamara's team stopped earlier. It's nearly impossible to see in the dark, and only a few officers have night-vision goggles.

My flashlight throws a narrow beam ahead of me. It feels pitiful against the density of the trees and what could be hiding in them.

Tension thickens the air as we move single file through the undergrowth. I keep my place behind two officers, exactly as instructed, careful not to crowd them. The radio crackles with short bursts of code and updates I don't understand. I barely register them anyway.

Thandi is tattooed on every thought, every heartbeat, every breath that leaves my body. My side, rebandaged, throbs, but nothing compares to the pain in my chest.

The clock is ticking, and every minute without her feels heavier than the last.

I think of Equinox at the edge of the woods, waiting for their signal, and glance at my watch again.

Thirty more minutes.

Eighteen hundred more seconds until they can deploy.

I've never been good at waiting.

Doing? Now that's something else.

Branches whip at my face and arms as we push deeper. Others crack underfoot, every step sounding too loud, too careless in the dark. Somewhere ahead, a police dog whines, vanishing again into the undergrowth. Another dog answers, low and intent, the sound threading through the trees.

My heart pounds so hard I'm convinced everyone can hear it. I breathe through my nose, forcing myself not to call Thandi's name. Forcing myself not to think about her and Daysha in Damian's grip.

"There's the rock!" A voice crackles over my earpiece.

Adrenaline jolts through my veins.

"Yes!" McNamara hisses next to me.

We break into a sprint, rushing until we emerge into a clearing. Here, the moonlight breaks through the trees, interrupting the darkness. It spills over the ground, catching on an irregular shape ahead.

A gray rock juts from the earth, just as Thandi described it, jagged and improbable, more sculpture than organic outgrowth.

My heart breaks into a million pieces as I imagine her young, hurt, facing a monster, and yet still brave enough to notice the one thing that mattered.

She was right.

I saw the shadows in her eyes when she told McNamara and her parents. I know she doubted herself, but dear God, my baby was right.

McNamara lifts a hand, halting the group. The unit fans out. Two officers peel left, two right, creating a loose perimeter. Flashlights sweep the ground instead of the trees.

The dogs surge forward the moment they're released. One K9 drops its nose straight to the earth at the base of the rock, and its handler crouches beside it, murmuring encouragement. Another dog circles wider, pulling toward the far edge of the clearing, claws digging into the soil.

My pulse roars in my ears. "What now?" I ask McNamara.

The detective steps closer to the rock, scanning the ground. "Now we let them work," she murmurs. "See if they can pick up a scent."

Translation: More waiting.

I nod, throat tight, fists clenching at my sides. Fear presses in on my chest. I don't let myself think about how long it's been since Damian dragged Thandi away.

What if we waited too long?

What if the trail has already gone cold?

"Detective," the handler calls from the edge of the clearing. "I think we've got something."

My entire body tenses; I spin, pivoting towards him.

"Ronan—"

I'm already sprinting across the clearing before McNamara can finish. "What is it?" I demand. "Is it her?"

McNamara sighs as she comes up behind me. "What have we got, Wallace?"

"Over here." The young officer pushes the brush aside, revealing a patch of flattened grass in the thicker undergrowth. "Something stopped here. Trail's a bit muddled, but Roxo's never wrong. It's still workable."

Still workable.

My heart stutters.

Workable means not lost.

Workable means we're not too late.

McNamara straightens. "Got it," she says quietly. "K9s in the lead. Everyone else, fall back. Single file. Watch your step."

Roxo surges forward, leash snapping taut as Wallace disappears with him into the brush. The second K9 and her handler, Irina, follow close behind. The woods seem to close in around us as the rest of the unit reshapes itself in their wake.

McNamara casts a sharp look my way. "Stay with me."

I nod, jaw clenched, even as every instinct in my body screams to run.

The air is cold, biting at my cheeks, and I welcome the sting. It feels wrong to accept any comfort when Thandi still isn't safe. But at least now we have momentum. Compared to the slow, careful progress earlier, the dogs are moving at a clipped pace, pulling us deeper into the woods.

Every few minutes, the moon breaks through the clouds, cold and distant—so different from the one that shone over us at the New Moon Festival. So different from the night Thandi and I first declared our love for each other. Then it promised warmth, love, and safety.

Now, it just seems like a warning.

I frown, quickening my stride. I refuse to believe this is it. Thandi and I have come too far for this to be the end.

The path curves ahead, the trees growing denser. Without warning, our forward movement stops.

"Wallace. Status?" McNamara snaps into her earpiece.

"Not sure," comes the reply. "You might want to see this."

"Roger that."

My heart is in my throat as McNamara and I approach the handlers.

"Show me," McNamara says, and Wallace nods. His headlamp casts a circle of light at our feet.

"There's at least eight of these out here," he says, nudging a discarded WhiffRush inhaler with his boot. "Not all new."

He hesitates, then glances at me.

"Some are bloody."

Ice threads through my veins. "Blood?" I choke. "Dear God, is it Thandi's?"

Wallace shakes his head. "Impossible to say. The dogs can distinguish between animal and human blood, but they can't tell us who it belongs to."

So it could be hers.

She could already be hurt—or worse.

The air leaves my lungs. For a moment, I can't think, can't speak. I can't imagine a life without Thandi; without her gentle presence, without her love keeping me whole. My chest heaves.

"Hey." McNamara places a hand on my arm. Behind her, the dogs keep nosing through the bushes. "We can't afford to think the worst. Damian was still bleeding when he entered the minimart. The blood could be his."

She makes a weary sound. "Besides, Thandi's smart and resourceful as hell. She won't go down without a fight."

I draw in a shaky breath.

She's right.

My baby is the bravest person I know. I can't give up on her. Not now. Not ever.

"Alright," I say. "Where do we go from here?"

"We keep moving." McNamara's jaw tightens. "We've got twenty minutes before your firm can be called in." She meets my gaze. "I'll keep my word."

I swallow. "Thank you, Detective."

"Let's go. The unit will sweep—"

"Detective!"

A young officer with dark curls jogs toward us, breathless.

"We need you. There's a vehicle hidden back here."

"Looks like he switched cars," an older officer with craggy features kneels by the sedan's front tire.

More WhiffRush inhalers litter the ground, a scatter of neon detritus.

"I don't understand," I grit, turning to McNamara.

Another officer answers before she can. "The vehicle isn't abandoned. Not quite. The depressions in the grass under the tires suggest that Patrick frequents this area. This is his usual rendezvous point."

The officer points at the inhalers. "Clearly, this isn't some master camouflage operation. I think the terrain is just too difficult for an old Subaru like this. I'm guessing the second vehicle is a pickup or SUV."

"A larger vehicle would leave tracks, wouldn't it?" I press, frustration lancing through me. "A trail we could follow without all of this—" I gesture at the dogs, the officers combing the perimeter, the wasted minutes bleeding away.

Thandi's sweet face flashes in my mind.

We don't have time for this.

"It's not that simple." McNamara shakes her head. "This isn't dry dirt or fresh snow," she says. "It's leaf litter, damp soil, and mud that shifts and settles. Tires compress it, then it springs back. Wind, animals, moisture—all start erasing the evidence within minutes."

"So there's nothing?" The words explode from my lips.

"There's *something*," she corrects. "Just not the smoking gun you're hoping for. A larger vehicle might leave impressions, sure, but not consistently enough to track direction. That's why we still need the K9 units."

The words land like a blow. My jaw clenches, but I nod.

McNamara's voice softens. "We're closer than we were before. Even if it doesn't feel like it." She shoots me an understanding look. "And the clock hasn't run out yet."

Fear perches like a wraith on my shoulders, but I loosen my fists, forcing myself to accept what she's saying.

"Alright," I say. "Then let's keep going."

We're only five minutes into chasing the new trail when we stop. Again.

I curse under my breath.

"What now?" I ask McNamara.

She heads toward Wallace and the other K9 handler at the front.

Instead of advancing, the dogs hesitate, mincing forward, then doubling back. Roxo noses a discarded inhaler, then whines, pawing at his muzzle.

"Something's wrong," McNamara mutters.

Wallace scrubs a hand through his hair as we approach. "Sorry, Detective. I don't know what's going on with Roxo."

"What do you mean?" McNamara asks sharply.

"He had the trail for half a second, then—" Wallace throws up a hand in frustration. "Lost it."

"It's not just Roxo," Irina says grimly, bringing her dog to heel. "Saya keeps circling." Her brow furrows. "It's like they're … confused."

I follow her gaze. The shepherd's ears are pinned flat. She lets out another thin whine and drops her head, nose skimming over the ground, only to recoil as though burned.

Panic claws at my throat. I glance from one dog to the other as McNamara's earlier words echo in my head.

The dogs are our only chance of finding Thandi.

If they're compromised….

"Can we help them?" I ask. "Figure out what's happening?"

"It's not that simple," Wallace says. "We've hit a wall. Something's contaminated the trail. There's no neat fix for this kind of disruption. We can't just hit 'reset' on their noses."

"He's right," Irina says. "We're also at an extra disadvantage right now because the ground keeps getting softer. I'm guessing we're closer to the lake. That *should be* good news, but the moisture is dispersing any scent they might have locked onto."

"So what? We're just going to give up?" I pace, anguish and terror building inside of me until I'm ready to explode. "There has to be something we can do. What about another dog?"

"That could take hours," McNamara says bluntly. "And it wouldn't change what's happening here. Without eliminating the contaminant, any K9 we bring in will struggle."

I clench my fists. "But—"

Saya circles a discarded inhaler and nudges it with her nose. The instant she makes contact, she yelps, recoiling with a sharp whine.

"The fuck—" Irina drops to one knee. "Saya, what's wrong?"

I stare.

The answer hits me like a bolt of lightning.

"It's the inhalers," I say.

McNamara turns. "What?"

"The inhalers are affecting them," I repeat.

"What do you mean?" Wallace frowns, steadying Roxo as the dog whimpers again, restless and distressed.

"WhiffRush is dangerous because it doesn't just affect the nose," I say slowly. "It changes perception. That's what's happening to the dogs now."

"I don't get it," Irina says.

"It forces the brain to treat everything as urgent." I nod at the inhalers scattered in the dirt. "Imagine being trained your whole life to listen for one voice. Now, instead of a soloist, you're facing a whole damn choir, singing all at once."

McNamara frowns. "So what we're left with," she says quietly, "is no signal. Just noise."

I nod. "They're completely overwhelmed."

Silence settles over the clearing, thick and oppressive.

The most suffocating weight remains from what is unsaid:

Our chance to save Thandi and Daysha has just slipped through our fingers.

"Fuck!" A cry tears its way from my chest. I double over as my body, no, my soul is wracked with agony.

To come this far only to be thwarted by James' evil feels like the universe's most cruel joke. Even humiliated and impotent, he's found a way to steal everything precious from me. First Mom, and now Thandi.

My sorrow builds to a crescendo. The world telescopes as sound drifts in and out around me.

"Alright," McNamara says. "Since we can't rely on the dogs to get us to the lake, we pivot."

Wallace nods. "Copy that."

"Get Parks back on the line and strip out everything that can't support a structure," McNamara continues. "I want a short list, not guesses. We need to tighten our radius."

"On it," someone calls from behind us.

McNamara barrels on. "Run property and forestry records in parallel—any old cabins, shacks, or inholdings near water. Flag everything that could shelter three people."

The rest fades into static around me. Each new command feels like another rush of sand through the hourglass, measuring what little time Thandi has left. I hear the team chatter about drones and thermal cameras, about deployment windows and visibility—all gambles, which need more time, more waiting. More seconds Thandi doesn't have to give.

McNamara is still in the middle of the clearing, calm and authoritative, issuing rapid-fire orders. I'm grateful for her persistence, but the knot in my stomach doesn't loosen.

I'm not law enforcement. I don't know their protocols or their equipment. But I *am* a scientist. Questioning assumptions is my business.

I stare up at the night sky. I'd feel a hell of a lot better about drones if the night weren't so dark, if the canopy weren't so thick. And thermal imaging only works if you know where to point it.

My panic intensifies, crystallizing into desperation.

We need something more precise.

More efficient.

We can't afford to lose another half hour, literally wandering in the wilderness.

I pace, forcing myself to think. My gaze moves from the dense vegetation to the trail of WhiffRush inhalers scattered over the clearing. At first, my mind freezes, too locked in panic and terror to form anything coherent.

I close my eyes and draw in a deep breath.

Slowly, the trembling in my hands eases. The fog lifts.

Of course, it's Thandi's voice that comes to me in the pit of my despair, wrenching me back into the light. My heart begins to race. Not with fear this time, but with something even more dangerous:

Hope.

The idea is wild. Totally improbable.

Which means it just might work.

And it's not like I have anything left to lose.

For it to succeed, though, I'll need a secret weapon.

I jog to McNamara, already reaching for my phone.

"Ronan." The detective starts. "What is it?"

"I have to call Equinox," I say.

I meet her gaze. "I think I may have something that can help."

Grace
Thandi

"Damian, why don't you say grace?"

Damian beams. "I'd love to, Mama."

I can't take my eyes off the hunting knife on one side of his plate. The keys are on the other—danger and freedom displayed in a single place setting. Any doubt I might have been clinging to evaporates.

Playing house won't be enough.

The only path to safety still runs through Damian.

He clasps his hands and squeezes his eyes shut. "Dear God, thank you for this yummy meal, for Mama Lana, and for my baby sister. Please watch over us and help us be a happy family forever and ever. Amen."

"Amen," Daysha and I echo.

A heavy silence settles over the room.

Daysha's hand finds mine under the table—small, cold, desperate—and I squeeze back, letting her know that I'm here, that I'll protect her no matter what.

Damian giggles.

The sound is high and eerie, wildly at odds with our drab surroundings and the tension threading through every breath.

"Mama's home," he coos, gripping his knife and fork. "We're all together now." His gaze locks on mine, burning with a misplaced devotion that makes my skin crawl, and my stomach churn. "Now we can have dinner like before."

Before what? I wonder.

Before, Tess?

Before Daysha?

Before his father shattered everything, we were?

"Yes," I manage. "Now we have dinner. Can you please pass me the salmon, Damian?"

"Yes, Mama."

I reach for the plate, and my blood runs cold as our fingers brush. I stiffen, fighting the instinct to recoil. The plate dips in my hands, wobbling dangerously until Daysha steadies it.

I shoot her a grateful look. "Thank you, baby."

She nods, eyes wide.

"Would you like some spinach?" I ask, loading both our plates with the salmon.

"Yes, please," she whispers.

"Good." I meet her eyes. "Everyone should clean their plates to grow healthy and strong."

"Like me, Mama?" Damian pushes his plate forward.

I bite my lip. "Yes. Just like you, honey."

We eat.

Damian hums happily, a tuneless little song, while cutlery clinks against the plates. I keep my voice steady—*maternal*—as I guide him through the meal, reminding him to sit up straight, to use his spoon, to chew slowly. He beams every time I praise him, soaking it in.

Daysha is quiet beside me, but I'm grateful to see her eating. I gently remind her to pace herself. After nearly a week of deprivation, too much too fast would only hurt her—and we won't survive this if one of us is sick.

She spears a carrot and glances at me. I offer a reassuring smile before turning my attention back to Damian.

"Mama's home!" he sings again, rocking in his chair, kicking his feet beneath the table.

I suppress a shudder.

My eyes never leave the keys resting beside his plate.

A twisted sense of déjà vu hits me. This meal is a gross carica-ture of my dinner with Ronan, the kids, and my parents. There's no warmth, no radical acceptance here.

No safety.

Only delusion.

And danger.

"Look, Mama," Damian says, beaming. "I cleaned my plate just like you asked. Now I'll grow big and strong!"

He flings his hands out with a flourish, and his elbow clips the small bowl of gravy beside him.

It tips.

Warm liquid spills across the table.

Damian's panic is instant.

"Oh no. *Oh no no no*," he wails. "I'm sorry. I spilled something." He rocks sharply back and forth. "Papa will be mad. Please, Mama, I don't want to go to the shed."

He grabs one of the paper towel squares I laid out as a make-shift napkin and presses it into the spreading mess. It soaks through immediately. With every second, his movements grow more frantic.

"Stop—stop—" He shoves himself back from the table so hard it shudders. The hunting knife skids, scraping against the wood. The keys bounce once, then clatter to the floor.

Daysha whimpers. She shrinks in her chair, eyes brimming with tears. She tenses, as if ready to bolt.

My heart thumps as the fragile balance we achieved careens into chaos. If Daysha runs, I don't know what Damian will do. The knife, teetering on the edge of the table, looms in my vision. I remember Spotsylvania and how fast Damian unraveled when he was cornered.

If he breaks his childlike persona, it's over.

I don't think. I move.

I'm on my feet and across the table in an instant, wrapping my arms around Damian and pulling him tight.

"Stop," I gasp, holding him fast. "It's okay. It's okay." I rock him gently, my arms locked around his trembling frame. "No one's going to the shed. Do you hear me? No one."

For a moment, Damian resists, still trapped in the spiral. He pants, breath ragged and uneven. His hand—slick with his own blood—slides toward the knife.

I freeze.

Every muscle in my body locks as I brace myself, my mouth already forming the words I'll have to say to Daysha—that I'll hold him back as long as I can, that she must grab the keys and run.

Then something shifts.

Like a switch flipping, Damian's body goes slack in my arms.

"No shed?" He rests his head against my chest.

My eyes fall shut as I draw in a shaking breath. *God. That was too close.*

"No shed," I say, and my voice is so strained, so hoarse, I barely recognize it. Gingerly, I reach out and pat Damian's hair.

He tightens his arms around me, burrowing closer.

"Thank you, Mama."

"I need my cherry now," Damian announces. He pulls away from me and stands.

The words are calm, almost matter-of-fact, but his body betrays him. He's jittery, his movements stilted as he crosses the room to the bag bulging with WhiffRush inhalers.

My stomach clenches as I watch him rummage inside, his fingers shaking. He pulls one out, raises it to his mouth, dispenses several pumps, and lets the empty plastic tumble to the floor.

"No shed," he mutters, already reaching for another.

He rocks back on his heels, closes his eyes, and takes another sharp breath. The words "no shed, no shed" remain a mantra on his lips as the cherry-scented air rushes into his lungs.

It's still not enough.

Damian grabs a third inhaler, and this time when he sucks in, something in him eases. His shoulders sag, and his frantic energy dissipates, replaced by brittle calm.

He releases a dry, rasping cough. For a second, his wheezing is so loud, I can hear the breath rattling in his chest.

I'm stunned. Three inhalers in less than five minutes is unheard of. I have seen what WhiffRush does to the brain, but watching him now, I cannot imagine what it is doing to his lungs. The stamina he showed in the fight with Ronan feels unreal in hindsight.

And yet Damian seems either unable or unwilling to register his body's warning signals.

That's when I understand.

It doesn't matter. He rushed to the FreshMart with a bullet lodged in his shoulder, and even now he smiles past the blood dripping from his fingers, because the worst of his anguish has never been physical.

It is emotional.

To Damian, WhiffRush is more than an indulgence or an addiction. It's medication.

When he is overwhelmed, when the past presses too close, this is how he survives: by numbing himself into something more manageable.

The realization terrifies me almost as much as the hunting knife. Because it means this moment of calm is borrowed. It is finite, measured not in minutes but in the number of inhalers left at the bottom of a grocery bag.

I need to think fast before the bubble bursts.

"Daysha, why don't you help me clean up?" I keep my voice neutral.

I keep my movements unhurried, guiding Daysha to the kitchen with me. From the corner of my eye, I note Damian drifting to the fireplace, humming to himself.

I open one cabinet, then another. Inside, I find paper towels, a half-empty bottle of dish soap, an unused bottle of vinegar, and a box of baking soda. I pull them out one by one, setting them on the counter as if this is nothing more than routine cleanup, even as my eyes catalog everything with urgency.

I don't know exactly what I am looking for, only that I will recognize it when I see it: something that could be used as a weapon. Anything that could buy us a second when we need it.

Daysha stays glued to my side. She peers into the open cupboard, then up at me.

"What are we looking for?" she whispers.

"For cleaning supplies," I murmur back, loud enough for Damian to hear. My hand closes around a bottle near the back of the shelf. "And," I lower my voice, "anything that helps us stay safe."

Daysha's brave, sweet spirit immediately shines through. A determined frown crosses her features. Leaning in close, she tugs on my t-shirt.

"Ms. Thandi," she whispers, "I want to help."

I glance over my shoulder.

Damian is sitting by the fire now, a faint smile tugging at his mouth. Dazed, he stares into the hearth, still under the heady spell of WhiffRush. Even from here, the cloying cherry residue lingers in the air between us. Dinner and the spill seem completely forgotten.

His back is to the table.

To the hunting knife—

And the keys on the floor, catching the firelight with every flicker.

"We need to get those keys," I whisper to Daysha. I draw in a breath, praying that I'm not making a terrible mistake—praying that I'm not putting her in harm's way. "If I distract him, do you think you can grab them and put them in your pocket? You'll have to be quick."

Daysha's lips tremble. Then she squares her shoulders. "I can do it," she says fiercely.

I pull her into a hug, holding her tight. "That's my girl. I'm so proud of you," I murmur. "I'll be right here. I'll make sure you're safe. Just wait for my signal."

She nods against my shoulder. "Okay. I trust you, Ms. Thandi," she whispers.

Warmth rushes through me at the weight of her innocence, her trust, but also her resilience. I think of her mirror, of how even alone, she used everything she had to keep fighting. Now it's my turn to see us through.

"Mama, is it bad that I don't want Papa to come back?"

I freeze.

Damian's voice shatters the quiet. He's half-turned toward us, his brow furrowed. The firelight limns his profile, throwing the acne scars on his cheek into sharp relief.

Daysha's glance darts to mine.

My hand shakes as I reach beneath the sink. My eyes widen as I pull out a bottle of bleach.

"It's not bad to want to be away from people who hurt us," I say slowly. "But let's not ruin our special evening by thinking about Papa." I force a smile. "Your sister and I are here. And since everyone has been so good, we can have dessert."

Damian's expression darkens, something flickering behind his eyes. For a moment, he loses his childlike wonder.

Then his face brightens again.

"Good!" he declares, turning back to the fire. "He's sleeping now anyway."

"Sleeping?" I repeat, my attention still fixed on the unexpected bounty of cleaning supplies spread across the counter.

"Mm-hmm." Damian chirps, tilting his head. "He was very tired. I don't think he'll wake up again."

Cold fingers squeeze my heart. I think of the mound of earth outside, of the loose dirt shifting beneath my feet.

God. Did Damian—?

My gaze drifts once more to the hunting knife resting at the edge of the table.

We have to get out of here.

Now.

I remember the two cans of peaches I spotted while making dinner. I grab them and dump them into the small pot on the stove. There is nothing to make a crust, but I find a half-empty bag of hardened brown sugar in the cupboard. I break it apart and pour it in with the peaches, bringing everything to a slow simmer.

This will have to do for a makeshift peach cobbler.

"Okay, honey," I whisper to Daysha. "This is what we're going to do. When I bring Damian the cobbler, I want you to grab the keys. As soon as you have them, come straight to us. We'll eat together by the fire and keep him away from the table." I search her face. "Are you sure you're still up for this?"

She swallows but nods quickly. "I'm ready."

"Good," I say, tenderness flooding my chest. "You're amazing." I bump her gently with my elbow. "Help me stir? Make sure all the sugar melts."

She flashes me a small smile and grips the wooden spoon. I keep one eye on her as I turn back to the cleaning supplies spread across the counter.

This part is for me alone.

My fingers close on the bleach and then the bottle of vinegar.

I break the seal on the vinegar, then pour some bleach into an old mason jar. I set both aside next to a bowl for later.

"Dessert's ready, Mama," Daysha calls out brightly, her eyes shining with determination.

"Good," I say, meeting her gaze.

It's now or never.

Hail Mary

Ronan

"Boss, we've retrieved the asset."

Ethan steps into the clearing, the rest of the Equinox team flanking him like shadows. In his hands is a small steel case, solid on three sides. Its muted glint catches the moonlight as he advances.

McNamara's unit parts without a word, clearing a path for him. I meet my head of security halfway, heart thumping in my chest.

"Ready?" Ethan asks, and I nod. I can't find my voice. Too much is riding on this for me to speak.

"Max," Ethan jerks his head at a muscular operative to his left, clad in a Kevlar vest over a thermal jacket. A comm wire disappears behind his ear.

He steps forward, gloved hands moving briskly over the complex locking mechanism. A soft beep punctuates the stillness before the latch swings open.

At first—nothing.

The entire world seems to stand still.

Then, a small pink nose peeks out, followed by a white-furred body.

ISO E Super stands on his hind legs and gives a squeak, his tiny cape lifting in the wind behind him.

The clearing falls deadly silent.

And then, from McNamara:

"You have got to be kidding me."

I raise a hand, a soft puff of air gusting past my lips. "Hear me out," I say quickly. "This is not as absurd as it seems."

McNamara folds her arms. "I'm listening."

"We lost the K9s," I say. "But mice have nearly ten times as many olfactory receptors as dogs. And ISO E is even more specialized."

I extend my hand, and Thandi's mouse races up my arm, nestling on my shoulder. "He's immune to the WhiffRush inhalers."

Wallace frowns. "How?"

"ISO's job is to isolate complex scent compounds," I say. "Allosteric modulators, just like the ones in WhiffRush. If those scrambled his signals, he'd be useless. So Thandi engineered him to be resistant."

I glance toward the tree line. "He can pick up where Roxo and Saya left off."

"Let me get this straight," McNamara says slowly. "You're telling me we're trusting a two-ounce rodent to lead us in the dark to Damian Patrick?"

I let out a short breath. "I know how it sounds. But no one takes Thandi's safety more seriously than I do."

My throat tightens, and I pause, forcing my voice to steady. "The truth is, we're at a dead end. We don't have the luxury of waiting for your equipment to magically point us in the right direction."

I jerk my thumb toward the woods. "We need a clean, reliable lead. ISO E can give us that."

I notch my chin. "Unless you have a better idea?"

McNamara is quiet. She sighs, tipping her head at Ethan. "What's your assessment?"

"Aerial and thermal are viable, but not optimal." Ethan folds his arms, widening his stance. "Your drones are likely ten to fifteen minutes out. Between the canopy, low visibility, and a remote pilot unfamiliar with the terrain, we'd be flying blind. If there's water nearby, it'll throw off the heat signatures. Thermal would light up every squirrel and possum in the woods."

He shrugs once. "If expedient extraction is the priority, I'd give the mouse a sixty-five percent chance of producing a viable lead faster than any other option we have."

"Amazing," Wallace whistles under his breath.

He looks to McNamara, voice rising with confidence. "Call me biased, Detective, but I think we should give it a shot. I wouldn't be in this job if I didn't think our animals could deliver." He tightens his hold on Roxo's leash. What do we have to lose? Tap the mouse in."

McNamara shakes her head, a short laugh escaping her. "All right," she says. "I'm convinced." She gestures toward me. "Show me what he can do."

Max steps forward immediately. From one pocket, he produces a length of thin black line attached to a miniature harness. He pulls out a small Ziploc of treats from his other pocket and hands it to me.

I lift ISO E from my shoulder and fit the harness around his torso, clipping the line into place.

Max steps back as I lower the mouse to the ground.

For a moment, ISO is perfectly still.

His nose twitches.

Then he leans forward, whiskers vibrating, tiny body angling toward the grass. He takes a few tentative steps, pauses, adjusts— then begins to move with purpose, tracing an invisible thread only he can see.

Wallace drops into a crouch beside me. "So how does this work?" he murmurs. "I don't see a scent article."

My lip quirks as I point at one of the discarded inhalers. "We'll use those."

"Seriously?"

I nod. "The molecules in them are almost identical to those he tracks in the lab."

ISO dashes across the clearing and veers, executing a quick end run around the discarded inhalers. He moves fast now, confident, nose skimming the ground as the leash traces a loose arc behind him.

Tiny squeaks burst from him as he goes—sharp, triumphant— echoing faintly through the trees as he finds each inhaler.

Wallace lets out a breath. "Well, I'll be damned," he murmurs.

ISO circles back at last, pausing at my feet, whiskers still vibrating with energy.

"Good work, buddy." I crouch, offering him a treat. He snatches it between his paws instantly.

I scoop him up, settling him into my jacket pocket, the leash feeding through my fingers. He's fully primed now, locked onto his mission.

I pivot, turning to McNamara and the rest of the team.

"Ready?" I ask softly.

Breathe
Thandi

"Peach cobbler is ready," I say, beaming down at Damian.

I balance two bowls in my hands, my body angled to block his line of sight to the table. This close to the hearth, the heat of the fire makes my sweats feel thick and oppressive against my skin.

Damian jerks to attention, eyes wide with wonder. "For me, Mama?"

"Yes, son." I smile. "Just for you. For being such a good boy today." I move closer, lifting both bowls in offering. "May I join you?"

"Of course, Mama." He scoots over immediately, making room beside him on the old tufted bench.

"Thank you." I hand him the bowl of warm, sweet fruit. "Your sister is washing her hands, and then she'll come join us, too," I say as I settle beside him.

This is it.

I can barely hear my own words over the blood rushing in my ears. Everything depends on the next few moments. I refuse to think about what will happen if we fail. Instead, I think of Ronan—and of Dad, with his unwavering optimism.

Neither of them would give up hope, no matter how impossible the odds might seem.

That means we can't either.

I glance over my shoulder and nod imperceptibly at Daysha. She bites her lip, then lifts her chin once in acknowledgment.

"Oh, good," Damian coos. He starts to twist around to look behind him, but I press a hand firmly to his uninjured shoulder, stopping him mid-movement.

"How would you like it if I told you a story?" I ask.

"A story, Mama?" Damian watches me with trembling excitement. "Like at bedtime?"

"Just like at bedtime," I say gently. "But we won't go to sleep yet."

"No sleep yet," Damian agrees solemnly. "Not like Papa."

A chill rushes through me, but I force myself to stay calm. I count under my breath, listening for Daysha's footfalls, praying she reaches the keys safely. I do not dare turn around. I cannot risk drawing Damian's attention to her.

"What story are you going to tell, Mama?"

"Hm?" I pull my focus back to his expectant face. I had blurted out the idea of a story without thinking, too intent on diverting his attention. Now my mind stutters, thoughts tangling uselessly.

"The story is..." I trail off, grasping for something—anything—when Dad's voice, strong and gentle, rises in my memory.

Suddenly, I know what to do.

"The name of the story," I say, clinking our bowls together, "is *Stone Soup*. Have you heard of it?"

Damian shakes his head, his mouth forming a perfect O of wonder. "No, Mama. How can soup come from a stone?"

"That's because it's a special soup," I tell him, keeping my voice warm, "where everyone works together to make it delicious." I meet his eyes. "Just like you, your sister, and I are working together now as a team. As a family."

"Just like a family," Damian echoes. He spoons the cobbler into his mouth. "Tell me the story, Mama."

I nod. "Once upon a time," I begin, telling it just as Dad once told it to me. Of course, he put his own spin on it, replacing the three soldiers in the original with a traveling band of three reggae musicians.

I tell that version now, my throat aching, my eyes going blurry as I think about my parents and how much love they poured into me, even when so much had already been taken from them.

The opposite of a man like Arnold Patrick, who chose only pain and selfishness.

I keep speaking. The three musicians have just gotten to the village when Daysha presses against my side, her bowl of cobbler trembling in her lap. She squeezes my hand so tightly her nails dig into my skin.

Our eyes meet for a second.

She did it.

I draw her closer, kiss her temple, then lace my fingers through hers. God, she is amazing.

I don't pause in the story, but for the first time, real hope swells in my chest. We're almost there. We only need to see our plan through.

I continue, my voice lifting as the musicians ask the villagers for ingredient after ingredient, each request sparking curiosity, then generosity, until the soup becomes something shared—made richer by everyone's willingness to give.

Damian is rapt. He fires off question after question, wanting to know what the soup tastes like, how the villagers celebrate, what the reggae musicians' island songs sound like.

When I finish, he releases a deep, satisfied sigh.

"Thank you so much, Mama. I love this story." His eyes shine as he looks into the fire. By now his plate is empty. I hand him mine, mostly untouched, and he accepts it with both hands.

"This is how it's supposed to be," he murmurs. "How a real family is supposed to be."

"Exactly." I smile, though my breath is coming faster, and a cold sheen of sweat breaks over my skin. My heart starts to gallop despite my efforts to calm it.

This is it—the moment of truth.

"Now," I continue, "we should work together to clean up. Everyone will have a special task—just like in *Stone Soup*." I tilt my head. "How does that sound, son?"

Damian brightens, sitting up straighter on the bench. "A special task?" he asks eagerly. "What do I get to do, Mama?"

"You can help in the kitchen." I nod in that direction. "It's an important job. I need you to make sure the pots and bowls are put away properly. And when you're finished, I need you to mix the two cleaners I've set aside and wipe down the counters."

Damian's chest puffs out with pride. "I can do that," he says at once.

"I know you can." I squeeze his shoulder. "Your sister and I will tidy up the living area while you work. We'll all be done in no time."

"Okay, Mama," Damian agrees, already rising to his feet. "I'll do it really well."

"I know you will," I say, watching him hurry to the kitchen.

The minute Damian turns his back to us, I herd Daysha to the front door. "The keys, sweetie," I whisper, my voice urgent.

She fumbles in her pocket and drops the cold metal into my palm.

Behind us, water begins to run. Damian hums to himself as he washes the empty bowls, the sound oddly cheerful as it drifts across the cabin.

I try the first key.

It doesn't work.

I try another.

Still wrong.

The water shuts off. Ceramic clinks as Damian wipes the bowls dry and stacks them neatly in the cupboard. He moves to the jars of vinegar and bleach I've set aside.

Each one on its own is ordinary, but the minute he mixes them like I asked, the cabin will be filled with toxic chlorine gas.

I'm no murderer, but I've apportioned just enough to make his eyes water, to leave him gasping and coughing—to irritate lungs already inflamed by WhiffRush.

There's only one problem:

If Daysha and I don't get out of here fast, it'll hurt us too.

"Come on," I mutter, my hands slick with sweat. The keys slip, and my heart lurches as they drop from my fingers. I duck at the last second, catching them before they can clatter to the floor.

I steal a glance at the kitchen.

Damian is pulling out a bowl and uncapping the bleach, a song still on his lips.

"Hurry, Ms. Thandi," Daysha whispers, her voice trembling.

I jam the next key into the lock and twist.

A click.

Then release.

"Daysha, run now!" I yell just as Damian begins pouring the vinegar.

We fling the door open and burst into the cold night air. Our hands are locked together as we race over the uneven ground. Pine needles slide beneath our feet, making the path treacherous. Frigid air cuts through my thin T-shirt, but I ignore it. Our breaths plume white in the moonlight as we push deeper into the darkness.

For a moment, nothing happens.

Then a plaintive wail tears through the night.

It echoes off the trees—wild and desperate.

"No! Mama, please!" Damian's anguished cry reverberates through the stillness. "Don't leave me again. I promise I'll be good, I—" His words dissolve into a violent fit of coughing.

"I'm scared, Ms. Thandi," Daysha whimpers, twisting to look back as we duck past the woodpile.

"It's okay, honey," I pant, tightening my grip on her hand. "Don't look back. Just keep going."

Ahead of us, the forest looms dense and forbidding. To the right lies the path Damian led me along earlier—firmer ground, clearer direction. To the left, the earth darkens and softens, slick with standing water, the lake glinting silver beneath the stars.

Which way?

Back the way we came, where it might be easier to find our way out—or toward the water, where Damian is less likely to follow?

A furious roar erupts behind us.

Damian bursts from the cabin, still coughing, charging toward us. The knife flashes in his hand.

I make a split-second decision. "Left!"

Daysha and I pivot, plunging through brackish puddles and skidding in the mud. She keeps pace at first, but she's smaller, younger, and has been trapped for days.

She's flagging. She won't last much longer.

"I know you're tired, baby," I urge, breath tearing from my chest as we keep sprinting through the darkness. "But don't stop. Just a little farther."

Daysha nods, gasping. She clings tight to my fingers.

I don't know exactly what waits ahead of us or how this will end. I only know we need to get as close as possible to the water—and the shed. If it comes down to it, every instinct in me says Damian will not follow us there.

It's a gamble.

But we are out of time.

We keep running, the lake drawing closer with every breath.

We crash through a curtain of reeds, and the lake opens up before us, black and glassy under the moon. The ground angles sharply at the edge, mud sucking at our shoes where the water laps against the shore. I skid on wet stone, and Daysha nearly goes down with me.

I brace, hauling us both upright as I struggle to get my bearings. Above us, the shed creaks and groans, swaying faintly on its stilts. Up close, it is even more forbidding—more ghastly—than it looked from a distance.

A dark shape lifts abruptly from the water with a splash, wings skimming the surface as it disappears into the reeds.

Daysha and I both startle.

Christ. I press a hand to my chest.

It's only a duck.

We dart forward, searching beneath the shed's spindly stilts for a way inside. I find an opening to the west of the structure, half-choked by weeds.

I know in an instant that my plan won't work.

The stairs have long rotted away, and even if we could climb inside, the entire structure is so unstable it would likely collapse around us.

For a heartbeat, I think I've made a terrible mistake.

Then I see it.

Half-hidden beneath the sagging stilts, slick with algae and tethered by a frayed rope, a small dinghy bobs against the shore.

Thank you, Tess. I lift my gaze to the dark sky as relief crashes into me so hard it almost hurts.

Maybe we still have a chance.

"Daysha," I gasp, steering her toward the boat. "Okay. Okay. We can do this. Come on, honey. We're getting in."

Murky water sloshes over my sneakers as I step closer. I brace one hand against the curved wood of the dinghy, holding it steady. With the other, I guide Daysha forward.

She lifts one leg gingerly into the boat, then hesitates.

"You're coming too, right, Ms. Thandi?" Her face is pale, her lips trembling in the moonlight.

"Of course, baby." I force a reassuring smile, even as my heart pounds. "I'm right behind you."

Daysha nods and steps into the dinghy, settling onto the narrow bench in the middle. I wedge the single splintered oar into her lap.

"Hold onto this as tight as you can," I tell her. "You think you can do that for me?"

"Okay," she says in a small voice, wrapping both arms around the paddle and pressing it to her chest.

"That's my brave girl." I brush my thumb gently along her cheek.

Leaning forward, I brace myself against the bow. The moon has climbed high above the trees, hovering like a jaundiced eye above us—cold, watchful, and unforgiving. Even in its pale light, I can see how badly my hands are trembling.

An owl hoots somewhere in the distance.

Then something crashes through the undergrowth.

I glance over my shoulder, and my blood turns to ice.

Damian is racing towards the shore, his face twisted with rage. The knife is a silver flash in his hand as he barrels toward the water's edge, heedless of the mud, the branches, the slick ground beneath his feet.

He's close.

Too close.

There's no time to climb in.

I have to make sure he can't reach Daysha.

I start pushing the dinghy toward open water, but the mud fights me at every step. My shoes sink to the ankle. I stumble, dropping to one knee.

"Ms. Thandi, hurry!" Daysha screams.

I scrabble for purchase, every muscle straining. The rough wood bites into my shoulder, but I don't stop. I can't stop.

"Hold on, honey!" I shout, panic bleeding into my voice as I shove harder, fighting the weeds and suctioning mud. The dinghy lurches, resists—

"Mama!" Damian roars as he tears through the rushes.

"Please," I gasp. "*Move.*"

My hands burn. My shoulder screams. The boat sways, shudders—

Then it breaks free.

The dinghy surges forward, gliding into deeper water as Daysha drifts out of reach of the shore.

"No! Ms. Thandi, please get in!" Daysha sobs, her small body shaking.

"I'm coming," I pant, stumbling after the canoe. Exhaustion deadens my limbs, slowing me as much as the muck, the weeds, and the terror clawing at my chest.

"Ms. Thandi!" she cries. "Please, please come!"

"Yes," I gasp, forcing my way through the reeds, my legs barely responding. I can feel the mud loosening its grip on my feet. Just a few more steps....

Behind me, the splashing slows.

Damian is in the water now, but only to his knees. He has stopped advancing. His gaze flickers wildly, darting past me to the shed looming in the darkness, its warped silhouette reflected in the lake. He shrinks back a half-step, breath hitching, eyes glassy with fear.

"Mama," he calls, his voice breaking. "Mama, please."

I turn forward again, my heart hammering. This is it. If I can just reach the dinghy—

"MAMA!"

The scream tears through the night.

I feel him before I see him.

Hands clamp around my waist, dragging me backward with brutal force. I cry out as my footing gives way, the world tilting violently. The sky spins above me for a heartbeat.

Then the lake surges over my head.

Cold water rushes into my mouth and nose.

I can't breathe.

My body thrashes as I'm pulled under, pressure crushing my chest, my lungs burning as they scream for air. For one terrible moment, there is only darkness and panic and the roar of water in my ears.

Then I break the surface.

I gasp violently, coughing as I'm hauled backward through the shallows. Reeds scrape my skin raw. My head knocks against submerged stones.

The shore slams into my back.

Damian wrenches me fully onto the mud, rolling me flat as I cough and retch, my vision swimming. Everything sounds distant, muffled—except Daysha's screams, splitting the darkness.

"Bad Mama," he snarls, his voice no longer childlike, no longer pleading. He straddles me, pinning my arms with his knees. His face looms above mine, twisted with fury and desperation. His lips peel back in a grotesque grin.

"This time," he pants, raising his arm, "I'll make it so you never leave me again."

The knife flashes in the moonlight.

Behind him, the lake ripples. Farther out, beyond Damian's reach, the dinghy drifts steadily into the night.

Daysha is safe.

In the space of a single heartbeat, I see Ronan's face, my mother's, my father's, Dani's, Fia's.

And finally, Tess.

I understand, then, that only one of us will make it home tonight.

The moon glares down at me, but the stars are gentler, scattered across the velvet sky. My breath sighs out of my lungs.

I'm sorry I couldn't finish it, sis.

But Daysha is safe. That's all that matters.

So I close my eyes.

And wait for what comes next.

Razor's Edge
Ronan

"I can't believe this is working," McNamara mutters.

We've covered more ground in the last twenty minutes than in the past hour, thanks to ISO.

The little guy rides tucked in my chest pocket. The line is slack in my hand. Every so often, ISO squeaks when he detects another molecular breadcrumb. I stop, let him down, and he darts through the darkness, mapping our next stretch with precision.

I reward him, scoop him back up, and we move again.

Soon, we settle into a rhythm. ISO may be tiny, but he's relentless. He never doubles back or hesitates. He just presses forward, treating the wilderness like his own personal maze.

No one speaks. The only sounds are the crunch of boots and the rasping of breath in the cold night air. McNamara keeps pace on my right, Ethan on my left. Their faces are equally grim in the thin glare of the team's headlamps.

We push through a knot of oaks and poplars until the ground turns spongy beneath our feet. The air shifts into cooler, heavier currents, and the vegetation thins.

All at once, the forest breaks open, and the lake spreads out before us, water glinting blackly under the stars. Pale sycamores cluster along the shoreline, their peeling bark mottled like camouflage. In the distance, darker shapes rise—rotting trunks, bare branches, and the skeletal remains of trees long dead.

I skid to a stop, pulse hammering. "We found it," I gasp.

We made it. Now Thandi just has to hold on long enough for me to reach her.

"Unbelievable," McNamara says at my elbow. She props her hands on her hips, surveying the watery vista.

ISO squeaks emphatically, jolting my attention back to him.

My lips quirk. "Sorry, buddy. Forgot to thank you for leading us through that last stretch."

I slip him a treat. As soon as he gobbles it up, I tuck him back into my pocket, fingers trembling. I'm already shifting back to McNamara when Ethan steps up beside her.

He looks past the thin line of sycamores.

"Canopy's opened up," he says. "Sightlines are clearer here than they were in the woods, though the far shoreline's still cluttered. No man-made structures visible. And with a lake this size, thermal's still a wash." He tilts his head. "What's your play, Detective?"

McNamara presses the ball of her foot into the marshy soil. "This ground wouldn't support a sandcastle, much less a cabin. My guess is Damian's holed up at a higher elevation on the western side—on drier ground." She lifts her chin. "We'll head that way, but get the drones up to confirm."

"Ronan." She pivots to me. "We'll take it from here."

I swallow. "What does that mean?"

"It means we're going in."

McNamara waves the veteran officer over. "Sullivan, you're with me on point. Wallace and Irina—Roxo and Saya will form the containment flank."

"Got it." Wallace gives a quick thumbs-up.

"Mandy, you're on drone duty."

"Yes, ma'am."

The detective circles back to Ethan and me. "Ronan, I need you with your security team in the rear. The less I worry about you getting hurt, the faster we can extract Thandi and Daysha."

I want to protest and argue for a place with better sightlines to Thandi, but I stifle it. She's right. I'm the liability here.

"Max, let's get ISO back in his carrier," I say, cupping our unlikely hound in my hands. "Looks like his work here is done."

Max nods, and once ISO E is secured, he takes him from me without a word.

By now, the entire MPD unit has assembled into their respective positions. Roxo and Saya pant softly, ears pointed, bodies alert as they tug at their leashes. McNamara adjusts her earpiece and glances over her shoulder.

"Ready?"

As I'll ever be.

I jerk my chin up. "Let's do it."

"Alright, team, let's roll out."

Everything seems to intensify then, the world concentrated and refracted through the prism of my fear—and the desperate hope that we can still save Thandi and Daysha. Ethan is at my side, shadowing my every step. Ahead, McNamara's team falls into the silence of a team deeply in sync.

The shoreline changes as we head further west. We're still on lowland, but far from the dense curtain of green we navigated before. The lake is deeper, blacker here, and far larger than it initially appeared. The air is musty and humid, and the grass gives way to clotted weeds and rushes. Sinking trees lift naked branches to the sky in an eerie, surrealist landscape.

I shudder, unable to reconcile the presence of so much water with the stark absence of life.

Above us, the drones wink in and out of sight. We move at a clip, punishing not in its intensity, but in the delicacy required to navigate the variable terrain. I grimace as my boot sinks into another fetid puddle of water.

"You okay?" Ethan asks.

I grunt, unable to shake the dread seeping into my bones even deeper than the dank or cold.

"About half a mile before we hit drier ground," McNamara says over the comm. "Parks says the cattails will thin out and the trees will start to close in when we're near."

I look up, instinctively scanning the shoreline for the transition she's noted. That's when I see the drones.

They're no longer combing the terrain in regular sweeps ahead of us. Two break formation and fly over the lake, slowing as they reach a point roughly halfway between our location and the distant shore. They hover there, holding their position, suspended over the dark water.

"Detective." Mandy's voice breaks over the line. "We've got something out here."

"Report," McNamara fires back.

"There's a vessel on the water. One person aboard. Small. Female. Breathing."

Hope soars and careens in the same heartbeat.

Just one?

Daysha?

Or Thandi?

As one, the officers break into a run. We surge after them, footsteps thudding against the earth.

"Who is it?" I press the comm unit tight to my lips. "Who's in the boat?" I shout. "Someone—say something!"

An eternity passes before Mandy's ragged breathing explodes over the line. Wind rushes through the connection. She says something, but it's partially swallowed by Roxo and Saya's barking.

"Mandy, what's our status?" McNamara snaps.

"We've got visual," Mandy says, breathless. "It's the child. I repeat—Daysha Howard is in the vessel."

Daysha only.

A cold sweat breaks over my skin.

Good. She's safe.

But God—my God—where is Thandi?

I no longer have a heart, just a gaping hollow in my chest where she should be. My eyes burn. I want to scream into the wind.

He can't. He can't take her from me.

"We'll find her, Boss," Ethan says. "We won't let this bastard get away with this."

I nod, numb. I realize that somehow—even when I saw Thandi collapse on the security footage, even as we lost the trail and found it again—deep inside, beneath the anger and fear, I never truly believed we wouldn't reach her in time.

Now I'm forced to face the bitter truth.

The force of her absence hits like a shockwave. I'm nothing but a charred shell, hollowed of every good thing that matters.

"Mandy, what is the condition of the vessel?" McNamara's voice breaks over the line again.

"Uncertain. There's visible rot, and water's pooling in the stern. It's shallow, for now, but I wouldn't count on it staying that way."

McNamara curses under her breath. "Then we don't have time to get the harbor unit out here. Mandy, I'm sending you in." She sighs. "Going in without a handle on visibility or depth isn't ideal, but nothing about this night has been."

"Copy that," Mandy says. "I'll approach on the leeward side and get her out fast. The canoe's most stable there."

"Good. The rest of the team sticks with the original extraction plan."

McNamara pauses. "Ethan, can Equinox spare an operative to back her up?" She presses on. "And if you're amenable, I'd appreciate your shadow. We're one down with Mandy in the water, and I need someone who can respond to whatever's out there."

"Not a problem." Ethan motions to a dark-haired man at his side. "Carlos, you'll support at the lake." He adjusts his earpiece. "Detective, happy to provide additional cover. I'll handle overwatch."

Ethan unzips the padded case slung over his shoulder and lifts out a long-barreled bolt-action rifle, the scope catching the light as he settles the sling.

"Viktor," he adds, already moving. "Stay with Mr. Thorne."

The blond tips his head and is at my side in an instant. "Yes, sir."

Ethan scans the rest of his team. "Move up to the shoreline and hold there. I need three thermal jackets ready." He nods toward Carlos and Mandy, already preparing to enter the water. "They'll be freezing when they come out."

Without a word, Max shrugs out of the jacket beneath his Kevlar vest. Two others follow, readying the gear for when the trio reaches shore.

By now, we're almost to where the drones still hover over the water. I crane my neck, desperate to get a glimpse. I won't believe Daysha is safe until I see her for myself.

The dinghy, battered and moss-covered, finally comes into view, little more than a splotch in the distance.

Daysha looks impossibly small in the center, clutching the broken oar to her chest.

I jog closer.

Fear for Thandi still claws at me, but for a fleeting moment, warmth blooms in my chest. After so many days of terror—of not knowing if Daysha would come back to us—I'm overwhelmed by the simple fact that she's here. Whatever happens tonight, she's proof that our efforts weren't in vain.

We slow to a stop, but McNamara's unit forges ahead, now joined by Ethan.

Carlos and Mandy wade into the water, swimming fast toward the canoe. One on each side, they take hold and begin guiding it to shore. Even from here, I can hear Daysha's sobs—and Mandy's low voice, murmuring reassurance.

The sound guts me. My fury at Damian Patrick flares hot and sudden. Four days in the clutches of a madman. Four days without love or care. And for what? So Damian could replay some twisted fantasy inherited from a man even more depraved than he is.

It's slow going, but bit by bit they draw closer, the water rocking against the dinghy as Daysha grips the oar with white-knuckled resolve.

Mandy and Carlos ease the canoe past a lump of driftwood.

I can see Daysha clearly now—her curls plastered to her forehead, her eyes wide with fear. The way she clings to the oar like it's a lifeline. Or a prayer.

Water has seeped into the boat, just like Mandy warned. It sloshes around Daysha's muddy sneakers—the yellow and pink Nikes Ricky once told me were her favorite. Of course, she's still wearing the sweats from the night Damian took her.

God. She must be freezing.

My gaze drifts to her sweatshirt.

And my stomach lurches.

I stumble, gasping.

She's wearing Thandi's hoodie.

That's when I fear the worst.

My hands shake so violently, I clasp them together, desperate to still them. I've never felt so helpless. Never known shame like this.

I tried so hard. And I still couldn't protect her.

With every passing second, hope crumbles through my fingers.

The dinghy scrapes through the shallows, creaking dangerously as Carlos and Mandy drag it onto shore. The moment the prow hits dirt, the Equinox team surges forward with the thermal jackets.

Mandy bends, draping one over Daysha's shoulders before lifting her gently from the boat.

"Daysha!" I call, my voice breaking as I rush toward her.

Her eyes widen. Fresh tears spill down her cheeks.

"Mr. Ronan!"

Mandy nods, stepping back.

I pull Daysha into a hug, rocking her against my chest. "Oh, sweetheart. I'm so glad to see you. So glad you're safe."

I expect relief—but Daysha doesn't melt into my arms. Instead, she pushes at me, her voice thin and panicked.

"No—please!"

I jerk back. "What is it?"

She clutches my jacket. "You have to hurry. He took her. He's hurting Ms. Thandi."

My blood goes cold.

"What?" I gasp. "Where?"

Daysha lifts her hand and points.

At first, I see nothing. Just a clump of dead trees and overgrown rushes gathered around a decaying shed at the far edge of the shore. I blink as movement flickers—too sharp, too violent to be the wind.

A flash.

Damian's pale form bursts through the brush, a knife glinting in his hand. His other fist is tangled in the back of Thandi's shirt.

She's limp as a doll as he drags her through the shallows, her small body scraping over rock, her head knocking against stone.

My world collapses.

Red explodes across my vision.

"Boss," Mandy snaps into her earpiece. "We have an active threat. Knife in play on the northwestern shore. I need you over there—now."

Rage and desperation claw at me. My body moves on instinct. I'm sprinting before I even register the ground shifting beneath my feet.

"Ronan—no!" Mandy shouts.

It doesn't matter. The hounds of hell couldn't stop me from getting to Thandi.

My eyes never leave her.

I've never run faster or pushed my body harder. My heart pounds, my legs cramp, my lungs burn. The ground is slick and treacherous, fighting every step. I leap puddles, skid through mud, teeter—then wrench myself upright through sheer will.

I'm closing the distance now, eating up the gap between Equinox and McNamara's unit despite their head start. Dark figures surge ahead of me, growing larger with every stride.

On the shoreline, Damian hauls Thandi onto a patch of grass.

She jerks awake, gasping for air.

My heart crashes against my ribs.

She's still with us.

"Come on, baby. Stay strong," I chant under my breath. "*I'm coming. I'm coming. I'm coming.*"

Pain rips through my side as my stitches pull and tear open again. I don't slow down.

Damian flips Thandi onto her back, straddling her.

From the corner of my eye, I see Ethan drop to one knee in the muck. He shrugs the rifle free of its sling, snaps the bipod into place, and settles behind it, bringing the scope to his eye.

"In position," he murmurs over the comm.

A breath ghosts from his lips.

"I don't have the shot."

McNamara curses and veers left, cutting diagonally through the marsh. Sullivan is right beside her. I carve a path of my own, seconds behind them— but still too far away.

The cattails thin. The treeline closes in.

Just a little closer.

My foot catches on the edge of the reeds. I scramble up the shore.

Damian lifts his arm.

The knife flashes coldly in the moonlight.

That's when I know I won't make it.

No.

No no no no no.

"Thandi!" The scream tears from my throat.

"Roxo—go!"

A growl rents the air.

Roxo and Saya explode past me. Tongues lolling, bodies low, they tear through the rushes and burst out the other side.

Roxo launches first, teeth clamping down on Damian's arm.

Saya attacks a heartbeat later, jaws locking onto his thigh.

Damian's scream is panicked. Feral. His body twists, the knife jerking and slashing as he fights to break free.

"Mama!" he shrieks. "Mama—help me!"

Saya snarls.

Roxo wrenches his head from side to side, refusing to release his grip.

Damian groans, clawing weakly at the earth. He strains, reaching for Thandi.

"Please," he sobs. "Mama, save me, I—"

A single shot splits the night. It echoes, ricocheting through the trees. For a heartbeat, everything goes still.

Then—a wet gasp.

Damian jerks. Blood froths at his lips. Then, he slumps sideways.

I turn, frozen in my tracks.

McNamara lowers her weapon. "That's enough."

I don't wait. I don't think.

McNamara shouts something.

Sullivan holsters his gun.

Behind me, Wallace and Irina crash through the brush, calling Roxo and Saya to heel.

I hear none of it.

Because there is only one thing that matters.

One person who matters.

Thandi.

She's backing away from Damian's body, eyes wide, sobs gasping from her.

I reach her and pull her into me, crushing her to my chest in a heartbeat. I kiss her face—her mouth, her hair—over and over. My arms shake.

I can't believe she's alive.

That she's safe.

She clings to me, her body trembling. Cuts mar her arms and side. Her palms are rubbed raw with blisters. Exhaustion threads through every breath she takes.

And still she's the most beautiful sight I've ever seen.

When she lifts her face to me, my heart shatters.

"You came," she whispers.

"Yes." My throat works. My eyes burn, tears spilling free.

"Always," I say.

"Forever."

Avengers
Thandi

It turns out, heaven looks like Ronan.

For a heartbeat, I thought it would be Tess.

In another life, that might have been enough—closing the wound, ending the pain. But I've changed.

Ronan has changed me.

I'm not dreaming of the past or some mythical afterlife. I want *this life*. Here. Now. I want to embrace love and everything this world still has to offer, with him at my side.

And I think, in the end, Tess would be happy for me. She'd understand.

When she was here, she never stopped moving—never stopped squeezing joy out of every moment.

Never stopped living.

She'd want that for me, too.

And now Ronan's arms are around me, cradling me against his chest.

I'm safe.

Back where I belong.

I can't help looking up at him in wonder, still reeling from teetering at the knife's edge to soaring into love's embrace.

"Babe," I whisper, my eyes filling again.

Ronan lifts me higher, kissing away my tears, even as his own cheeks remain wet. "I'm here, sweetheart," he murmurs. "And I won't ever let you go again."

Warmth rushes through me, chasing away the bile of terror and the chill of the night air. "Thank you," I blurt, clutching his shirt. "Thank you so much."

"For what?" Ronan's eyes soften as he smiles at me. In the moonlight, he's even more beautiful, more devastating than I remember.

He kisses my cheek. "For loving you? For needing you here?"

I nod, my throat clogged with everything I don't know how to say.

"Look at me," Ronan says gently, tipping my chin until I meet his gaze. "Baby, you're my whole world. My life. My breath. What are you thanking me for?"

His voice roughens. "When we came here tonight, I wasn't just trying to save you. I was saving myself."

His words pierce straight through me, stitching together places I never thought anyone could reach. My tears spill over again.

"I love you," I gasp. "I love you so much."

"I love you too," Ronan vows, bending to claim my lips.

His mouth slants over mine, and I part my lips, welcoming him in. I need his warmth—need him to fill me until there's no room left for fear.

The kiss is fierce and tender all at once, holding our hope and our relief in equal measure. I moan softly, leaning into him, meeting him breath for breath. For a moment, time seems to still. The world narrows to just us, shimmering with the joy of somehow, against the odds, finding our second chance.

I close my eyes and press closer to Ronan.

I think I'm finally beginning to understand what Dad meant about trust. About holding on, even when it doesn't make sense.

"Thandi?" McNamara approaches, a tired smile softening her features. Now that my heart has slowed, my panic ebbing, I'm aware of the buzz of activity around us. "How are you feeling?"

"Detective." I draw in a shaky breath. "A lot better than I did thirty minutes ago. Thank you—for everything."

McNamara shakes her head. "Just doing my job. I'm glad it worked out in the end."

She tilts her head toward Ronan. "Besides, if we hadn't brought you and Daysha back, I'd have *him* to contend with."

She throws her head back and laughs—full-throated and unguarded. For a split second, I glimpse the humor and warmth she usually keeps suppressed.

"I've never met a man more allergic to following orders than your boyfriend," she says, shaking her head. "Still, his quick thinking bought us precious time tonight."

A sheepish look crosses Ronan's face, but he shakes his head. "Detective, nothing compares to what you did in the end. I have Thandi back because of you. I'm forever in your debt."

"How about we call it even?" McNamara exhales, rocking back on her heels. Her lips quirk. "And you can both thank me by staying out of trouble."

It's my turn to laugh. "Deal."

"Good." Her tone shifts, gentler, but all business again. "We have to move you out of here. The area has to be secured, and you both need medical attention. Thanks to Mandy, EMS is already on-site."

She gestures toward the shoreline. "Ethan will head back with you."

The minute she mentions medical care, I freeze. I'm not worried about a few cuts and bruises. But Ronan—

My lips flatten in dismay. "Ronan, your stitches! Put me down."

Ronan shrugs, but he does set me on my feet. "I've already torn them once. What's a second time?"

"What?" I'm beside myself. "Babe, what are you thinking? You'll have scars now."

"Good," he says emphatically. "I never want to forget the moment you came back to me."

My lips part. I don't know how to counter that, so instead, I thread my fingers through his. He squeezes my hand, and together we thank McNamara again, then head along the shoreline toward the medics and the rest of Ronan's security team. Ethan meets us halfway, rifle slung over his shoulder.

We walk in silence.

There's a hum of activity here, too. Black-clad security personnel are moving about. Some are packing up weapons and other equipment; others are giving clipped orders into their earpieces. The rest are clustered near an ambulance angled several feet away from the water, on the firmest ground.

Ethan waves and begins ushering us over. "Come on, you two, let's get you taken care of."

The back of the ambulance is open, its interior washed in soft white light. A stretcher waits nearby, still folded. A dark-haired man stands off to one side with a thermal blanket draped around his shoulders, answering questions from an EMT.

A female officer and Daysha are seated together on the open bumper, both wrapped in silver blankets. The woman's arm is tucked around Daysha's shoulders, her head bent close as she murmurs something. Another EMT crouches in front of them, checking Daysha's pulse and temperature with gentle efficiency, speaking softly as he works.

My heart lifts. I break into a run.

"Daysha!"

She looks up, eyes widening. Her lip trembles, and then she's crying in earnest.

I reach her, and we have our moment—laughing, crying, clinging to each other. I pull her close, cupping her face between my palms. "My sweet girl," I whisper. "You made it."

She's so brave, so brilliant. I don't think I could have survived this without her.

"Ms. Thandi," she hiccups, her chest rising with each shaky breath. She wraps her arms tight around my waist. "I was so worried about you. So scared."

"It's okay," I murmur, rubbing her back. "We're safe now. We made it."

Ronan stands beside me. With the adrenaline fading, I notice the shadows beneath his eyes and the faint limp in his step, no doubt from the wound in his side. The other EMT casts him a critical glance.

"All right," she says. "You're up next." She points at his ribs. "We need to take a look at that inside."

Ronan opens his mouth, but I shoot him a withering look before he can object.

"Yes," I say firmly. "He'll go in."

"Fine," he mutters, without heat. He squeezes my shoulder and presses a quick kiss to my cheek before stepping into the ambulance.

The female officer laughs, standing. "Hi, I'm Mandy," she says.

I keep one arm around Daysha, but free the other to shake her hand. "Thandi," I say, kissing the top of Daysha's head. "Thank you for looking out for her."

"Not a problem." Mandy winks at Daysha. "Besides, she made it easy. She's a rockstar."

I grin as Daysha lifts her head with pride.

"She is, isn't she?"

"Sorry to interrupt." The EMT who was attending to Daysha appears at my elbow. "But I need to look at your wounds, too."

Sighing, I reluctantly release Daysha. "Will you keep an eye on her?" I ask Mandy.

She doesn't get to answer.

A siren wails in the distance.

A second ambulance jolts into view along the dirt path, headlights slicing through the darkness, before it comes to a stop near the shoreline. It barely settles before the back doors fly open.

There's a moment of stillness.

Then a woman jumps down. She's frantic, her gaze darting left and right.

"Mom!"

Daysha bolts from my side before I can even react.

Aliyah's head snaps up. Her face crumples, disbelief collapsing into relief.

And joy.

Then she's running too.

They collide halfway, Daysha slamming into her arms. Aliyah drops to her knees, sobbing openly as she crushes her daughter to her chest. She cups Daysha's face, pressing frantic kisses to her cheeks, her forehead, her hair, touching her again and again like she needs proof that she's real.

"You're here," she keeps whispering, shaking her head. "You're here. You're here."

I stand frozen, tears streaming freely now, my hand pressed to my mouth. The knot of pain that had crystallized within me—layer by layer, over two decades of desperation and fear—finally fractures and gives way.

It's over.

Daysha is safe

Damian is dead.

I finally did right by Tess.

A gentle hand touches my elbow.

"Come," the EMT says softly. "Let's get you checked."

The world slows. The chaos fades.

Daysha and Aliyah have gone home, wrapped in joy and relief.

Only Ronan and I remain. McNamara asked me to linger a little longer to give my statement. I don't mind. Because once I turn my back on this place, I never want to return.

It's time to turn the page.

"You okay?" Ronan asks, nudging my shoulder.

We're huddled together on the ambulance bumper, wrapped in blankets. Someone mercifully found coffee, and steam curls up from the cups, warming our hands.

"Yes," I say, smiling up at him. "Finally."

His eyes soften as he leans in to kiss me again.

I sigh. Equinox is packing up. Ethan gives quiet instructions as the team moves through the clearing. Once Ronan and I were bandaged, they all came over to introduce themselves. They're an amazing group, capable, steady, and kind. I'm deeply grateful for every one of them.

Max, the bruiser of an operative who somehow makes even Ronan look lean by comparison, ambles past carrying a small case. He pauses, opens it, and a pink nose darts forward to snatch a treat. An unmistakable red cape flutters in the breeze.

"Ronan." I freeze. "What is ISO E doing here?"

"Oh…" Ronan rubs the back of his neck.

By the time he finishes explaining the dogs, WhiffRush, and his last-ditch decision to bring in ISO E as reinforcement, I'm crying all over again.

I glance around the clearing, and for the first time, I really see them—the unlikely Avengers Ronan somehow pulled together, just to save my universe.

Now I understand McNamara's earlier comment about his ingenuity.

God. What did I do to deserve him?

"You're crazy," I murmur, pulling him down to me again. "Absolutely crazy."

In his arms, I'm lost and found all at once. My heart beats strong and sure. I rest my head against his chest and feel the echo there.

"Thandi?"

McNamara approaches, her voice tentative. It's the first time I've heard her sound unsure.

"Yes?" I ask, lifting my head.

Then I see what she's holding.

The coffee slips from my fingers. I barely register Ronan's voice—rough, urgent—over the rush of blood in my ears.

"We found this in the cabin," McNamara says quietly. "Among several other children's things." She presses her lips together. "It's outside protocol, but I thought you'd want it."

My hands shake as I reach for the wreath. The artificial flowers are still bright, still beautiful.

Just as they were the day she disappeared.

Tess.

It looks so much smaller, so much more delicate than I remember.

"Baby—" Ronan breaks off, helpless.

Only then do I realize I'm crying. Crying so hard I can't see the past, the present, or the future.

Ronan's arms close around me as the sobs tear free, raw and relentless.

I press the garland to my chest, rocking back and forth.

And nothing, not even Ronan, can console me then.

Tess
Thandi

The day dawns bright and clear.

Even though what we've come to do is difficult, it doesn't feel heavy. Instead, it feels inevitable.

Overdue.

It is.

Ronan is next to me, gentle and supportive in his sharp black suit. On my other side, Mom, Dad, and Ricky hold hands. Mark and Nancy—Dad's musician friends—have set aside their usual bohemian flair and, like us, are dressed in somber black.

The sweet, haunting music rising from their instruments plucks at the grief in my chest.

The last two weeks have come in wave after wave of emotion—pain, relief, joy, and an ocean of sorrow.

In the end, we didn't use Daysha's mirror to escape. But she freed someone else.

When the drones swarmed Damian Patrick's property, they followed the pale, flashing light into the woods, where her mirror reflected again and again.

There, deep among the trees, was a darkness no light could ever cleanse—a burial ground for innocence.

Tess was waiting there too.

Twenty years too late for rescue.

We never stopped waiting either.

Now, she's finally home.

My eyes fill again, and Ronan pulls me close as I clutch the urn to my chest.

"I'm here, baby," he murmurs.

I smile up at him, grateful beyond words.

"Ready, Peanut?" Dad asks, his voice hoarse with strain.

The last two weeks have been hard on all of us, but perhaps most demanding of him. From the moment we found Tess, he poured every waking hour into a single project—a custom columbarium. He called it his life's work: dedication, memorial, and sculpture in one.

It rises from the earth now with impossible fluidity, a delicacy only a maestro—or a father's loving hands—could achieve.

Dad didn't try to capture Tess's face. Instead, he gave her motion—metal arcing upward, petals scattering in her wake, as if she's slipped free of gravity itself.

Set into the curve of the sculpture is a small recess holding a photograph of Tess and me. It's from the summer we spent at Grandma Moses' lake house—the year we lived in the water, daring each other to jump farther, scream louder, live bigger.

We're still in our swimsuits, arms looped around each other's waists, hair wet, skin warm from the sun. We're wearing wacky sunglasses. Mine are star-shaped; Tess's are oversized pink hearts.

The camera flash went off too fast. Instead of looking at the lens, we're grinning at each other.

That's always been my favorite part.

Below the photo, there are no dates. No beginning. No end.

Just her name.

Theresa Elowen

And beneath it, in curving letters:

Loving Daughter, Sister, and Best Friend

In our hearts forever

It only makes sense. I know when the story breaks, when the messy details become public, they'll call her missing.

But the truth is, she never left.

She's been with us every step of the way.

Mom steps forward first, one hand resting on Ricky's shoulder. Bending, she places the wreath at the base of the sculpture. The flowers spill outward in a soft halo of color, bright against the stone. Her shoulders shake, and she doesn't try to hide the quiet sobs that slip free.

Dad comes around her then, wrapping one arm around her, the other drawing Ricky close. The three of them stand there together, holding one another upright.

Ronan's hand tightens in mine.

I step forward, the urn smooth and heavy in my hands. Weighted not with our grief but our love.

The opening is already there, discreetly set into the curve of the piece.

I pause, lean in, and place the urn inside.

It's a perfect fit.

I withdraw slowly and step back into Ronan's arms.

Dad moves forward without a word. He closes the panel, pressing it into place until it is flush with the sculpture's surface. His shoulders hitch, and he rests his palm there for a moment.

Later, I know, it will be sealed for good by another sculptor and dear friend.

For now, we form a circle.

And as if by some unspoken signal, we reach for one another at the same time.

As one, we lock hands.

And then, we let her fly free.

Release
Ronan

Two months later

"Today is the long-awaited arraignment of Astor Pharmaceuticals CEO James Astor," a news anchor's voice drones from the screen mounted behind the driver's seat of the Equinox SUV.

The media scrutiny around the kidnapping—and everything that followed—has been relentless. Ethan insisted on a security detail the minute we decided to go to the courthouse.

Thandi reaches across the seat and twines her fingers with mine. "Are you sure you want to do this?"

She's wearing a yellow sheath dress today, one that brings out the warmth of her skin and the highlights in her hair. Of course, she's radiant. She always is. She's my sunshine. I smile, tugging her closer, and the tension that's been humming through my limbs all morning eases.

"Yes," I say. "I need to."

I lift her hand and press my lips to her knuckles. "What about you? Are you okay? I won't feel bad if you want to turn back."

Thandi shakes her head with a soft smile. "I'm good. I want to be here to support you."

The wave of emotion that hits me is sharp enough to steal my breath. My love for this remarkable woman clenches my lungs. Somehow, even after everything she's endured, she still makes room to worry about me. To offer her strength.

There's no minimizing what happened that night in the woods. The road back hasn't been easy.

Damian may be dead, but that doesn't mean the world—*her* world—simply resets. Thandi's physical wounds have healed, but grief doesn't obey timelines. She's still carrying what she and Daysha survived. Still processing saying goodbye to Tess.

Some nights she wakes up panicked, shouting, and I hold her until the terror loosens its grip. The therapist she and Daysha are seeing has been a gift. Healing moves on its own schedule, in its own rhythms, and all we can do is honor them.

But there has been joy, too.

A grin spreads across my face as I lift her hand again. The three-carat pink diamond solitaire on her finger catches the light from the window, glittering with the rosy tints of dawn.

"What?" Thandi asks, noticing my expression.

"Nothing," I say. "Just thinking about making you my wife."

She makes a small sound of pleasure and rests her head against my chest, her other hand curling at my waist.

"You make me so happy," she whispers, and my heart swells in response.

I can't resist pulling her onto my lap. I cup her face in my hands and kiss her. Our mouths meet, and for a moment, the world narrows to the warmth of her body, the sweetness of her scent, the quiet certainty of us.

Yes. Joy. So much joy, anchored in the woman I've chosen and who has chosen me back.

By the time we pull apart, James feels like little more than a footnote—a smudge I'm eager to wipe from our rearview mirror.

"Mr. Thorne, Ms. Elowen," Max's voice comes over the intercom. "We'll be approaching the courthouse in ten minutes."

Thandi and I straighten, putting ourselves to rights.

On the screen, the news has shifted, a grim headline ticking across the bottom:

Body Found in Woods Identified as Serial Kidnapper and Murderer, Arnold Patrick.

Over the past few weeks, the steady stream of discoveries has continued as more details about Damian's past and the victims in the woods have emerged. McNamara and her team have done heroic work, but Arnold Patrick's crimes run so deep that many questions may never be answered.

What is clear, though, is how he died:

A knife wound.

From his own son's hand.

It's chilling.

I will never grieve Damian, but since the story broke yesterday, a feeling has been trapped in my chest, like the dark beating of moths struggling to break free.

We know now about his father's physical abuse, the emotional terror, the relentless cruelty. And in some feral, unguarded place inside me, I recognize the shape of that damage.

I understand what it's like to live under a brutal fist.

I stare down at my hands.

Maybe, in the end, Damian understood something I have always resisted.

Sometimes the harm can't be fixed.

Sometimes you have to put the monster to bed.

As we make the final turn toward the courthouse, my hand tightens around Thandi's. The thin, woven bracelet Winston gave me slips past the cuff of my shirt. Two small beads hang from its ends—one polished wood, the other impenetrable onyx. Growth and strength, according to Winston. As usual, I have no idea how any of his mystic interventions work, but I'm all for good omens.

More than that, with the moths still beating hard, asking for vengeance, it's a reminder of what a father's love can be.

A reminder of what can grow in the light instead.

The courthouse looms ahead. Max pulls up along the side of the building, away from the knot of reporters gathered on the front steps.

With Ethan guarding our flank, Thandi and I slip inside and await James' judgment.

Of course, despite Ethan's best efforts, it's impossible for us to go unnoticed. Thandi and I take our seats anyway, declining the press clustered along the aisle, hovering like vultures. We're not here to validate James with a spectacle.

Thandi is small and sure beside me, her hand warm in mine, as we wait for the proceedings to begin. The room is packed—every seat filled by someone Astor has harmed.

Since the connection between WhiffRush and the kidnapping came to light, the trickle of victims has become a flood. I've tried to keep my focus on Thandi's recovery, not James, but even I understand that today is only the beginning. Astor's cruelty has birthed a hydra of civil suits, too many to count.

Ousmane sits a few rows ahead of us, his maroon boubou dark and immaculate, his posture rigid with restraint—the lead plaintiff in a growing class action brought by dozens of small business owners locked into Astor's failed franchise model. He and his wife, Mariama, grip each other's hands, their eyes fixed on the empty judge's podium.

A few rows to the left, a cluster of youth advocates drafts a dispatch—heads bent over screens, fingers moving fast.

At the front of the room, a woman kneels beside a motorized wheelchair, gently lifting a bottle of water to her daughter's lips. The girl's head is braced by soft guards, her body stilled by straps designed for support, not restraint.

Marnie Peters.

Her mother, Lucy, murmurs something I can't hear, her thumb at Marnie's chin as she waits for her to swallow. It's hard not to look at them without rage searing my chest. The Peters became a national touchstone after they nearly lost their daughter—bright, vibrant Marnie—when her care facility replaced the medication that managed her cerebral palsy with PlayMist EDU.

I draw in a breath. Today isn't about their cases, but I understand why they're here—why none of them can look away. My fingers worry the woven cord of Winston's bracelet.

Ousmane, Marnie, Lucy—they're all hoping today's outcome will be their good omen.

A murmur ripples through the assembly as James enters from the side door, his movements clipped.

He surveys the room, the tight set of his jaw betraying his irritation. When his eyes land on me, they pause before sliding forward again. He settles at the defense table, leaning back as if the entire proceeding were an inconvenience. Two attorneys flank him, already murmuring to each other, while his longtime lawyer Griffin takes a seat behind them.

The door opens again, and the room rises as the judge enters. Her expression is composed, her eyes clear as she takes her seat at the bench.

"Please be seated," she says.

The hum of conversation falls away at once.

The clerk opens the proceedings, formally calling the case.

Everything moves more quickly than I expect. Appearances are noted. Thandi gives my hand an encouraging squeeze.

Then the charges are read:

Nine criminal counts, including IP theft, securities fraud, criminal negligence and reckless endangerment, obstruction of justice, and aggravated corporate misconduct.

Bail is set at an astronomical thirty-one million dollars.

A cheer goes up in the room. James braces as if struck, his expression darkening. His lawyers lean toward him, whispering urgently, but he stares petulantly ahead. Across the room, Ousmane presses a trembling hand to his lips and lifts his eyes to the heavens.

Of course, this is not the end, but the universe Winston so fiercely believes in has delivered its good omen.

As for me, I feel … nothing.

It shocks me.

I've been dreading the arraignment for weeks, somehow expecting that James would bluster through—that power and greed would prevail over the arc of justice. But now that the charges have been read, something cracks open inside of me. The moths break free, leaving nothing behind but indifference.

And relief.

Now that the moment of reckoning has come, instead of the bile of schadenfreude, I feel disconnected, untethered from James and his malice. I've been so focused on my baby, making sure she's recovering, that somewhere between the rescue, Thandi's love, the unyielding support of Winston, Iris, and Fia … I've healed too.

Maybe this was the growth Winston wanted for me.

Not just him. Mom too.

The road Thandi and I have traveled has been long and pitted with thorns. Yet, the moment I stopped hiding, the moment I revealed the truth of who I was to Thandi, something began to bloom in place of the burrs of my father's abuse:

Love, trust, and resilience.

I may have abandoned the Astor name a decade ago, but only Thandi's love has given me the strength to finally relinquish James Astor's hold on me.

Only through her love have I become the man my mother wanted me to be.

The smudge has been wiped from the mirror.

I am no longer James' son in any way that matters.

Releasing a sigh, I glance one last time at the man who was once my father.

Then I turn back to Thandi and pull her into my arms again.

Sweet
Thandi

"You've got a little powdered sugar."

"Where?" I lift a hand to my face.

"Here." Ronan pulls me into his arms and brushes his lips over mine.

I moan and soften into him, the last wedge of funnel cake trembling in my hands. "Babe…"

"Yeah?" Ronan grins, tugging me closer. "Want me to get the rest?"

I shake my head, then draw in a shaky breath, trying to calm the spike in my pulse and the heat in my veins. I'm already melting from his touch. I don't know if I'll ever get used to this need—this craving for Ronan that refuses to be tamed.

I smile, looking up into his whiskey-colored eyes, the hot caress of his gaze lingering on my face.

Good thing he's just as wild for me.

"Come on, be good," I say, stepping back and slipping my hand into his. "We only have about half an hour until The Sugar Hill Spark."

I polish off the pastry and wipe the sugar from my hands. Ronan lets me tug him forward, and we weave through the crowd toward the pavilion, where the show that ushers in the park's evening lights will soon begin.

When Ronan wraps his arms around my shoulders, I curl into him, taking in the riot of sound and color around us. Sugar Hill Park doesn't dim in the fall, it sharpens. The cold bites, the mascots glow brighter in their fur-lined outfits, and the screams echo even louder in the crisp air.

A roller coaster thunders overhead, followed by a chorus of delighted shrieks. Metal rattles, gears grind, and music blares in competing keys, each attraction insisting it deserves the most attention.

I glance up at Ronan's strong profile and feel a rush of tenderness.

In a way, this is where it all started. Oh, of course, there was the youth center, our consultation—even Tino's, but this is where we first acknowledged the truth between us.

Where we first opened ourselves to trust, desire—

And then love.

We've overcome pain, separation, Damian's and his father's cruelty. And now the rainbow on our horizon feels brighter than all the park's blinking lights.

I make a happy sound and slip my hand into Ronan's pocket, the weight of my engagement ring both alien and comforting. The woman I am now—at peace with the wounds of her past, cherished in the surety of love—feels almost like a stranger. I never thought I could experience this much joy.

"What?" Ronan asks, looking down at me.

"Nothing." I rest my head against him. "Just thinking about us."

"Mm." He kisses my temple. "Tell me more."

"I'm just happy," I say softly. "Just grateful to have you with me."

"Baby," he breathes, then I'm lost in his arms again. His kiss steals my breath, and by the time he pulls away, we're both trembling.

"Okay." I nudge him. "Enough of that. Let's explore a little before we have to head to the pavilion."

"Fine." Ronan laughs. "Let's see what's out there."

We pass a cluster of concession stands where indulgent flavors are coming to life. The air smells like syrup and hot oil. Kettle corn bursts in rapid pops, and every few minutes, whiffs of cinnamon and fried dough drift on the wind.

We amble past. Leaves skitter across the pavement, scattering in bright spirals around our feet. Everything is loud, crowded, and a little overwhelming in the way happiness sometimes is.

Ronan keeps his arm around me, a comforting weight at my side. Every few steps, he murmurs close to my ear: *You okay? Hungry? Warm enough?*

I nod, smiling, because I am. Because he's here.

Because he loves me.

I am wooed, swooning, happily on my feet.

We slow down, pausing to marvel at an acrobat in a sequin-studded bodysuit contorting into impossible shapes. Halfway through the performance, Ronan slips away from me. He returns with a steaming cup of hot chocolate mounded with so many colorful marshmallows, I'm convinced he asked for every flavor. He presses it into my mittened hands, folding my fingers around the cup until the heat sinks through the wool.

"Drink," he says, his voice brooking no protest, as though somehow hot chocolate is essential nourishment.

Well. Who am I to turn down sweetness?

I laugh and take a sip, nearly burning my tongue, marshmallows bumping against my lips.

A bell clangs in the distance, followed by cheers. Above us, the Ferris wheel turns slowly, while the coaster climbs again, click by click by click. After weeks of sorrow and the intensity of James's arraignment, the silliness—the wonder of it all—feels like blissful release.

Everything is moving. Everything is loud. Everything is alive.

And somehow, right in the middle of it, with Ronan's arm around me and warmth pooling in my hands, I feel perfectly still. Perfectly grounded in the promise of possibility, in the new beginning he helped me believe in the first time we were here.

We keep walking, the midway bright around us. Ronan's thumb brushes absently at my sleeve as we merge with the easy drift of people who aren't in a hurry to be anywhere else. I feel … light. Still glowing from the way he keeps looking at me like I'm his treasure.

In the winding section called Candy Cane Lane, vendors flank us on every side, selling everything from mass-produced foam Captain Funnel Cake hats to intricate, handmade art. At a stall displaying wood carvings, a flash of color catches my attention—pink and purple, cutting through the noise and motion. Against the muted wood, the girlish tones stir something wistful inside me.

I step forward as if in a dream.

"Baby?" Ronan asks, trailing after me.

"I—" I shake my head, drifting closer. "Just … one second."

The artist, a young woman with a patterned headwrap and paint-stained fingers, smiles as we enter.

"Welcome. These are all my work, carved from maple wood," she says. "Let me know if you have any questions."

I nod, gazing at the shelves in wonder. The stall is filled with small nature carvings—trees, animals, flowers—furtive creatures caught mid-motion. Everything looks touched by a human hand. Loved into being.

All of it is stunning, but nothing distracts me from the spark that grabbed my attention—a carving on the smallest display table at the edge of the stall.

I lift the figurine, turning it in my hands.

I'm immobilized, submerged in the current of memory.

I gasp.

The twin tributaries of nostalgia and grief rush beneath my feet.

Two sparrows, carved from pale wood, perch on the same slender branch. One leans forward, the other slightly back, as if they've been caught mid-play. Tiny flowers dot the branch between them, delicate and vibrant. One has pink wings. The other's are purple.

An ache sears through my chest.

I cradle the carving as if the birds might startle if I move too fast. The wood is smooth beneath my fingers. I can almost see us—two little girls with garlands in our hair, beads clicking as we run, laughter spilling between us. Tess's purple beads swing as she turns. Mine, pink, catch the sun.

"Do you love that one?" the artist asks gently.

I swallow and nod, pressing the carving to my chest. "Yes," I manage. "I really do."

Ronan kisses my forehead. His hand rubs slow circles over my shoulder. When I look up, his eyes are full of compassion.

"I've got it," he murmurs, already reaching for his wallet.

I don't protest. I just turn to him, letting his arms come around me, the carving tucked between us. For a moment, the noise of the park fades—the rides, the music, the laughter—and all I feel is love.

Love strong enough to live alongside memory without breaking.

Love strong enough to hold me up so I don't break anymore.

Grateful doesn't feel like a big enough word to capture what he's done for me.

But as Ronan's chin rests against my hair and his arms tighten around me, it's the closest one I have.

We step back into the flow of the park. I loop the bag's thin paper handle around my wrist. Ronan keeps his arm around me.

Neither of us speaks.

But it's all right.

It's a comfortable quiet. A shared one.

The ache inside of me has eased, not gone, but folded gently into everything else.

Ronan slows, and I feel the shift in his body as his gaze fixes on something ahead.

"What is it?"

"Come on," he says, grabbing my hand. He moves so quickly, I have to run to keep up with him.

"Ronan, stop! Where are we going?"

He glances back at me, eyes dancing with mischief. "Trust me. I have to do this."

"Have to do what?" I ask, stumbling as he pulls me toward a row of game booths twinkling in neon.

"Just wait," he insists.

We skid to a stop, and I see it immediately.

The high striker towers above us, all flashing lights and ridiculous bravado. The metal column is painted in Sugar Hill's unmistakable colors. At the top, instead of a bell, is a grinning funnel-cake cut-out—the Captain himself—his powdered-sugar uniform rendered in cartoonish layers. Every time someone swings the mallet, a puck rockets upward, sparks flashing along the track.

"Oh god," I say, already laughing. "Seriously, babe?"

Ronan grins, unabashed. "Oh, yes."

Prizes are stacked behind the counter. Rows of smaller plushies—turtles, frogs, rabbits, and a medium-sized bright blue wolf—line the shelves. Looming behind them on the top rack is the grand prize—the biggest teddy bear I've ever seen: Cream-colored, nubby-furred, and so large its head almost brushes the ceiling.

A crowd jostles. Two contenders line up ahead of Ronan, faces set with determination.

The first man swings, muscles straining, a puff of air bursting from his lips.

The puck flies up—

And climbs halfway up before clanging to a stop.

The man drops the mallet with a muttered curse.

"Nice try. Better luck next time." The attendant hands him a turtle from the bottom shelf to a smattering of applause.

The second man does better. His swing drives the puck higher. Sparks skitter up the column, only to stall just short of the top—about two-thirds of the way up.

Impressive, but not enough.

Captain Funnel Cake stays stubbornly unlit.

Our second hopeful wins the blue wolf, lifting it triumphantly above his head as the crowd cheers wildly.

Next to me, Ronan is a ball of anticipation. "Damn, he almost got it," he mutters.

"Almost?" I shake my head, laughing. "It's impossible. It's probably rigged."

"Impossible?" Ronan steps up before I can utter another word. He slips out of his jacket with deliberate ceremony. Draping it over my shoulders, he tucks it around me like a cape.

"Watch this," he smirks.

The attendant glances up, one brow lifting. "Well, folks," he announces, his voice carrying over the crowd, "looks like we've got a serious contender."

Laughter ripples outward. More people drift closer, drawn by the promise of a spectacle.

"You're insane, you know that, right?" I say as Ronan rolls his shoulders and stretches his arms, warming up. He cracks his fingers, then steps back to me.

"Utterly." He bends, presenting his cheek with exaggerated solemnity. "A kiss, please, my lady. For good luck."

I roll my eyes but kiss him anyway, my heart doing a little tap dance in my chest. Because whether he rings the bell or not, I know what he's doing—why he's choosing this.

I clutch the gift bag against my wrist, blinking back tears.

Because behind the mischief, behind the performance, there is a much more tender truth: Ronan saw my sadness, and he wants to cheer me up. To ease my pain—even if it comes at his expense.

Even in this silly way, he is protecting me.

Just as he has done again and again.

I squeeze his hand and give him another kiss for good measure before releasing him to take his position.

"After all that buildup," the attendant turns to the crowd with a theatrical flourish, "can he deliver? Just so everyone knows—the biggest prize won tonight was the wolf." He gestures to the empty spot behind the counter. "And that took everything the last guy had."

The crowd cheers. Scattered voices shout words of encouragement. Others tell Ronan to give up.

Ronan approaches the platform, unfazed. He lifts the mallet, shifting it from hand to hand—testing its weight. Then, he braces his legs far apart and takes a breath.

Everyone quiets.

For a heartbeat, the world slows.

Ronan raises his arms.

And swings.

The mallet smashes down, the impact echoing with a clang. The puck rockets upward, sparks flashing along the column as it climbs—past one marker, then another, each higher than the last.

I stop breathing.

A ripple of excitement moves through the crowd.

The puck clears the blue wolf threshold.

The crowd yells.

The puck wavers, hesitates—then surges again, inching higher.

Higher—

And strikes the target.

Captain Funnel Cake lights up in a blaze of color, sparks exploding as a triumphant digital tune blares. The sound is ridiculous and glorious, an impossible anthem of victory and love.

The crowd roars.

I squeal, bouncing on my toes, adrenaline crashing through me. Ronan turns just in time for me to throw myself into his arms. He lifts me, spinning us as the noise swells around us. Any lingering weight in my heart dissolves.

My laughter breaks free.

The moment narrows to us—Ronan's hands at my back, his forehead resting against mine, both of us grinning like two silly kids.

"Show-off," I say breathlessly.

"Only for you," he murmurs.

"Thank you," I whisper, melting into him.

"Ahem."

The attendant appears at our side, hauling the giant teddy bear with both arms. It's nearly as tall as I am. The crowd laughs again as he deposits it into Ronan's hands.

"Congratulations," he says with a grin. "That was amazing."

Ronan looks from the bear to me and winks. "Told you I could do it."

And as he hands it over—this absurd, oversized proof of joy—I can only think one thing:

I'm truly, finally where I belong.

Spark

Thandi

After the Sugar Hill Spark, we lingered at the park's diner-style restaurant for dinner. Now, sated and content, we walk back to the parking deck hand in hand. Ronan carries the gift bag since I refuse to stop clutching the bear. I tighten my arms, pressing my face into its soft neck.

I'm still floating, still tingling from Ronan's chivalry.

I release a happy sigh, and he glances over at me. "Should I be jealous? That bear is getting pretty handsy," he says with a laugh as we step into the elevator.

I rest my head against his shoulder. "What can I say? I have a thing for big softies."

Ronan huffs, but he's grinning like a maniac. He kisses my cheek, and I can't remember ever feeling this free.

The elevator dings, and we step onto the basement level. It's late enough that the space is almost empty. Family rhythms and kids' bedtimes mean most of Sugar Hill's visitors leave just after sunset. Even if we'd forgotten where we parked, finding our car would have been easy.

The Maybach gleams under the garage lights. Ronan slips the gift bag onto the back seat, then circles around to open the passenger door for me.

Still paranoid about paparazzi or overzealous fans, Ethan made us promise to park in the covered deck, choosing a corner spot backed by concrete on two sides. That way, no one can drift close to us without being seen.

The privacy is meant to afford us safety, but now that we're in the car, it's giving me other ideas.

My heart is full, my pulse still thrumming after a day steeped in joy. Heat spools through my veins.

As soon as Ronan gets in, I don't give him a chance to start the engine. I slide across the seat, my sweater dress brushing his thighs as I move. I feel the strength in his shoulders as I settle over his lap. His warmth presses against my chest. The steering wheel nudges my back.

Ronan's eyebrows shoot up even as his arms tighten around me

"Well," he says, voice deep with amusement, "this is nice."

"Mm hmm." I nuzzle his neck. "You going to do anything about it?"

"Maybe," he rumbles. "What do you *want* me to do about it?"

"This."

I lean forward.

The moment our lips touch, the world fades away. Ronan cradles my face, meeting me with a gentleness that's almost reverent. I can feel the softness of his lips, the way they move against mine—each touch a slow act of devotion. His breath is sweet, his tongue sinful, and I let myself sink into his caress, my body responding with a flicker of fire.

When I finally pull back, Ronan's breath is shallow, his eyes dark and hot.

"Thank you for today," I whisper, molding my body against his. I'm so hungry for his warmth, his strength—for all of his tenderness—that it feels like I will never get close enough. I grip his shoulders and, slowly and softly, begin lapping at his neck.

"Thandi—" Ronan groans.

"Hm?" I suckle at the tender skin beneath his jaw, and his voice tapers into a moan.

He calls my name again, his voice low and thick. It's not a question. It's a plea—an incantation. I trail my fingers up his chest, slipping under his shirt, to his skin beneath. His breath stutters, and I lean closer, the intoxicating scent of him filling my lungs.

"Fuck, baby." Ronan leans back against the headrest. "What's gotten into you? Not that I'm complaining."

"What's gotten into me? You, hopefully," I say with a smirk.

Laughter explodes from him. His fingers dig into my hips, shifting me against the ridge of his erection. "I think I can manage that," he says huskily.

"Good."

His gaze locks onto mine, and for a second, I think he's going to say something. But he doesn't. He just pulls me closer, his mouth finding mine again—this time more insistent. His thumb traces my cheek.

"You really want this?" he murmurs. "Now? Here?"

"Yes. Now. Here." I rock my hips.

Ronan glances at the exposed passenger window. "But what about—"

I grab the giant teddy bear and stuff it against the glass, then curl my arms around his neck, again. "You were saying?"

"Well," he says, his tone warm with amusement, "I guess that settles it."

I lick the corner of his mouth, squeezing my thighs around him. "Stop talking and kiss me," I say.

So he does.

Our moans tangle together. Ronan's hips surge up to meet mine even as his hands slip beneath my dress. They roam over my skin, finding the center of my back, unclasping my bra. I shiver as the rough pads of his fingers trail down my spine.

Ronan places a burning kiss on my collarbone. "You're beautiful, you know that?"

I can't respond. I can barely hear him over the blood rushing in my ears.

I whimper as he caresses my ribcage, his large hands coming up to cup my breasts. He circles me first. Then he presses and teases me through the soft weave of my dress. Sparks burst behind my eyelids, and all my thoughts scatter.

"Ronan," I gasp.

"So, so, pretty," he breathes. Ronan brushes my shoulder, his fingers skimming at the edge of my neckline, then dipping into the deep V.

He kneads me, tracing my curves before easing my right breast free, lifting it until my nipple, taut and swollen, is exposed above the neckline of my dress.

Ronan's eyes droop. His lids go heavy, gaze glittering as he stares at my nakedness.

I prickle with heat. I should feel self-conscious, but I only feel desired, cherished—caught in an all-consuming fire.

He holds my gaze, and then he's bending, drawing the sensitive peak between his lips. The first touch of his mouth nearly unravels me. I shout, clinging to him as my world tilts.

Ronan growls. He nips the rigid point before yanking my neckline down, freeing both breasts. He kisses my tender flesh, his stubble grazing my skin. I moan, writhing as his mouth widens, taking more of me in. I feel sensitive, full, a livewire that could trip at a moment's notice.

Thank God I'm not alone in my torment.

The sounds Ronan is making are voracious, tortured, as if just playing with my breasts flays him alive. He pulls one dark peak between his lips, suckling hard, then releases it with a sullen pop.

I gasp at the wet, aggressive suction. My skin is on fire. I cry out, thrusting upwards, my chest bowing outward, begging for his mouth.

His wicked tongue steals out, laving one bud and the next. When his teeth close around the tip of one breast, I cry out as a shockwave arcs through me. I shudder violently, singed by the lightning in his touch.

"I want you so much," he groans. "I'm going to make you feel so good."

"Yes. Show me. Help me," I plead. I grab his hand and press it between my legs, to the wet aching center of my need. "I need you, Ronan."

A feral sound snarls from his chest. "Anything you want, baby. Always."

The air between us is alive. Ronan's hands find the hem of my dress, pulling it up to expose the curve of my waist. I shiver, not from cold, but from the way his touch feels like a promise. Inside the car, the only light comes from the faint glow of the dashboard. It's enough to see the hunger in his eyes, the way they dart between my lips and my breasts still lifted in offering to him.

He kisses my ring first.

Then his thumb presses my clit. He caresses me so thoroughly, so hotly, my head spins. My thighs slacken, falling wider apart. A rush of wetness has me clenching with need.

Ronan makes a sound of pleasure, holding me up with the strong bar of his arm. He strokes me again, spreading the evidence of my desire.

"That's it, baby," he purrs. "Let me feel everything."

I moan long and deep. I'm spiralling, my hips seeking in an urgent rhythm. The ache inside me grows to a fever, a yawning chasm with only one cure.

"Please." I clutch at Ronan, fumbling between us, unzipping his fly. His entire body jerks when I close my hand over his length. I stroke him, smoothing precum over his dick with each pass. I love the weight of him in my hand, love the way he feels like velvet over steel.

I love the way the vital pulse beneath my fingers tells me how much he wants me.

"Fuck, Thandi," he groans, throwing his head back. "You have no idea what you do to me."

"*Now*, Ronan. Please." I guide him to my entrance. I'm trembling, my heart pounding in my chest.

Ronan stills. His breath is shallow, his eyes dark with something I can't name. He grips the back of my neck, squeezing just the way I like—that pitch-perfect pressure, hovering on the point of pain.

"You're mine," he growls.

Then he enters me, hard and fast.

The sensation strangles the breath in my throat. The stretch is deep, almost more than I can bear, but he's already moving, cupping my ass, pumping me on his length. It's perfect, exquisite. Ecstasy blooms and refracts in the slide and retreat of his body against mine. I feel every inch of him, every heartbeat, every movement.

And I know, without a doubt, that he is right.

I belong to him.

The feel of him is electric. Ronan's hands grip my waist, the heat of him searing into me. He pulls almost all the way out and pushes back in. This time the penetration is slow, deliberate—like he's savoring me. I moan, and he kisses me again, more deeply, more passionately, consuming me with every breath.

Wet silken sounds punctuate the silence. Ronan thrusts in an implacable rhythm, tracking my response, adjusting to me with every flicker of my eyelids, every whimper of breath. Breaking me down and building me back up again.

We're both trembling, teetering on the edge, but I don't want it to end. This dance, this union, is all I've ever needed.

Ronan brushes his mouth over my lips, then he pulls back, pressing our foreheads together.

"I love you," he whispers.

That's all it takes, and I'm tumbling over the precipice.

Ronan holds me as the tremors rock me to my very core. Then he groans, and his own body gives in, his release filling me in a warm rush.

We come down slowly. He caresses the swell of my hips, and I let out a soft sigh.

There's no rush, no urgency—just the quiet intensity of two souls in perfect alignment. I can taste the salt of his skin, feel the lingering warmth of his desire.

"That was amazing. You were perfect." Ronan strokes my back, his fingers tracing sweet sigils over my skin.

A wave of emotion rises in my chest, so powerful it almost hurts. The park, the laughter, the tiny wood figurine, the bear wedged awkwardly behind us—every small joy of the day stacks gently on top of the trials we've survived: the fear, the distance, the nights when love felt like a broken dream instead of a promise.

Yet somehow, we made it through grief, danger, and doubt—so that this moment, this shimmering bond between us, doesn't feel stolen, but inevitable.

Ronan cups the back of my neck. His hands settle at my waist, drawing me closer. I lean fully into him, melting.

"I love you," I vow, unable to hide the joy in my heart—or the way my voice shakes.

Then I tilt my head back, surrendering to his kiss, to his touch—to the way he makes me feel like I'm the only other person in the world.

Forever
Ronan

Six months later.

We didn't do Montego Bay like Winston and Iris.

We did Bali instead.

The ocean roars like a heartbeat. Late afternoon light spills across the sand, gilding the water in rose and gold. The air smells of salt, jasmine, and frangipani. It's almost sunset, and the whole world seems to hold its breath, waiting for the sun's slow descent.

Fia was right: The light in Bali really does have its own color.

I'm a nervous wreck as I wait for Thandi to come down the aisle. I know the moment she does, I'm going to fall apart.

I wouldn't have it any other way.

Not when it means a lifetime of Thandi's smiles—her love, her laughter.

Not when it means forever.

"You okay?" Fia whispers, reaching over to squeeze my hand. She's radiant in coral silk, her dark curls pinned up and threaded with baby's breath.

"I keep having nightmares that we don't have the rings," I mutter.

She rolls her eyes. "What kind of best woman do you take me for? Relax. I've handled everything."

She has.

She's been the mastermind behind the entire wedding. I'm useless with event planning, and Thandi, humble as ever, would've been happy with a courthouse ceremony. So Fia stepped in, with a little help from Dani.

The care they've put into every detail takes my breath away.

Warmth rushes through me as I take in the crowd of friends and family gathered to celebrate us.

Iris sits in the front row, elegant in a pale lavender dress, her face soft with emotion. To her left, Trent bounces Junie in his lap, coaxing a gummy smile from her. Carmen is just behind them, checking her makeup discreetly in her compact. Janice from the youth center is here too. She and Aamir are getting along famously, their heads bent close together in conversation. And there's Fred, looking calm and happy at last.

I'd like to think Mom is here too, somewhere, watching over all of this.

And of course, Tess.

Dani's wife, Evelyn, is our officiant. It turns out she's not only an incredible somatic therapist but also ordained. The band begins to play, and her pale sage kaftan flows around her as she turns to face the aisle.

It's time.

The violin notes swell, rich and aching, and my heart pounds in my chest.

The crowd rises.

Daysha comes in first, scattering petals ahead of her, her blush-colored dress fluttering around her knees. Ricky follows, solemn as a judge, holding the rings like sacred cargo. He's grown taller these past months—more confident, too.

Dani strides in next with calm purpose. Somehow, Fia convinced her to trade her signature black for striking emerald. She smiles as she takes her place across from me beneath the bower.

And then the moment of truth.

My anxiety swells to a crescendo with the music and evaporates the instant she enters, replaced by joy so deep it steals my breath.

Thandi.

The love of my life.

She's so beautiful that I can't catch my breath.

She is radiant, glowing in the lanterns flickering to life along the aisle. The spaghetti straps and gently draping neckline of her dress are soft and utterly feminine—just like her. White liquid silk skims her curves, falling in an elegant column to her ankles, the fabric luminous against her skin.

In her hands is a cascade of frangipani, apricot, coral, and blush petals spilling downward, warm as sunlight. The scent reaches me even from here: creamy, sweet vanilla drifting on the sultry breeze.

My throat aches at the significance, the nod to memory and healing.

Behind her ear is a single frangipani—an homage to childhood garlands, now laid to rest.

Winston leads her down the aisle in a charcoal three-piece suit and mint silk tie, his locs pulled back into a neat queue. Besides me, he's easily the most emotional person here. His eyes shine, glossy with love and pride as he looks down at his daughter.

Thandi walks with him, barefoot across the sand, crushing Daysha's petals underfoot, releasing more sweet perfume with every step.

Our eyes meet, and something breaks loose in my chest.

God, she is stunning.

Not just in the way she looks—though she is breathtaking—but in the quiet radiance of her heart. Knowing the depth of her kindness, her courage, and her capacity to love makes my eyes burn with tears. It makes me want to shout my gratitude to the world.

I can't believe we have a lifetime together.

That I'll have forever to cherish her.

She reaches the dais and turns to me, and I'm trembling as I take her hands in mine.

"You're perfect," I whisper.

"So are you." Her eyes shine. "I can't wait to be your wife."

That hits me right in the chest. I swallow, blinking.

Did I mention she's perfect?

The world narrows to the sound of the ocean, the rise and fall of her breath, and the way her eyes hold mine.

Nothing else exists.

A soft clearing of a throat pulls us back.

Evelyn steps forward, her kaftan stirring in the breeze. When she speaks, her voice is warm, carrying easily over the sand.

"We are gathered here," she says, "surrounded by water, light, and love, to witness something both ancient and entirely new."

Her gaze moves between us. "Thandi and Ronan have chosen each other—not out of convenience or expectation, but out of courage. Out of trust. Out of a love that has already been tested and has only grown stronger because of it."

Evelyn opens her hands. "Before we begin the vows, I invite everyone here to take one breath together. To arrive fully in this moment—a moment not to be taken for granted, because it was fought for and hard-won."

She pauses.

Eyes flutter shut. Chests rise and fall. The tide breaks softly against the shore.

Then we continue.

She smiles. "Ronan, Thandi, I invite you to recite your vows."

My pulse hammers as I lift Thandi's hands and kiss her knuckles. Her skin is soft, her delicate perfume wrapping around me. The pink diamond on her finger catches the last of the sun, lit from within—like her, like me.

I rehearsed these words a hundred times. I even have a folded printout in my pocket, just in case emotion stole my voice.

But looking at Thandi now, at her sweet face and her big brown eyes, I know I won't need it.

I couldn't forget these words if I tried.

They're already written on my heart.

"Thandi," I begin. "I knew from the moment we met that you were my destiny—everything I'd dreamed of and didn't know I needed. I was grieving, wallowing, selfish—hiding behind brittle bravado. You shattered it with a single look."

I laugh softly. "You've wrecked me in the best way ever since. Through your brilliance, your compassion, and your strength in the face of unimaginable grief, you showed me what true bravery looks like. You inspired me to be a better man—stronger, steadier, kinder. A man with intent and purpose. Because that's the only kind of man worthy of standing beside you."

I hold her gaze, lifting her hands to my lips once more.

Ricky steps forward, raising the satin pillow. I take Thandi's band and slide it onto her finger. It's rose gold, with a delicate halo of diamonds echoing her engagement ring.

"Thandi, you are my dawn every morning. The sun in my sky. The very heart in my chest." My voice thickens. "It would be the honor of my life to cherish you, protect you, and love you for all the days of my life."

She makes a small, broken sound as tears spill over her cheeks. Smiling, I cup her face, brushing them away with my thumbs.

"I love you, Thandi Elowen."

Thandi

I stare into Ronan's eyes, take in the rows of smiling faces around us, and can't quite believe I'm here. Can't believe the joy overflowing my chest after a lifetime of guilt, grief, and doubt.

And it's all because of the man standing in front of me.

The man who showed me what true safety feels like—who even now is catching my tears.

The man whose love is so big and so bright it chased away my fear.

I look up at him, my heart aching with answering love.

He looks so handsome in his soft taupe suit, the tailored cut emphasizing his broad shoulders. But it's his pale pink tie—the quiet nod to my hair—that undoes me all over again. I grip his hands as his vows strike a chord so deep in me that not even the earlier violins could compare. I'm vibrating with love, with passion, with a peace I never imagined possible.

When Evelyn turns to me, I can hardly catch my breath.

"Ronan," I begin, sniffling as I let out a watery laugh. "You keep saying I'm brave, but I learned that from you."

His hands tighten around mine.

"For twenty years, I tried to outrun grief and loneliness. I told myself I was never enough. I fought so hard to remember my past that I missed the most important truth—that love doesn't ask us to forget ourselves."

I squeeze his hands, grounding myself in his warmth. His love.

"In your arms, I learned how to trust enough to surrender. How to accept that needing help isn't a weakness." My voice trembles, but I don't look away. "And most of all, your love showed me how to be myself—to see all that I am, not just the other half of a broken mirror."

I take a shaky breath and slip the plain rose-gold band onto his finger.

"Ronan, you're my rock—my harbor in the storm, my soft place to fall." My voice wavers. "You lifted me up and believed in me when I couldn't believe in myself. I am undone by your strength, in love with your laughter, your irreverence—and yes, your stubbornness."

Ronan snorts, and I grin through my tears.

"Every day beside you is filled with so much joy that I'm still pinching myself. I love you more than I have words for, and I can't wait to spend my life as your wife and your friend."

"Thandi," Ronan breathes.

He lifts me off the ground, gathering me against his chest. I loop my arms around his neck, still clutching my bouquet, never breaking eye contact. His amber gaze burns with love and devotion, and in it I see tenderness, laughter, and the lifetime of happy endings we'll make together.

I lean forward. Ronan bends to meet me—

"Ahem."

Evelyn claps her hands, laughter in her voice. "Jumping the gun, are we?"

Ronan and I both jerk back.

Laughter ripples through the crowd.

Of course, I'm laughing and crying too.

Behind me, Fia dabs at her eyes. To my right, even Dani looks misty-eyed. Daysha and Ricky stand arm-in-arm, faces bright with impish grins. And Mom and Dad—

My heart contracts.

They're holding each other, smiling through their tears.

The wind rushes forward, frangipani blossoms trembling in the bower overhead. The warm scent of vanilla surrounds us like a blessing. I close my eyes and breathe it in. There is no more terror. No more darkness.

Only healing, redemption, and the unending sweetness of love.

"Ronan Thorne and Thandi Elowen," Evelyn says, spreading her hands with a grin, "I now pronounce you husband and wife."

She winks.

"Now you may kiss the bride."

Ronan's arms tighten around me as we turn to each other.

"Thank you for loving me," I whisper.

His eyes glisten. "Thank you for being the best part of my life. I love you, baby."

I smile, trembling with the beauty of the moment. I'm safe. Cherished. Whole.

And now Ronan and I get to build a whole new mixtape of memories together.

His masculine scent fills my senses—fresh, familiar, comforting.

Our lips meet.

And we seal forever with a kiss.

Fin.

Post Script

Bouquet
Ronan

Music swells. Laughter bright and easy fills the air.

I can't take my eyes off Thandi as she moves to the center of the room to throw the bouquet.

Guests trail behind her, ready for their chance.

At her elbow, Janice says something. Thandi throws her head back laughing, and my world stops spinning for a moment. I don't think I'll ever get over how beautiful she is.

And now she's my wife.

Wife.

Warmth rushes through me as I bring my champagne glass to my lips.

I love how that sounds.

I can't wait to show her how much later.

My gaze returns to the knot of hopefuls. The bouquet toss, it turns out, is an equal opportunity affair. All the single people have gathered—both men and women.

Plus Daysha and Ricky, of course, who are leaning forward, knees bent, positioned like footballers waiting for the snap. They whisper together, exchanging grins. Instead of going alone, it looks like they're making a coordinated play for the bouquet.

I can't help laughing at their antics.

The adults' excitement is a bit more contained, though there are some clear contenders. Janice and Carmen have taken off their heels to aid their chances of success. Aamir's pretending to be nonchalant, but I don't miss the way he's rolled up his sleeves.

Trent unsurprisingly is going all in, and he bounces on his toes after handing Junie to Iris.

And then, there's Aliyah and Fred, more tentative on the edge of the group, but my heart goes out to them both for taking a risk on love again.

I amble over to Fia, who's parked near the edge of the dance floor, a champagne flute balanced between her fingers.

I lean against the sideboard, nudging her with my elbow. "What? You're not giving it a shot? I know how competitive you are."

She shoots me a look. "Roncito, when have I ever been a romantic?"

"Oh, come on." I grin. "It's tradition."

She rolls her eyes. "No thanks, I'll pass."

I touch my glass to hers. "Hey, you never know. Life is funny. Six months ago, I'd never have believed I'd be married to the love of my life."

Fia's quiet. Her expression softens as she looks out over the group and then back up at me. "You're right. This turned out amazingly, didn't it?"

"It did. Thanks to you." I squeeze her in my arms. "Thank you for everything. For making today perfect."

"Of course." She tightens her arms around me. "I am so happy for you and Thandi. The two of you are beautiful together."

"Thanks." I swallow past the emotion in my throat.

Her eyes go to the crowd again, and for a moment, I glimpse wistfulness and a hint of weariness in her gaze before she conceals it again, her charismatic mask falling back into place.

"Hey," I say softly. "You okay?"

"Hmm?" she says, startled. "Just a bit tired. I didn't sleep much last night."

"Too much prep?" I ask. I know how much work she put into the wedding and reception, and I feel a pang of regret at being the cause of her exhaustion.

Fia smiles. "Oh no, it's nothing like that. The staff here is amazing. We finished all the details well ahead of schedule." Her brow furrows as she glances at the dancefloor again.

"So what happened?"

Fia rubs her eyes. "There was a mix-up with our bungalows, and Trent and I ended up having to share."

"What?" I straighten. "Why didn't you say? Should I speak to the manager?"

A hint of color touches Fia's cheekbones. "No, it's fine. It's only for a couple of days. Besides, thanks to Junie, Trent is marginally less annoying."

I frown. "What—"

"Ready?" Thandi yells.

She turns, waving the bouquet above her head.

A roar goes up from the group. She hasn't even thrown it yet, and already there's some friendly jostling.

The bouquet arcs through the air—fragrant blooms spinning in the light.

Daysha and Ricky dive for it.

Aamir lunges, teeters, and crashes into Fred. They both go down in a tangle of limbs.

Aliyah leaps with surprising grace. She reaches— The bouquet grazes her hand ... then slips through her fingers.

The bunch keeps sailing until the last of the group comes barreling our way.

Carmen lifts her skirts and sprints towards us. Janice is right behind her, followed by Trent.

"Go, Carmen!" Fia screams. "Show these bastards what the Zamoras are made of!"

My shoulders shake with laughter.

Well. That confirms she hasn't lost her edge.

Carmen and Janice are neck and neck—so close now we can almost touch them. Janice leans right, but Carmen edges forward.

She's going to cinch it.

Until an unsuspecting waiter picks that moment to step out of the kitchen with a plate of hors d'oeuvres.

His eyes widen when he sees the two competitors racing towards him.

Too late, he blinks, yelps—and crashes straight into them.

"Damn it!" Carmen hisses.

They go down fast in a tumble of swearing and helpless laughter. The tray goes flying, clattering across the floor. The poor waiter keeps apologizing, but thankfully, no one is hurt.

Faced with a suddenly clear field, Trent looks around, disoriented.

He skids to a stop.

The bouquet plummets.

And lands squarely against his chest.

He reaches, catching it out of pure reflex.

A stunned beat passes.

Then he looks from the bouquet to Fia, one brow lifting.

He loosens his tie and ambles over, stopping only when he's in front of her chair.

Trent's lips spread into a grin.

"Guess that means I'm next, huh?

Stay Connected

Loved this story?
Join my private reader list for behind-the-scenes notes, early looks at upcoming books, and exclusive bonus content.

☞ stay.devinem.com

www.ingramcontent.com/pod-product-compliance
Lightning Source LLC
Chambersburg PA
CBHW031332020726

47499CB00005B/1237

* 9 7 8 1 9 7 0 2 7 1 0 1 0 *